The Fall of Cthulhu
Volume II
An Anthology of Dark Stories

Edited
By

Douglas Draa

COVER ART

"Fogalypse" By Manooze
freeimages.com
"Shattered Horror" by hyena reality
Image courtesy of FreeDigitalPhotos.net

GRAPHICS

Nathan J.D.L. Rowark

First Edition

Horrified Press

ISBN: 978-1-326-31172-8

Table of Contents

The Heart of Heka
Craig E. Sawyer

The drinks were not too watered down tonight at the Brass Rail; and that's saying a lot for a place that usually smelled like stale beer and twenty dollar snatch. There was only one pretty girl in the whole joint and her name was Jenny K. She had been a prostitute when a brooding Percy Hero first met her on the streets—and now she had moved up the ladder of life to that of a low-rent stripper.

She was chaos with great tits.

Percy moved the leg of a dark-headed, gyrating, stripper to one side in order to get a better look at his watch. His partner Jake was late again. Jake would be late to his own funeral one day, he thought. The smoky neon gave the place a dreamy atmosphere. It was like being transported to a heaven for sinners, complete with all the trimmings: a Hank Williams Lost Highway—fucking nirvana.

The walls were painted with smoke-stained mahogany and regret.

Percy ordered another double Jack, and a cold beer. Two men fought at the bar over some dirty blond, as he retreated back into the smoky haze to his usual dark corner table. His partner Jake had called him an hour ago, going crazy about some huge job in the sticks. It was supposed to be a very rich score, one that promised to keep them both in strippers, drugs, and booze for a long time to come. He was a little skeptical, because *Jake the Flake* had a way of stretching the truth a mile. The man could make shit smell good on a hot day.

The front door suddenly blasted opened and in walked an excited Jake. He spotted his partner immediately and sauntered over. He plopped down in the chair in front of Percy and waved over the waitress for two shots of Jack. He looked excited beyond measure and, of course, he was high out of his mind.

"You're late," Percy said.

"I'm always late; it's part of my charm."

"So, what's this job you were going on about over the phone?"

"Whoa, slow down, partner. I wanna have a lap dance, maybe a couple of drinks, and then we will get into the gritty details," Jake mumbled and whistled to the waitress.

As the waitress made her way over, she was suddenly intercepted by the leggy stripper by the name of Jenny K. Jenny took the drinks from her and sauntered over to the table and sat in a surprised Jake's lap. "Hello there boys," she purred, "how they hanging?"

"Whoa Jenny, is Percy here not getting the job done for you these days?"

"He's doing alright—except for not calling me back for the past forty-eight hours. Where have you been?"

Percy fumbled in his jacket for his pack of crumpled smokes, eventually fishing out one with his lips. "I've been around. I don't know what you're talking about."

"What's her name?" Jenny K. sneered as she snatched his cigarette from his hand, taking a long drag before putting it put out on the table. "No smoking in the bar."

"When the hell did that start?"

"New policy for assholes," she said and made a b-line to the nearest pole.

Jake started to snicker. "It must be that time of the month."

"Ok, what about this score you been going on about?"

Jake took another shot and got comfortable. He said he was hanging out the other night at a back-country poker shack the called *The Wild Deuce*. It was a church of sorts for Jake, where he worshiped chance on a nightly basis and lost most of what he and Percy made from their heists. He wasn't going to tell his partner that he was in the hole for ten large; but the more that Jake drank, the more the truth started to emerge.

"You lost your ass at the table again?"

"I had a bad run, nothing that can't be fixed with this job. I met this old guy at the table and he offered us the opportunity of a lifetime."

"I need another drink for this," Percy said.

Jake said that after an intense game. A hand where he blew his entire wad on a pair of kings: that was when he started talking to the peculiar old guy. The codger wore dated clothes and a monocle of all things; a fucking, goddamn, monocle. The crazy coot reminded Jake of the monopoly guy, but half of his face was paralyzed or something—creepy guy.

Well, the monopoly guy had taken him to the shed for fifteen grand that night.

"I thought you told me ten grand?"

"At first, yeah, but then I borrowed five from the house."

Jake was just about to get up and leave when the old man asked him if he wanted to earn some *real* cash, and if he did this job for him, he wouldn't owe the house or him a dime. He just wanted him to break into a rundown ole mansion in the country a few states up in Rhode Island and retrieve a small antiquity that was stolen from him.

"What is this antiquity?"

"Get this shit: he said it was a petrified heart, or some shit."

"What the hell?"

"I know—right?"

Jake asked the man why he would want such a weird thing and not money or jewels, but the man insisted that it had value for him—that he also had more than a passing interest in rare and unique antiquities. That it was a matter of life or death to him. Jake didn't quite understand what the man meant, but he nodded his head. He would have agreed to just about anything rather than get his legs broken for owing the *Deuce* money.

"I told the guy right then and there: I'm your man."

"You mean you told him that *we're his men*?"

"Yeah, that's what I said."

"Well, keep going."

"This is where the story gets as crazy as that ole wino *Red Bananas*. He said that the heart was suppose to be cursed or something. That it had belonged to a crazy cult, called the *Cult of Heka*, yeah, that's what he said—Heka.

"You're pulling my leg…right?"

"What I'm telling you is the biblical truth of what the old guy *told me*. Not only will this crazy old codger pay *my* debt to *The Deuce*, but he will also give us twenty grand each upon delivery of this thing."

"You sure he said all this?" Percy asked.

Yeah, the guy said his name was Doctor Jonas Raspin. He said he had strong associations within distinguished archeological circles in the states; and on many occasions, he had commissioned his own scientific expeditions around the globe. He was on such an trip six months ago in the Valley of the Kings, in Egypt, when he came across a hidden tomb; and within that tomb, he discovered a vile containing the legendary petrified *Heart of Heka."*

"Ok, you've got my attention…keep going," Percy said with a sly smile.

"I couldn't remember every detail, so I switched on my phones recorder...here you go."

There was a pause, and then someone clearing their throat before they started to speak. The voice sounded clear and educated with a slight accent that Percy could not place.

"The story goes that the heart had belonged to a ruthless, mad Egyptian Pharaoh named *Heka Khafra Ayubid* who was obsessed with achieving immortality on Earth. He believed himself to be a descendant from some *Great Race* that had pretty much died out thousands of years ago. He scoured the land in search of any magic or knowledge that could help him achieve this goal. He was led to believe that ritual sacrifice would bend the gods to his desires, so he sacrificed hundreds of his own people in mass ritual killings. He would cut out their hearts under the light of the moon and consume them, but he still aged.

He swathed the land in red until until he crossed paths with a magician named Maze Coptos Atum. Maze was to be the Pharaoh's next sacrifice, but this man was no ordinary man— maybe not even human at all. He was a high cleric of the Old gods and their chief god, *Yig*: a dark supernatural being from the beyond the threshold of this reality. Some say that Maze could change into a giant lizard, and that he had been banished from the kingdoms of the skies and now was cursed to walk upon the earth, others say that he had made a deal with the god of serpents and the darker dimension; but whatever Maze Atum was, he was the wrong man to try and sacrifice.

Atum told the power-hungry Pharaoh that he could help him achieve his wish to live forever. That he could summon the god *Yig* and make a pact to obtain his immortal heart. Once that had the heart of a god beating within his chest—he would not age for a three thousand year cycle, that upon stealing the heart, *Old Yig* would fall into a deep sleep for the time, but after that time was up; he would awaken and come for his heart, unless the same magic ritual was enacted on the very last hour of the three-thousandth year deadline, but by doing the ritual in the first place, it opened a doorway between this world and the dark dimension that Yig and his kind were locked Into. If he was to regain his heart, then he would usher in others like himself, and then our world would be thrown into bloody chaos for eternity.

The Pharaoh was intrigued by the magician's proposal and told him that he agreed to do what he asked, as long as the magician fulfilled his end of the bargain. The legend goes on to say that the magician tricked the Pharaoh into becoming a sacrifice himself—that the ceremony of immortality required a body descended from the legendary Great Race. It was the crafty magician Atum who gained immortality by placing his soul within the Pharaoh's body with a stolen god's heart."

The voice broke up a little bit as it finished the story. He said that the heart was lifted from him in Egypt and brought back here to the States, where it was most likely sold into the black market. He then hired a local detective named Eddie "The Rope" Mars to hunt it down and he did; but shortly after Mars had called me from a payphone and was rambling incoherently about hunched backed men wearing grey suits following him, and then he disappeared off the face of the Earth.

Jake's phone suddenly switched off.

"What happened?' Percy said.

"My memory must have run out," Jake said as he snatched up his phone.

"What happened then?"

Jake picked up the story where the phone had left off.

He said that after the old man told about the last guy having vanished, that he started to get cold feet. Jake asked for more money, so he doubled the price. "After we shook on it, he wheeled himself back from the table by pressing a button on the arm of his chair. He had been sitting in a motorized wheelchair the entire time, unbeknownst to me. A thick blanket lay over his two legs. He patted his uncooperative members as if petting a dog."

Satisfied, Raspin told Jake to meet him here at this table two days from now with the retrieved item; he would need to take with him a lead box that was in the trunk of Raspin's car and a map that will lead you to the mansion which is located just north of a town called Arkham. He then grabbed Jake's arm and squeezed tightly to bring home his point. "Tell me that you understand. You must place it inside the box."

Jake looked up at Percy to see what his reaction was to this incredible story.

"You're telling me the truth? All of it?" Percy asked while raising an eyebrow.

"Of course…"

"You sure that you weren't the one to get offered the job for ten-thousand, and now that you got it doubled, you're bringing me on board?"

"You were on board from the beginning pal."

As Percy walked to the door, a leg wrapped itself around his chest.

The leg belonged to the sultry Jenny K.

He could smell her heat coming from between her thighs, her sparkling green eyes were nearly hypnotic, but he didn't have time for this.

"You're no fun tonight," she purred and continued to contort her body in all manner of seduction. "Don't call me when you get back," she smiled.

"Easy," he replied and then walked away.

"I hate you," she spit. "You will never get this again."

"I will make you eat those words," he relayed coolly and then caught up with Jake at the door.

Much later, the two would be thieves pulled onto a long, gravelly, dead-end road in the cold northern back country of Rhode Island about an hour before midnight. They pulled their car off the small road and parked it behind a thick grove of trees. Jake pulled out a pistol from his belt and checked the clip and then placed it back. He then brought out two black ski masks from the glove box and tossed one to his partner, then placed the other over his head.

He then produced a small plastic vial. He popped the tiny lid from the vial and shook out a large bump of coke onto the tiny web of flesh between his thumb and index finer. He held out the web of his hand to Percy. "Here, for good luck."

"Naw, I'm good."

"It's for good luck, asshole. We always take the bump."

"Give me you hand, asshole," Percy said and sniffed.

"That's the spirit, pal! Now we're ready for action," Jake squealed.

They then exited the car and ran off into the night.

It was fairly easy for him to jimmy open a pair of French doors. Once Jake entered the dark room, he reached down and switched on a small flashlight.

Percy entered behind him and tapped Jake on the shoulder to alert him to the face of a *giant snarling lion* that was just inches from his face. Its ivory fangs and eyes glowed in the pale light.

"Jesus, that thing scared the daylights outta me."

The gigantic room had a high ceiling and was stocked full of stuffed beasts from every corner of the globe—as well as strange artifacts and weapons of antiquity.

In the far back of the room there was a giant aquarium that took up an entire wall from floor to ceiling. It was massive enough to hold a whale. Jake shined his light into the Sea-World-worthy cask. It was reinforced with triple-paned glass and glowing security sensors. The light could only cut through the murk a few feet, but it was enough to show parts of an enormous marine like creature. It had massive appendages.

Jake put his face closer to the glass.

A massive bubble burst in front of his face from beyond the thick glass. The thing inside had trapped air under one of its dark folds and as its massive frame shifted slightly; it forced the air upwards making a moaning thunk. "Holy....," Jake said as he back up quickly.

"Over here," Percy said.

He was pointing at one of several massive glass display cases. Inside the nearest case was a jeweled sword with a heavily sculpted gold pommel. Its long grip was decorated with swirls and its cross was comprised of two winged dragons with *lapis azuli* beads for eyes. An inscription on the case read: *Charlemagne's coronation sword.*

"That would look good hanging over my television—those jewel's real?" Jake said.

"I'm no museum curator, but an underground collector would give millions for this," Percy said with wide, greedy eyes.

"We should take it then. The old man said we could take whatever."

They suddenly heard footsteps in the hallway and keys jangling on the outside the door.

Percy quickly cut the light and both disappeared into the shadows.

The large wooden double doors slowly creaked open and a bright light from the hallway illuminated the room. The person who entered was wearing a blood-red cloak. It sleeves were embroidered in gold trim, the overly large hood pulled over his head to hide his face. The cloaked stranger went to a nearby case and pulled a chained, silver key from around his neck and unlocked it. He then reached into the case and pulled out an impressively long dagger.

A clumsy Jake bumped into a stuffed *Howler Monkey* that was mounted to his left and caused it to rock back and forth from its rope vine that hung from the ceiling.

The strangers head whipped around to the direction of the noise.

He started to make his way toward Jake's hiding spot without making a single sound; the dagger held up in a stabbing position.

Jake held his gun in a ready position as the cultist made his way closer and closer to him; but just as he was about to pull the trigger, another one of them stuck his head into the doorway and croaked to his comrade that the ceremony was about to begin.

The first hood took one more glance around the room, then closed the case and left the room.

After a moment of safe darkness, they both switched on their flashlights again.

"What the hell was that?" Jake snorted. "It was like something out of a bad horror flick. You see that pig sticker that guy had?"

"Let's keep our minds on the task and get what we came for."

Jake's flashlight beam crossed over a large case that sat near the center of the room. Inside the case was a single item: *The Heart of Heka.*

"Holy shit—jackpot," Jake whispered.

"Hey, let me see the key that old man gave you."

Jake pulled it from his pocket. It resembled the key that the cult member carried.

"This is too easy," Jake smiled as he hurriedly placed it into the lock on the case.

"I know it is. That's what has me worried," Percy said.

The case made a small clicking sound as it opened; and Jake didn't waste any time going for it. The heart felt cool in his hand and it made him feel monstrously strong—invincible. It was like when he had just polished off a fifth of liquor and was bulletproof.

Percy pulled out the small lead box from his backpack and held it open at Jake. "Put it in the box."

Jake pulled out his gun pointing its barrel in Percy's face.

"You double-crossing bastard," Percy growled

"Sorry bud. But there was more to this deal than I let on. Strangely enough: you being delivered here was a big part of it.

"What are you talking about?"

The old man knew all about you, said something about you being a descendent from kings. He said your real name was Ayubird or something. Whatever, the guy is a nut-job, but he's a rich nut-job."

"My grandfather's last name was Ayubid."

"Whatever pal, I'm supposed to take you down to the basement for a ritual or something.'

"I wouldn't move around too much if I was you,' Percy said with a wry smile.

"What're you talking about?"

"Look at your arm."

The place was so dark that Jake didn't realize the case was swarming with dozens of *Death Stalker Scorpions*; and several of them were now covering his arm and shoulder.

"Get them off of me, man," Jake whimpered.

Percy came up with his own gun and pointed at his double crossing friend.

"Why should I save your ass?"

"We're pals, you and me. You wouldn't do this to a friend. I admit—I was an asshole."

Against his better judgment, Percy took the blade of the sword and brushed off the deadly creatures.

"Thank God," Jake exclaimed with a huge sigh of relief, but as he stood back up, he still had the barrel of the gun pointed at his partner. "I really am thankful, but you were stupid to do that. You know my real best friend is Mr. Benjamin Franklin, and by the way—Jenny K is with me now.

"I wouldn't trust her if I was you," Percy smirked. "She's deadlier than those scorpions."

"I would just shoot here right here, but the old man said there was a bonus in it for me if I delivered you before midnight."

"Didn't the old man say that thing was cursed?"

From behind the stone heart emerged another lone scorpion that dug its singer into Jake's chest. Jake's dropped the heart and it busted into a hundred pieces on the marble floor.

"We all get what we deserve," Percy said to his backstabbing friend.

As Jake fell to his knees convulsing he started to laugh hysterically.

"What's so damn funny?" Percy asked.

"I put some sleeping powder in that bump of coke you sniffed, and it should be kicking in…right about now," Jake said before collapsing to the ground.

Percy's his vision started to blur as he stumbled into one of the cases. His legs started to go numb. He only made it a few more steps before he fell to the ground.

Percy awoke with a sharp pain in his right shoulder and the strange harmonies of what sounded like a choir all around him. He tried to move, but could not. He was tied down to a long stone table with a tight rope across his throat. His gaze was forced upward toward a high wooden ceiling. Large metal sculptures hung down from sturdy fixtures. He could barely make out the dozen or so men standing around him chanting, each wearing several strange masks, some crocodile-headed, others dogs and birds.

The strange hymn suddenly came to an end.

"Bring out the master!" the man hissed.

Percy could hear the hum of a motorized wheelchair, and he knew instantly it was Jake's old man from The Deuce. In Raspin's lap was the lead box. "Greetings, Percival Hero Ayubid, I hope you are not too uncomfortable. I would say it's going to get better, but that would be stretching the truth. Let me first introduce myself. I am Maze Coptos Atum, and I need your body to be a vessel for my stolen heart."

"How in the Hell is that possible? I don't understand. I saw the Heart shatter."

"It was just a replica...a MacGuffin to lure you here. The real one beats within my body," and with that he ripped his shirt open to revel his pulsating chest. "However, the human body can only be a vessel for its immense power for so long, and even then it must be the body of a descendant of the Great Race. In your veins flows the blood of that race. I need it in order for the Heart of Heka to sustain me, and must be done before the stroke of midnight chimes, or the wrath of the Great Old Ones will be unleashed.

The others started to chant again, as Atum was helped up from his chair.

Percy had been trying to get to his knife in his pocket the entire time and had managed to lift it to his side with his long fingers. He moved his body from side to side, slowly eating away at the rope holding his right hand securely to the table.

The chanting had reached a crescendo.

Percy tried to move his eyes as far to the side as they would go to see what was going on. He managed to capture glimpse of the old man as he opened the box.

The dark priest that stood nearby ripped Percy's shirt to expose his chest; then, he took the dagger and lightly drew a bloody line across Percy's heart area. The heart within Atum started to beat louder as it radiated a faint red through his taunt skin. The beating mixed with the rhythmic chants seemed to change the room. The walls seemed to close in and the ceiling got lower.

Raspin ripped open his shirt. "We must hurry, the two thousand-year mark is almost upon us, and *Yig* will awaken soon to reclaim his heart.

Blood started to rise to the surface of Atum's skin and eventually shot forth from his chest.

The head priest raised his dagger over a doomed Percy, but just as the tip of the blade lowered.

A gunshot suddenly echoed through the great hall.

The serpent priest grasped his throat and made a high pitched moan as blood gushed from a smoking bullet hole.

Percy had managed to loosen the rope; and through intense pain, plunged the knife into the old mans chest, but as its tip snapped off after penetrating the flesh and hitting something stone like. "No, you fool!" the old man wailed, his eyes now a deep yellow—his skin now old and loose hanging over his bones. "You have doomed the entire human race."

The Heart pushed its way from his sucking chest and fell to the ground, still beating ferociously, before being trampled by the fleeing cultists as they ran from the hail of bullets coming from the mysterious rescuers gun.

A lean figure walked out from the smoke and pushed back her long blonde hair from her face. "What are you waiting on, cowboy," Jenny K asked Percy with her signature purr, "a written invitation?"

Percy leapt from the table, as they both ran for the door.

A terrible crash from above shook the entire mansion.

Water gushed from above like a waterfall, followed by a deafening roar.

It was minutes until midnight, and the Dark God would soon be fully awake
Percy stopped running and turned back.

"What the hell are you doing? We have to get out of here," Jenny K yelled.

"Everything about the story has been true so far, so that means the Old One is about to wake up unless we do something to stop it," he said as he made his way back to the real Heart of Heka.

He reached down and lifted the up the Heart. It had grown to seven times its normal size, but shrunk back down to the size of a human's heart again in his hands. It started to beat furiously in his palm. He wasn't sure what to expect, but the pain was beyond anything that he could have imagined as he held it against his chest. The artifact became semi-transparent as it started to enter him. The world ceased to move, and all of the sounds around him muted.

The drinks were not too watered down tonight at the Brass Rail—and that's saying a lot. There was only one pretty girl in the whole joint and her name was Jenny K. She had almost betrayed the man she loved; but instead, she saved his life.

She glided in through the front door with long legs and a short dress. She carried a small suitcase in her hand. She leaned over and kissed before taking a seat across from him. "Somebody in a black sedan was following me, but I lost him on tenth," she said and then lit up a smoke.

"That's alright; we are going to be on the other side of the ocean by tomorrow," Percy said as he finished off his drink.

"What about money?"

He picked up his backpack and plopped it on the table between them. "Don't worry about that. We just have to visit a friend that deals in antiquities in Zonguldak, Turkey named Richter Hynes before we start our permanent vacation." Percy unzipped his bag just enough for her to see the jeweled pommel of a sword.

"We should do one last shot here before we go," she said as she pulled a bottle from her purse and held it up.

"You're a regular girl-scout," Percy grinned.

She filled his glass up, then leaned over and grabbed another glass from a nearby table and poured herself a shot.

"I'm gonna miss this tomb of a town," he said as they clanked her glass and threw back his.

She didn't' say a word as the two of them stood up and left the place.

After a beat she spit her shot of whiskey onto the sidewalk and wiped her lips.

"You were right to call this place a tomb."

Percy grabbed the edge of a street sign as the world began to spin. "What did you do?"

"I just gave you a shot of poison," she said candidly, then stood up, picked up his bag and tossed it over her shoulder, just as a black sedan pulled up beside them.

"You did say that I couldn't be trusted... right. I got the lowdown on the mansion, and all it had to offer, from a guy I knew named Eddie Mars. We had a thing while he was doing some detective work for that crazy old guy."

A square jawed Eddie Mars stepped out from the driver's side and made his way to the back of the car and opened the trunk.

"I thought we had something? You had something for me once," Percy said as he started to tremble.

The only thing I *have* is a meeting with a dealer of antiquities in Monaco who used to be a heart surgeon, and I don't wanna be late, and after that maybe someplace tropical."

That was the last thing Percy heard before everything went black.

The Guards of the Stone
Carl Thomas Fox

I wish we never found it now. It was better to have left it alone, to float in the water unnoticed. But because of it, I can no longer rest. I can no longer find peace. All because I know they were watching me.

Please leave me alone. Move me so I can't see the lake. They are watching me. They blame me for releasing it, and I know it is coming back. We have only postponed the inevitable.

I was a student at High Gates University, in the small town of Dunsmouth. A simple town, not much happened. Days turned into weeks, weeks turned to months, and you get the picture. The perfect kind of town to study archaeology, you get so much free time to study and research. In particular, I needed to. I was a high flyer on the course, studying directly under the magnificent Professor Glen Howard, who became famous several years ago when he came across a series of tunnels and caves in the hills overlooking Dunsmouth, once used by smugglers.

Other than the time the banality of Dunsmouth offers, another thing that helps with the study of archaeology is the Craft Lake in the outskirts of town. A popular tourist location, renowned for large fish, warm water that allows people to float effortlessly, and the towering trees that surrounded it. Craft Lake was affectionately known by archaeology students as The Fossiled Lake, for it regularly spewed forth a relic of the past.

You see, it was well known that Craft Lake was formed by an asteroid that hit many centuries ago, burrowing a great hole into the ground. In time, this hole filled up with water over the asteroid that was still buried deep in the ground. In addition, several streams merged into the lake, filling it over, before travelling several more miles south to reach the Miskatonic River.

Whenever a storm brews, and Dunsmouth was known for its frequent storms, the water of Craft Lake churned and twisted, and the morning after strange things were found ashore. Namely, fossils left from early centuries. Fossils of insects, marine life, dinosaurs, and humans throughout the ages. Fossils and artefacts, a never ending supply of research for us students.

There were rumours a few years back about extraterrestrial fossils, housed within the asteroid that were freed by the churning waters, for the military came to explore the waters.

Anyway, I digress. What I am revealing to you happened in my final year of studying, when I was appointed as Howard's personal assistant. It was after another frightful storm in the fall, on September 21st, one that shattered many windows and roofs within the town. It was a storm unlike any other. I remember, earlier that evening, watching the black clouds ink over the sky, like the ink left by an octopus when it flees or fights. The sky roared to life with heavy thunder and lightning, sending rain down in impenetrable sheets.

At one point, whiLst working on my thesis of the evolution of early humans, I could have sworn I saw handprints on my window. That was an impossible notion, my room was five storeys up. Nonetheless, there were two handprints. Closer examination showed it to be an illusion from the running rain.

The next morning, we were amazed to hear on the news about several accidents in mental hospital from patients suddenly acting irregularly and violent. It was as if the storm awakened something deep within them, making them all lash out. I admit, I had many dreams that night, of walking through a strange, ancient city, feeling something following. Something whispering in the darkness.

No matter, I put that aside, it did not matter. What mattered was that there was a storm, and that meant only one thing. Not wasting a moment, I called on Howard, amazed to hear he suffered from similar dreams, out pushed it aside. We rushed through the wet town and we came down to find what novelties the Craft Lake had provided for us.

Upon arriving at the lake, we came across the usual insect fossils scattered amongst the fallen red and golden leaves. Fossils that were starting to seem dull as it was what we have always seen. But that was until Howard suddenly gave out an ecstatic yelp. He had found something.

Watching my footing, I charged over the slick, wet ground, coming across Howard, knee-deep in leaves, silt and mud, looking at a monolithic stone. The thing was enormous, of a black stone I couldn't really place, covered in inscriptions. The images did not correspond to any language I had read, and not even to Howard who ran his fingers over them in amazement.

As well as these strange symbols, we also found pictures, relief carvings of humanoid figures praying before a creature. Although not clear, this 'god' appeared humanoid, but a giant, with great wings and what looked like a crown of horns down coming from its head, almost like long, flowing locks. Images also showed this was a lesser form of a larger, similar looking deity.

But the other figures, those worshipping it, looked thuggish and malformed, maybe some strange tribe of Neanderthal. But the language showed intelligence beyond the Neanderthal.

Other than that one image, there was no more.

As we looked over the strange stone, both our eyes were drawn to the exquisite podium it rested on. It was cracked, and appeared hollow. Even hollow, that podium must be made of a dense stone, to hold the monolith. How did the primitives carve it?

Reaching in, coming across slime-encrusted water and weeds, Howard gave an almost orgasmic look on his face as he started pulling out fossilised bones. He pulled out femurs, humerus bones, rib bones, and all other parts that showed a human. A human of gigantic stature. But then he started pulling other bones. Bones that did not make sense for they seemed bat like, particularly of the wings, but of one the size of a man.

Most likely a pterodactyl.

As Howard pulled the bones out, we both agreed this skeleton was probably put together as an image of this winged god, using bones of different sources.

Then, he came across the skull, and it was a monstrous thing, probably taken from a malformed sea creature. Although vaguely human, there was no jaw bone. Instead, under the fanged upper teeth, there was evidence of mandibles, as if the lower half of the face opened into a maw. And when I say fanged upper teeth, they were large and serrated, appearing as if they could tear anything apart. The cranium was massive, almost reminiscent of the skulls found in Central America. But this cranium was not just long, it was wide. In addition, it was in segments, meaning that the brain inside pulsated, something I had never seen in any life form.

Then those eyes, my god those eyes. The sockets were deep set and large, and the curvature of the forehead showed a monstrous brow.

Whatever this skull belonged to, we did not know. It was unlike anything we had ever encountered before.

The day was growing late, and Howard was desperate to find out what this was. Therefore, asking me to remain behind, assessing the monolith and any nearby debris, he rushed off back to the university. Without any hesitance, pulling out my pocket torch, I began looking around the marshy ground, looking through every shard of rock. I didn't need to worry police or complaints. The whole town knew all students searched the shoreline of the lake. Within a few hours maybe, the next day at the least, the whole shoreline will be swarmed with archaeology students from here and nearby universities.

Nonetheless, my search was very lacklustre, disappointing and fruitless with me finding only rock. Nothing else showed similar engravings or pictures. Just usual fragments of bedrock, a few simple fossils of insects, and not much else.

The monolith just appeared to be by itself, a lone anomaly. Nothing connecting to it, nothing about it seeming to fit into regular understanding.

It just didn't make sense.

I needed for it to make sense.

Focusing all my attention onto the monolith, I looked more closely at the carvings and engravings. Although this must have been deep under the lake, there was no sign of water damage, no algae or any other plant life. In fact, the carvings looked too perfect. Cut in exact angles, smooth and with precision. There were no mistake cuts, no flaws in the stone.

Looking at it, I was starting to think this might be a fake. That someone planted it during the storm, a cruel hoax at the idea of finding a new culture and civilisation.

Just as this thought came to me, I heard a splash in the water, the definite rush of someone coming out. I was half expecting a group of frogmen coming out, the hoaxers clothed in wetsuits to see their success.

Turns out I was more correct than I thought.

The moment I saw them, fear overwhelmed me and I leapt to my feet, running behind a series of bushes. Panic filled me, I could not feel anything than terror.

These beings were not men. I didn't know what they were. They were tall, hulking creatures, their large hands and feet were webbed, each holding three digits. Despite their size, they did not sink in the mud; they barely left any prints, as if the webbed feet acted like a pair of snowshoes. The flesh was black and scaled, and seemed to be pulsating as if the flesh itself were breathing. As the mouths opened, to speak in strange clicking noises, I saw hundreds of savage teeth and a long tongue. But the eyes; large and empty, glassy misty orbs. They all carried primitive weapons cared from bone. Savage spears, axes and swords, sharp and deadly.

They were not trying to find me; their focus was all on the monolith. They seemed enraged, finding the empty compartment at the bottom. Suddenly, one of them turned, sniffing the air. It was looking in a direction I knew all too well, towards whatever those strange fossils were.

Howard.

Trying to remain hidden in the shadows, I slunk away from the lake, using the wet, leaf-carpeted back streets for shortcuts. Backstreets us students knew all too well, using them for our needs whenever the strains of study became too much. At times, I saw many students indulging in these pleasures.

Nonetheless, I soon arrived at the university, going in through the back way, heading straight for the research lab in the basement. As I was nearing it, I started second guessing myself. Did I really see those things emerge from the water, or was it someone trying to play a prank on me? Either, my answer came to me when I came across Howard, and nothing could prepare me for what I saw.

A bloody pile of bones and torn clothes.

That was all that remained of Professor Howard, and not a sign of the fossilised bones.

Nearby, I found Howard's recorder, which he used to record all his findings. It was beeping, showing there was no more recording space. Determined to understand what had happened here, after my obvious reaction of spilling what little was in my stomach all over the floor, leaving a pain in my stomach, I pressed 'play'.

'Although the subject shows humanoid proportions,' said the voice of the man that lay as a pile next to my vomit, *'the actual structure deters away from any homo species. The bones appear honeycombed, yet are as heavy and dense as steel. The wings, first thought to be artificially*

attached, have actual joints connected to exaggerated scapula bones showing these wings were meant to be at the back. As for the cranium, I ...'

The voice stopped speaking; only becoming muttering and clanging. Vaguely in the distance, I could hear Howard speaking to himself, trying to find a hand that had fallen on the floor.

Suddenly, there was a shriek unlike what I have ever heard, followed by a strange garbled roar, which in turn gradually heightened to an ear-piercing shriek that I instinctively held my hands to my ears, dropping the recording in the process, shattering as it hit.

Did those things get here already? The room was brightly lit, there was nowhere for them to hide. I had to get out of here.

Not wasting a single moment, I ran out of the room, bouncing up the stairs into the darkness of the upper corridors. If those things were capable of killing a man like that, I did not want to see them. I needed somewhere to hide.

Upon reaching the main floor, which consisted of three central corridors that all tapered off from, I charged down the middle corridor, heading for the main doors. Outside, that was the safest place to be.

But that was when I saw them, their silhouettes hitting the large glass doors. I came to a skidding halt, only to run back up the corridor, hoping to reach one of the side ones and find another way out. Ahead, against the rear wall, I saw a flickering light, the flashlight of the night guard. Seeing this I thought I was safe.

Then I saw it.

As the flashlight was moving back and forth, it caught something, the shadow hitting the rear wall, showing it was not far from me. The shadow was a skeleton, and had great wings that were stretched out, a thin membranous film stretching between the digits. Between the bones of the skeleton, that moved with a will of their own, a few strands of flesh.

Seeing it, I knew what this was, I recognised the bone structures. I recognised that enlarged cranium, pulsating. It was the skeleton we had discovered. What I thought were horns were actually tentacle-like protrusions, each writhing with a mind of its own.

Before the night guard could even react, the thing charged at him. I will never forget that hollow sound of bone hitting the tiled floor. The inhuman clicking and clacking, the shrieking from the night guard. The thing started roaring, loud and monstrous at first, only to grow high-pitched. Although the flashlight dropped, spinning in the floor, I was often shown a shadow of the thing hoisting the poor security guard up, it was twice his size, and it was eating him. As it was eating him, I saw the gaps between bones filling up, as if flesh and organs were reforming.

Soon, only bones remained of the guard as the monster dropped it. That was when it looked at me, the flashlight stopping to throw the shadow on the back wall. But it was in a different corridor, it was the shadow looking at me. It knew I was there.

That was when I heard it. Not a voice in my ears, but a voice in my head. As it sent the thoughts, the tentacles stood erect, vibrating as if sending out the message. It was thanking me for freeing it, from taking me away from its captors. It then showed me images. Images of its past, a hybrid formed from its original host, to enslave the primitive races of Earth. But they fought back, aided by servants of another monstrous deity. They hacked the being apart, flaying the flesh from the bones, and encasing it in stone, forever watching over it. Then, the images showed what it intended, of it reformed whole, winged, humanoid monstrosity with a tentacled face that it would become? Then it returning to the lake, becoming something else. Something beyond terror and monstrosity. To become its true host. All before returning to its true home to summon others like it.

Screaming in panic, I ran towards the door, only then remembering the lake creatures, who smashed the window in.

19

My heart stopping, I went into a nearby room, knocking over desks and jars filled with various specimens, in a wild struggle to reach the door. Behind me, I heard sounds of inhuman screams and the tearing of flesh. I dared not to look back. At one point I felt a large, wet, strong hand grasping at my ankles as I crawled through the door, but that hand was soon pulled away.

I was able to crawl to safety, running as fast as I could. At this point, I do not remember much, I was delirious, screaming at the op of my lungs about everything I saw. I heard people shouting from their homes, telling me to shut up, but I kept on ranting, not knowing where I was.

That was when I heard a screeching and saw two bright lights coming straight at me, and I fell into deep darkness.

***

After my car accident, I was rushed to hospital, where I scared many staff and patients of my ramblings about the things I saw. I had only minor injuries, but because of how I was acting, I was sent to the psychiatric ward. No matter what they pumped me with, I kept on ranting.

Of course, the police investigated. There was no sign of Professor Howard, or the security guard. Although there were signs of vandalism at the university, no signs of violence. Then, to my horror, no sign of the strange creatures I described, or the dark monolith.

Who won the battle? The worshippers, who I now knew to be guardians, or the god they tried to remain hidden? Did they take everything back into the lake with them, or was it all in my head? Did those creatures inhabit the asteroid that formed the lake, or were they here before everything, and buried under the asteroid?

Whatever the answer, I do not know. Even as I write this as part of a therapy exercise in the psychiatric ward, I still cannot find answers. But every night, I look out my window, which has a clear view of the lake, and every day I see those glassy eyes poking out, looking at me. They know where I am.

Every time I look, my blood runs cold for the lake seems to be growing darker. Darker as if there was something growing under the water.

Crawling Chaos Theory
Kevin Wetmore

Wayne clutched his briefcase close as he sat between the two silent agents. His hair fell down in front of his glasses in thick, black waves and he nervously brushed it aside for the fourth time in five minutes. The agents on either side of him, huge men that made him feel dwarfed, staring straight ahead, neither speaking nor engaging him or their surroundings in any manner. This was the third and hopefully final time he was brought in by the Federal Bureau of Investigation.

It was like this every time.

He remembered the first time they brought him in. He had just finished teaching his course on advanced topology for undergraduates (which, by the way, he could teach in his sleep - that day had been a discussion on separation properties) and was in his office at Miskatonic prepping for his graduate seminar on differential geometry when Tweedledee and Tweedledum here knocked on his door.

"Professor Wayne Park?" said Tweedledee (Wayne thought for a moment and realized he has never heard Tweedledum's voice. He bet it sounded almost exactly like his doppleganger, though, and left the thought behind as they drove on down route 1.)

Upon confirmation of his identity, the men showed their badges, announced that he was needed in Boston and allowed him only enough time to put a sign on the classroom door of his seminar class letting them know that afternoon's session was cancelled.

Then, as now, they drove down to Boston, headed downtown and entered the garage for the Federal Building, taking him down even further once they entered the building.

The first time, they brought him to what he thought was an interrogation room. One way mirror, check. Table with two uncomfortable chairs facing each other, check. Fluorescent lighting, check. It was all cliché and more than a little unsettling. He was put in the chair facing away from the door. He was certain this was for effect and was determined not to let them see he was rattled in any way. He had done nothing wrong. He was, however, curious as to why the federal government wanted him.

They had kept his briefcase, allowing him nothing in the room, not even his cellphone. He wasn't bored. He was never bored. He was, however, slightly offended. Why did he have to cancel his seminar if they were going to play "hurry-up-and-wait"?

The door opened and a new suit walked in. This one was different. Shorter. His facial expression was neutral, but it could not mask the intelligence (Wayne thought "cunning") that lurked right behind it. His movements were precise, exact. Not fussy, but organized and confident. He was empty handed. Tweedledum was with him and stood by the door, wearing sunglasses inside, which Wayne had always thought was kind of silly.

Crossing around the table to the other side of the room, new agent pulled out the chair, sat down and simply looked at Wayne. It was not staring. It was not meant to intimidate. Wayne realized it was almost scientific. He was a new specimen and was being examined before any theories could be advanced about him. So he studied back.

Gray suit, tailored (Wayne could not afford custom suits at his salary), no visible jewelry, no visible scars. His black hair was starting to grey at the temples, but he was that sort of face that could have been anywhere between thirty-five and sixty. The most apt descriptor Wayne could think of was "nondescript."

Finally, the man across the table spoke. He spoke from memory, consulting no notes.

"Wayne Park, age thirty-three. Undergraduate degree in physics from Stamford, Ph.D. from M.I.T. in mathematics, with a dissertation on non-Euclidean geometry and chaos theory, which is what brought you to our attention in the first place. Parents were Korean immigrants, now deceased. Owned a convenience store in San Jose. One older brother, doing a stint in Salinas Valley State Prison in Soledad for armed robbery. You've been to visit him only three times since he went in. Not too much in common to talk about, I guess."

He waited for a reaction. Wayne refused to give him the satisfaction, but was now even more confused and anxious.

"Assistant professor of Mathematics at Miskatonic University. Up for tenure next year. You live alone. No significant other, no kids. Avid videogamer and you play the piano. Raised United Korean Methodist but stopped going once your folks passed. Do I have your attention?"

"Yes. But I cannot say I am too impressed yet, a good google search would turn up most of that. What is going on here?"

The man continued to study him before continuing.

"I'm Special Agent in Charge Hogue. I head up a small division of investigators who deal with the unusual." He let that land and watched to see where Wayne went with it.

"So...the *X-Files* is real?" Wayne chanced a smile. He always joked when nervous.

"I would not know, Dr. Park. My division deals with science and threats to our way of life beyond human. For the past century, this division within the bureau has existed to combat sentient beings and their human allies who are working against the best interests of this planet."

Wayne said nothing.

Hogue pulled out his cellphone, punched in a code and brought up photographs, which he scrolled through and showed to Wayne. The first showed a group of agents standing on a ship with several longshoremen in handcuffs. As he looked closer he realized the men were all deformed in some way.

"Innsmouth, 1928. A raid on the Massachusetts coast to destroy a colony of Deep Ones."

"Deep Ones?"

"They're a race of humanoid aquatic beings. Fish-men, if you will."

"But 'Deep Ones'? I mean I know there are no poets in the FBI, but you couldn't come up with a better name than 'Deep Ones'? Do you call aliens 'Space Ones'?"

Hogue just stared, then scrolled to the next photo. "Waco, 1993." The image was of a wooden building with flames bursting from it.

"Wait, I thought the Branch Davidians were a radical Christian sect. Are you suggesting the botched raid was a cover story for something else?"

"That's the story we released to the media. Vernon Howell, who called himself 'David Koresh', was engaged in radical religious rituals. He was in the midst of opening a dimensional rift to bring a being that is seemingly a living fire, named Cthugha, into this world when the FBI intervened to end the ritual. All involved died at the scene."

Scroll. Third image. A covert photograph, taken from a distance through a telephoto lens. A desert. Fighters in desert clothing with their faces covered holding large guns. They were on one side of the image, on the other side were a group of individuals similarly attired, but the faces were not human but reptilian. "Sana'a, Yemen, 2015. a parley between Islamic radicals and a race of serpent people that live under the desert."

"I still don't know what..."

"They are followers of a radical but minor Islamic prophet and mathematician named Abd al Azrad, a pseudonym that means 'Worshipper of the Great Destroyer', who lived and died in the eighth century. Al'Azrad wrote a prophetic book called *Al Azif*. Here is a page from the book."

Hogue reached into the inside of his jacket and pulled out a folded piece of paper. he opened it up and handed it to Wayne.

Wayne looked at it. It was a printout of a scanned page from an ancient manuscript.

"Bullshit."

Hogue said nothing.

"You say this guy wrote this in the eighth century?" He pointed to a line of text. "If I'm reading this right, this is quantum mechanics. We didn't start even thinking about this stuff until the eighteenth century. You're telling me a minor Islamic prophet was writing about physical phenomena on the nanoscopic scale twelve and a half centuries ago?"

"Not possible, I know, and yet there it is." Hogue held out his hand expectantly and Wayne, against his wishes, handed the paper back. Quickly and meticulously it was folded and gone.

"I assume you read Arthur C. Clarke?"

The question was such a non sequitur that Wayne had to replay it in his head to hear what it actually asked.

"Yeah, sure."

"Any advanced technology is indistinguishable from magic. Al Azrad wrote what many think is a 'magic book.' I assure you, Professor Park, I believe it is more accurately an advanced mathematics textbook and that is why you are here. Your background is perfect for an experiment I'd like to try.

Reaching into his other jacket pocket, he handed Wayne another piece of paper. Wayne began to study it.

"This is…"

"Wait! Shut up!" Then, realizing what he said, he grimaced, but without looking up from the paper said, "Sorry, just…let me look at this.

The clock ticked.

Wayne looked up. "May I have my computer from my briefcase?"

Hogue nodded and Tweedledum opened the door in response to an almost immediate knock. His breifcase was handed into the room and the agent drew the laptop out, handing it to Wayne, who immediately booted up and began entering data.

After fifteen minutes, he turned the screen to Hogue, who had waited patiently, watching him work without saying a word.

"This is remarkable. This is an algorithm designed to map out the hyperbolic topography of local space anywhere in the universe, and then straighten the curves, so to speak. It introduces an angle into the curve of space."

"And something could presumably come through that angle, yes?"

Wayne stopped and considered. "I hadn't thought of that, but yes. If something exists outside the curvature of spacetime, this algorithm would allow it to enter through the angle created. But that's easily solved." He entered in several more lines of equation and showed them to Hogue.

If you alter the equation like so, it erases the angle and instead forms a non-Euclidian 3 space over it."

Hogue raised an eyebrow.

"OK, here's a metaphor. If this original equation creates a door in the universe, changing it this way closes and locks the door and builds a wall in front of it. Like so." One final keystroke and something in the universe shifted.

It was not so dramatic as flickering lights or vulgar as a scream, but something had definitely changed in the world.

Hogue's phone buzzed. He picked it up. Pressed in a code, stared at it and then turned the screen to Wayne.

The screen showed a video of a cell not unlike the one he was in. Because of the size and resolution of the screen he was having a hard time making out the image. It appeared to be a translucent mummy with a head that looked vaguely canine, but also resembled a misshapen ape. Its eyes, yellow slits deeply recessed in the holes of its face burning over a snout filled with crooked fangs, stared at the camera taking the video, on the wall above it. Its expression was pure malevolence. Then, all at once, it was not there. It had vanished, not looking at all like a bad special effect, but that it simply ceased to exist.

"What the fu…"

"That was the cell directly below this one." Hogue put the phone down. "We had captured a dimensional shambler and one of our consultants had devised equations to bind it to that room. You typed code into your computer and it was returned to its lower dimension and, I can only assume, the door was shut and the wall built. This, Mr. Park, is why we brought you in."

"I have no freaking clue what is going on," Wayne answered simply.

"You're here to save the world."

Wayne began to smile. "I'm being punked, right?" He looked at the mirror and waved. "I'm on camera right now. Who set this up? Timothy? Dr. Chaterjee? Seriously, who?"

Hogue's expression did not change. "You are on camera right now. And no, you are not being 'punked.' The camera is for archival purposes only, although a psychiatrist will watch all interviews with you to ensure we do not miss any potential issues."

Hogue reached across the table and set down a tablet with inscriptions in Latin and a series of sigils and runes. "This is a summoning ritual to open a gate to Yog Sothoth."

"Seriously, who thinks up these names?"

Hogue's expression remained unchanged. "Dr. Park, I encourage you to take this seriously. What I am about to reveal to you is classified top secret, known only to a handful. If you read the forms you signed before you were ushered in here you know that to reveal anything that you have seen, heard, done or said today will result in your immediate arrest and imprisonment for the rest of your life."

From the matter of fact way Hogue said it, Wayne knew, in his heart, he was not being punked. He suddenly felt a chill and his anxiety level shot up. He figured the best plan was to wait.

"I take it from your silence," Hogue continued, you understand the gravity of the situation. We are at war, Dr. Park, a war that threatens our entire existence."

"Wait, this al-Azrad guy - he has inspired some sort of terrorists?"

"No, sir. This has nothing to do with Muslims, the Middle East or any terrorism. This has to do with genuine terror. We are a small group of scientists and agents who are fighting beings from other stars and other dimensions that seek to destroy our world, as well as their human agents."

"OK, now it feels like you are punking me again."

"No, sir." Hogue laid a series of photos on the table between them. Blurry images, all, but they showed a variety of strange creatures, in many cases attacking human beings. In other cases, the entity was clearly dead, placed next to some common item to give a sense of its size, whether that common item was a boot or a tractor trailer. Although Hogue had said they were not terrorists, Wayne was reminded of the photos of dead bodies shown in the press when a famous terrorist was killed. A bloody, beaten formerly evil thing sat in the center of the photo, looking rather pathetic as it lay on a sheet or on the ground, lifeless but still horrific.

Hogue reached into another pocket and pulled out a flash drive.

"This contains a scanned copy of the *Al Azif*, from which that summoning spell was taken." He pointed at the paper with the "spell" for summoning the monster with the silly name, as Wayne thought of it.

"I want you to take both. Take a couple weeks. Familiarize yourself with them."

"To what end?"

"I'm taking the fight to them. These beings exist because they understand the mathematics that allow them to move through hyperspace into other dimensions. You have the exact right set of skills to close the doors. I want you to close the doors so there are no more incursions."

"Do you really think a set of computer programs can shift reality like that?"

Hogue smiled for the first time. "Clark, remember? You're going to use chaos theory and hyperbolic topography equations to work magic and close our universe off. Agent Smith here will escort you back to your university. Get to work, we'll be in touch soon."

The second time he made the journey from Arkham to Boston was very different and he was very different. A true academic, after returning to his apartment from his first visit to FBI headquarters in Boston, Wayne began to research the *Al Azif*, the beings Hogue mentioned and the mathematics that supposedly shaped their ability to enter this reality. The more he researched, the more obsessed he became. He knew Hogue was probably tracking his computer and phone and knew everything he searched for, read and asked about. The more he dug, however, the more frightened he became. He cancelled classes for the week, feigning illness. He stopped going out, and then stopped ordering food for delivery, keeping the windows covered. He cancelled classes for a second week with no explanation. He had not showered for six days, slept for seven or turned on his computer for two when a pair of agents entered his living room.

He didn't know how they had gotten in, and he panicked, attacking one with his laptop. Later, he was not certain if the other hit him with something or grabbed him hard and injected him with something, but he was unconscious in seconds and woke up in the same room as last time, handcuffed to the chair.

Hogue sat across from him, staring, silent.

Wayne slowly came back to himself and then everything flooded back and his panic began to rise again.

He felt strong hands push him down into the chair and hold him in place.

"I don't think that is necessary, Agent Smith. Professor Park will settle down and we'll have a nice chat."

Wayne forced himself to breathe and control his anxiety.

"There, now. See? Please wait outside while we have a chat." The hands left Wayne's shoulders and he heard the door behind him open, close and lock.

Hogue smiled. It was not comforting. "Told you," was all he said.

Wayne felt tears begin to roll down his face. He was well and truly losing it.

"It's all real and none of it is. The world is…"

"I know, settle down," comforted Hogue, at least as much as he could comfort.

"I have begun to hear the baying of a hound. It's not like it is in another apartment, it's like someone is watching it on television in a car driving past, but it is getting louder."

At this, Hogue looked at the mirror in a meaningful way, then turned back.

"Please," begged Wayne, "don't make me do anything more with this stuff. I am going crazy. I just want to…"

He could not complete the thought as Agent Hogue leaned across the table and slapped him hard. Wayne was shocked, but it had the intended effect, which was to focus him.

"Professor Park - Wayne, I'm not going to appeal to your sense of patriotism. I'm not going to appeal to your sense of humanity. I'm going to appeal to your sense of self-preservation.

"We knew you had stopped working since you have not logged on in two days. We need you to step up your game. Focus up and create a series of algorithms that close the gates in spacetime. If you do not close our reality off from these beings, that hound you hear will find you. And you'll be lucky if it does, as there are other entities that no doubt are now aware that you are working to banish them."

"What? No! I want out!" Wayne began to cry again.

"There is no out except to close the doors."

"HOW?" Wayne leapt up.

Hogue did not react at all. Just looked at him until he sat back down again, meekly.

"The last time you were here, it took you less than twenty minutes to banish a dimensional shambler that you did not even know existed. You have the knowledge to do this. You lack the will and strength to face the reality that is and the reality that must be."

Wayne looked up. "Must be?"

Hogue cleared his throat. "Explain chaos theory to me."

"What?"

"What is chaos theory?"

Wayne's mind reeled. Then he said, "It's the study of dynamic systems. Small differences in initial conditions means that radically different outcomes can be reached by altering just a single, small element. In other words, nothing is truly predictable. The present determines the future, but the approximate present does not approximately mandate specific futures."

"Yog-Sothoth knows the gate. Yog-Sothoth is the gate. Yog-Sothoth is the key and guardian of the gate. Past, present, future, all are one in Yog-Sothoth. He knows where the Old Ones broke through of old, and where They shall break through again. He knows where They have trod earth's fields, and where They still tread them, and why no one can behold Them as They tread." Hogue recited from memory.

"That's from *Al Azif*."

"Yes. You have read it. Good. Thus you have beheld them as they tread. They are terrifying. They would unmake reality."

"So they hate us?"

"Do you hate the termites that infest your house? No, you simply eradicate them and never give them a second thought. We are as termites to them. Those earlier incursions, the photos I showed you? They are nothing compared to what could happen. Self-preservation, Dr. Park. Yog Sothoth knows past, present and future. But chaos theory says the future is unpredictable, because variables and random events change every possible outcome."

Wayne began to calm down.

"You can write the algorithms that close those gates. You are the chaos that even in a deterministic system changes the outcome. Go home. Shower. Eat a good meal. Then start again. Agent Smith and his associate will return to get you in two weeks. I expect you to have something for us by then."

Wayne did as he was told. He showered. He went out and got kimchee like his mom used to make. He then opened his laptop, opened *Al Azif* and opened the universe. He understood suddenly how to shift everything. And then he realized more. It was as if a darkened landscape was suddenly made visible by lightning. He saw it all laid out as it truly was. He also saw his own fate, and knew he had to change it.

He sent an email to himself, knowing it would be read. Hogue had given him two weeks. He only needed one. He simply sent an email saying, "I'm ready."

For the third and hopefully final time they wended their way through Boston traffic. They entered the parking garage. This time they did not make him wait. Hogue was already waiting in the room when he arrived.

"You look much better than when I saw you last, Dr. Park."

"Because I know the answer. Topological mixing."

"Explain."

"Some chaoticians don't like topological mixing. They say chaos is only determined by initial conditions, but topological mixing says systems are dynamic and evolve over time. If we anticipate the potential mix points, we can overlap them or mix them."

"I think you lost me there."

Wayne grinned. "Any given region in phase space will eventually overlap with all other given spaces. So rather than close the doors, I have linked them all together. Any gate which opens will open on infinity. Any being summoned or attempting to manifest on our planet will manifest only at the end of time. All points except zero lead to infinity, and thus we are safe."

He handed a flash drive to Hogue who took it and placed it on the table between them.

"Put that in your system. Run the algorithms. All points except zero will be closed literally forever."

"What about zero point?"

"You don't have to worry about that. Nothing originates at zero."

Hogue smiled. "Well, it appears my faith in you was not misplaced. You have done a great service to your nation and humanity. I need not remind you that you are sworn to secrecy about all of this."

"There is one last issue."

Agent Hogue raised an eyebrow.

"I know you like to tie up loose ends and I know I have a dangerous amount of information that can, according to you, compromise national security."

"I assure you the government is not in the business of eliminating..." Hogue began, and stopped as Wayne unbuttoned his shirt and pulled it open.

"We both know that's a lie, and that is why I have this." On his chest, over his heart was a new tattoo. Hogue could not begin to describe what it looked like with words, but he immediately recognized a variety of aspects of the design. Wayne decided to help him understand. "It is a blend of a Poincaré map, a probability algorithm and several sigils from the *Al Azif.*"

It was the first time Wayne had ever seen Hogue surprised.

"How did you...?"

"My older brother? Before he tried to stick up that restaurant, he worked in a tattoo parlor. In Soledad he kept his work up. You remember what you said when we first met? That he and I didn't have much in common to talk about? You're right. But I always ask him about his interests and the last time I went to visit him he had some new ink. He told me how he tattooed himself and others behind bars with everyday items. The funny thing about being a genius is that I have an audiographic memory. Someone tells me something once and I retain it forever. So I decided to ink myself. You like it?"

He began to button his shirt back up.

"I'm not sure I follow you, Wayne."

"Call it insurance. I know that you are planning on offing me. Oh, don't try to deny it. You'll make it look like an accident: an 'accidental' radiation exposure at the university, a hit and run at an intersection as I walk across the campus, maybe a 'home invasion gone wrong' staged scenario in which a wetwork team breaks into my apartment and leaves me a corpse. Eliminating me is the only logical option, given your goals."

Hogue remained inexpressive.

Wayne tapped the tattoo under his shirt. "This is a gate opening glyph. If I die an unnatural death, my body will become a gate itself, allowing untold horrors into the world. If I die a natural death, of old age in my bed, then it is just an interesting tattoo." Wayne smiled. "You're the one who gave me the idea - appealing to self-preservation, remember? Well, I have just transformed myself into the zero point."

"What happens if something happens to you and it's not us?" the agent asked.

Wayne's smile widened, "Well, now you have a vested interest in keeping me alive, making sure as you follow me that your agents know the Heimlich Maneuver, have the right blood type for an immediate emergency transfusion, ensure I never get mugged, be ready with an ambulance, you know - keep me from harm for the rest of my natural life."

Hogue's expression still remained unchanged. "I suppose you're going to blackmail us now, demand money."

Nope." Wayne stood up. "I want to be left alone. I want the gift that I gave the rest of the world - to live the rest of my life without having to fear horrible death. So call it off and your agents only follow me from now on in order to ensure I live a long, happy life."

Hogue sat, staring at him for what seemed like an eternity. Then Wayne saw something shift in his eyes. A decision made. He picked up the phone, punched in seven numbers. "The delivery for Park is cancelled." He punched another key and set the phone down.

"Satisfied?"

"Immensely. If you change your mind, remember what happens." Wayne turned to go.

"Didn't think you had it in you, Park," Hogue called from behind him.

Wayne turned back and smiled one last time. "Because you don't actually understand chaos theory, Hogue. While initial conditions may set up a series of events seemingly predictable based on past behavior, the deterministic nature of these systems does not make them predictable. And when you introduce something as random as a human being simply wanting to survive, well, a way is found to change the outcome. Have a good day, Agent Hogue."

And he walked out of the building into a long, happy life.

From Cronus to Cthulhu
John Kaniecki

Immortality, my dear friend, is a bitter curse. I know what I possess is sought more diligently then gold, silver or diamonds. It is even more attractive then that most coveted intangible, a thing called power. Perhaps if there was indeed a Fountain of Youth. Ah to be eternally young that would have definitely improved my situation. But alas I am condemned to hobble about this cruel Earth perpetually an ancient man. Believe me when I say, every day I feel my age. My bones ache in misery singing harmony with my soul. What is my age you may ask? More centuries then you can count on your fingers and toes. Suffice it to say I've been around.

I must disguise my words with frail ambiguities. There is a whole cabal of us old timers that walk the dusty roads of Earth. We have none to thank but Satan himself for our nasty ordeal. Well now, perhaps I am shifting the true blame from myself. After all it is not every person who sells their soul to the devil for eternal life. Most that do were far more clever than I and had other benefits tossed in to fatten up the deal. Alas I signed my name in blood simply in exchange for eternal life. I must sigh in grief to say I got what I deserved.

This story it is not about me. In fact it is not really something I experienced, at least not first hand. My tale is a story that needs to be told. Yet, it will not be something that would reveal my identity. It is only that fact that emboldens my tongue and loosens my pen. I would like to have a little payback to my foe. I would like to shine a light on the Prince of Darkness if it only be a frail candle. It is not such that I have compassion on any that would follow in my steps. We who have signed the oath are a despicable lot, the scourge of the Earth.

If there is one pass time I truly enjoy in my perpetual elderly years it is reading. I have passed through the phases of carnal pleasures. I have tried every drug and have investigated all forms of lustful desires. These were temporary fixes that satisfied for only a brief moment. They soon grew old and stale. It came to my realization that the tempting fruits of Satan were in fact all appearance and no substance. Empty promises are the contents of the whole rotten barrel. But reading, now that is a grand adventure.

Alexandria was my favorite hang out place. That was a library beyond description. I have never seen a worthy rival. It was there that I studied most diligently. Morning, noon and night I could be found pouring over the papyrus manuscripts. It was not the great knowledge that I was accumulating that motivated me. Rather it was the joy in the journey. In all the world I had found one thing that I truly enjoyed without measure. Far much better then eating, mind you. Indulging the pallet leaves one's physical frame in agony. Reading however sharpens the mind all the while entertaining.

It was the subject of Cronus that really caught my interest like none other. That he predated the Greeks was no secret. According to the 'official' myth Cronus had sired a slew of whole host of children. These grew to become the deities of Greece after they did in their 'father'. As true with all religions, the faith was not a search for truth but rather an exercise in control. None could dare question the status quo. To deny the doctrine was heresy and punishable by death. I of course being immortal had no fears of death. But to spend eternal life in a dismal dungeon cell was less attractive then death.

In Alexandria there was a select few who practiced the dark arts. They evoked the pantheon of gods of Egypt. I infiltrated their number. Now, I know that I am risking exposure. Perhaps some of that small, select, group were miserable creatures like me who had made an 'oath' in blood with Satan. If that is so please do not attempt to decipher my identity. Rather think of me as one who is keeping the flame of Cthulhu burning bright.

Who is that you say? Allow me to continue with my story dear friend and I shall reveal all. Whether you chose to believe it or not is really irrelevant. I am simply relinquishing my responsibility and performing my duties. My hands shall be washed clean of all blood guilt. That is all the matters to my selfish self.

Now, the worship of the Egyptian gods by my companions was simply a ruse. In Alexandria the masses still clung to their deities despite their defeat to Greece. But as the military goes so follows the divine. The power of Set, Osiris, and company was simply dismissed with a mocking laugh by the conquering legions of Greece. So a small group of zealots clinging to the banished faith posed no threat whatsoever. But the cover of the book was switched and the pages soaked with blasphemy. For our exclusive party was dedicated to the illegitimate son of Cronus. His name of course was Cthulhu.

At the time I thought that perhaps this was pure foolishness. Like so many Gnostic organizations, knowledge of the group and doctrine was revealed in greater clarity the deeper one progressed. I was an initiate and pure novice. Still it became apparent to me that this sect of Cthulhu was throughout the entire world. In fact I vividly recall viewing a map of extremely accurate depictions of what would one day be called the Americas.

When Rome in it's arrogance came and burned the library of Alexandria I wept for my virgin mistress. To this day in horrible nightmares I can see the flames burning. I would prefer the torments of hell over those hideous fires I witnessed. Gone was all the knowledge since the dawn of creation that were contained in that massive collection. Papyrus full of wonderful words now nothing more then ashes of mourning. My associates too vanished like smoke in the wind. I, not knowing anything further then my local association, could not flee to join others elsewhere. I had no place to seek out the bastard son of Cronus. But still in my heart I held a home for Cthulhu. And not in my head alone but in my head. For in my brain I never lost focus of the elder of the dark gods. Why you may ask? Well let me tell my tale.

Over a dozen and a half of centuries had passed and the whole world had been turned upside down. The barbarians of Europe fueled by their sciences had risen from their caves and bearskins to become unrivaled masters. In fact the fought two world wars amongst themselves to decide whom of their number would dominate the Earth. Millions upon millions had perished in the madness. But personally, for me, it brought me to my knees in wonder. For the coming of the reigning of the pale man was foretold centuries ago by the followers of Cthulhu.

Ah and then my tale begins in utmost earnest. I being a man of darkest skin tones decided that this insanity of the Europeans held nothing but woe for me. The lure of mammon that captivated these conquering colonizers repulsed me. I headed for the deepest jungles of Africa to her secret cities. It was an attempt for me to escape the reality of the changing world. I knew sooner or later I would have to come to terms with the new elite. Eventually I left the solitude. It was, in fact, a move of necessity. To stay any longer would have brought suspicion as to why this old man did not die. It was a dilemma that I have faced constantly in my many years.

Fresh out of the woods, so to speak, I had to acclimate myself to reality. So much had changed! The advances of technology amazed me. I was seduced by the information explosion. Above all was the superfluity of books. I was truly overwhelmed and began to devour the innumerable volumes of literature. And there I discovered open to the world like the noon day sun an author by the name of H.P. Lovecraft. A man who openly talked about Cthulhu. I was both amazed and impressed. It could not be some coincidence. If only I had time to have rise in the ranks.

Astrology is one of the most arcane arts. As such it is one of the most difficult. Contrary to the host of frauds and fakes astrology is useless to determine ones immediate future. True the lining of the celestial bodies does leave an indelible mark on a person. Much in the same way as a brand on a cattle. But the stars are indeed an extremely accurate indicator of the seasons. I am not of course talking of spring, summer, fall and winter. Rather there are epochs or ages. The dawn of science was one era. In fact it is the period which is in dominance now. But it is waning and fading with a rapid retreat. Of course it may not seem so but I am confident of this truth.

The ancient texts talked of the times when the fires would descend. This would occur after the name of Cthulhu, the one who sleeps has been proclaimed. I had watched with horror as the United States dropped not one but two atomic bombs on citizens of Japan. The nuclear fission bombs literally burned as the sun albeit in brief flashes. Without a doubt this was the fulfillment of the prophecies.

It is true that I knew little of the faith the I am such a devout follower. Yet I knew the basic tenets that I was instructed in almost two millennia ago. It was the tale that exposed the truth from Cronus to Cthulhu. I will now expound upon that mystery and then bid you a hasty goodbye. All the while to my compatriots I have news of the most wicked nature. That is we have been betrayed!

Coming to the United States in the turbulent times of the sixties brought upon me anxiety. There was of course the racial struggle surging. The African American man was demanding equality. Also social forces were resisting the capitalistic system for a more sharing and equitable one. Neither of those causes gave me the slightest interest. I had no concern for any other save myself. It was the answer to Cthulhu that I sought out. Allow me to truly confess my hopes. It was my greatest expectation that through the power of that dreaming deity that I could overcome my curse of Satan. I intended to pit the son of Cronus against the Prince of this World.

Cthulhu is in fact a creature of cruelness. Perhaps my attraction to him was that I saw so much of myself in my dark master. Evil however does not negate intelligence. The dreaming deity lay in his dormant state awaiting a time when he could be ushered into the world of living. Of course it would be his task to conquer and rule. It is in the ruling aspect that my hopes lay. For who can rule the world alone? Does not one need a government or some other association? It would be better to rule on Earth then to wander as some hopeless vagabond. Ah to be a priest in the order of my master.

So it was in the course of my travels that I ran across a man whose name I shall not reveal. He is dead, I assure you. His throat was slit with my own hand. I feel a slight measure of remorse for doing this individual in. He was a wicked man. But then again, if we are to talk in candid honesty, most men are wicked to one degree or another. Who is there without sin? This man practiced the dark arts of voodoo and had a knowledge of Satanic ritual. But those two aspects held little attraction for me. I was well versed in both fields already far beyond the proficiency of this man. What he had that I desired was a set of papyrus scrolls.

How such an individual had attained this most rare and precious treasure I did not inquire. Certainly not at first. In fact I had to play a ruse that I had no knowledge of the immense value of the writings, let alone my personal passion. I have learned over the years the subtle arts of the conman. Never show your lust. It will only raise the price of the ante.

This man had bonded with me. I however had long since discarded any love or affection. Not because I am a cruel and hard man. Rather it was a task I undertook as a necessity. I have buried my wife a dozen times. I have said goodbye to dear friends scores of times. It got to the point where the misery of the coming loss outweighed the happiness that friendship could provide. So I in a world of billions walk alone. Except of course with the others who have taken the 'oath'. But I desire nothing to do with such wicked creatures. It is true that I am a fox but the others they are dragons. For unlike me, one who has rejected Satan, the majority have embellished their dark lord.

It was after some years of interaction and feigned friendship with this person of interest he finally let me in on his secret. There was an island, I shall say no more than to say it was in the Western Hemisphere. It was very tiny and out of the way of the shipping lanes. No humans lived upon the small outcropping. There shipwrecked upon the shore was a vessel that had sailed from Egypt in ancient times. I learned the history of that voyage from the papyrus writings I discovered on board. The captain wished to salvage the knowledge of the most ancient Egyptians. He and his crew were patriots longing to restore defeated Egypt to it's glory. Understanding that knowledge is power he took his treasures to preserve them. Unfortunately somehow he was shipwrecked upon this nameless atoll.

His misery was my salvation, and my friends demise. After personally visiting the deserted island I indulged myself in the murder of my associate. He, in fact, had done me the greatest service ever rendered unto me. What a cur I am to have repaid him in such a way. But necessity can bring harsh extremes. Besides this man was a dark fiend and truly deserved a brutal demise. At least that is how I justify my guilt.

It was a sheer delight to be reintroduced to the ancient texts I had once adored so many years ago. It was like walking in another time. For a while I felt at home. Hope filled my heart and life was pleasant. I even dared to thank God for his mercy and kindness. And then, as an eagle flying over at the greatest heights and then miserably plummeting to the ground, I fell from jubilation to utter horror. A grim misery beyond anything I had ever experienced. I came to know the truth about Cthulhu the illegitimate so of Cronus.

Mister H.P. Lovecraft was a most clever man. His fanciful words brought the dreaming god into the psyche of humanity. He did this in a bold way. Truly during his lifetime he received almost no attention. But after passing into the shadows of death many have come boldly forward to give praises and accolades. The majority I suspect are those secretly involved with the cult that I was once an initiate in so many years ago in Alexandria. Of this I must now speak on.

Allow me to boldly state the we have been duped. According to those ancient tomes that I viewed the time of events had been reversed. The fall of the stars should have proceeded the proclamation of the great name of Cthulhu. I will now give you the exact details of why that is.

Cthulhu was never truly the illegitimate son of Cronus. Rather that claim was to bring him on the level of that deity and his offspring. The truth is far too shocking for humanity to accept. That this Cthulhu, this creature whose semblance was so far from human, that he could be best described as a monster. That this being of the great beyond was dominant over the so called gods as a giant over ants. Truly then none would pay homage or bow the knee to the modern rulers. All would seek out the ancient one. At least those with sense.

Portraying Cthulhu as Cronus' bastard son was a way to turn away those who happened upon his doctrine. That was the first effort of the powers to be. To diminish Cthulhu into the oblivion of obscurity. If there were no adherents to awaken the sleeping god, then there would never be the call. That attempt, as we are all aware now, has failed.

So then came the call from one H.P Lovecraft. We can only suspect the motivation of his premature beckoning. Perhaps he was fooled into taking the actions that he did. Yet his writings contain such an intimacy of knowledge that I would have to rule this motive as impossible. I believe that this Lovecraft purposely spread the name of the great Cthulhu prematurely to awaken him too early.

I attribute this to no other quality then excessive adoration. It is the only explanation that makes sense with all the facts that I have gathered. What would motivate a mortal to do such a deed? Indeed that word 'mortal' is truly the key. For H.P. Lovecraft knew that if he had done what was proper and kept his mouth silent, the time of the coming of his master, would have been out of his lifetime. So he took it upon himself to awaken the sleep god a little bit earlier. I suppose he reasoned that Cthulhu once awakened could complete the task of his return.

But the stars are most powerful. Are they not the eternal markers? Do they not continue in their immortality steadfast. Empires rise and fall. Ages and epochs they come and go. But through it all there is a consistent factor, the stars. As such the authority of their council is absolute.

Cthulhu you see was a god from a far away distant time. He and his kindred minions had lived in their epoch. Great and wonderful as they were they were still no match to the eternal ever present stars. In their wisdom they clearly saw what was to come. Through arcane knowledge and dark calculations they contemplated the future. If only they could bring the stars to Earth at the precise moment, they could in fact skew the orientation of the universe. The timing needed to be precise. The grand overlords of the past needed every smidgen of power the could muster. Cthulhu could have successfully returned. I have no doubt to this conclusion.

What else could one say? That the words of mighty Cthulhu were false? Surely he has not returned, that is obvious to all! And so I say this to those who work and plan, that your plans have been frustrated. Yet allow me to finish this proclamation with hope. There was more written in those papyrus papers then I have revealed. Contingency plans just in case. Truly great is the wisdom of Cthulhu. I do not know if Cthulhu has returned to slumber after his early awakening. I cannot see into that nether world of gray. Both I do know this that the great Cthulhu lives. Where there is life there is hope. I will inform you all of those secret writings I have discovered. I will not repeat the mistakes of the past. I after all have all the time in the world.

Innocence and Blood
Kevin Henry

It was an unusually gray day in southern California and I watched the rain beat down on my windshield as I drove to a job. I was missing home and in a surly mood.

I'd come to California looking for new opportunities but the charm had worn off and the years had flown by. Now California was like the old slut you wake up beside after the alcohol has worn off and you see her with her makeup smeared and her hair knotted up and you just want to slip out before she wakes up. All I wanted was to get back home. Back to New York. I figured after one more good job I could do it.

Earlier, I had gotten a call from this dame about some urgent business. She wouldn't meet in my office. I had to go to her. No problem except she lived in Arcadia, which is the playground of the rich and beautiful. Not my crowd but the money spends good. I strapped on my heater, hopped in my boiler and breezed off.

The address she gave me took me to a ranch in the Valley. The Von Junzt ranch to be exact. I'd heard the name in passing. They were old money. Just what I needed. Most of their kind are inbred lunatics.

The spread was impressive. The ranch must have been twenty acres or more, mostly oak trees. They had kennels, stables, and tennis courts. The mansion itself was huge, with all sorts of European style columns and such.

Pulling my bucket up in front of that finery was like flopping a turd down on a dinner table in front of the Queen of England.

I straightened my tie and headed for the front doors.

On both sides of the heavy, stone stairs leading up to the front of the mansion were square pillars with odd carvings. One in particular caught my attention. It looked like a man with bat wings and tentacles on his face. I felt a chill in my bowels as I passed it. Must have been the Chinese I had for lunch.

Before I could knock, the front doors opened and I found myself staring at the ugliest mug I ever saw. He was like a brick wall with a nice suit and shiny shoes. His skin had a greenish tint and there wasn't the smallest glint of intelligence in his small, black eyes.

"Brock Dedman, here to see Mrs. Von Junzt," I said, not even sure if this gink could understand simple words. He must have been savvy because he let me in.

The place was fancier on the inside than out. There were paintings on all the walls and vases on pedestals in every corner. Each one was probably worth more cabbage than I'd see in a lifetime.

I nosed around for a few minutes. The dummy at the door didn't seem to mind. Something about the place seemed off kilter. There was a sickening, sweet smell, like perfume on a corpse. The place reeked of decay and death.

Finally, the lady of the house came to meet me. She fairly floated down a set of circular stairs, dressed like she was going out for a night on the town. She wasn't what you'd call pretty, but managed to be alluring all the same. Her face was thin, with sharp cheek bones. Her eyes were large and fierce, almost magnetic. I couldn't stop staring at them.

"Brock Dedman," I said, introducing myself. I put out a mitt for a shake, to which she simply smiled. It was like a snake's smile, cold and dangerous.

"I know who you are, Mr. Dedman. Follow me, please."

I followed her through several rooms until we ended up in a greenhouse. The air was thick and wet. Large drops of moisture ran down the glass walls and dripped from the glass ceiling onto the plants below. Exotic plants filled the place, none more bizarre than the white lotus blossoms, with their pale petals shaped like the faces of small dead men.

"I hope you don't mind talking here, Mr. Dedman. The greenhouse soothes me."

"What's the job? Suspect your husband of stepping out on you? Former business associate blackmailing you?"

"My daughter has been kidnaped," she said very matter-of-factly.

"How long she been missing? And how do you know she was snatched and didn't just run off? Kids do that sometimes."

She stared at me with those large, predatory eyes that I couldn't look away from.

"Who would run from this?" She asked, as if I was a sap. I didn't say it out loud, but the place looked to me like what you'd call a gilded cage.

"She is six years old. She's been missing for two days."

"What's the little darling's name?"

"Dorothy Anne."

"Can you think of anyone who'd want to harm your family? Have you received a ransom note?"

"There will be no ransom note. She was taken by her uncle Ervin."

"Ok," I said, scratching my head. "If you know who did it, why not go to the police?"

"No law enforcement. This must be handled discreetly."

"I'm a gum-shoe, Mrs. Von Junzt. I ain't no dropper."

"By your reputation, you are known as a man who can handle himself. I expect you to handle this situation to my satisfaction."

"You know my fee?"

"Money will be of no consequence, but time is of the essence. I need her back within two days."

When I inquired as to the time frame, she said Dorothy was taking medicine for some rare illness and needed another dose by that time or it would be curtains for her.

After getting details about Ervin, I left. Apparently there had been a rift between him and the rest of the family over some religious dispute. This had happened recently and was suspected as the motivation for him taking the girl. Like I said, lunatics.

I checked all of Ervin Chandler's known numbers and addresses but hit a brick wall. He wasn't at the house he shared with his wife or the one he had bought for his mistress. The next day I did some major leg work. I looked closer into Ervie and found a warehouse he owned through a dummy corporation. I doubt if his own family knew about it. It was my next stop.

The warehouse was a broken-down building on the margin of the city's business district. It was dark when I arrived which suited me just fine. The kind of work I was about to engage in blurred the lines of legality and I'd just as soon not be seen doing it.

I gained entrance to the warehouse though a side door. It was locked but I knew how to overcome such obstacles, hence the blurred legality. Anyways, once inside I gave it the up and down. There must have been thousands, maybe millions of dollars worth of stolen stuff. Apparently Erv wasn't satisfied with his trust fund.

The ground floor was unoccupied so I found a stair that led down. It's always bad to go down into the darkness of a place you're not supposed to be at in the first place. Nothing good ever came of it.

At the bottom of the stair I found a closed door. I smelled the same odor I had detected at the Von Junzt mansion. It reeked of rot, decay, and death. There was light coming from under the door so I knew someone was waiting on the other side. Not being one to favor caution, I barged right in like I owned the place.

On the other side of the door I met the second ugliest mug I ever seen. This one looked like he could be the brother of the doorman at the mansion. I didn't give him time to act. I played him a symphony of chin music that would have made Joe Louis proud. The bird just stared at me with those dead eyes. He didn't even flinch.

He whacked me on the beezer so hard I saw stars. I came back at him with my best work but to no avail. He swatted me again and I went reeling on the floor. I knew I couldn't take much more of that kind of hammering. This Bruno had mitts like anvils and meant to croak me.

I was behind the eight-ball, so I pulled out my bean shooter and clipped him good. I was astonished when he didn't seem to notice. The ape stepped up and walloped me hard. My heater went flying. He gave me a pounding like I never took before. He showed me how my teeth looked outside my mouth and all covered in blood. I felt ribs crack. Darkness was closing in quick.

When I got the chance, I scrambled to my gat like a rat to the last ball of cheese on earth. When I felt the cold metal in my hands again I turned and gave the bastard a severe case of lead poisoning. He didn't care. The lug picked me up and tossed me through the doorway I'd come through, into the wooden stair-railing. A piece of railing broke off and I picked up a board with a nail in the end. The sonofabitch might grease me, but I'd make him remember me in the morning.

When he came for me again, I struck his noodle with the board, driving the nail straight into his brain. He stiffened up and fell square on top of me. He weighed a ton and smelled like a graveyard.

After rolling the stiff off me, I reloaded. No chance of surprise now. Everyone in a two block radius must have heard that commotion.

There was a door at the back of the room, so that's where I went. It was locked, naturally, so I finessed it with the heel of my right foot. It gave way and I entered.

I saw a man holding a little girl against the far wall. More important to my immediate well-being, I also saw two more of those dead-eyed man-mountains rushing me. I remembered the first palooka going down with a nail in his head, so I plugged both his buddies in their noggins. They dropped like a can house chippy's underwear on half-price night.

My vision was blurry by that time and my aim wasn't what you'd call steady. Still, I trained my rod on the man holding the girl.

"It's over Erv. Give her up and you walk away from this."

He held a silver letter opener to Dorothy's neck. It wasn't a knife, but it would easily penetrate soft little-girl flesh and tiny arteries.

"Back away," he said. "I'll do it. I swear, I'll kill her right here."

I stared at him for a moment. He was nervous and sweaty. His hands trembled. His eyes were wide and his breathing came quick and shallow. Little Dorothy was a real doll though. She stood quiet and still, not aggravating the situation.

"I don't think you want to do that Erv. You took her for a reason and I don't think it was to kill her. Her family wants her back now, though."

"Those fiends? You don't understand. You don't know what they want to do to her."

"You're right Erv. Why don't you tell me? Fill me in."

"They're sick. I couldn't let them do it. I won't let them ruin everything."

"Ruin what? You're not making much sense and I'm getting tired of holding this iron."

He rambled on about his family being in some cult. I got tired of listening and took a step forward. He got a squirrelly look in his eyes and pushed the tip of the letter opener tight against the girl's skin. A single drop of blood trickled down her neck.

I tried reasoning with him but his disposition only deteriorated. I recognized the look in his eyes. It was the same look I'd seen in husbands before they redecorated the living room with their wives brains, and in desperate souls before stepping off a ledge to paint the sidewalk red.

I pumped a slug into his brain.

Little Dorothy didn't seem to be much worse for wear. She was a real trooper. When I picked her up to get her out of there she smiled up at me.

"I'm special," she said.

"I bet you are," I said with a wink. "I bet you're a regular princess."

She reminded me of the kid I left behind in New York. At least, that's what I imagined she had looked like at that age.

I regretted wrecking my daughter's life. Sophia. Beautiful name. Beautiful kid. I left her and her momma because I couldn't hack the job I'd signed on for. The job of husband and father.

I wasn't cut out to work in the local grocery store, coming home to the wife every evening, chatting about the banality of life over the dinner she spent all day cooking for me, arguing over how much she could spend each week on her hair and shoes, going to church on Sunday and pretending not to recognize the same stiffs sitting in the pews that I'd seen coming out of the bars and strip joints on Friday night.

No sir, that wasn't the life for me, but I was going to do right by Sophia, though. When I went back.

I didn't take Dorothy home after the warehouse. Something was gnawing at the back of my mind. Something I needed to check out. I needed to do some research before going back to the ranch so I took Dorothy to stay with a friend.

Velvet was her stage name but I knew her as Rose. I'd known her since she was a kid. Rose was a good girl with a lot of baggage. She danced at a titty bar called the Blue Iguana to pay the bills, but always dreamed of going to school to be a lawyer. Just like I dreamed of going back home. Time had a funny way of slipping away with your dreams, like a thief stealing your life savings a few dollars at a time. Before you know it you're flat broke and turning tricks in skeevy alleys to get by. Time was a bastard like that.

It was three a.m. when I knocked on Rose's door. I knew she would be home from her shift by then. When she opened the door, she was still wearing the makeup she wore on stage, dark around the eyes and heavy on the lipstick. She didn't look happy to see me.

"Brock. Holy shit! You look like warmed over death."

"Thanks. Got tired of having my features in the same place all the time. Thought I'd get them rearranged."

She opened the door wider to let me in and saw Dorothy peeking around my leg. "Who's this? Brock, what have you got yourself into?"

I didn't give Rose any particulars, but told her I needed to stash the girl for a day or so. She didn't know from nothing about watching kids, but I sweet talked her into it. She let me use her bathroom to clean up and stitch my face back together. I flipped her a fin to buy the kid something to eat, then headed back to my place.

My friend Johnny Walker helped me get to sleep, but I kept dreaming about being chased by creepy little girls and tentacled men rising from the ocean.

The next morning I made arrangements to meet with a college professor who owed me a favor. Dr. Philip Ashton was an expert on occult stuff who I'd helped out of a sticky situation involving a curvy student and a batch of compromising photographs. I made the six hour drive to San Francisco to meet with him at his office at the Golden Gate University.

Dr. Ashton, a man a fragile constitution, was shocked to see me in my current bruised and battered state. I assured him that everything was under control.

"Doc, I need to know if you recognize this design," I said, laying a sheet of paper on his desk. On the paper I'd drawn the tentacled man with wings that I'd seen carved in stone at the Von Juntz mansion.

He looked as if he'd seen a ghost. He locked the door, poured us both a glass of Scotch, and sat nervously in the chair behind his desk.

"Where did you see that?"

"Carved into a stone pillar. There were other symbols but this is the one that stuck with me."

"Why do you need to know this? Is there a connection with a case you're working? If so, drop it. Drop it immediately."

"Can't do that doc. I'm balls deep in it now. A young girl's life may be at stake."

He downed his Scotch and poured a new one.

"There is a book called Unaussprechlichen Kulten, also known as the Black Book. It is the book of unspeakable cults. The first edition appeared in 1839 in Düsseldorf, Germany. Few copies still exist. An edition is known to be kept in a locked vault at the Miskatonic University library. Some few book collectors and occult scholars have managed to find it over the years."

The doc took another swig of his drink.

"I convulsed in instinctive nausea when I looked upon its cursed pages. The symbols and hieroglyphs in that book were never meant to be seen by Man."

"What's in the book? And what's it got to do with this octopus man?"

"The text of the Black Book contains information on cults that worship pre-human deities. This tentacled being is one of them."

"So, people worship Mr. fish-face?"

"His name is Cthulhu. He is one of the Great Old Ones, a race of ancient, powerful deities from space who once ruled the Earth and who have since fallen into a death-like sleep."

"People believe in this nonsense?"

He leaned forward in his chair and fixed me with a withering stare. "Do not discount that which your mind cannot perceive, Mr. Dedman."

"You believe it?"

His hands trembled as he answered. "Let's just say that I've seen too much not to believe. A wise man once said *'The most merciful thing in the world, I think, is the inability of the human mind to correlate all its contents.' Life is a terrible thing, Mr. Dedman. From beneath the reality we know sometimes peer horrible hints of truth. It is these things which haunt our dreams at night."

"This cult, what do they want? What's the goal?"

"To bring the Great Old Ones back. Through arcane ritual and human sacrifice they hope to open a portal that will bring them back to rule again. Tonight is a significant time for them. An aligning of--"

"Human sacrifice," I repeated. I suddenly felt like I'd been kicked in the gut by a donkey. "Gotta go," I said, heading for the door.

"Don't go poking around, Mr. Dedman. These cults are dangerous."

"So am I."

I couldn't stop thinking about little Dorothy Anne. Such a sweetheart. And her own family meant to sacrifice her to some old gods that didn't even exist. That was what Ervin meant to save her from. I blew his brains out for doing the right thing. I'd set things right. I didn't know how exactly, but I'd find a way.

The drive back to Pasadena was agonizing. I finally pulled up out front of Rose's apartment about ten-thirty p.m. A strange sense of urgency made me take the steps two at a time. When I stood in front of her door, I saw it wasn't shut and locked like it should have been. It hung open just a crack. It had been forced open.

I pulled my heater and slipped into the room. The only light came from the neon sign outside the window, bathing the room in alternating blue and red. I immediately smelled the stench of rot and death, just like at the Van Juntz mansion and at Ervie's warehouse.

I made my way through the apartment, staying low and quiet. Near the bathroom, I found Rose on the floor. Her head was twisted around backwards. She stared up at me as she lay on her stomach. Her beautiful, dead face was blue like a corpse, then red like some hellish specter. Blue then red. I got sick and puked all over her carpet. I felt bad about it but I guess she wouldn't mind. Not now. Not ever again. She was a good girl. She didn't deserve this.

There was no sign of Dorothy Anne.

I knew who had taken the girl and what I had to do. Sure, they were her family, but this wouldn't be the first time someone had needed protection from their own kin and it damn sure wouldn't be the last. Family have a way of hurting each other in a way no one else can.

As my trusty snub-nose .38 wouldn't pack enough punch for the party I had planned, I went to a friend to pick up additional supplies. I picked up a Colt M1911A1 .45 and an Ithaca 37 shotgun with double-ought buckshot rounds. I also grabbed a machete, which piqued the curiosity of the party supply merchant. As usual, he asked no questions. He did require payment up front, however, as these sorts of parties were the kind people frequently didn't walk away from. So much for my New York homecoming fund.

As I drove to the Von Juntz ranch, the rain was falling again. I ditched my boiler along the road before anyone at the mansion could see the headlights and went the rest of the way on foot. The dogs in the kennels must have smelled me because they were kicking up a racket. They were only doing their job but I cursed them anyway.

I made my way through the dark to the back of the mansion. There was one big-and-ugly guarding the door. As stealth was still the name of the game, I pulled out the machete and hacked him up real good. I kept slicing and he kept coming. He came at me with missing fingers and hands lopped off, with his insides hanging outside and with half his face missing. Finally, after I took off his head, he stopped moving.

There was something doc Ashton had said about seeing too many things to not believe in all that supernatural jazz. I was beginning to see what he meant.

I gained entry to the house and tip-toed ever so softly down a dark hall. I was holding the shotgun at the ready, aimed at head level.

The goon who got the jump on me was quiet as a mouse fart. I felt his cold, clammy hands around my throat before ever hearing a sound. Those paws were like a vise and they squeezed the strength and the fight right out of me. My vision got blurry and then everything went black.

***

When I came around I was in a large, shadowy chamber. From the echoes of voices around me, it must have been a basement. My head throbbed and my throat was raw.

When I tried to move, I realized that I was lying bare-chested on stone and my hands were tied to metal rings in the floor. Noticing that I was awake, the voices hushed up. I saw a familiar figure in front of me.

"Good evening, Mr. Dedman," Mrs. Von Juntz purred. "How good of you to join us. And, how very predictable."

"Sorry about that. Must have left all my good tricks in my other jacket."

"You're about to perform the greatest trick of all . . . bringing back the Great Old Ones, our Masters from Beyond."

"Thanks, but I'll pass. I'm not really into old ones. I like mine young. And alive."

"Like Dorothy Anne?"

My heart leaped into my throat when I saw little Dorothy step up from behind Mrs. Von Juntz. She held a dagger in her tiny hands.

"I can see by the look of terror and revulsion on your face that you're confused, Mr. Dedman. You thought we were going to kill her?"

"Ervin. . ."

"My brother and I disagreed over the meaning of the ancient texts. It's not the loss of Dorothy's life, but of her innocence that the Old Gods require. In addition to that, and the ritual we will now perform during this once in a millennia alignment of the heavens, the Old Ones require the death of a hero. That's where you come in."

"You got me all wrong. I ain't no hero."

"Do you believe you were chosen at random, Mr. Dedman? We know everything about you. We know that you are as sentimental as you are tough. We know about your white knight complex and your weakness for saving young girls because of the one you abandoned in New York."

"You got my number do you?"

"Indeed. And soon the Old Ones will have your life."

Mrs. Von Juntz led the congregation, which consisted of about twenty geezers in robes, in a chant. They looked to a circle painted on the floor in the center of the room. There were weird symbols painted inside it. The chanting went on for several minutes.

While their attention was elsewhere, I worked to get my hands free. The rope that held me was silky. Probably had some ritualistic meaning for them but it was easier for me to slip out of. I worked hard to look like I wasn't doing anything but lie there. I was close to getting free when the chanting stopped. Mrs. Von Juntz turned back to me.

"On this special night, the Cosmos aligns. We say the ancient words. We work the old magic. Now, we give you innocence and blood."

She pushed little Dorothy forward. The girl approached me slowly, holding the dagger in front of her. She knelt down in front of me and smiled.

"I'm special," she said with that sweet smile.

"Don't do this honey. You don't have to."

She raised the dagger and, just like she was taught, plunged it into my chest.

It went plenty deep, but not deep enough. She wasn't strong enough to do the job with one stab. As pain exploded inside my chest, I pulled my right hand free of the silky bonds. The congregation gasped in horror as I pulled the dagger from my chest. Blood oozed down me in a warm, sticky torrent.

I cut my other hand free and stood to see a half dozen of the dead-eyed stiffs coming for me.

My blood fell to the floor and a tremor shivered through the ground. I thought it was an earthquake but it was something much worse.

It was Them.

Long, slimy tentacles rose up from what had been a solid floor seconds earlier. They started snatching up the robed geezers and pulling them down into whatever hell they existed in.

I saw my clothes on the floor near the door and ran for them, praying that my party favors were there. They were. I raised the shotgun and squirted metal. The stiffs' heads turned to mush.

I watched as Dorothy was pulled into the tentacled hell. I tried to grab her but was too late.

That was when I felt the pain in my back. Turning, I saw Mrs. Von Juntz with the bloody dagger in her hand. She was about to stab me again when she got whisked away by the tentacles. I smiled a little.

In moments, the tentacles receded back into their netherworld and the floor was solid again. Something had mucked up their plans. Maybe the planets were out of alignment now. I didn't die as planned. The window of time for Their liberation was past.

I put my back against the cold wall and slid down to sit on the floor. My breath came in ragged gasps and I felt my life leaving me.

I realized that evil was not just an abstract concept for philosophers to debate. It was real. It would always be there on the outside trying to get in. Things turned out alright this time. The good guys won. But what about next time?

As I sat with my lifeblood pouring out, the worst thing was that I would never get back to New York. I would never be able to set things right with Sophia. I guess a part of me always knew I never would.

I thought of my little girl as I slipped down into the darkness.

Quote from 'The Call of Cthulhu' by H.P. Lovecraft

Legacy
Josh Phillips

I cannot guarantee the truth of the following story, because after suffering the whims of creation and the reckless abandon of the cosmos, I cannot guarantee you the preservation of even the faculties of my mind. I only write this in the hope that it will bring you to afford me some vestige of forgiveness. I do not expect it, however, and can only surmise that the following tale will be the final utterings of a madman to be pondered by psychologists long after I am gone.

It was a chilly evening in September of 1982, a week before I was scheduled to fly out to Sydney, Australia for my first semester studying abroad. I ignored the cold weather to visit my 90 year old grandfather and play our weekly game of chess.

Frank was an avid explorer and traveled much of the world in his youth. On this night, when I told him I was preparing to leave for Sydney, his eyes lit up in genuine fascination but were lined with fatigue and a sadness that seemed unwarranted.

"You'll like Australia, Richard," he said, the bishop in his hand suspended in midair as his eyes rose to meet mine. "It's an interesting place."

He set the bishop down, capturing one of my pawns and, I noticed, exposing his queen to potential capture. His eyes met mine again, and for the first time in a long time I became aware of just how old he looked. His face was ragged, wrinkled, pocked with moles, his eyes were sunken, his ears looked too big for his head, and the few remaining wisps of hair were gray and unkempt. He suddenly looked tired; death was inevitable and no amount of chess would keep it at bay.

I studied the board in front of me, gingerly touching my rook and thinking through all the possibilities.

"You've been there?" I asked, already knowing the answer.

Frank nodded. "When I was much younger. Before the war."

He meant World War II. I moved my rook to capture his queen.

Frank seemed to consider his next words carefully. "There's an old shipwreck off the coast of New Zealand that you may find interesting. Just north of a city called Oamaru."

"You were on it?" I prodded, hoping for another interesting tale of his travels.

"No, but I always wanted to see it. Maybe you could send me photos."

I returned my attention to the game board, where my grandfather was moving his second bishop. I realized that I had fallen into a trap.

Frank looked up at me with a mischievous grin, placed the bishop, and said, "Checkmate."

I stared at the board in disbelief.

"You sacrificed your queen," I said. "Brilliant."

"For the greater good," he replied.

I stood and shook the old man's hand. "I'll beat you one day."

"You have before."

I smiled. "Not in a long time."

Frank laughed, and I walked him back to his room. Before closing the door behind me, he asked one more time about the shipwreck. I casually told him I would do what I could to take a few photos and send them back, and that he would be hearing from me soon.

The next week I flew from Boston to Los Angeles where I met Robert Burton, a classmate of mine, at the airport and we took a 15 hour flight over the Pacific. When we arrived, I spent the first day finding my assigned dorm room and acquainting myself with the University of Sydney. I also met my roommate, a man roughly my age from Perth by the name of Lucas Walker, and we agreed to have lunch at a nearby diner with his girlfriend, a cheerful blonde girl from Perth named Jessica King. I invited Robert as well.

I'm not sure why I began speaking of my grandfather, but at some point I told the group about my last conversation with him. The more we spoke of the derelict ship on the coast of New Zealand the more the group felt inclined to join me on my expedition. Lucas pointed out that we had plenty of time to book a flight to New Zealand and see the sights.

My preparations for international travel included some additional money to encourage spontaneous trips like this, so I found myself on a plane to Christchurch, New Zealand with Robert and two new friends the very next day. From there, we rented a car and drove three hours south on New Zealand's State Highway 1. On the way I learned that Lucas was in his third year of university. When I asked him why he still lived in the dormitory, he simply shrugged and said he liked meeting new people. Besides, if we hadn't been assigned roommates he wouldn't be going on this fantastic adventure to explore a derelict shipwreck in New Zealand. I couldn't help but appreciate and share his enthusiasm.

My grandfather had given me a set of instructions to find the shipwreck since it was not marked on any map or near any road, but I clearly failed to follow them since we eventually found ourselves in the city of Oamaru. Although no map contained the location of the wreck, I bought one at a local convenience store to help us pinpoint its location. It showed only tracts of farmland leading up to the coast, so I asked the man behind the counter if he knew anything about the shipwreck. He said it ran aground in shallow waters about a mile off the coast, so we would have to take a ferry.

My grandfather hadn't mentioned this. I could sense Robert's growing unease as the conversation continued, but I chose to ignore him. I asked the attendant where we could charter a ferry and he gave me the name and number of a local service. I thanked him and stepped outside to use the payphone.

Before I dialed the number, Robert interrupted me. "Are you sure about this?"

"We've come all this way," I said. "We can't give up now."

"How much do you think it will cost?" he asked, but I could tell money wasn't the root of Robert's concern. He was looking for a reason to back out.

I flashed a smile. "We'll find out if you let me make this call."

It rang a few times before a gruff, masculine voice with an Irish accent answered. At first he hesitated when I mentioned the wreck, but agreed to take us out first thing tomorrow morning. I was surprised at the price of the ferry; it was much higher than I expected, but still well within my range. I agreed to meet at his dock in the morning, then hung up.

Robert gave me a look that was filled as much with anger as it was apprehension. I reminded him that he didn't have to accompany us and he could just as easily stay in the hotel tomorrow and wait for us to return. He didn't seem to like that idea, either. When I told Lucas and Jessica, they were ecstatic and picked out a hotel near the north end of town that had a decent view of the waterfront.

That night, my dreams were filled with horrible visions of a city beneath the water with dead streets and quiet buildings covered in dripping green mucus. I wandered the dark city, alone amongst its towering Cyclopean structures, calling for anybody who may be within earshot until I realized I could be giving away my position to any who may be interested in causing me harm. Somehow I knew I was in a dream, but it was the most real, tangible, and lucid dream I had ever experienced.

43

I started running, my footsteps echoing off the hard stone walls, my breath quickening more from fear than exertion. I wish I could say I had a sinking feeling that someone or something was watching me, but it was in fact the opposite. My existence was insignificant; it seemed a higher being had already judged me and found me so unremarkable that it hadn't even bothered to silence my existence. It was a soul-crushing realization that propelled me into running down those barren streets to escape my meaningless fate. But each street, each alley, each crumbling building was as empty as my own existence. If any creatures existed here, they must have understood my utter inconsequence and retracted from my approach in complete disgust.

When I reached the end of this ancient dying city, the ground shook beneath me and a deep rumble crescendoed behind me. It sounded as though something were pushing aside the very earth, peeling away layers to crawl out of the massive tomb that had confined it. When I slowed and turned around, I saw a glimpse of a great series of tentacles shaped roughly in the formation of what I would describe as a hand or some other appendage completely alien in nature. It wrapped around a towering skyscraper, cracking the massive structure's midsection as it lifted its horrible frame. I saw more tentacles, glowing eyes, and massive wings that unfurled into the sky. I knew immediately that I was witnessing something known only to those who practiced dark arts and called upon the denizens of furthest reaches of Hell; and in that moment I knew that it was all real, and this beast would escape its underwater confines and consume the earth as a mere afterthought.

I awoke in a sweat, gasping for breath. The hotel room spun about me, but I managed to swing my feet off the bed and place them onto the floor to steady myself. The dream had felt so real that my hands were shaking and I could not get the image of the beast out of my mind. It was only an outline and a vague collection of strange details. The draconic wings, the burning eyes, the tentacles; I could remember them easily enough, but the entire form was blurry. Simply trying to recall it made my head spin again, and so I vowed not to make any more attempts to do so.

Robert sat at the edge of his bed with his head in his hands, muttering quietly to himself. I asked him what was wrong as I carefully stood and dressed myself, but he gave no response. When I suggested we get some breakfast he hesitantly acquiesced.

Lucas and Jessica were already at a table, quietly drinking coffee. I gave them a perfunctory greeting and they barely looked up to mutter a half-hearted response. There was a hearty helping of eggs, hash browns, and sausage patties but I didn't have much of an appetite, and as I watched the others I realized they didn't, either.

"Everything all right?" I asked, forcing myself to bite into the sausage.

Jessica shrugged. Lucas tried, in vain, to tell me everything was fine, but his demeanor belied his anxiety.

"Do you want to turn back?" I asked the group. At first I wasn't sure why I asked, but now I know it was because in actuality I wanted to turn back. Now I wish I had listened to my own instincts.

I was only half relieved when all but Robert said they wanted to continue. Robert finally spoke and admitted he did not want to continue, that he'd had a horrible dream that seemed more like a premonition.

Dread crept through my bones. I dimly wondered if it was the same dream I had, but instead of asking I told him to finish his breakfast. Lucas and Jessica exchanged a knowing glance as they silently poked their food.

The ferry was small, but the driver said it could carry one mid-sized vehicle if necessary. His name was Gilliam MacLeod and he was a gruff, brawny man with a large graying beard and a patchy red beret on his head. His terse demeanor implied he didn't like us very much, but it wouldn't stop me taking his ferry.

I made sure I had my camera on me, a 35 mm Kodak I had bought from a local shop in Boston several months ago in preparation for my international travels. I tested it by taking a few shots of MacLeod as he untethered the ferry's moorings and started the engine.

The mood on the ferry was much lighter than it was back at the hotel. Everybody, including Robert, seemed to be in high spirits, and I attributed to the fresh air. But as we approached our final destination, my heart started thumping in anticipation. After two days' worth of traveling to see the wreck, I couldn't help but imagine it would be incredible and unforgettable.

The sun had completed roughly a quarter of its journey across the sky when MacLeod pointed out the wreckage in the distance. I used my telephoto lens to zoom in and caught the faint outline of a teetering ship, a small vessel with a single mast and triangular sail. I was immediately disappointed; I had imagined some large clipper or three-masted barkentine, but this was a recreational luxury vessel.

I handed my camera to the others one at a time and they shared a similar resentment. Still, we had come this far and I had no intention to turn back now. I doubted that MacLeod would agree to refund a proportion of the payment equal to the time we did not use if we turned back now. So I said nothing and patiently waited to reach the boat.

It took another 15 minutes before we reached the yacht. MacLeod cut the ferry's engine and let it drift as we clambered to the side to view the wreckage. The yacht had run aground on shallow waters and now leaned starboard. Its sail was mostly destroyed, shredded into ragged strips by the elements over the years. The wooden hull was punctured in several places, but I could just make out the name painted on the side in an olden time font: *Alert*. A strange name for a ship, but at least it didn't adhere to the cliché of taking the name of a beautiful woman.

MacLeod cranked the engine long enough to bring us to the starboard side of the *Alert* to observe the deck. Most of the planks that made up the deck were rotting and it had collapsed in several areas. I was no sailor, but I could tell by its design that it was a very, very old ship.

"How old is it?" I asked MacLeod.

"Almost a hundred. It ran aground shortly after it was boarded by a hostile ship in the Pacific. Tthe few survivors swam to shore."

Sighing, I produced my camera and dutifully snapped a few shots. I zoomed in on the name of the ship and snapped another photo, zoomed out and got one of the entire deck, then turned the camera 90 degrees to take a vertical shot of the single mast and its torn rigging.

When I lowered the camera to check the number of shots remaining, I noticed MacLeod in my peripheral vision glaring at me, his eyes squinted in what I can only describe as a hateful leer. I glanced in his direction and made eye contact, but quickly averted my gaze and returned my focus to the camera. When I put the camera back up to my eyes, MacLeod walked away. The engine started a few seconds later.

"Are we leaving so soon?" Lucas asked sarcastically. It seemed he was also disappointed with the small ship.

The ferry started moving. I said nothing because I was also happy to be leaving, although I did not want to admit it. The ferry picked up speed and started turning toward the *Alert*.

"Hey, watch it," Lucas called back to MacLeod.

The ferry continued to accelerate and both Jessica and Robert let out a shriek. I called for MacLeod to stop but the driver remained silent as the ferry slammed into the aft deck of the *Alert*. I steeled myself against the ferry's railing and managed to prevent myself from going overboard, but neither Robert nor my camera were so lucky. The camera dropped into the ocean and disappeared beneath the murky surface as Robert went over the railing and crashed into the deck of the *Alert*, shattering several rotten planks of wood.

A sharp pain stabbed my forehead and I put my hand against it, feeling the warm wetness of blood. I brought my hand back down and stared at the red on my fingers for a moment before something cold and narrow pressed against the back of my head.

"To your feet," MacLeod said, jabbing the object against my skull. My head swam, but I understood that the Irishman was holding a gun to my head. I stood and MacLeod urged me forward with the barrel, forcing me to join Lucas and Jessica near the edge. They were both crumpled against the railing, gripping various parts of their bodies in pain. Lucas's arms wrapped around his ribs and he seemed to be struggling to breathe, while Jessica's left arm was twisted in an unnatural direction.

MacLeod stepped away from me and cut the engine. If I had known better, I would have leapt overboard at that very moment, but my mind was cloudy and failed to fully comprehend the danger. When MacLeod returned, he motioned both Lucas and Jessica to climb overboard onto the *Alert*. At first they refused, but when he threatened to blow my brains out they complied, helping each other scurry over the railing despite their obvious wounds. Robert stirred and pushed several loose boards away, revealing a long, bloody gash on his right leg.

Lucas helped Robert to his feet and wrapped a strip of the old sail around the injury. MacLeod pressed me forward and I joined the others on the leaning deck of the *Alert*, now convinced that the Irishman was going to abandon us out here.

I was genuinely surprised when MacLeod stepped off his ferry and joined us on the deck. He pointed to a large hole on the port side of the deck and told us to move toward it. The four of us surrounded the hole and peered in, seeing only darkness below. Robert pitifully moaned that he wouldn't enter, but when MacLeod fired a shot into the air Robert was the first to descend. I followed closely and helped Lucas and Jessica climb down in once I found my footing. The smell of rotting wood permeated the air, and something crunched beneath my feet.

MacLeod produced a flashlight and clicked it on, illuminating the lower deck. I could now see that the innards of the yacht had been gutted, leaving only the bottom portion of the hull intact. Water filled at least a quarter of the interior on the starboard side, and whatever wasn't submerged had been covered in algae and other slick, viscous green ooze. A few pads that may have once been mattresses or pillows pooled in one corner of the water, but otherwise the innards of the ship was devoid of any remnants of the past.

We were ushered away from the hole so that MacLeod could join us below deck. He then prodded us to move along the slippery surface toward the bow of the ship where the wood joined at a point. Robert moaned pitifully as he limped along, occasionally slipping. I offered him a hand and did my best to keep him steady as we carefully moved forward.

About halfway to the bow we stopped at a cavernous opening in the ship's hull that led into a sickly scented descending cavern. MacLeod ordered us in, and my mind raced, considering possible escapes. Robert panicked and for a moment I thought maybe I could use his sudden conniption as a distraction. MacLeod fired another shot in the air, but this time the bullet was aimed toward us and lodged into the deck above our heads, bringing down splinters and soggy wood around us. Robert calmed and hesitantly moved into the cavern as I followed, still steadying him with one hand. I glanced at Lucas and Jessica behind me and they both looked pale. Lucas was moving slowly, grunting at every effort, and Jessica was softly moaning and whimpering in pain. I seemed to be the only one relatively unharmed, which meant when it was time to make a move I would have to be the one to do it.

When we descended 20 feet into the sloping passageway, we could see a glowing light just ahead and around a bend. We descended another 20 feet, rounded the bend, and were met with an open cave that housed a vertical glowing disc hovering a foot above the soppy ground. Damp mud squished beneath our shoes as we entered the room, gasping in awe at the sight before us.

The disc's edges rotated in a slow clockwise motion, although if I had to describe what exactly was rotating I could not. It was as though wisps of energy moved around a center in a circular motion, and within that circle was an image I will never forget: Tall Cyclopean structures of an alien architecture covered in green mucus against the backdrop of a red sky, latticed by empty streets. Although the color was muted, it seemed to be the very image in my dreams that haunted me the night before. Jessica let out a horrifying shriek of madness when her eyes fell upon it, and I could not help but feel as though the very boundaries of sanity were being torn asunder within my own mind. I struggled to keep breathing, to remember where I was and to continue formulating an escape.

MacLeod forced us to line up within several feet of the glowing tapestry, threatening each of us with his firearm until we complied. Our backs were to the portal, and I was sure that at any moment the giant creature's great appendages would travel time and space to snatch us from our place on earth. MacLeod moved near the entrance of the cave and produced a well-worn leather-bound book from a knapsack on his back.

"Do you lot know what this is?" MacLeod said, hefting the book open and flipping to a particular page. "I would wager not. It's no matter to you, but it's the single most dangerous book in the universe. It contains detailed secrets of all corners of the cosmos, from the Black Goat of the Woods with a Thousand Young to the mysteries of the sons of Yog-Sothoth to full descriptions of the many masks of Nyarlathotep."

I had no idea what strange aberrations MacLeod spoke of. Standing near the portal made it more and more difficult to concentrate, to think about anything other than the pit of despair and madness we had been led into. The fabric of our very minds was being assaulted, and any effort expended on listening to the ramblings of MacLeod could potentially shatter our defenses. I was only barely able to simultaneously fight the impending insanity and heed MacLeod's words.

"If you were to read these things," MacLeod continued, "you would likely be driven insane. Too true, I've known a few unfortunate souls who slipped into that fate. It's only through dedicated study and careful planning that I've avoided plunging into the horrifying depths."

MacLeod then focused on a page in the book and began to chant. The words were like nothing I had ever heard before, barely naught but congealed muffles and strange guttural growls. As he spoke, something crawled upon my skin and the portal behind us shimmered. Beside me, Robert fell to his knees and gripped his head with both hands. His mouth opened as if to emit a scream of terror, but no sound came from him. Flashes of pain erupted in my head and I fought back my own screams of pain.

"Ph'nglui mglw'nafh Cthulhu R'lyeh wgah'nagl fhtagn."

MacLeod could not have recited the book's incantation for very long, but it felt like an eternity before I was able to muster enough willpower to overcome the pain and the horror rising within me. MacLeod uttered a final rasping phrase in English: "And there he must stay." And then he slammed the book shut, snapping me out of my painful trance.

My body ached but I could not move despite my sudden lucid state. MacLeod approached Robert and shoved the blubbering mass of a man into the portal. "And there he must stay," MacLeod repeated.

Robert's body dissolved into the portal. He didn't even have a chance to scream before his body was torn asunder and added to the collection of energy swirling around the picture of the city, which I now understood must be called R'lyeh although I had no idea how I knew. Lucas and Jessica remained absolutely still, clutching their heads, lost in their own madness. MacLeod shoved Jessica in next, and her body dissipated, too. The portal was no longer muted; the red sky of R'lyeh was as vibrant as a burning fire.

Finally I recovered control over my body and lunged forward, grasping for MacLeod's gun but instead sending the book into the corner of the cavern. We struggled for the gun, and although I was weak he was an aging man who could not overcome my youth. I finally gripped the gun and pulled it free from his grasp, then jumped in shock as the gun discharged point blank into MacLeod's chest. The Irishman's legs went limp and he nearly fell, but he held on to me to steady himself, pulling me in closer. I could smell fish and whiskey on his breath.

"And there he must stay," MacLeod said one final time before his eyes rolled into the back of his head and he went limp. I shoved the body into the portal and watched as it dissolved and became one with the gate to R'lyeh.

The cavern was suddenly filled with silence. Lucas remained kneeling on the muddy floor, holding his head and muttering to himself. I pulled him up, collected the leather-bound book, and together we escaped the cavern, returned to the surface, and made our way back to the mainland on MacLeod's ferry.

I will never be able to fully explain – or share – the images that pervaded my mind on our way back to the mainland.

I did not attend university that semester. Neither Lucas nor I recovered from our experience in the cavern beneath the grounded *Alert*, but at least I escaped with my mind intact. I cannot say the same for Lucas. I contacted his family and they retrieved him, only to discover their son had been driven utterly insane. He was admitted into a mental health facility shortly after, and I do my best to visit him at least once a year. It appears, now, that he will outlive me.

I returned to my grandfather's residence to question him, as I now believed that he had sent me to New Zealand for the specific purpose of sacrifice to some dark god lying in wait beneath the Pacific. However, when I returned I found only the chess set we had played upon so many times and morose staff members who relayed to me the news of his passing. He had gone quietly in the night, they said, and felt no pain. I, on the other hand, felt only rage.

As I packed his things, preparing to bring them to my home in Arkham, Massachusetts, I looked upon the chess set and recalled our last conversation. He sacrificed his queen – *for the greater good.* Had he been talking about the chess game in that moment?

I found his journals as I was gathering his belongings, and spent a summer reading them. My grandfather, Francis Wayland Thurston, had discovered a cult attempting to awaken a sleeping god in his early years. What the cult failed to do, a small crew on a yacht by the name of the *Alert* succeeded – although by mistake. My father stole the *Necronomicon* from its place in Miskatonic University and, through years of careful research, found the ritual that would bind Cthulhu and return him to his rest in R'lyeh, the underwater corpse-city existing in a universe of non-Euclidean geometry; a ritual so grisly and disturbing that it must only be carried out once every 15 years.

The last few entries of my grandfather's journals revealed that the ritual had not been performed in some time, and so he was required to resort to any means necessary to ensure its success. I expressed an interest in visiting Australia and New Zealand, and so he regretfully capitalized on my upcoming travels and my own personal curiosity. I now know that he did not do this out of malice, but out of a sense of self-preservation – not only for his life, but for that of the entire world's.

I tell you all this now only because I must relieve the burden. I lay on my deathbed, awaiting my final terrible judgment, and have no successor to perform the tasks I have carried out for the majority of my life. With Frank and MacLeod both gone, I was forced to undertake their terrible work lest Great Old Cthulhu escape his prison and consume the Earth. Cthulhu is not the monster: I am.

None have believed my tale. I write this final piece in the hope that someone will take it to heart and carry out the mission that I can no longer fulfill, as my grandfather did before me and as I did after him.

It is, after all, of the greatest importance, for at the time of this writing *I have not completed the ritual for 14 years.*

Perchance to Sleep Perchance to Dream

A Cthulhu Story

Owen Morgan

Boston, Massachusetts, February 13, 1928

I awoke to a gentle rapping upon my bedroom window. To my left, a branch brushed against the glass, undoubtedly driven by a storm gathering at sea. I fetched my robe and made my way down to the kitchen. The wonderful scent of bacon and eggs greeted me. Miss Pond, the housekeeper, acknowledged me with a smile.

I returned the smile. "Has the paper arrived?"

She shook her head. "No, Mr. Simpson, and I dare say with all this snow, one will be truly fortunate to see any missives either."

Ravenous, like a man deprived of food for weeks, I devoured the meal. Just as I handed the plate back to her, the phone rang in the library. I excused myself and picked up the receiver. The line was terrible as if talking to someone underwater.

"Hello, Hiram is that you?" I shouted down the line.

"Yes, it is I. Horrible line. I need to see you."

"Very good. I shall send my driver to pick you up."

An hour later, both bathed and shaved; I awaited his arrival in the parlor. At the chime, Miss Pond made her way to the door. I could hear Hiram's distinctive Oxford accent from across the hall. He entered my comfortable abode minus his boots.

"Please don't tell me you came here barefoot?" I smiled.

"Nonsense, dear boy, I merely took my boots off at the door. Must be two and a half feet of snow."

He sat beside the fire, rubbing his hands. "Thank you for sending your driver. I am afraid there is little time for pleasantries. Robert, do you remember my great uncle, Filbey? He passed on last week. I told you about him during the Great War."

"Oh yes, he was the propertied one. He owned land just outside of Arkham?"

"Quite so," he said tugging at his wax handlebar mustache, "I'm glad to see that near death experience with the Bosch hand grenade did not dull your memory. Well, the thing of it is, he's left me some rather interesting things in his will."

"Such as?"

"A warehouse along the river, a farm to the north of town, a hunting lodge on the border with New Hampshire, and most curiously, the deed to a private sanitarium. Also, his assemblage of weapons and other odds and ends he had been collecting from some dark corner of the world."

"Most interesting. Do you require any assistance?"

"I do indeed. But this storm has paralyzed the city. One can only imagine the dreadful job of traveling along the country roads." He became quiet as if pondering some weighty matter.

"I don't mean to pry, but is something bothering you?"

He sighed. "He left me a piece of personal correspondence. I read it on the way over. He wrote, *be both armed in the mind and the body.* What do you think he meant?"

I shut my eyes and massaged my temples. "I assume that is not all he wrote?"

"He went on at length about dark and mysterious things he'd seen in Central Africa, the South Seas Islands, and the Hinterland of Brazil. All manner of most unchristian things I can assure you."

"To your question. I think he means for us to be cautious and to arm ourselves against attack."

"But by who?" He lapsed into silence for a couple of seconds. "I have no enemies. At least none of which I'm aware."

"Perhaps members of the family who felt you profited too handsomely by the will?"

"Ahh… yes, that is a point and a good one at that. The Americans were nonplussed at the reading. But the British side of the family, especially after the trip across the Atlantic, they were most upset. Still I can't see anyone taking a sword-cane to me."

A low thud against the front door interrupted our discussion. I opened the door, and a bitter wind slashed at my robe. I looked down to see the evening edition of the Boston Advertiser half entombed in snow. Retrieving the paper, I presented it to Hiram.

He glanced at the front page. "Seems a trifle early for the evening edition."

"Perhaps the paperboys are trying to make up for the lack of a morning one?"

I tended to fire as he read. "Any news of when the storm might pass?"

He cleared his throat. "The Navy its sending it ships down to Florida. Apparently the seas are too rough. I fear we may have this snow around for some time."

"I propose we head out this weekend and do a tour of your properties. I will send my driver back to your home in the morning. You can furnish him with a list of things you may require. We will take the train."

"Capital idea."

"Would you mind if I call in on my sister? She lives in one of the small towns just along the line."

"Of course not. I believe our last exchange of correspondence happened four months ago when I sent her those books on ancient languages."

***

A lead-colored sky pressed down on the world. I looked for the sun. It appeared as a white haloed disk between vaporous tendrils. I found no comfort in its presence. The train steamed into the station. We left Hiram's luggage to the porter, who struggled with its considerable weight. The conductor punched our tickets and pointed us to our carriage.

When seated, I took out a pen and notepad. After I jotted down a couple of lines, I turned to Hiram. "May I ask what was in your baggage?"

He licked his thumb and turned the page of his book. "Hmm… oh my bags? Yes, I brought several changes of clothes. A couple of books and my toiletries."

I smiled. "Perhaps one of those books is War and Peace?"

"War and Peace? Heavens no, I had to read that at Oxford. I have no intention of reading it more than once. Why would you think I would bear that tome?"

"My driver commented on the weight of your bags and I noted the difficulty of the porter at the station."

He closed his book and leaned in, although no other soul was present. "I didn't want to alarm anyone, but I brought a few firearms with me."

I paused and considered my words. "A couple of pistols?"

"Yes, a Webley, a Colt, and, of course, a shotgun and a Trench Sweeper. I suspect the weight comes from all the ammunition."

"A Thompson Submachinegun?" I tapped my pen on the leather cover of the notepad. "I dare say you are taking the warning seriously."

He patted my shoulder. "I did not serve as a line officer for four years just to be killed by some irate distant cousin who felt cheated."

I did have to admit I felt some comfort with the thought of all of those weapons. I placed the notepad in my vest pocket and snuggled in the corner of the padded bench in the hopes of retrieving some of the sleep I failed to catch last night.

***

The jerking of the carriage tore me from my slumber. I glanced at Hiram. His face buried in some tome. He looked to me. "Excellent, now that you are awake. We can venture to the dining car."

We sat before a white linen table cloth. The water teeter-tottered in the glasses. No doubt the train was making good time. I tucked into a beautiful New York Steak. Hiram offered me one of his potatoes. "Please have this, you appear a little too thin for my liking."

Thanking him, I took the potato. "I have to admit I have not been sleeping well. Also, my appetite is voracious, but I am losing weight. Beyond all this, I keep seeing shadows out of the corner of my eyes."

He crossed his silverware. "For how long?"

"Oh, I would say ten days now. I did see my doctor. But he said I am in top physical condition."

He signaled the waiter for another bottle of beer. "Well, the shadows are a symptom no doubt of your fatigue. And the lack of sleep is brought on by stress. Although this wouldn't explain your ravenous appetite. Is something bothering you?"

"Yes, my sister has been up to some, well, unladylike activities. I'm not only concerned for her, but the family's reputation as well."

"What has she done?"

"After finishing her degree in psychology, she took to traveling unescorted to see magic shows in New York and Boston."

He stifled a laugh. "Please, I beg your forgiveness. But from what you are describing she is an educated woman who enjoys magic shows."

I licked my lips. "But she likes this group of charlatans who practice hypnotism. An underhanded method for taking in gullible people and separating them from their money."

"I served in India. This is merely another version of an Oriental practice. Why not stay your concerns until you have spoken with Natalie?"

I nodded in agreement, but in no way felt convinced.

***

As we alighted from the train, Hiram pointed to a slight figure wearing a trench coat and a gray fedora. "I believe that is Natalie."

"Don't be preposterous, Natalie would not wear men's clothing."

As we approached, the diminutive figure waved to us. Natalie doffed her hat and gave me her best smile.

"I... Natalie why are you wearing those men's clothes, didn't you receive the dresses that I sent to you from mother?"

"Oh yes, I did, thank you so much," she stood on the tips of her toes and kissed my cheek, "I just thought a trench coat more fitting given the inclement weather.

52

I regained my composure, after all, I had survived a year in the trenches, I could withstand her masculine attire.

Natalie took us to her truck. Hiram offered to drive, but she declined. The truck's small cab made for a cramped drive along the frozen, muddy way. We spoke little, and this lent me to observing the dead thickets on either side of the road. I caught a flicker of movement from the corner of my eye. I jerked my head to look out the cab window. A tarp covering a pile of wood on the flatbed obscured my vision. Natalie brought the truck to a stop. She turned and peered into the gathering twilight. "Did you see a bear?"

"What... I, yes, it must have been a bear. It was large and moved with such speed."

"Yes, there are lots of bears around these parts. The locals call them Bruins. That's why I've got myself a twelve gauge. I don't want any bears pounding on the back door."

Hiram smiled. "A wise precaution. Reminds me of seeing off Jackals in India."

I decided to break into the conversation at this point. "As I said on the phone, we're taking a tour of Hiram's inheritance."

Natalie put the truck back into drive. "And which one do you wish to see first?"

"We would like to see the private sanitarium."

Natalie smiled. "Would you mind if I tagged along Hiram?"

"By all means, given your education. On which part of the human mind did you concentrate your studies?"

"Dreams, the subconscious, and hypnosis."

***

Natalie brought the truck up to the sanitarium gates. A guard approached, his flashlight lancing through the blue-black of the night. He motioned for Natalie to roll down her window. The guard pushed up the rim of his hat with his flashlight. "What are you doin' here?"

Hiram waved at him. "Pardon me, but I am Hiram O'Brien. I am the owner following the passing of my great uncle." He passed on the appropriate paperwork.

The guarded nodded. "My apologies, sir. I was told of a new owner." He signaled for the other guard to raise the barrier.

We parked near the front entrance. I opened the door and stood down into ankle deep snow. Muttering, I made my way to the double iron doors. At our approach, one of the doors opened. An orderly, with a stern, no-nonsense air stepped into the opening. "Good evening, Mr. O' Brien."

Hiram nodded. "Good evening. Where is the Head Doctor?"

"Sorry, the doc, he's got a mass of problems to deal with. He'll be tied up for a while."

The orderly lead us to a round room with a polished floor that reflected a number of powerful white lights set into the ceiling. A man sat behind a u-shaped desk. He paid us no heed as he made notes. I introduced myself to the orderly and said, "Who exactly is in charge here, and what is the problem?"

The orderly stiffened. "Doctor Philips has been running the place for well on five years now. Shortly after Christmas, about a dozen of the crazies, sorry, patients started to get violent. Couple of the boys got black eyes or lost a tooth for their troubles."

"Yes, I imagine that would consume his time."

He pressed his back against the corner of a wall, almost as if, protecting his back from an expectant attack. "Those were bad enough. But then there's patient X, he makes most of us feel on edge."

Natalie stepped up beside me. "Did someone just drop off this man at your front door?"

53

"Yes, Ma'am, the thing of it is, he fell asleep the day after we admitted him. He's been asleep for over forty days now. His eyes are always moving beneath the eyelids. Docs call it deep sleep. That's not the worst part. Once a day, he speaks in his sleep. No one can figure out what he's saying. All I knows is he's not speaking no English."

Hiram raised an eyebrow. "Thank you, mister?"

"Catcher, sir, Frank Catcher."

"Could you direct us to Doctor Philips? I'm positive he won't mind speaking to me."

The orderly signaled two more men to follow him down the hallway. I palmed the Webley beneath my coat. Hiram noted my gesture and nodded making the same patting motion over his jacket pocket. The orderlies stopped at every intersection and checked around each corner. After ascending a flight of stairs, Catcher pounded on a steel door. A view plate in the door slid back. A gruff voice called out, "Doc's busy."

"That's true and all, but the new boss is here."

The jingling of keys heralded the opening of the door. A tall man with a purple, welt under his left eye ushered us inside. Four patients restrained by straitjackets thrashed on their beds. Some cursed or spluttered half intelligible phrases or broken sentences. The orderlies shepherded us towards a man dressed in a long white coat, splotched with brown stains.

Hiram stepped forward. "Good evening, Doctor Philips. I am Hiram O'Brien."

The man regarded us with glassy, red-rimmed eyes. "Good evening to you, Sir. Please pardon my appearance. One of the patients had a violent episode last evening."

I pointed to the stains on his shirt. "Is that dried blood yours?"

Looking down, he shook his head. "Not mine. The patient vomited on me." He made to speak further but then stopped.

"Good doctor," I prompted, "we are aware of the unusual behavior of the patients since the arrival of an unidentified man. Please leave nothing out. We will have little difficulty believing anything you have to tell us."

He gave a deep sigh. Catcher brought up a high-backed chair for him. He sat and rubbed his chin. "Patient X, as you know, came to us last month. After he collapsed into unconsciousness, he begins to speak in tongues. Nothing we have tried can revive him."

Natalie sat on the edge of a vacant bed before him. "Is the language Latin, Ancient Greek, Babylonian?"

"Who are you," he frowned, "a dabbler in ancient languages?"

"No," she straightened, "I completed my psychology degree last fall."

"Too bad, my dear, believe it or not, a degree in ancient languages would be of greater use than anything else at this time."

I could sense my sister's growing agitation. "Pardon me, Natalie. Sir, what time of the day does this man speak in his alien language?"

"Eight in the evening, regular as clockwork. He prattles on for about three-quarters of an hour then lapses back into sleep."

I checked my wristwatch. "It's almost eight. Do we wait eighteen minutes?"

Doctor Philips stood giving us a knowing look and led us to a private wing. An orderly opened the cell door. Inside the mystery man slept on his back, arms crossed in a manner that reminded me of my grandfather's funeral.

Hiram cleared his throat. "Doctor, have you attempted to record his words?"

"We've tried on two occasions. The first time the recording was of poor quality. The second recording was destroyed in the last round of violence."

"Doctor Philips," Natalie suggested, "perhaps we can try and record his words again?"

The doctor made arrangements, and an orderly wheeled a playback-only device into the room. I took out my pocket watch and waited for the appointed time. At precisely eight o'clock, the man's eyelids shot open. His eyes continued to move back and forth as if in the deepest part of sleep. Natalie started the machine as the man spoke in a tongue beyond my ken. I looked around the room and saw no indication of understanding from anyone. At fifteen to nine, he ceased speaking and fell back asleep.

Natalie stopped the recording. No one spoke a word. A clamor from downstairs crashed upon our thoughts. Doctor Philips sighed like a man dealing with unruly children rather than another possible outbreak of violent behavior. He opened the door and called to the orderly down the hall.

The exchange left no need to guess at the situation. "Lady and gentlemen," he said in a halting voice, "the patients are up in arms again. Please follow me. I'll see you get out through another door."

Doctor Philips and Hiram took the lead. Natalie tried to keep up, clutching her notes to her chest. I brought up the rear. The ravings grew louder and from time to time I glimpsed shadows behind opaque windows. A chant grew from the bowels of the building, muffled by concrete and steel. As Doctor Philips opened the door, it seemed all the patients had added their voices to the damnable mantra.

Hiram placed a steadying hand upon the doctor's shoulder. "You may well need to contact the police."

Doctor Philips opened the door and called after us. "I shall take that under advisement."

***

I might have found my sister's home charming if not for the events of the previous day. We huddled around the fireplace. My coffee sat neglected beside me. I listened as my sister as she poured over her notes and consulted her books.

Natalie made her way over and sat beside me. "I think, I've managed to figure out a few lines of the man's infernal jabbering."

"What language was he speaking?" I enquired.

"Some of the words are Latin. A couple come from the ancient civilizations around the Fertile Crescent. However, one word stood out to me, Cthulhu. I found two references to this word in one of my more obscure texts."

Hiram checked the sights on his pistol. "What is a Cthulhu?"

She cleared her throat. "Cthulhu is said to be an entity that has resided on Earth since time out of mind. The man, I believe, was not babbling, but having a conversation with Cthulhu."

I raised an eyebrow. "Why does he speak with this thing?"

"My books noted a cult that venerates this creature. Cthulhu slumbers somewhere beneath the seas and awaits the right time to awaken and walk the Earth like a titan."

I crossed my arms. "This Cthulhu is contacting a madman to know when to wake up? Natalie I know you like magic-."

She shot up like an arrow. "Do you have a better explanation? All the patients turning violent at the same time or the sleeping man's strange language or that chanting?"

I held up a placating hand. "Let's say this is possible. What do we do?"

Natalie sat. "The man seems to always be in the deepest sleep. He is susceptible to suggestion."

"You mean hypnotism?" Hiram probed.

"Yes, I've read several books on the matter."

We took to planning our great gambit before retiring for the night. Our hope lay in the orderlies and not the inmates controlling the sanitarium. At first light, I opened my eyes to see Hiram holding the phone to his ear. He shook his head, placing the receiver in the cradle.

"Who were you calling?"

"I tried to call Doctor Philips. The phone must have rung eight times. Then I heard someone pickup, but they did not speak."

***

Despite the fresh snow, Natalie sped us along the road. No one spoke. She brought the truck to a halt before the gate. No guard greeted us. I stepped outside and checked the guard box. With no one present, I lifted the barrier. I felt a certain disquiet around the building. I might have preferred to hear the chanting over the stifling silence.

Hiram, armed with a Colt, used the barrel to push open one of the twin doors. Unlike our first visit, only half of the lights flickered in the reception area. I drew my pistol. We moved along the same route as the previous day, stopping at each hallway intersection. As we ascended a flight of stairs, a bullet sang past my right ear. I looked around in a near panic trying to spot the shooter. A man, dressed in the blood-splattered uniform of an orderly stood at the top of the stairs, a pistol in his hand. He fired another shot before Hiram took aim and returned fire. The bullet struck the man in the stomach. He made not a sound but tumbled down the metal stairs.

Hiram thundered up the stairs. We moved up at his signal. He pointed down the hallway. The bloody bodies of orderlies and patients littered the way. For the first time, I heard Hiram swear. He holstered his pistol and unslung the Thompson. "Sorry, everyone but we must assume the inmates are in control."

As we turned down the corridor, a score of patients lunged towards us. Some sported crude clubs, scissors, or even the odd knife. I glanced to Hiram. He shook his head and pressed the Thompson to his shoulder. We opened fire. The reports crashed upon our ears and set them to ringing. Hiram and I continued shooting until only a mass of twitching limbs remained, the floor slick with blood. Hiram took to reloading our weapons. My hands proved unsteady for that task.

As we shadowed down the hallways, the patients began their chant anew. We pushed on the door to the special wing. The door gave way after pushing with our combined might. As I stepped through, I found the obstruction. A hill of humanity, no more than a mass of arms and legs piled against the door. Doctor Philips lay among the corpses.

"They took a lot of the bastards with them," Hiram pointed with his Colt at the patient's bodies.

Hiram helped Natalie navigate the carnage. He moved to the last door before the unidentified man's room. "I think we must assume the patients are going to make their stand in there. We can't risk using the Thompson lest we kill him in the crossfire."

I checked my Webley and muttered. "Six bullets between me and oblivion."

Hiram opened the door, pistol in hand.

After a couple of seconds, we moved down the hall. Hiram knelt beside the wall to the left of the nameless man's room. He craned his neck in an attempt to see between the door and the frame.

A blur of motion and a glint of light on metal. A hurled knife embedded in his left shoulder. Hiram opened fired. One round shattered the glass part of the door. Some shards tore into the attacker, and a crimson smear coated a portion of the frame. I jumped forward as Hiram pulled out the blade. I shouldered the door. A mass slammed into me, and I slid across the floor. I looked up into the eyes of an unhinged man. The report of a pistol deafened me; while my assailant toppled.

Hiram helped me up. Natalie hurried past us. Hiram helped me to a stool. He left me to recover my senses.

Natalie sat on the edge of the bed. She began to converse with the man. Hiram guarded the door while I observed. Natalie, from my perspective, appeared to perform magic. She managed to engage the man in conversation. He replied to her inquiries in English, his Baltimore accent betraying his upbringing.

"Do you speak with the creature called Cthulhu?" Natalie asked.

"Yes, I can hear it in my mind. Even from its lair beneath the sea."

"Why does it speak with you?"

"I'm an astrologer. It wants to know if the constellations are right for its return."

"And what did you tell Cthulhu?"

"I told Cthulhu that the constellations are not right."

"Will they be in alignment soon?"

"Yes."

She turned to me and whispered. "Cthulhu will keep asking until the time is right. We must deprive this creature of the man's knowledge."

"Then tell the creature that it must slumber on for many years for the constellations are not favorable," I replied.

Natalie spoke in a soft and reassuring way to the man. "I want you and Cthulhu to rest now. Sleep. For the time is not right."

***

The Baltimore Police Inspector almost chewed off the end of his pencil listening to our account. I would not blame him for thinking, perhaps; we too should join those who dwelt within the sanitarium. But his investigation confirmed the uprising by the patients. The inspector found on balance our ordeal harrowing enough without adding court proceedings to our list of concerns. Of course, we left out the Cult of Cthulhu from our explanation. Just a classic case of inmates running the asylum. I must confess, my hunger is remorseless, and I catch strange shapes out of the corner of my eyes with increasing regularity. If this Cthulhu communicates by telepathy with the insane, is this his plan for me?

Dreams of Dead Gods
Matthew Wilson

London, 2015

I.

Richard knew Cthulu dreamt when the winged, red eyed things fell out the clouds.

"Stop staring, fool and get on that gun," Maxwell screamed as the foul smelling demons beat their wings to slow their speed and kicked snipers from off the hollowed out buildings to fall screaming in the city debris below.

There'd been no resistance after Cthulu killed the king, he had all the power and the humans he allowed to live after their short unsuccessful war against the lord of other worlds were ready to call it quits. But when Cthulu dreamt of monsters, the people of London ruins #1 felt justified enough to defend themselves without souring the exiled god's feelings.

"Stop yellin' at me," Richard moaned, cutting his hand as he cocked the wall mounted machine gun and tried to collect his mad spreading thoughts like marbles dropped from a bag into *something* of a competent plan.

Too many soldiers screamed as the horned things with claws carried men up to sufficient heights and dropped them like keen hawks would turtles to break their shells and sink their fangs into the warm, exposed insides.

Maxwell showed you this 100 times, Richard thought, blinking at the smoke, trying to ignore the adrenaline that pulsed through his hands making them shake too wildly, everything moved far too fast.

If what Cthulu dreamt came to life, then why couldn't he dream things to help humans through long winter famines or construct hospitals and schools from nothing? But Cthulu was homesick and often dreamed of the wildlife back in his own realm, these ghoulish, pregnant things that favored the night.

"Pull, click, fire," Richard repeated like a child learning his ABC's, in the gutted public library remains that was now used as a dirty hospital, he'd found the remains of hardback books, promises of better worlds where people had actually used schools to learn alphabets rather than assemble rifles for when Cthulu took forty winks.

His feet left the floor when sulfur stinking fire belched out the greased end of the cannon and punched him to the floor like a mules kick.

"Shoot the sky, not the ground, you idiot," Maxwell said, shaking his muddy blond hair out his eye and using a half filled beer crate to reach the trigger, leaned into his weapon so not to break his shoulder. He fired with more promise into the poisoned clouds where monsters screamed than his brother.

The missiles that men had fired at Cthulu in the early days of combat held all kinds of hazardous waste that lab men swore would remove a tentacle or even one of the exiled gods evil eyes, but they had no experience in these matters and only succeeded in melting the trees every time the yellowed clouds spilt with acid rain.

Drunk on the gun-smoke, Richard struggled to his feet, thinking of the stories dad told to stop them weeping with fear at night. How when he was 11, he'd watched cartoons on something called a TV and swam with friends in the river before the mutilated bodies had polluted them to such a degree that not even weeds could grow within them.

"I can do this," Richard said to steel himself and fired with little accuracy and more a gut feeling that the more steel in the air; the better. He stopped breathing when more through inevitability through the monsters numbers than skill, he clipped one green wing and watched it fall with gruesome beauty, smashing into a burned out car in the streets below.

"Holy hell, I got one," Richard cried out in dumb amazement.

"Fantastic!" Maxwell scorned as he reloaded with bandaged fingers. "Now get another."

No one dared disturb Cthulu from his dreaming, his temper could easily destroy this world, so it mattered little that a few humans died when he dozed after a hard day being tyrant. He could do so much more damage when awake.

Luckily, Cthulu was greedy and felt 8 hours sleep a day was a missed opportunity, there was much to conquer and he'd do none of it being asleep.

"That fat turd has to wake soon," Maxwell said. "Just try holding out a little longer."

The call to hold fire came several minutes later with a fresh ration of cold water for the survivors who'd remained at their guns. The ones who hid underground would be lashed or deprived of rations for a week. If not for cowards such as them, then Cthulu would never have dragged himself through the wormhole in the first place.

"Get your rest while you can, ladies," Maxwell finally broke into a smile now he could sit and rest his scars. "Our tentacle king is a hard worker; the poor dear will wear himself out and be dreaming again in no time."

"I think *we're* the only ones still alive," Richard said, feeling no need for an official newsletter, but he was quite surprised when he heard hurried footsteps coming up the bullet chipped staircase at quiet a pace.

The messenger boy carried an official stamped slip of paper and an apology for their loss. The winged things had struck further into the city than was first thought. Richard and Maxwell's father was dead; no more dreams remained for him on any world.

II.

"I don't think this a very well thought out plan," Richard said, picking barb wire of long forgotten battlefields out of his trousers before he risked tetanus. Didn't soldiers bury land-mines round here? Cthulu was a well-known night owl, so although the dark lowered the risk of being spotted, Richard wondered why Maxwell had dragged him here this late.

"Shut it and pass the bag."

Cthulu felt it an insult to have something as low as human guards surround the landmark building he'd made his lair and threaten to murder friend or foe he found on his property. A king liked his privacy. A god needed no protection against mortals. Sometimes, superstitious women left food or pennies out here as an offering for mercy in the coming bloody times, but a merciful god *wasn't* a successful one.

Guts empty, Maxwell squatted at the mess of food and nibbled at a rotten apple he thought half edible when he knocked out the worms.

"This unspoken wars gone on too long," Maxwell said to himself as much as Richard, "with dad alive there was something holding me back from going postal... now Cthulu doesn't get to push us around any-more."

Richard gulped and took the gun his brother offered him. "Maybe we should re-plan this when we're not so emotional." Richard knew there was no room for graves like the old days. The body parts that hadn't been devoured by giggling winged demons were quickly burned to lower the risk of infection through mortar scarred streets.

Once, this Westminster building had been decorated with angels, since they'd interfered with Cthulu's ability to sleep, he'd scratched out their eyes for fun and settled down for a well-deserved rest. Like a clumsy child with blood-colored crayons, he'd cut wings and fangs onto the old illusions of angels for devilment.

"Stop shakin', you'll blow us sky high," Maxwell hissed in the pregnant blue moon whose light carried chemicals burning bright as sapphire witches candles.

"People tried to blow this guy back to hell before," Richard said. "There's no way we can destroy him with only a few sticks of dynamite stolen from the armory."

"I promised to pay them back, didn't I?" Maxwell said with sudden heat, disliking his good name being blackened. He'd no idea how the lead from the church roof had gotten in his bag that one time, but at least dad had eaten well when he'd pawned the precious metal to desperate cannon builders.

"We don't have enough kick here to kill that demon," Maxwell lamented, making sure the explosives were still good and dry. "But I figure we got enough to bring this whole building down on him… we'll make him a prisoner, buried under 100 ton of earth."

"I still don't think—"

"Dad told us to stick together," Maxwell interrupted with surprising softness for his character. "A dad that this *dreamer* killed… are you in?"

Maxwell had saved his brother from being devoured by starving humans in the food riots and though the constant drive to stay alive had hardened his heart to stand a chance against a cold world, from to time; Maxwell was capable of reforming *some* gentleness that made Richard grateful he was kin.

"Dad said bloods thicker than water," Richard supposed there was no one thicker than him for agreeing to this. Nodding, he let Maxwell take his hand, and quietly lead him inside, to where king Cthulu watched the cosmos from his stinking pit.

III.

The Westminster bell hadn't rang in thirty years, not since Big Ben had disturbed king Cthulu's sleep and he'd crushed it in his fist. The smell of blood made Richard's head swim but afraid to be alone; he could no more turn back now than make the clouds clean again. Cthulu had doodled more ghastly images on the walls, highlighting the madness of his own world.

Years ago, bloated, badgering MP's had argued over matters of the day here, planning a poor defense against tyrants through a wormhole, now this building of bitter ghosts was filled with yellow-eyed icy like tentacles pulsing like exposed brains around the crumbling ceiling.

Each twitching limb, pregnant with parasites and the rotten meat of previous intruders seemed to act like a water divider throbbing toward the sensation of their heat. Their poisoned thorns clicked like crab mandibles, snipping dazed blue-bottles from the stale air.

"Stay by me now," Maxwell said in a daze, unable to process the insanity of Cthulu's lair as hungry bats fed up in the high timber beams, leaping upon any flickering spider's shadow their copper colored eyes detected.

"I'm not going anywhere," Richard whispered, "Hopefully."

Cthulu's tentacles lining the floor like poisoned tree roots heaved with great labor since his body still wasn't used to this atmosphere were covered with a thick, ugly Rhino like hide and Richard wondered how much sensation the exiled god had in them. Would the building shake vile thunder if Richard so much as stubbed his toe against one?

Controlling his breathing with great difficulty, Richard took two fistfuls of dynamite as ordered and started climbing over the dust smeared chairs where once fat judges and public speakers had tried to pass their laws.

"Easy, Jesus," Maxwell sang out when Richard lost his footing and a chair cracked like an old man's spine when it caught him.

"I can't see nuffin', I said we should have bought torches."

"Slave?" A voice called from the dark, a wheezing, diseased sound like a corpse swearing revenge from the deep. "Leave your offerings outside, I will not be disturbed now."

For a moment, Richard looked at Maxwell and Maxwell looked right back. Had that just happened? The tentacles twitching in the walls picked up their masters fury and swelled, engorged with blood as dust rained down from the ceiling, the floor shook in its effort to shoo away the little mating bugs.

Something came.

"Get it done, do it now!" Maxwell said, disposing of any secrecy as he spat on is hands for friction and turned the small wrist watch connected on the explosive to 4 minutes. Dad had only taught him how to tell the time last week; if Maxwell promised to be good – to look after his brother -- he'd promised to teach him how to whistle as well.

Now there'd be no more lessons. No more memories of dad but Maxwell's anger and sadness at his leaving.

"What number comes after four?" Richard asked, trying to set the detonator to a sufficient number to make a run for it before the fireworks blew him back to Cthulu's hell.

Maxwell picked up a rock in frustration but felt it fall useless from his fingers before he could nick Richard's arm when he heard something scrape its massive body through a cracking door. The creatures skin was the color of faded manuscript, yellowed like an-other world sun, an older, neglected star.

King Cthulu was no portrait, his mouth twitched with mini-tentacles like worms pricked onto a fishing hook, his claws punched into the wall, straining, shifting his weight along the bloodied floor and though Maxwell squinted, he saw no legs, only more damn tree trunks.

"Ah, heroes then," Cthulu's face wasn't designed for smiling, but there was wicked humor in his eyes as he settled further in the room, enjoying the peace before a battle. "I do like fools who don't turn back."

Maxwell dropped his bag and raised his rifle. His lieutenant would be up in two hours and find him missing from his machine gun nest; he wouldn't have let the brothers come on this suicide mission, with the monsters of Cthulu's dream, there were few enough soldiers to begin with.

Now, Maxwell wasn't worried about being put on a charge for being AWOL, or even having his soul devoured as all fools before Cthulu were prone. All Maxwell could think of was getting back to his brother; Richard was useless on his own.

"You're supposed to be sleeping," Maxwell moaned, trying to keep Cthulu's attention on him. "Does his *majesty* want a teddy bear to help him go bye-bye?"

Cthulu's eyes saw beyond *one* world. "I smell one of greater fear than you, boy. Where is the other?"

"I'm here alone," Maxwell lied, having greater experience of deceit, feeling guilty for all the times he'd swindled Richard out his war rations. There was so much to apologize for, all those times he'd been a bad brother, cultivating in dragging him here to halve Maxwell's anxiety of facing cruel gods.

"Humans are poor liars," Cthulu noted, unimpressed, it was any wonder the puppet government he'd set up to take the fire out the human rebellion had convinced anyone that things were fine. "But you won't hide food from me."

Richard cocked his weapon for effect. "I'm enough for anyone," his shaking hands threw off his fire and Cthulu laughed as bullets riddled the bare masonry above his winged head. Richard's muddled brain reacted before he was aware of giving his body the order to dive as a broken bust of Queen Victoria pitched from her podium on the wall and missed his head inches.

"Ah, dinner *and* supper," Cthulu said pleasantly.

Richard liked to get people's attention; he succeeded when he pulled the pin on his explosives. "I don't need to aim to get you with this."

"Maxwell, wait. That wasn't the plan."

"Get out of here, Rich," Maxwell demanded. "It'll be worth the big bang to see the look on this guy's face."

Cthulu had slit his father's throat while he slept, he'd stood alone before the armies of his jealous brother and crushed cities single handedly for praising other gods than him. "What do you know of fear, boy?

"Your biographer said that even gods may die," Maxwell hoped, having been home schooled Lovecraft's *good book* in the early years of Cthulu's reign. "Let's see how reliable a Providence hack can be."

Richard watched his brother charge at Cthulu, in the way of his freedom, his heart thudded too loud, but despite Maxwell's mouth being open, so Richard knew that he was screaming, all Richard could hear was the ticking of the damn detonator.

Cthulu lost his humor when Maxwell got close enough to hit a barn door and howled as saliva coated bullets tore into his side, blowing out three Elephant tusk like ribs. "Don't sting me, bug," Ctulu hissed.

Maxwell flew briefly as Cthulu's bloodied wing unfolded and struck him across the chest, breaking one arm that Maxwell tried to bring up in vain to block the blow. Strangely, there was no on pain as he lay down, fighting sleep which curiously descended upon him.

"That's unpleasant," he noted with a rare absence of cursing and flinched when he heard gunfire.

Richard was being a poor solider, ignoring his retreat orders. He was coming to save the day! Groaning, feeling his bloodied ribs prick into his vital organs; Maxwell managed to blast off a final salvo that missed his brother's head by inches.

Maxwell liked getting people's attention. "I said go away," it hurt his ego for other people to see him cry. "Cthulu – hey, rat-face!"

There was too much blood in his throat, his voice was weak and had the substance of dust to shout out again. Maxwell tried whistling to get Cthulu's attention, and blew several useless raspberries before he remembered dad was supposed to teach him how to do it like a pro.

He watched Richard dart through the falling debris of Ctulu's rage, the walls shook with his hatred of mankind, but despite being tired, Maxwell realized he still saw the funny side as he patted the detonator like a loyal puppy on his lap. He wished Cthulu well on their journey together, and didn't hear the explosion when the white light burned away his tears.

IV.

In the gunpowder stained dawn, Richard broke his fingernails crawling like a dog up the mountain of rocks that had once been London Bridge. The sun came through the ugly clouds and though it invited new diseases, Richard opened his collar and let the heat warm his face.

He didn't know how long he'd been out, but the houses of parliaments remains seemed to have burned for a long time. The last thing he remembered was that something cold and wet had struck his head, propelling him forward, and then Maxwell – God, Maxwell!

Weeping, Richard limped forward to the dirty river Thames, purposely not thinking, washing his face in the rubbish cluttered water, trying not to see the tentacle-faces of dead gods staring back.

Scary World
Spencer Carvalho

Along the coast of Florida away from the kid friendly amusement parks there was a year round haunted house called Scary World. It had gained a word of mouth reputation as America's best haunted house.

A long line of people waited outside the entrance to Scary World. They passed the time by talking to each other but stopped when they heard horrible screams coming from within the haunted house. As the screams became louder more of the people in line became quiet. It reached its peak when a woman ran out of the entrance to the Scary World screaming and crying. A man in overalls and a hockey mask carrying a chainsaw ran out behind her. He stopped near the entrance while she kept running to the parking lot. The people in line were impressed with the terror and cheered. The man with the chainsaw turned to the crowd and lifted his mask. They all cringed and the ones with weaker stomachs were close to vomiting. The face revealed beneath the mask was grotesque. His skin was gone. The red meat underneath was bloody and wet. His eyes were black and lifeless. He stared at the line of people who became completely silent. Without pupils no one could tell who he was looking at so they all feared that he was staring at them. Then he spoke.

"Sometimes they get away."

Then he pulled the mask down and walked back inside Scary World. Underneath his mask was a huge smile because KC loved scaring people. He loved it more than anyone else who worked at Scary World and his love of the job was what made him the best. Right after he passed the entrance where he was out of sight of the people in line Sally, the ticket taker, told him that Martin wanted to see him. Martin was the owner of Scary World and also a vampire. When KC walked into Martin's office he saw a guy wearing glasses sitting in a chair across from Martin's desk. They both stood up when KC walked in.

"KC, I want you to meet Lyle Crumb," said Martin.

KC and Crumb shook hands. KC took off his mask and Crumb backed up when he saw his face.

"Oh, hold on a minute," said KC.

KC's face changed into a normal human face and his body shrunk to a smaller size. The large overalls became loose.

"Is this better?" asked KC.

"I guess," said Crumb.

KC looked at the slack from his oversized overalls.

"Don't worry. I'm wearing spandex shorts underneath here."

"Crumb here is a new employee," said Martin.

"What kind of monster are you?" asked KC.

"I'm not really a monster... I just um... "

"He's a werewolf," said Martin. "A recently turned werewolf."

"Oh really," said KC. "For how long?"

"Oh uh, about a month now," said Crumb.

"Huh, so how do you like being a monster?" asked KC.

"It's all a bit weird."

Martin and KC laughed.

"It sure is," said KC.

"Crumb here had a problem with the law," said Martin. "He wolfed out and went on a rampage."

"Did you kill anyone?" asked KC.

"Only some cows," said Crumb. "I woke up on a farm. They found me naked and covered in blood near some dead cows. Now there's a warrant out for my arrest."

"Since when did it become illegal to kill cows?" asked KC. "You know, if killing cows is a crime then the fast food industry should be in more trouble than you."

"I thought you could show him around," said Martin.

"Sure, why not," said KC.

"You're in good hands," said Martin. "KC is my best guy."

KC left and Crumb followed behind him. They went to the employee locker room where it was quieter.

"Are all the people here monsters?" asked Crumb.

"Yep," said KC. "This place is a safe haven for monsters of all kinds. It's also a place to find work. It can be pretty tricky to find a job when you can only work at night or need full moons off."

KC took off his overalls which he hung in a locker and put on a t-shirt. He then switched his size 18 boots for some better fitting sneakers. KC noticed Crumb's nervousness.

"This is all new to you, isn't it?" asked KC.

"Yeah."

"Don't worry. You'll get used to it."

"So what are you?"

"I'm a boogeyman. I feed off of fear. So you can see how working at a year round haunted house is the perfect job for me."

"What do you mean? How do you feed off fear?"

"It's a very complicated biological process but the simple version is when people become afraid they put off a pheromone. I absorb it through my skin and it makes me stronger like spinach for Popeye. I love this place. I really do. Before I started working here… "

KC trailed off. He collected himself and tried again.

"Life was difficult before I started working here. I had to scare people just to stay alive, usually children because adults tend to chase you with weapons. Not anymore. Here, people want to be scared, they pay for it, and there are so many people. I've never been this well fed. I love this place."

A black cat walked out and rubbed against KC's leg. KC kneeled down.

"Come here little guy," said KC.

KC picked up the cat and started petting him.

"This little guy is Cat Damon."

KC turned his attention back to the cat.

"You're the kittiest cat in the whole wide world. Yes you are."

KC looked up at Crumb.

"He's normally more cataonic."

KC waited for Crumb to laugh. There was no laughter.

"I'm better at terror than humor," said KC.

"Does he belong to a witch or is he a shape shifter or something?"

"No. He's just a regular, normal cat. Although some people around here think he's an ancient Egyptian god trapped in cat form. But I don't think an ancient Egyptian god would be so interested in laser lights."

The door opened and someone else walked in. He was wearing at zombie mask.

"Hey Shane," said KC.

Shane took off the mask and Crumb was surprised by how much Shane looked like a male model.

"Hey," said Shane. "Stay back, I have a bit of a cold."

"Shane's a fairy," said KC.

"I've never heard of a guy fairy," said Crumb.

"Then you've never been to San Francisco," said KC.

KC waited for someone to laugh. There was no laughter.

Shane pulled out a tissue.

"Where do you think baby fairies come from?" asked Shane.

He sneezed and glitter came out. Crumb stared confused.

"Did you just sneeze glitter?" asked Crumb.

"Yeah," said Shane. "And I fart rainbows."

Shane headed toward the exit.

"See you guys later," said Shane.

"Bye," said KC.

Crumb waved goodbye as Shane left.

"Is he kidding?" asked Crumb.

"I wish he was," said KC. "It's so weird."

Crumb noticed a sign on the wall the said made by Gremlins.

"I noticed that there are made by Gremlins signs all throughout this place."

"Oh yeah. Gremlins are very handy at making things and this is probably the one place in the world where they are given credit for their craftsmanship. Visitors assume the signs are jokes but that's on them. You'll never see them but they keep this place running smoothly."

Crumb looked around the locker room.

"Good job guys!" yelled KC.

There was no response. The room remained quiet but hidden from their sight the Gremlins smiled and cheered.

"I'll give you a more thorough tour tomorrow during daylight hours," said KC. "Let's go to a bar."

KC and Crumb left Scary World and walked a few minutes until they reached the shore where they found a bar on a pier over the water's edge.

"My girlfriend works here," said KC. "She's an Encantado."

"What's that?"

"Brazilian water fairy. She's got a great sense of humor. She's the one who came up with my name, KC."

"I don't get it. What does KC mean?"

"It's for KC and the Sunshine Band. They had that song. I'm your boogeyman, that's what I am, and I'm here to do, whatever I can."

They walked inside where Crumb saw various types of monsters. He also saw the most beautiful woman he had ever seen singing a song in Portuguese on stage. When the song ended she ran over to KC and gave him a kiss.

"Alesandra," said KC. "This is Crumb. He recently became a werewolf."

"Hello," said Alesandra with a thick Brazilian accent.

"Hello," said Crumb.

KC turned his attention back to Alesandra.

"You look beautiful," said KC.

She smiled.

"You're full of compliments."

"I like to make you smile."

A group of four old guys at a nearby table were playing cards and smoking pipes. They looked like regular old men except that they had algae-green skin and hair. Crumb also noticed when he got closer that they had gills. One of them started talking to KC.

"Hey there," he said with a Czech accent.

"Hey guys," said KC. "How're you all doing."

"Not as good as you," said one of the old men.

KC laughed as he hugged Alesandra closer to him. KC turned to a confused Crumb.

"These guys are Vodnici. Vodnici are water spirits. Nice guys."

Crumb looked at their card game.

"Who's winning?"

"I'm the lucky one now," said one of the Vodnici. "Not sure how long my luck will last. I've heard rumors among the water sprits that some local death cult is trying to awaken Tulu."

"You mean Clulu," said one of the other Vodnici.

"No," said another. "I think it's Kutulu."

The last Vodnici gave it a try.

"I'm pretty sure it's Kutu."

Alesandra gave it a try.

"Thu Thu."

KC laughed.

"That's not even close to right but it's so adorable. Thu Thu."

KC laughed some more.

"Thu Thu sounds like the name of a bunny rabbit."

"I believe it's most commonly pronounced Cthulhu," said Crumb.

"Cthulhu again," said KC. "It seems like there's always some stupid death cult trying to wake him up."

"Yeah, but the rumor is that these guys are actually getting close. Normally those weird Cthulhu death cults search for Cthulhu in the South Pacific but it appears that one of them finally figured out that the Bermuda Triangle might be a good place to search."

"So Cthulhu actually exists?" asked Crumb.

"Of course he exists," said one of the Vodnici.

"Thu Thu," said KC again as he laughed.

"Why would anyone want to awaken a giant destructive monster?" asked Crumb.

"The decisions of stupid men are beyond understanding," said one of the Vodnici.

"Being part of a death cult trying to awaken a world destroying monster seems crazy," said Alesandra. "It still makes more sense than being Amish."

Out in the Atlantic Ocean in the very center of the Bermuda Triangle a death cult chanted aboard their luxury yacht. They stood around in hooded robes all reading from their e-book versions of the Necromonicon. Deep below them in the ancient city called R'lyeh an elder god named Cthulhu started to wake.

Everyone with miles of the Bermuda Triangle felt a slight earthquake while everyone in the world felt their subconscious anxiety turning into fear. They did not know the source of their dread but could not deny that it was there. The fear was so great that a large number of the Earth's population lost control of their bowels and crapped themselves.

Back at the bar everyone felt a strange sensation, especially one of the Vodnici who excused himself to the bathroom. Everyone at the bar felt fear creep into them except for KC who felt great.

"Did anyone else feel that?" asked Crumb.

"That was awesome," said KC. "I feel great."

The water below the death cult's ship began to stir. A large creature emerged from the water destroying the ship in the process. All the members of the death cult died which seemed appropriate.

It was a few hours later when a siren ran into the bar and told everyone that a large monster was approaching. They asked her what it looked like. She described it as looking like a dragon with an octopus head. She said it was scaly, had claws, and wings.

"That sounds like Cthulhu," said Crumb.

"You mean Thu Thu," said KC.

KC waited for someone to laugh. There was no laughter.

"Thu Thu is funny," said KC. "If you're not laughing that's on you."

"Does anyone know how to stop him?" asked Crumb.

There was silence.

"He is much older than any of us," said one of the Vodnici. "His ways are the ways of the ancient."

"You know, Martin's pretty old," said KC. "He might know something."

KC, Crumb, Alesandra, and one of the Vodnici went back to Scary World to talk to Martin. They found him in his office and explained that there was a Cthulhu sighting.

"So what can we do?" asked Crumb.

"It's hopeless," said Martin. "This is an elder god of immense power. There is no hope."

"Let's get drunk," said the Vodnici.

"That's your solution to everything," said Alesandra.

Cat Damon walked into the office. Crumb picked up the cat and placed him on Martin's desk.

"Cthulhu is an elder god," said Crumb. "Some people think that this cat is an ancient Egyptian god trapped in cat form. Maybe a god could be powerful enough to battle another god."

Everyone became silent as they turned their attention to Crumb and the cat.

"If you are an ancient Egyptian god now is the time to do something amazing."

The cat started licking its genitals. KC was the only one who laughed.

"You guys are a bunch of downers," said KC.

"The world is coming to an end," said Crumb. "How can you be so happy?"

"I feel great," said KC. "I've actually never felt this good."

"Part of the Cthulhu prophecy says that the entire world will feel fear when Cthulhu awakens," said Martin. "Since KC feeds off fear he has never been this powerful before. You know, KC might have a chance of stopping Cthulhu. Since he just woke up he's still groggy and at his weakest. You won't be able to kill him but you might be able to knock him out."

"Hey, I'm Mr. Positivity right now so let's go for it," said KC. "Why not battle an ancient giant monster? Sounds like fun."

They all made their way to the beach.

"I think I can hear him," said Alesandra.

Then they saw it, a giant monster slowly wading through the water towards the shore. It was a hideous and slimy creature.

"How long has he been asleep?" asked KC.

"He slept dreaming for eons," said Martin.

"So much for beauty sleep."

KC waited for someone to laugh. Nothing again.

"Alright I guess I should get started," said KC.

KC turned to Martin.

"I'll try to finish this before daylight so you can enjoy the show."

"So, how are you going to do this?" asked Crumb.

"I can shape shift. The more power I have the more powerful a form I can take. The entire world is terrified. With all this power flowing through me I can transform into something pretty powerful. I can transform into a creature born of fear. A being that represents the subconscious terror of a nation. Born from the deaths of thousands."

KC started to change as he ran into the ocean. He took off his shirt and threw it in the sand and removed his shorts when he hit the water. They were unable to see him as he changed but Crumb knew what he changed into when he heard the roar. It was a roar that he had known since childhood. It was a roar that sounded like a monster and metal. It was the roar of a creature powerful enough to stand against the almighty Cthulhu. KC had transformed into Godzilla.

"Holy crap," said Crumb. "This is gonna be good."

Alesandra started humming Godzilla by Blue Oyster Cult.

The two massive creatures approached each other. They stopped arms distance apart and stared at each other. Cthulhu roared at KC. This was a sound that could make most men's heart stop. KC gave a thumbs up to his friends back at the beach and back handed Cthulhu across the face. The monsters were far off so they couldn't be sure but they thought they saw KC give them a wink. The features of Cthulhu's face were alien but they could all see that it was angry. Then the true battle began.

The two beasts charged at each other. KC made use of Godzilla's thick legs and drop kicked Cthulhu. Both creatures landed below the water. The impact sent a small tidal wave that landed at the feet of the people watching. When the monsters emerged from the water they began battling again. Cthulhu swiped its claws and fought the way a wild animal would fight with unpredictable ferocity. KC knew some boxing so he bobbed and weaved while throwing jabs and the occasional roundhouse. Cthulhu swiped wide and KC ducked underneath. KC seized this opportunity and attacked with an upper cut.

KC's friends cheered for him.

Cthulhu jumped onto KC and digged its claws into him. KC let out another familiar Godzilla roar. The pain was immense but KC then remembered he was in the form of a monster with long, sharp teeth and bit it on the neck. He then shook his head the way a dog does. Cthulhu backed off. KC then kicked it in the crotch where he assumed the genitals would be. There was no reeling on the ground in pain from the monster like he had hoped for. Cthulhu charged KC who used a judo move and flipped it over his back and then placed it in a sleeper hold. KC felt the tentacles from Cthulhu's face grab at his arm around the monster's neck but he held on. Then the tentacles began to secrete slime and this allowed for it to turn around. The two monsters were trapped in a death lock. The monster's giant wings expanded and started flapping. They started to lift them out of the water and into the air and continued to rise until they were high in the clouds.

"Oh my God... zilla," said Alesandra.

Then Cthulhu let go. KC would have plummeted to earth but he had wrapped his tail around his enemy's leg. KC weighed his opponent down like an anchor and they both started to drift downward. KC pulled himself upward and clawed at Cthulhu's wing's creating a rip which made them both plummet back down. As they fell KC remembered what he had learned from countless action movies and maneuvered himself so that he was on top and would try to use Cthulhu's body as a cushion. He had no idea how well this Godzilla body would handle the fall because transforming into a giant monster and falling from the sky was a new experience for him.

They both landed a few miles from the shore. The impact was strong enough that it appeared on seismic charts. Both monsters sank beneath the water. The people on the shore waited for someone to appear. They continued to wait as nothing happened. They became worried fearing that both of them had died either from the fall or from drowning.

Then they heard a noise. It was the unmistakable sound of a Godzilla roar. They saw KC emerge from the water dragging behind him an unconscious Cthulhu. In order to keep Cthulhu asleep KC dragged him back to the underwater city of R'lyeh. When KC approached the shore he transformed back into human form where Alesandra greeted him with a towel and a hug.

"Great job," said Martin.

"That was amazing," said Crumb. "It was by far the craziest thing I have ever seen."

"Are you okay?" asked Alesandra.

KC smiled and then spoke.

"Thu Thu."

KC waited for someone to laugh and finally they did.

"There is one thing that is bothering me," said Crumb. "Why didn't you change into King Kong?"

"Isn't it obvious?" asked KC. "Gozilla's cooler."

Showdown at Port Innsmouth
Phil Morgan

It was raining. It was always raining in Port Innsmouth. It was best that way, the soft and insistent patter of precipitation was a nice and soothing way to keep all the Olde monsters sleeping.

The rain didn't bother me. I was a detective and I had a case. Nothing kept me from seeing a case to the end, even death.

Yeah. I'm dead. Don't make a big deal about it, okay? The name's John Kaiden and because I'm the Ghostly Detective, some wit decided to call me the Inspectre once and it stuck.

I really didn't care what people called me, the dead had no time for such trivialities. The dead also couldn't be driven insane. That came in really handy in this place.

The *Shadow* was the mythical realm where everything that could happen did, often violently and with complete disregard for the rules of polite society. It had many cities and many towns where Gods and Monsters of all stripes flocked with their own kind. There was Evercity, where they only turned off the lights after the Apocalypse, and Futuretown, where the mad scientists and aliens got to share the same universal bathrooms, and the Flipside, where the Fae let it all hang out. This was Port Innsmouth, the go-to place for everything that had the putrid stink of the Elder, of the Olde Ones.

Each city had its own unique look. Evercity had neon noir, Futuretown had gleaming skyscrapers and streams of flying cars, the Flipside… well, the Flipside defied description.

Port Innsmouth was dark and dreary, the waterfront of the Gods. Narrow twisting alleyways, rickety shantytowns, fishwives bustling about their smelly business, none of it mattered to me. The dead don't have time for scenery.

I was tracking an elusive quarry. He knew I was on his trail, knew I would relentlessly follow him until we were standing face to face. He didn't care. He was going to make me find him. It was just his way.

I pushed open the splintery wooden door of Flotsam's Folly and if I had been alive, I would have recoiled in disgust. It wasn't the smoky air or the heavy smell of so many power-drinkers drowning their misery, it was the general psychic miasma, the aether of the place. It was dark and stinking, evil and miserable. I would find my quarry here.

I scanned the room as only the dead can scan a room. I could See all there was to see and trust me, it wasn't pretty. Webs of sin with cloudy wisps of madness drifting through them littered the room. Dark desires and forbidden ambitions floated through the smoky air.

There were the usual assortment of mutated fish-men and robed figures bent crookedly over pints of hot grog. There were more notable names at the warped and filthy bar or skulking in the shrouded booths. I saw little Suzie Nightmare reading from a battered copy of the King in Yellow and laughing in all the right places. Johnny Encantado lounged at his reserved table, a brightly colored and very deadly coral snake winding itself around his unnaturally long, pale fingers. He noticed me looking and tipped his head in a mock greeting. I studiously ignored him and checked out the rest of the room. A long-faced author was dreamwalking through the bar, staring intently with his dark and piercing eyes. He had a battered notebook out, frantically scribbling details so his waking self would remember them. Finally, I saw my quarry.

Simon Le'Chance, the Infinite Man, was average height with brown eyes, brown hair, and tan skin. His features were bland, unforgettable. He looked like nothing more than one of those composite photos of humanity, the every man.

I knew, however, that Simon was no ordinary man. He had been a string theory physicist and a damn good one. Legend had it, he had built a machine of some sort to reach across the dimensional barriers. When he had switched it on, something went wrong (or right, depending on how you looked at it) and all the infinite versions of Simon Le'Chance had been compressed into one body. For one moment, Simon Le'Chance had been a God within himself and it had nearly driven him mad, which made Port Innsmouth the perfect place for him.

"Finally found me, I see." Simon said as I floated over to his table. I was a ghost but I had the unique ability to make myself solid, to concentrate and make my ectoplasmic form tangible. If I really concentrated, I could summon up a Ghostly Gun that fired Ghost bullets which was as handy as it sounded in my line of work. "I thought I outsmarted you this time."

"You always come to this bar to hide." I said.

"I do? Well, nobody told me that!" he said angrily and grabbed a passing figure. "Do I always come to this bar?"

The creature, a horrible half man-half monkfish (I think, don't quote me) pulled back in fear and then reluctantly nodded. Simon pondered that for a minute while still holding the poor, sniveling mutant six inches off the floor.

"Simon." I said pointedly and he looked at me questioningly. I gestured at the fish-man and Simon tossed him aside like a ragdoll. He was wearing a glamour of himself as the Golden Gloves champion because in some distant reality, he was. Simon could take the form of any version of himself that existed in the multiverse, all of them quite mad like the original.

"What is this about, John? Can't you see I'm busy being crazy here?" he sighed.

"I can see that and that you are terrifying the mutants. Do you have any idea how hard it is to terrify mutants?" I replied.

"Maybe they are afraid of you? Ever think of that? You are some freaky ghost gumshoe, you know."

"No, it's you. Trust me on that Simon." I said gently. Hell, Simon even scared me and we were friends. Well, as much as anybody can be friends in the *Shadow*. "Now finish that foul brew you are swilling and come on. We've got a case."

"What the case?" he asked.

"We have to stop Those Who Wait in the Dark from waking an Elder God." I said, even my dead voice showing a tinge of fear.

"Oh, it's Tuesday then." Simon rolled his eyes and knocked back his grog.

****

He was right. It was Tuesday. Of course, it was always Tuesday in Port Innsmouth because Tuesday was the most evil of days. People thought Monday was the most evil and don't get me wrong, it was evil. Nothing, however, matched the banality of Tuesday, British soap operas weren't even a close second.

I steered Simon towards my car, which was an endeavor akin to herding a cat and a rabid cat at that. He was always getting distracted, often dangerously so. He once told me it was because he could See all the timelines, all the possibilities. Having that curse would cause the best of us to get sidelined once in a while.

Finally, we reached my car. I drove a remodeled 1922 Riddle motorized hearse, I was the Inspectre after all. What did you expect me to drive? A sports car? A hearse fit my theme perfectly.

Simon grinned delightedly as he always did when he saw my car, ripped open the reinforced suicide door, and bounded into the passenger seat. Simon was a nearly-mad scientist but that didn't preclude him enjoying the simpler pleasures in life. He groaned appreciatively as he sank into the expertly hand-crafted leather seat. I climbed in the driver's seat in a rather more sedate fashion than Simon.

Simon was quiet as I fired up the engine and steered into traffic. Immediately, we were surrounded by ancient roadsters and horse-drawn carriages driving far too fast for everybody's good. Gaslights basked the streets with a warm, smoky glow that did little to dispel the aura of overwhelming madness. Occasionally, great misshapen birds of prey had been known to swoop down and snare an unsuspecting car but luckily none were out tonight... or they had already eaten.

"So, what's the big deal? It better be good this time. I was perfectly fine brooding over my grog at Flotsam." Simon finally broke the silence. I certainly wasn't going to break it, the dead have no use for small talk.

"Some rube named Aaron Fell got his grubby paws on a batch of Primordial clay and proceeded to sculpt a statue of Dagon. Now, he and his people have spent the past 30 days weaving some complex and highly disturbing ritual to bring him back from his watery grave. We are off to stop them." I explained.

"Dagon? I thought he was some moldy old Mesopotamian fish god. He isn't one of the Olde ones."

"Well, conventional wisdom is wrong about Dagon. I mean, he was a moldy old Mesopotamian fish god but he was actually one of the Elder. He was cast down with all the others of his kind with the first light of Heaven and now he sleeps his sleep of death. If Fell has his way, the alarm clock is about to sound." I said grimly. "We cannot let that happen for a multitude of reasons, the death and pain and madness it would cause and, most importantly, the really large sum of money I get paid when I stop it."

"I thought the dead didn't need money."

"We don't but it sure does come in handy. Cleaning supplies able to get ectoplasm stains out of leather isn't cheap, you know." I replied.

"How much?" he asked.

"Six figures and that is just the retainer." I answered honestly. "You'll get your cut."

"Good. They just doubled the price of absinthe at Flotsam." He said, sitting back in the seat. With a sudden movement, he shot back up to stare at me. "Who would pay you six figures to stop a plot by somebody I have never heard of?"

"It was anonymous." I said.

"An anonymous job? Isn't that what got you killed in the first place, an anonymous job? Why in the world would you take another one?" he demanded.

"A six figure retainer. Besides, you can only die once. After that, it's all gravy." I said and pressed down hard on the accelerator.

****

If you were conducting a highly dangerous, undeniably secret, and completely insane ritual to awaken a sleeping, dead, Elder god, you would probably choose a locale more suited to the undertaking. You know, something like a fog-shrouded moor or a dark and stinking swamp but that wasn't the way things worked in the *Shadow*.

The parking lot lights were blazing when we pulled into the Port Innsmouth Convention Center and Juice Bar (and you will avoid the juice, if you know what's good for you). The lot was nearly full, I had trouble finding a parking spot large enough for my car. Long streams of tourists queued up, waiting their turn to get into the Center, all of them wearing garish Hawaiian print shirts, socks with sandals, and Bermuda shorts. Nothing was scarier than a tourist in the *Shadow*.

I ghosted through the driver's door as Simon stepped out of the car and onto the pavement. We met at the front of the car, shared a look, and headed toward the Convention Center as one.

We walked past the long line of tourists with Simon tossing me puzzled glances. Occasionally one of the tourists would recognize one of us and whip out a cellphone to take a picture. I wished them the best of luck, only specialized and highly dangerous cameras could photograph me. As we passed the ticket booth, Simon pulled up short.

"Aren't we going to buy tickets?" he asked, puzzled.

"Oh, of course we are!" I said through a gritted smile as I dragged Simon away. Once we were out of earshot of an overly watchful (and too curious for his own good) scalper, I snarled at Simon. "I never buy tickets!"

"Well, that's no way to be! What kind of agent of Good are you then?"

"The dead kind, now follow me and don't say anything." I growled.

I didn't buy tickets because I wasn't there to be entertained, I was the entertainment. The eternal showdown between Good and Evil, between light and dark, sanity and madness drew all sorts of voyeurs. Long ago, the movers and shakers in the *Shadow* had figured out how to profit from said showdown. Far be it from me to line their pockets any more than I already did.

After a few minutes of brisk walking (and can I stop right here and say how much I hated brisk walking? It was unendurable when I was alive, now that I was dead, I had even less patience for it) Simon and I rounded a corner to confront an unconscious security guard next to an unobtrusive and very definitely locked steel door.

"Okay, do your thing!" I said to Simon.

"Looks like somebody already has. Maybe we can just go home?" He replied, nodding to the guard. I gave him my best stern look and he shrugged. "Okay but it's your funeral."

"It wouldn't be the first time, now get a move on. We don't have all night to stop the insane megalomaniac from destroying all of Creation. Also, there is a new episode of Supernatural on tonight and I think it's the best comedy on television right now." Even I had my addictions.

"Whatever you say, boss." Simon grinned suddenly. "What do you want? What do you need? Perhaps a dark avenger of the night?"

He twisted an ornate dial on his belt buckle and his form began to warp and shift violently. In a flash, Simon Le'Chance was gone and in his place stood Simon Le'Chance. He was tall and muscled, his features hidden by a night blue cowl. A long and tattered cape on his back whipped in the mild breeze and steely eyes glared out at me, admonishing me for not buying tickets probably.

"Beware denizens of the night, the scourge of crime has entered the building. Mr. Mystery at your service!" Simon said, his voice a deep and menacing growl.

"No." I said sternly. "Pick somebody else."

"You'll never get justice that way but it's your dime." He growled and twisted the dial again. His form whipped and shimmered and suddenly, a new Simon appeared. He stood jauntily, his posture showing his roguish nature. He wore tattered yet sturdy khakis, a battered hat, and worn boots. His chest was bare, only suspenders and a loose vest covering it. In his left hand, he held an uncoiled bull whip; in his right, a vintage .45 caliber wheelgun.

"Simon Le'Chance, treasure hunter! At your service!" he said, his stubble-covered cheeks widening into a grin.

"Not just no but no way in Hell. We don't have time for all the paternity suits that will pop up before you can open that door. Pick again."

"You really are no fun at all." Simon said, pouting. "Oh well, I was saving this one for a special occasion but I guess another End-of-the-World will have to do."

Again, he twisted the dial and his form became a violent blur, spinning, shaking, twirling, growing larger with every moment. With a start, the blur coalesced into a form. He stood nearly eight feet tall and my first impression was somebody with too much time on their hands and not even sense had spent two months in a junkyard creating a Halloween costume.

He was more machine than man and the parts of him that were still flesh were horribly disfigured. Even in the places that weren't burnt or scarred, Simon had carved designs in his skin or inserted fetish jewelry. His hair had been shaved into a severe (and probably illegal in many states) Mohawk. One entire arm was missing and in its place was a decidedly vicious appendage covered in spikes and blades and ending in a wickedly hooked claw.

"Simon Le'Chance, cyborg, here to kick ass and chew broken bottles and I am all out of broken bottles." He said, his voice mechanical and terrifying. What sort of world could produce such a monster? I decided I didn't want to know.

"The door." I pointed and he casually ripped it off its hinges and tossed it fifty feet over his shoulder as easily as you or I could litter a gum wrapper. He stepped through the mangled doorway, the large spikes on his shoulders doing even more damage to the broken and twisted frame.

"This is all going to end in tears, I just know it." Even the dead were permitted their pessimism.

****

The crowd screamed its bloodlust, shaking the very rafters of the Convention center. It seemed the main event had already started without us. Simon and I looked out from the darkened tunnel where we were hiding.

A group of young superheroes called the Misfits from Justiceville were getting their asses kicked by a mob of hooded and disfigured cultists. Apparently, being mutated was a job benefit when one was working for the Elder. Presiding over it all was a tall hooded figure on the stage. At his side was a glowing clay statue.

A slender girl covered in what appeared to be bone armor was struggling with a trio of cultists, her bone spear barely keeping them at bay. There were sudden flurries of movement as a speedster laid low dozens of hooded figures before being tackled during one of the brief moments he was visible. A massive and dull looking teen was spinning and flailing and thrashing as countless enemies clung to his massive frame, hoping in vain to bring him down. Two magicians, a black boy and an Asian girl stood back to back tossing small magicks to little effect. Crumpled in a heap at their feet was a chubby kid, unconscious but still glowing from his power to manipulate the visible spectrum.

"See! I told you Mr. Mystery was a perfect choice!"

"A perfect choice? The last thing this place needs right now is another superhero." I groaned. "Now, go do your thing!"

"Where will you be?"

"Where I always am, right behind you." I replied.

"We really need to renegotiate my contract." He rumbled and then leapt into the fray.

He hit the crowd of cultists like a bomb. At first, they tried to fight him but he was just too fast and deadly. He laid them low with every sweep of his massive mechanical arms, he stamped and twirled, danced and surged. After a moment or two, the cultists were on the verge of being routed.

It was then Aaron Fell decided to get involved. He threw off his robe and stood defiantly on the stage, all eyes turned to him. He was tall and powerfully built. His skin was mostly gone, only patches of flesh appearing here and there amid the sea of blood, scabs, and pus that dominated his body. He thrust his arms out violently and said Words that made the soul shiver in revulsion.

The moment he finished speaking, a purple flash covered the room. Both Simon and the Misfits were immobilized, paralyzed by the magick. I was unaffected, either Fell's spell didn't affect the dead or he hadn't noticed me.

"Step out of the dark so we can see you, dead man." Fell's voice rang out over the center as his followers grabbed the paralyzed heroes.

"How did you know I was here, Fell?" I asked as I walked into view.

"You aren't the only one who can See the world, Inspcetre." He smiled evilly. "Besides, who do you think hired you?"

"Why would you pay me to stop you? That makes no sense at all." I asked warily. I needed to buy time, needed to concentrate without giving away my intentions.

"Stop us? You are here to finish the ritual. We need your ectoplasmic form. You exist between life and death, between solid and ethereal. You will be the perfect vessel for Dagon, the ultimate form for him to inhabit. He will ride you as he returns the universe to its original, perfect form." Fell grinned insanely and the glowing statue beside him began to pulse and writhe evilly. "Dagon thanks you for your sacrifice."

"And I thank you for the retainer." I replied.

My arm snapped up. In my ghostly hand was my Ghostly Gun. Fell's mouth dropped open in shock. He, like most people, had no idea I could control my ectoplasm in such a deadly manner. I took a moment to aim carefully and shot him right between the eyes. He flipped head over heels off the stage and all Hell broke loose.

The second the ghost bullet had struck him, his paralyzing spell had broken. Suddenly, the cultists found themselves in far too close of a range to Simon and the Misfits. With an explosive roar, they surged to their feet and struck out at their foes. It only took a moment and the cultists broke and ran.

Fell took that moment to rise up from where he had fallen. My ghost bullet hadn't killed him, he was too powerful, too inhuman. He screamed in rage, locking eyes with me. His gaze promised tortures undreamt, pain unimaginable. I shrugged at him, the dead have no fear of threats.

He began to say his Words and a hooded cultist appeared behind him. Viscously lashing out, the cultist struck down Fell. He didn't kill him but the force of the blow rendered him unconscious.

I stared at the cultist and he pulled down his hood to reveal Johnny Encantado. He gave me a jaunty salute, grabbed the clay sculpture of Dagon from the nearby table and bolted for the exit. I took off after him, yelling fruitlessly for Simon to follow. The massive fray of enraged superheroes, frightened cultists, and one very large, nearly-mad, cyborg scientist was too much for me to fight through. The last I saw of Encantado, he was pushing open the exit door.

****

All that was left was mop up duty. Simon and I left that to the Misfits, nobody was better at mopping up henchmen than superheroes. I think it has something to do with professional rivalry.

We didn't speak as we left the Center, Simon having long since reverted to a more normal form (at least, what passed for normal for him). I counted my lucky stars, usually he picked something like a hermit or a street mime after a big fight. This time, he was only a hippie (the lesser of three evils).

I pulled out of the parking lot and headed back into the infamous traffic. Simon was silent for a long while then he turned to me. He didn't speak, just stared but I could tell something was on his mind.

"What?" I finally asked, exasperated.

"See what happens when you take anonymous jobs? Are you ever going to learn?"

"Nope, the dead don't learn." I said with a hint of humor. "Besides, I knew you would have my back. I wasn't worried."

"I won't always be here to take care of you and what does it say about you? Having to rely on a madman to cover for you? That's not exactly a good plan, man." He said, lighting up a crookedly hand-rolled joint. "Maybe you should find a new business."

"I have a new business. I have to hunt down Johnny Encantado and retrieve that damned statue before he finishes Fell's handiwork." I said grimly.

"Don't worry about Johnny. Somebody else takes him down. Fell's plan never works, man." He said, his voice dreamy from the smoke.

"How do you know that?"

"I can See, even better than you or Fell. The Elder don't awaken in any of our lifetimes." He explained and I looked at him peculiarly. "Well, deadtime in your case. Anyway, the Elder don't return during man's time in the universe and why you may ask? Because the forces of Good are always there to turn them aside. Whether it's Allen Crowley in Evercity, or the Cerberus Convention in the real world, or you right here? Humanity wins every time because you never give up, never give in. Compared to your tenacity? The Elder gods are nothing but a bad dream."

"If you weren't nearly mad I would be a lot more confident in what you just told me." I said after a moment. "Either way, the job I was paid for is completed. I will be sending you your cut as soon as I drop you off."

"Great! There is this new bar called Flotsam's Folly I have been wanting to check out!"

"I'm sure you will fit in there nicely." I grimaced.

Strange and Distant Shores
James Pratt

Failing to convince the pilot to wait, Klauser could only watch from the airlock as the shuttle undocked and began maneuvering for its return trip home. In less than two hours it would be on Earth whereas Klauser was stuck in space till the next shuttle. He couldn't blame the pilot for being in a hurry though. With the sky literally falling, space wasn't what it used to be.

Grabbing the tether-line, Klauser pulled himself hand-over-hand to the airlock's inner hatch. Mounted beside the inner hatch was a control panel complete with over-sized buttons to accommodate his spacesuit's bulky gloves. At the push of a button, the outer hatch slid shut and the airlock began to pressurize. Despite his temperature-controlled suit, beads of sweat trickled down the back of Klauser's neck. He'd heard rumors that it was so hard to keep personnel on the stations, the military used convicts and deserters for long-term staffing. Klauser figured the only thing worse than being trapped in space was being trapped in space with a bunch of deviants.

Taking a deep breath, Klauser pushed the inner-hatch release and stepped through. Waiting for him on the other side was a stout woman in a military jumpsuit. The next few moments were spent in uncomfortable silence as the woman simply stared at him before Klauser realized he was still wearing his helmet. Having been mesmerized by a horizontal scar running across the woman's left cheek, he made a mental note not to stare at it once his helmet was off.

"Welcome to Space Station Charybdis, Mr. Klauser," the woman in the uniform said after he removed his helmet. "I'm Corporal Ellis. I'll be your liaison."

Removing one of the spacesuit's heavy gloves, Klauser shook the corporal's outstretched hand. "You can call me Mario. Nice to meet you."

"I have to admit I was a bit surprised when I read your file," Ellis said with a polite smile. "When they said they were sending somebody to upgrade the solar array, I thought they'd send someone-"

"Older?" Klauser replied, talking as he removed the rest of his spacesuit.

"I was going to say more experienced."

"Technically I'm the most qualified team-member for this job but to be honest, the decision was mostly based on practicality. I also happen to be the most expendable."

"Why do you say that?"

"Everybody else on my team has a background in theoretical or particle physics. They're the ones who figured out how to deal with the solar flares and came up with the idea for the causality array."

"The what?"

"The solar array. You know, the thing that's going to save humanity. I just helped build it. My background's in applied physics with a minor in engineering."

"Meaning?"

"The rest of my team studies the building blocks of reality but I know how to build stuff and use tools."

"You're right. That does make you the most qualified one for this job. So how much training do you have in space travel?"

"An eight hour crash course."

Ellis's smile wavered a bit. "Is this your first time off-planet?"

"I've been up in a shuttle a few times but this is my first time on a station."

"That's okay," Ellis said, leading Klauser out of the airlock and down a large hallway. "You pick up most of the important stuff as you go along."

They passed large work and storage areas where men and women dressed in jumpsuits toiled at various jobs. Most of the workers gave Klauser a passing stare and most of the stares were merely curious but a particularly rough-looking trio watched him with an intensity he didn't like.

"We call this part of the station the Dungeon," Ellis said. "It's where the machine shops and warehouse are located."

"Some of the people back there were wearing jumpsuits without any military markings," Klauser said. "Are they civilians?"

"They're contracted labor."

"Contracted through whom?"

Ellis rounded on him, smile in place. "Why do you ask?"

"No reason, just making conversation."

"Can I give you some advice about space station protocol?"

"Yeah, sure."

"There are only three rules you'll need to obey when you're here. Work hard, never go anywhere without a military escort, and only ask questions that pertain to your job. Do that and you'll be alright. Fair enough?"

Klauser nodded. "Fair enough."

"Okay, let's get you settled in then we'll go to the mess hall and get something to eat."

"That's okay. I'm not really hungry."

Ellis looked him in the eye. "Yes you are."

"Oh. Okay, I guess I am."

***

A few hours later, Klauser and Ellis sat in the dining hall. The room itself was reasonably clean and in good repair but only half the lights worked, filling the hall with deep shadows. Served by contracted labor, the food was slightly better than Klauser expected in that most of it was the prepackaged bachelor-chow he lived on back home. Ellis's demeanor had changed from friendly helper to something a bit more reserved and so, after a few awkward attempts at small talk, they sat in silence.

"So you said your background's in applied physics, right?" Ellis suddenly asked.

"Yep. That makes me the odd man out."

"Does that mean the other physicists treat you differently?"

Klauser chuckled. "No, they invite me to all the meetings."

"And they don't hold anything back from you?"

"Why would they? We're all working on the same goal."

"And you understand their work?" Ellis asked.

"I can't honestly say I understand every facet but I have a pretty good grasp."

"Can I ask you something?"

"Um, sure."

"What the hell is going on?"

"You mean the sunspot activity? There are several theories. The one that most-"

"Give me a break," Ellis interrupted. "That's a cover story they're feeding the public."

"What are you talking about?"

"I know what solar flares can do. Whatever's happening out there, it's not the sun acting up."

Klauser shifted in his seat. "Okay, what do you think it is?"

"I have no idea. I mean I've heard things, but…"

"But what?"

Pushing her tray aside, Ellis leaned in. "My brother was on the Ymir Deep Space Station. I need to know what happened to him."

"Nobody knows what happened to-"

"Wrong again. A friend of mine in Special Ops smuggled me the last few minutes of video feed before Ymir Station went dark."

"Are you serious?" Krauser asked, pushing his own tray aside and leaning in. "What did you see?"

"The station was disappearing in chunks. Not breaking apart but…just collapsing into floaty bits."

"Like when you have a weak video signal and the picture starts to pixelate?"

"Yeah! Exactly that, only it wasn't the picture. It was the station itself. Sometimes the floaty bits would just vanish and sometimes they'd come back together rearranged all wrong. And the same thing was happening to the crew too. God, they were screaming the whole time. Even the ones who got rearranged so they didn't have mouths were still trying to scream. And… something even worse was going on."

"Worse than that?"

"Some of the crew didn't…pixelate, as you put it. Pieces of them just tore loose and vanished. It's like something was eating them alive. I don't know what happened to the Ymir station but I know it wasn't sunspots."

"No, it wasn't sunspots," Klauser admitted. "But I can't tell you anything. You told me there are rules on a space station. Well, you have your rules and I have mine."

"I gave you those rules as a favor. Now you own me a favor. Tell me what's really happening."

"Look, I'm sorry about your brother but-"

"What's a causality array?"

Klauser blinked. "What?"

"When you first got here, you said your team came up with the idea for the causality array. We were talking about the solar array but you called it the causality array."

"Did I say that?" Klauser asked and Ellis nodded. "And your brother was really on Ymir Station?" Ellis nodded again. "Dammit. Okay, okay. I'll tell you what I can but you have to keep it to yourself. Deal?"

"Deal."

"It's called Non-Causality Phenomenon or NCP for short. It was first detected indirectly by astronomical anomalies. Stars weren't where they were supposed to be. They really were, of course. Something was messing with their light, making it look like they were in different positions. Then the deep space probes started sending back really weird readings before going dark. It wasn't until the phenomenon reached the first manned space stations-"

"Wait a minute," Ellis said, voice dropping to a growl. "You mean they knew about it before Ymir?"

"Up till then, we had no idea what it could do. It was moving through the solar system like a wave closing in on Earth. Readings from the deep space probes showed that the phenomenon was preceded by a burst of quantum activity. Using particle physics and our satellite ultrastructure, we figured out how to create a defensive shield around Earth fairly quickly. Space Station Charybdis is the broadcast hub of that shield."

"In other words, the causality array."

"Right."

"Okay, so what's a causality array?"

"Do you know what causality is? I mean from a physicist's perspective."

Ellis shrugged. "Every action has an equal but opposite reaction?"

"That's part of it. It basically means very event is predicated on a previous event. That's how things work in the observable universe. The only exception is quantum or subatomic space where events can happen spontaneously, i.e. non-causality."

"That's what NCP is? Spontaneous events?"

"It's a little more complicated than that. You also have to factor in dimensional topology. See, what we think of as space is actually an intersection of the spatial dimensions we call height, width, and depth plus the dimension of time. In other words, space-time. There are all sorts of spatial dimensions out there, intersecting to create other space-times we can't even imagine. But all these universes share one thing."

"Quantum space?"

"Bingo," Klauser said, giving Ellis an appraising look. "You're a bright one, corporal. So the theory is some event in another space-time is creating ripples that echo through quantum space and into our space-time. These ripples are the Non-Causality Phenomenon. It overrides the laws of physics and makes our space-time behave very differently."

"And that's bad?"

"As far as we can figure, NCP uses a macro-variation of something called quantum tunneling to remove matter and energy from our universe and send them to space-times they weren't designed for. I imagine the...pixilation phenomena you saw on the video was Ymir Station and its inhabitants getting quantum tunneled bit by bit into another space-time."

Ellis considered that for a moment. "What about the people being torn apart?"

"No idea. Maybe it was a gravitational anomaly pulling them in separate directions at once. We still don't know everything NCP can do."

"How do you defend against something like that?"

"The causality array maintains the integrity of space-time by broadcasting a corresponding wave frequency that cancels out the quantum ripple. For now, anyway. The closer the NCP wave gets to Earth, the stronger the quantum ripple will become. That's why I'm upgrading the broadcast hub."

"Okay, one more question. Why the story about solar flares?"

"The powers that be figured blaming solar flares would be better than simply admitting we don't know. People tend to panic in the face of the unknown. Now can I ask you a question?"

"Go ahead."

"Why don't you already have someone trained to do maintenance on the array up here full time?"

"The technology is proprietary and your company won't train any of our personnel."

"That's...exactly the answer I was expecting. I always figured patent laws would be the doom of the human race."

Ellis motioned to someone across the room. "Private Waverly will escort you to your quarters. I'm sure you're in hurry to finish up and get back to Earth so when you're ready, we'll suit up and I'll take you outside so you can get started."

"Outside? As in, outside the station?"

Ellis nodded. "Your company keeps the array technology locked up in a utility dome on the outer hull."

Klauser winced. "So we have to space-walk to get to it?"

A tall man, lean as an athlete and with recruitment poster good looks, appeared beside Ellis. "Private, please escort Mr. Klauser to his quarters. He's bunking in Room 12, Section D."

"Yes, ma'am," Waverly replied in a crisp voice. "This way, Mr. Klauser."

***

Taking in the scenery, Klauser trailed behind the Private Waverly. The station's interior was larger than he expected but legions of stacked crates created corridors within corridors. Distracted by a hint of activity in a dark alcove, Klauser suddenly realized Waverly was nowhere in sight. Rushing ahead, he came to a T-intersection. Hesitating a moment, he proceeded to the right where he paused after encountering an inexplicable salty ocean smell. Rounding the next corner, Klauser found himself surrounded by the trio he'd spotted earlier.

"Howdy," one of the men said. Built like a scarecrow, the man flashed a gap-toothed jack o' lantern grin.

Klauser swallowed. "Hi."

"I'm Norwich," the man continued then pointed to a tall, scowling man with massive shoulders and coal-black hair braided into a long ponytail. "That's Hess. He don't talk much."

"I...I'm Mario," Klauser said, trying not to stare at Hess's nose. Broken and smashed numerous times, it lay almost flat against the big man's face. "Mario Klauser."

The third man extended his hand to Klauser. "Nice to meet you, Mr. Klauser. My name is Josiah Marsh."

Klauser tried not to wince as he shook the man's hand. Pale and hairless as a mushroom stalk, the man had bulging eyes, an almost non-existent chin, and freakishly long, bony fingers. His grip was cold and clammy yet surprisingly strong. Wattles of flesh on the sides of the man's neck fluttered with each breath he took. Standing within a foot of the man, Klauser realized he was the source of the inexplicable ocean smell.

"So you're the guy, huh?" Norwich asked.

"Pardon?" Klauser replied, tearing his eyes away from Marsh.

"You're the guy that's gonna go outside and crawl around on the station."

"I have to do a spacewalk if that's what you mean," Klauser confirmed.

"You're crazy, man," Norwich laughed. "There's things out there."

"Out there?" Klauser repeated. "You mean in the vacuum of space?"

Norwich nodded. "Hell yeah."

"What sorts of things?" Klauser said, smiling as if to play along with the joke.

"Things brought here from strange and distant shores, Mr. Klauser," Marsh said. "Things that thrive in the vacuum of space and don't show up on video screens."

Klauser snorted. "No offense, but that sounds like a line from a bad movie."

Hess reached for Klauser but Marsh stopped him with a gesture. "It's all right. You heard Mr. Klauser. He meant no offense."

"Yeah, that's right," Klauser insisted. "It was a joke."

Norwich poked Klauser in the chest. "It's the truth is what it is."

Klauser held up his hands. "Fellas, I'm sorry but I have no idea what you're talking about."

"I come from a long line of prophets," Marsh said. "There was a time when I turned my back on the gods of my forefathers and picked a more conventional one. I even ran with the Flat

Earthers for a time. That's how I ended up here by way of prison. But I've seen the truth. It was revealed to me in my dreams. Now I preach it to my fellow lost souls."

"That's…um…noble of you," Klauser said. "Giving them hope in a place like-"

I don't give them hope," Marsh interrupted. "Hope is a liar's game. I give them truth."

"I see," Klauser said.

Marsh smiled, revealing double rows of piranha teeth. "As do I. I've seen the city in the ocean, the tomb-city where the true god of this world lies dead and dreaming. And I've seen the stars. It's the stars that tell the tale."

Klauser shook his head. "Sorry, still lost."

"What do you know about waves, Mr. Klauser?" Marsh asked.

"A wave is a disturbance that travels through matter or space," Klauser quoted.

"Accompanied by a transfer of energy," Marsh added. "Most people think of water and the ocean when they hear the word 'wave', but there are other kinds. Sound waves, for example. And just as there are other kinds of waves, there are other kinds of oceans. Time is an ocean, as is space. That's the part the others got wrong. The tomb-city doesn't lie in a watery abyss. It lies in distant depths where the oceans of countless space-times mingle together."

"Almost sounds romantic," Klauser said.

"The stars are almost right, Mr. Klauser," Marsh continued. "The Lord of the Lost City stirs in his sleep. As his dreams echo through the starry abyss, their passage creates waves which ripple across the face of Creation. And just as the ocean tide comes bearing things from foreign shores, so too do these ripples bring with them things born of foreign space-times."

"That's what I was trying to tell you," Norwich said.

"What was that about stars?" Klauser asked.

"You know," Marsh replied. "You've seen them too."

"Why are you telling me this?" Klauser demanded.

"Why am I telling you the truth?" Marsh shrugged. "Because it's my job and my calling."

"What am I supposed to do with this…truth?"

"If and when you return to Earth, become a prophet and spread the word," Marsh replied. "If the human race can't die with dignity, at least it can die knowing the truth."

"Mr. Klauser?" a new voice asked.

Klauser turned and saw Private Waverly standing nearby. "I…uh…guess we got separated," Klauser said, hurrying over to Waverly.

"Sorry about that," Waverly apologized. "This place is like a maze so it's easy to get lost. Well, let's get you to your quarters."

"Sounds good to me," Klauser said, looking back for one last glance at the trio.

"Have fun out there," Norwich said.

***

"It was the craziest stuff I've ever heard," Klauser said, telling Ellis about his encounter with the trio as they dressed for the spacewalk.

Ellis shook her head. "They really need a better screening process. Station life is hard enough on normal people. It makes people who start out crazy even crazier."

"Do you know anything about Marsh?"

"After he started gaining a following among the civilian staff I did a little research on him. Turns out he was part of a cell of Flat Earth insurgents who were going around bombing scientific research facilities. Their favorite targets were scientists researching space-fold technology.

Apparently they thought somebody was going to open up a doorway to hell. After he was arrested, he found a new religion."

"Or rediscovered an old one," Klauser mused. "Had you heard any of that stuff before? Alien shores and all that?"

"Mythologies evolve just like everything else. His stuff is just sailor lore reinvented for a bigger setting. Every culture loves its tall tales and always finds a way to hold onto them."

"Yeah, but this was, I dunno, different. He seemed pretty lucid. And the stuff he said about the stars being right…"

"Listen," Ellis said. "You're in a strange place and out of your element. That leaves you open to all kinds of crazy talk that you'd normally dismiss. Don't let it get to you."

"You're probably right. Still…Have you seen anything, you know, unusual on the station? Or maybe…outside?"

"Nothing that couldn't be explained away as a technical glitch."

"Then why are you bringing that ion-rifle?" Klauser asked, nodding toward the weapon hanging from her right shoulder.

Ellis shrugged. "Um…standard procedure."

"Of course. I just wonder… Marsh said something about things that don't show up on video screens."

"What, like vampires?"

"Vampires from foreign shores," Klauser murmured.

"What?"

"It just made me think of what you said about the crew on Ymir Station being torn apart as if-"

"They were being eaten alive," Ellis finished.

"Maybe we should get going," Klauser said.

Ellis nodded. "Ready when you are."

Suited up, they went out through the air lock and climbed onto the surface of the station. Magnetized boots kept them safely anchored to the station and a magnetized sled did the same with Klauser's gear.

"So far, so good," Klauser said into his helmet-comm as he remotely guided the sled along.

"Don't jinx it," Ellis replied, ion-rifle in hand. "This is just…"

Klauser glanced at Ellis. "Just what?"

"Did you see that?" Ellis asked, squinting into the distance.

"See what?"

"I thought I…Never mind. Let's get moving. We have a twenty minute hike."

They traveled the rest of the way in near silence. Consisting of three cuboid sections arranged like a horseshoe, their mile long trek across the station's outer hull took them from the tip of one outer section to the middle of the inner section.

"Thank God," Ellis said when the dome came into sight. "Let's get this over with."

"I…Did you see that?"

"Now you're seeing things too?"

"I could have sworn…" Klauser pointed ahead. "There it is. Do you see it?"

Floating in the air was a bell-shaped thing trailing tentacles behind it. Streamers of light flickered across the thing's transparent surface, surrounding it in a ghostly halo.

"What is it?" Ellis asked, raising her ion-rifle.

"Strange and distant shores," Klauser said.

"What?"

"Something else Marsh said. That thing…it looks like it could have come right out of an ocean abyss."

"What are you talking about?"

"Maybe Marsh was right," Klauser mused. "Maybe the NCP wave brought something with it."

"Look, there's another one!" Ellis cried, pointing at a darting, translucent shape. "What do we do?"

"What we came here to do. If these things are connected to the NCP wave, the upgrade to the causality array will take care of them."

"At least they don't seem to be AAAHHH!!!" Ellis cried out as a toothy shape more mouth than body clamped onto her arm. "It bit through my suit!"

"Get to the dome! We can repair it once we're inside!"

"But-"

"Go!"

Moving as fast as she could, Ellis made her way to the dome while Klauser brought up the rear. Bobbing, darting shapes were all around them now with more appearing by the second. Some wiggled or unfolded into existence like a sleight of hand trick while others simply appeared out of thin air. There were more bell-shaped things and sinuous quicksilver shapes, but new things were also appearing. Some glowed so bright they looked like tiny stars. Others were living geometries, fiery lattices folding, unfolding, and rearranging themselves into countless configurations. There were things that seemed little more than glaring eyes and gnashing teeth, and shifting things whose appearance changed depending on the angle from which they were viewed. Perhaps the worst were the oozing things that resembled living tumors whose movements hinted at both a dim intelligence and burning hunger.

Klauser focused on the utility dome which seemed a thousand miles away. He saw Ellis enter the outer hatch, pressurize the airlock, and stumble through the inner hatch into the dome. At the rate the sled moved, he would be there in less than a minute but that minute might as well have been an eternity. Every second some impossible new thing appeared, dragged from whatever alien universe that spawned it into Klauser's own space-time by a wave of force beyond comprehension. Some of the things were in fact vulnerable to the rigors of deep space, collapsing into themselves and imploding the moment they appeared. Others were made of sterner stuff, or of stuff born of conditions even harsher than airless, frigid space.

As Klauser approached the dome, something emerged from a dark recess and skittered toward him. Covered in overlapping plates, at first glance it resembled a giant lobster with the addition of an enormous pair of membranous wings folded across its back. Then the thing reared up, revealing a face that resembled a cluster of fist-sized spheres lit by a pulsing glow. The thing's forelegs ended in prehensile tri-pincers that held a cylindrical object which looked both manufactured and organic. As the lobster-thing raised the object and pointed it at Klauser, the object's tip began to glow. An electrical burst streaked past Klauser, striking the lobster-thing and sending it careening off into space. Turning Klauser saw that Ellis was outside the utility dome.

"Are you crazy?" Klauser asked.

"Comes with the job," Ellis replied.

"We should be safe in here," Klauser said once they were inside the dome. "The causality array is broadcasting toward Earth but the dome and the station's hull are vibrating at the same frequency as the array."

"That thing I shot," Ellis said. "It…It was holding a weapon, right?"

"I…don't know. Let's just assume it was."

"I heard rumors of deep space probes finding signs of intelligent life, but-"

"No time for speculation. If the NCP wave is close enough to make those things manifest this far inside the solar system, it'll soon overwhelm the causality array. We need to finish the upgrade or it's goodbye Earth."

"Fair enough," Ellis said, watching through one of the dome's viewports as the lobster-thing spun end over end on its journey into the void.

"Remember what I said about being safe in the dome?"

"Yes, what about it?"

"I'm going to have to shut down the hub for about ten minutes while I replace the hardware. The array itself has enough residual energy to keep broadcasting for another twenty minutes while the hub's down but-"

"The dome will be unprotected?"

"Right. You're a bright one, Corporal Ellis."

"Okay, just do it. Maybe those things have already forgotten we're here."

"I'm sure they have," Klauser muttered as he went to work.

Klauser worked in silence while Ellis kept watch. He was almost finished when Ellis said his name.

"What? I'm trying to...Do you hear that? Sounds like the wind. You don't think-"

"Klauser," Ellis repeated.

Turning, Klauser started to say something but the words stuck in his throat. Something indescribably foul was manifesting nearby. As if pumped through an invisible hole, it bubbled and oozed into existence. Floating in the air, the thing was a living tumor not unlike those things Klauser had spotted earlier but much larger and far more mobile. Ropy tendrils emerged from puckered orifices randomly scattered across its pitted surface, blindly groping about the dome. Whatever the tendrils touched smoked and dribbled away as if drenched in acid. Suddenly the thing paused. Bobbing on phantom winds, it began drifting toward them.

"Dear God," Ellis whispered, raising her rifle.

"Don't miss," Klauser said. "One stray shot will-"

"I know."

Channeled by a beam of ionized particles, a dozen megavolts of electricity arced from the tip of Ellis's ion rifle and struck the floating cancer-thing. A high-pitched keen filled the air as chunks of it flew off and vanished, perhaps sucked back to whatever alien space-time spawned it. Within moments, gelatinous flesh flowed together to seal the crater left by the blast.

"Aw, crud," Ellis muttered.

"Almost ready," Klauser said. "As soon as the frequency modulator finishes calibrating-"

Ellis raised her rifle for another shot when a tendril whipped across the room and knocked her aside. As she tried to rise, a carton fell off a shelf and struck her in the head. Ellis collapsed and lay still.

Finger on the virtual keypad that would reengage the broadcast hub, Klauser turned to check on Ellis. Looming above him, the floating cancer-thing filled his field of vision. Gritting his teeth, Klauser hit the button. The broadcast hub activated, filling the thin air with a frequency-pulse still trying to match the NCP wave. Shredded by the clash of frequencies, the invisible essence of space-time parted like a torn curtain. Waves of psychic dismay washed over Klauser as countless alien horrors strained against the reverse flow drawing them back to their native space-times. As the cancer-thing faded, Klauser glimpsed what lay beyond the tattered fringes of known space-time. A city that dwarfed Space Station Charybdis or any of the works of Man, its perception-skewing architecture hinted at an alien geometry born of spatial dimensions outside the ones Klauser or any human being knew.

Klauser's mouth hung open in horror but it wasn't until he glimpsed the things emerging from the city's impossible angles that he began to scream. He was still screaming when Ellis slapped him across the face. Klauser blinked. The city was gone. Equilibrium between the NCP wave and the causality array achieved, space-time was restored.

"You okay?" Ellis asked. "What happened?"

Speechless, Klauser could only shrug.

***

A few days passed before another shuttle arrived to take Klauser home. Ellis and Klauser avoided talking about the dome incident until the final moments when she accompanied him to the docking bay.

"Are you going to tell me what you saw?" Ellis asked.

"The same as you."

"You're lying." After few moments of silence, Ellis turned to Klauser. "Is it over?"

"There's haven't been any reports of new NCP events. Maybe the wave's come and gone. To answer your question, yeah, as far as we can tell, it's over and that's all that matters. I…Hold on a second. Wait here."

Klauser left Ellis and rushed over to a familiar trio unloading supplies from a cargo container. Grabbing Marsh by the shoulder, Klauser spun him around and pinned him against a stack of crates.

"What the hell is it?" Klauser demanded.

Hess reached for Klauser but Marsh stopped him with a gesture. "You saw it, didn't you? You saw the Lost City."

"What does it mean?" Klauser asked through gritted teeth.

Marsh gently brushed Klauser's hands aside. "It means you know the truth."

"But…It's over, right? The wave, the…the dream, it's moved on, right?"

Marsh smiled. "To quote the Prophet, *'That is not dead which can eternal lie, yet with stranger aeons, even Death may die'*."

"What does that mean?"

"You'll know soon enough. Now that you've seen the city, you're connected to it." Marsh laid a hand on his shoulder. "You're a prophet, like me. And like me, he'll come to you in your dreams."

"Who?" Klauser cried as Ellis approached and the trio walked away.

"It's time to go home," Ellis said, leading him to the airlock.

"Who?" Klauser was still whispering as the shuttle undocked and began maneuvering for the journey home.

The Condo Over in Innsmouth
Stephen R. Wilk

I had, of course, heard of Innsmouth long before I laid eyes on it. It was the year I graduated from college, and before settling into a workaday job, I was embarking on a backpack tour of New England, sightseeing and doing a little historical and genealogical research. I had no car, but was traveling by bus, train, and bumming rides. Leaving Boston, I intended to strike out along the North Shore, and I took the train from North Station to Salem, where I visited all the standard tourist sites, but also visited the small and nondescript Peabody-Essex Institute, which still occupied its old and classic building, along with a modest modern extension to the side. This obscure museum also housed an important genealogy and historical archive. Most people knew it as the home of the Salem witchcraft trial documents, but it was also a treasure trove of other old documents, including those about my own family, as well as the record of other North Shore towns, including Innsmouth.

From Salem I went north to Beverly and Rowley and up to Newburyport, with its quaint shops and touristy boutiques, then planned to continue north across the Manuxet to Innsmouth.

At the Newburyport Historical Society I read up on Innsmouth, and found the old and crumbling books in their collection much more forthcoming about the history of the town than guidebooks or Wikipedia were. That seemed odd, and I wondered if it might be worthwhile to try to update the entries myself.

The town had been founded in 1643, had been a center of shipbuilding, and had, like Boston, Salem, and other nearby ports, carried on heavy trade with the Orient and the South Seas. Unlike Salem, the trade had not slackened during the nineteenth century, partly, no doubt, because of its deep harbor that allowed the inner port to be used up to the present day. Also in the same century it had turned to manufacturing, taking advantage of the Falls of the Manuxet to drive the belts of machines to make shoes and weave cloth. There had been a plague and riots in 1846, but the books had little about this.

After the Civil War there had been a decline in the town's fortunes, and for a time the only notable business had been the Marsh refinery and the Marsh fishery, with the smiling Marsh Codfish mascot. There always seemed to be plenty of fish around Innsmouth Harbor, even in the present day, and species that were commercially extinct elsewhere continued to thrive there.

One of the darker truths of Innsmouth's past was its insularity. Foreigners did not settle there, and there was evidence that Portuguese and Poles who had tried to settle there had been dissuaded in violent ways. The Innsmouth town website pointed out that Innsmouth today actively welcomed everyone, and displayed a photomontage showing people of all colors and nationalities shopping, playing, and working in the modern and brightly decorated streets of the Innsmouth waterfront.That was the picture Innsmouth strove to present -- a happy, vibrant community, now isolated only from the economic ravages that beset the surrounding towns, with no slums or decay.

One of the things they didn't celebrate was an odd story I'd come across, first published in the 1930s by an obscure author named Howard Philips Lovecraft. Lovecraft was one of the stable of fantasy writers whose stock in trade was the atmospheric tale celebrating ancient evil and transdimensional malignities, especially in his native New England. The only reason that I knew of him was that there had been a volume of his works published by a small press in the late 1960s when adult fantasy had been the rage. His stories had been revived along with better-known authors like Robert E. Howard, Clark Ashton Smith, and Arthur Dunn. But the single volume apparently didn't sell well -- Lovecraft's archaic prose wasn't a good fit for modern sensibilities, I suppose – and he remained known only to aficionados like myself, while Clark Ashton Smith's stories inspired a gout of bad movies by the likes of Roger Corman. One Lovecraft story that attracted my interest concerned the evil inhabitants of the real-life town of Innsmouth who had made a bad bargain with amphibious creatures to revive the flagging fortunes of the town, and had paid a dear price for it. Even shortly after Lovecraft's time, however, Innsmouth had been a successful city, so why he had chosen to write such a story remains a mystery to me. The Innsmouth website, naturally, had nothing to say about this.

The next morning I caught the Innsmouth bus in front of the Rite Aid drug store. There were only three other passengers. I asked them why, and was told that they had missed the company bus that Marsh Industries for the out-of-town workers. Two of them were coders, writing software for MarshSoft.

The town itself was isolated from its neighbors by the marshy areas common to many North Shore coastal towns, but as we approached I could clearly see the new roads and bridges, and the commuter rail train that ran along the same bed the old Marsh-built private railway had run.

The bus came south into town along Federal Street, passing by the exotic and well-appointed Hall of the Esoteric Order of Dagon on New Church Green before rolling past a row of old turn-of-the-century houses, all beautifully restored and kept up. We crossed the Manuxet River on the new bridge and pulled into the broad Town Square. We were let off in front of the large and modern Gilman Inn. As the bus pulled away I could see a Rite Aid, a new Supermarket, and several little bistros and restaurants lining the square.

The streets were full of people, and I walked around taking in the sights. I found the Library not far from Town Square. At the front desk I asked if they had a genealogy department, and was told that they didn't get many requests for that, but there were some books in a small office on the second floor. The woman fronting the main desk passed the responsibility for that onto one of her staff, and escorted me to the room herself.

The room was surprisingly small, with a couple of shelves, containing fewer books than I would have expected, along with a few file boxes of material. My disappointment must have shown in my face, because she explained that there had never been much public interest in genealogy or family history in the town. The families were very much aware of their own histories, and kept it to themselves. The material in this room, she told me, were donations from scholars and libraries elsewhere, intended to fill the gap. She showed me where copies of relevant books were. She would return later. I should just try to keep things neat, and not open more than one file at a time.

I went through the bound family histories first, and I could see that all of them came from elsewhere. They barely touched on Innsmouth families at all. The town histories, as well, all dealt directly with the surrounding communities Again, the information about Innsmouth was slight, and included only the most cursory information. What sort of town is it, I wondered, that did not indulge in a little local boosterism?

The boxes containing random papers were actually more useful. They were marked by who had donated them, and did not appear to have been classified. Much of it was photocopied from other books, or from original handwritten material. There were pages showing genealogies of people who had come from Innsmouth – very few of these, and mostly from colonial days.

One box covered the Plague of 1846. There were copies of old newspapers, diary extracts, part of a government report. There was even an excerpt from someone's thesis on 19th century plagues. The plague was one of the most important events in the town's history. Had a written town history existed, this would have formed a chapter in it. From the estimates, it must have carried off fully half of the adult males in town. Yet there was no identification of the illness. The author of the thesis thought that it was some form of influenza that might have been picked up in China and brought by one of the trading ships.

When I opened one box I had to smile – it contained that story about Innsmouth by the virtually forgotten Lovecraft, copied from its original publication in 1936.. The unnamed contributor must have submitted this because it was one of the few references to the town in any form. I flipped quickly through the photocopied pages, refreshing my memory of the story about an amateur historian and genealogist (not unlike myself) who investigates the crumbling and decrepit town of Innsmouth. He is able to worm the secrets of the town from the garrulous town drunk, Zadok Allen. The narrator at first does not believe the story – that the failing town prospered because Captain Marsh had struck a deal with undersea dwellers who sent fish to the town, and gold, apparently, but which ultimately demanded that the townfolk practice their pre-human religion and intermarry with them. This produced a town of amphibious half-breeds, who became progressively less human and let the town decay around them.

Lovecraft actually named the Marsh family and identified their businesses, instead of setting up some fictional counterpart. If the Marshes learned about the story, they wouldn't have been at all happy. Part of me wondered if perhaps they had a hand in suppressing the work.

Beneath the photocopy of the story, I found copies of hand-written notes. They seemed to convey the same story as that told by Zadok Allen, but were fragmentary. Someone must have found Lovecraft's notes for the story.

They were in the form of fragments of sentences, written out quickly as if in a stream of consciousness flow of material. At times the pencil seemed to be starting another thought before it had completed the previous one, as if rushing to keep up.

As if he were transcribing what someone else was saying.

No! That was absurd. It must simply be the way he composed his ideas, imagining them coming rapid-fire from the mouth of an inebriated informant. The story they told, though disjointed, had more detail than the published story. There was mention of the great Festival in the Town Square, the Exhibition of the Deeps, and a description of some of the rites in the hall of the Esoteric Order of Dagon.

Here was a list of names, with notes saying that some were still active, while others were changed. Here a list of dangerous streets. And this page had descriptions of.... Horrible things. Cannibal feasts. Mutilations. Things that would never have been published in a journal of pulp fiction sold on a newsstand. Was he letting his imagination run wild?

I got up from the table and walked around, needing to clear my head. I went out of the room and down the hall to the bathroom, where I splashed water on my face. Looking into a clear mirror in a scrubbed restroom, it was hard to believe that there was anything to the fantastic story. I made my way back to the room, and found that the papers were gone from the table. In fact, the entire box containing the papers was gone. I looked for the place it had been on the shelf, but the box wasn't there. I decided that the librarian must have come in, seen the room with papers on the desk, and thought I'd simply left them there. But surely she saw my pack...

My pack was gone! It wasn't on the chair where I'd left it. Did she take that, too? I ran down the stairs to the main desk, but I couldn't find her. I asked at the desk about her and about my pack, but nobody seemed to know anything. They told me that I shouldn't leave my things unattended, even in as safe a place as Innsmouth. If I would leave my name and information, they'd let me know if they turned anything up. In the meantime, I should report it to the police.

I did, although the reporting took longer than I thought. I was told it was very unlikely that my pack would be found, but they would make every effort nonetheless. The police didn't seem interested in the disappearance of the librarian. I told them that I would be staying at the Gilman. Despite the hotel's impressive appearance, it had inexpensive rooms.

There is something about being the victim of a crime that makes you feel very vulnerable and conspicuous. I felt as if many eyes were watching me as I made my way to the hotel and checked in. The price I paid for the cheap room was that it seemed set off from the other rooms on the third floor, hidden away behind the ice machine, which leaked in its niche and gave a subtle fishy odor to the room containing it. I ran the key card through the slot on the door, and it opened easily onto a clean and spacious room.

After I inspected the room I went down to the lobby and got a bowl of soup and crackers to eat in the coffee shop, then took the stairs back to my room. I thought I saw movement down the end of the hall where my room was, but I found no one there. I swiped the card key and went in.

I was suddenly quite sure that someone had been in my room. I couldn't tell you why. I closed and locked the door and set the chain bolt, then quickly searched the room. The sliding door/window onto the balcony was closed and latched, and the connecting door to the next room (which could apparently be opened to make the adjoining rooms a suite) seemed to be locked. There was no overt sign that anyone had been in here, aside, perhaps, from that fishy odor from the ice machine, but I was certain that someone had been.

Why? With the theft of my backpack I had nothing to leave in the room, but perhaps my intruder had not known that. Was that glimpse I had on arriving on the third floor – unexpected, as I had walked instead of taking the elevator – the intruder hastily departing just before I could catch them?

I should have gone back to the front desk and complained, but I realized that I didn't want to do that, either. I didn't know if I could trust them.

What could I do? The door was locked, but I had locked it when I left for the coffee shop, and someone had still gotten in. The connecting door was locked on my side. The hall door was also latched with the chain bolt, but it looked a flimsy thing. I dragged a chair over and wedged under the door latch. The friction between its angled legs and the carpeting would hold at least for a time against any attempt to open the door. Not trusting the connecting door either, I managed to push the desk in front of it. The only unbarred way in was the balcony.

I decided to stay awake and not take off my clothes. I turned on the television, but with the sound muted, so I could listen for suspicious sounds. I no longer felt tired.

Nothing happened through the early evening, and there were no unusual noises. When I looked out the window, the part of the square I could see looked normal.

About ten o'clock I turned off the room lights. I turned off the television and lay down on the still-made bed, shoes and all. I strained to hear the noises around me. Footsteps in the street. A car suddenly accelerating. A call across the square. Doors opening and closing down the hall, and occasional footsteps in the hall. The intermittent whirring of the ice machine.

Sometime around midnight there was a change. I could sense people at the door in the hall. A look at the light coming through that narrow illuminated strip beneath the door confirmed it, however – there were shadows there, occasionally moving. I could have gone to the door and tried to look through the peephole there, but I didn't like the notion. It was better to figure out what to do if they suddenly tried to open the door. I should have done something earlier, during my precious free time, instead of watching the television. But who knew my suspicions would turn out to be real?

I got off the bed as quietly as I could, and just as quietly stripped off the sheets. I knotted the two sheets together with a secure knot and went softly to the balcony sliding door, unlatched it as quietly as I could, and slowly slid it open.

Both balcony and street seemed deserted. I put the sheet through the railing and tied the other two ends together so I had a continuous loop . I didn't need to get to the ground. All I had to do was get to the balcony below, which my sheet would easily reach.

I heard a *chink!* From within the room behind me and swiveled to look. The swinging of the chain told me what had happened – the plate attaching the chain bolt to the wall had somehow been released. The bolts holding it in were phony, or something. The chain and the wall plate now hung down from the end connected to the door, swinging freely back and forth.

Then suddenly, with a loud bang, the door was struck. It would have burst open and swung wide, had it not been for the chair wedged under it. As it was, the door only moved a couple of inches. There were moans of animal rage and frustration.

I didn't wait to listen. At the first assault, I swung over the balcony and slithered down. I glanced into the room connected to this balcony, the one below mine, and saw that it was dark and apparently untenanted. I hastily undid the sheet knot, whipped it down, attached it to my new balcony, then slithered down again. The chair would not hold up long against that determined attack. I was able to get down from that balcony to the street by using the decorative features on the hotel wall. I dropped to the ground. Should I go down the alley behind the hotel, or out into Town Square?

I didn't know what the alley lead to, and decided to chance the square. The sooner I got away from the vicinity of the hotel, the better. I went down Eliot Street, then onto Bates and went away from the ocean. I had come into town from the north, and thought that might be a way there.

I turned north up Adams street, headed towards the Manuxet. Where were the bridges that crossed that river? I wished that I had paid more attention to the map. Then I recalled that I still had my phone, and called up an app that would give me a map. Yes, sure enough, the rail station was only a couple of blocks away. Maybe I could get a train.

As I looked down the street, I saw many more people seemed to be out and around. Worse, I noticed the flashing red and blue lights of an Innsmouth Police cruiser. My instinct was to stay away from even the police. The paranoia was sinking in fast, but I embraced it. Paranoia might just keep me alive.

The station was brightly lit and busy. The people there seemed to be simply looking, not waiting for a train or a cab. I think they were scanning the people coming in to the station. What was I to do, then?

It struck me that even if I didn't take the train, I could walk the tracks. It seemed to me less likely that people would be watching the tracks than the streets. On the roads I would inevitably have to cope with the bottlenecks of the bridges that I would need to cross to traverse the marshy environs of Innsmouth, and those few bridges could be watched. But the railroad bridges might escape their notice.

I circled well around the station and picked up the tracks at Bank Street, which ran parallel to the river. The rails crossed the Manuxet on their own bridge, and I was able to go across this unseen by staying low.

I crossed River Street at grade and continued on. The heavily-used railway was mercifully free from the brambles that hugged the banks. My course was roughly parallel to the Rowley Road, which would cross in front of the tracks ahead. I checked behind me to see if there was a train coming, and was surprised to see an undulant motion on the Road. I could hear sounds –

suggestions like the bestial howl on the other side of the hotel door, a wet flapping and slopping, and the sounds of much motion. There came a powerful fishy smell.

A large crowd was coming. If I stayed on the tracks I would surely be seen, so I pushed myself into the bushes on the sides of the cut, hoping to conceal myself there. I could clearly see the spot where the road crossed the tracks ahead, and the crowd seemed destined for that point.

I confess that I was not sure that what I saw was reality or a nightmare hallucination, brought on by my memory of that story and reading the notes of Zadok Allen. They came in a limitless stream – flopping, hopping, croaking, bleating – a parade of inhuman figures illuminated by the parchment moonlight. They went upright on two legs, but seemed more frog than human, their skin a fish-belly white. The fishy stench was overpowering. I stared at the stream of Bosch-like creatures and shuddered at what they might do if they caught me. What if some of them decided to turn down the railway, instead of continuing on the road? Then I saw a police car drive up. "Innsmouth Police" was written on the side in reflective letters, and I saw that the driver and passenger were both those Things. The car drove slowly and ponderously over the tracks, stopped there for an eternity as the passenger looked down the railway, looked right at me in my hiding place, then drove off.

I wanted to lose myself in unconsciousness, but I feared what would happen. I willed myself to stay awake. The herd dwindled down. The sounds grew less and the odor dissipated. I waited after the last one (I hoped) had passed. I waited one minute…two…three. It seemed clear. I had better cross now before the pack came back down the road. I prepared for the dash across the exposed road. Just as I sprang, a hand caught my by the shirt collar and hauled me back.

I was jerked around to face three men in loose-fitting clothes. They had wide faces with neck wrinkles that suggested gills, large, bleary liquid eyes and wide mouths. They stank of fish – how could they have snuck up on me? The one with his hands on me narrowed his eyes and said, "Where do you think *you're* goin'?"

At that point, I did faint.

I awoke to bright sunshine. I saw immediately that I was in some large office with large windows, a couple of stories up. I was on a couch, and alone in the room. I sat up and tried to figure out if this had been some weird dream or a reality. Where was I?

I sat up, checked myself for injuries, then got up and looked around. The desk was almost bare, with desk set and blotter and a computer.

Looking out the window I saw that I was above Town Square. My backpack was there on a chair.

What do I do now? My instinct was to grab the backpack and run, fast, anywhere. But surely those who brought me would have posted a guard. I unzipped my bag to see what was in it, and if anything else had been put in there.

As I did, the door opened. A very ordinary-looking man looked in. No gills or fish lips. Business casual clothes.

"Good. You're awake. Wait here a minute. The Boss would like to speak with you."

The door opened wide, and I suddenly noticed how big a door it was – much wider than a standard door. It needed to be. The figure that came through had a substantial girth. It wore a generously cut business suit, and the corpulent belly extended far out in front.

The head was almost as extreme as those flopping monstrosities from last night. Bloated and wide, with a fish-belly white color, a wrinkled neck with those quasi-gills. No hair, virtually no ears, and those huge, staring eyes that were looking right at me, unblinking. I didn't know what to do. So I did nothing.

The Thing finally shut the door behind him and walked with a swift and easy gait to the desk.

"You haven't run," he said, in a wet, gurgly voice, " There may be hope for you yet. Sit down." By way of illustration, he sat down himself, in a chair that I hadn't noticed was custom-made for his size. He took a slim cigar from a holder on his desk and lit it.

"What.. what's going to happen with me?"

"That depends upon how you answer some questions. Sit." It was a command. I sat.

He drew on the cigar and blew out the smoke. It was disturbing to see some smoke curling out from those neck wrinkles as the smoke escaped through openings there.

"We found your pack, and what you were reading. You'd read that story before, hadn't you? Hadn't you?"

"Uh...yes. I found it in an old book."

"You had a copy of that in your pack, too. Is that why you came to Innsmouth?"

"Yes...yes. That and genealogy."

"So. Who's your family?"

I told him.

"Hm," said, at last "No obvious link to the Families. Let me see your face. Lift your chin! Yes, possibly. It would be good for you if there is."

"Why?" I ventured to ask.

"Why?! Because Innsmouth people who leave Innsmouth are drawn back here, like a salmon to its spawning ground. We are drawn to the rivers of our youth. If I let you go, what would you do?"

"I...don't know." What could I say that would convince him to let me go? What could I say that he'd believe?

"An apt answer. You're clever and adaptable. I don't like to throw those qualities away. Do you know who I am?"

"You're the Boss."

"Yes. I'm also Barnabas Marsh. Obed Marsh was my grandfather. How old does that make me?"

I had to think. "You'd have to be over 150. I think.. 168 years"

" You're good at math. And you have read that damned Providence man's story. Do you believe it, now?"

"I guess I do."

"You should. It's all true. Ever since they published that book we've tried to suppress it, but you can never clean up all the pieces. That story was a wake-up call. It made us look around at what we were and what we'd become. Even if we disdain the Upper World, letting the town decay only called attention to ourselves. The wretchedness of the town repelled visitors, and that was good for a while, but it was only a matter of time before the pressure of your neighbors would force others in. So we polished the town and restored it. We built modern industries, but always with our own people in charge. We are the shepherds , and the surface people are our unaware flock."

"But you killed all those people in the Plague. You sacrificed people to Dagon and Cthulhu. Those notes..."

"Oh, yes, those notes. We should have paid closer attention to what was going on at the library. Nobody really knew what our librarian had been hoarding. We've taken the files, and she is being ... re-educated.

"Yes, we killed off many in the town, but it was necessary to keep our secret and to maintain order. As for the sacrifices, they are necessary. We sacrifice our own people, too. Did you know that? That whelp from Rhode Island didn't, because all he had was the word of an old drunk. You really should thank us. You know what a Shoggoth is? Yes, I see you do. Even the Old Ones couldn't control them. We keep them at bay with rites, but those demand payment in blood. If not for our work – including the sacrifice of our own – your precious land would have been overrun by them by now."

"But you sacrifice to Cthulhu. It says in the…"

"We sacrifice to Cthulhu, who is very real. He does lie dreaming in his city of R'lyeh. And as long as the rites are performed, and until the stars are right, he will keep dreaming. When he awakes the Earth will be transformed, and the lucky will be the first to die. Would you like that to happen?"

"No. Of course not."

"Neither would I. That's where I differ from my mother and my grandmother. They worship Cthulhu. But do you think I *want* to give all this up? To let that great monstrosity simply rise up and smash all that we've built? To take all that human potential that we can use to our own advantage and simply eat you all? We who remain will be reduced to ranks of simple worshipers. I'm not ready for that. We will see to it that Cthulhu will never wake.

"To prevent that, we need to find ways around the rites. We need to find ways to prevent his knowing when 'the stars are right'. And in that, we have found the help of you surface-dwellers helpful. While we grew torpid, doing things the same way for millennia, you have been developing science and technology. You have found ways to alter the physical world, and your information technology has caused knowledge to be transmitted widely and rapidly. We have learned and developed so much since putting your people to work on the ancient texts."

"Here," he raised an electronic reader, "is the Kindle edition of the *Necronomicon*. It was once the deep secret of a very few who jealously guarded the knowledge. But by studying this and cross-referencing texts, our team has learned how to keep Night Gaunts at bay, and how to fence in the shoggoths. And soon, I hope, we will know how to keep Great Cthulhu in his slumbers.

"So there's your choice – will you join us? I'm sure we can find a place for you in the organization. Join us and live, because if He awakes, or if the shoggoths break out, you will die horribly. "

"But I'd be a participant in your actions. I'd be helping to enslave humanity."

"Don't be so dramatic. As far as we're concerned, we're your shepherds already. And if we left you to yourselves you'd kill yourselves off and poison the earth "

"Couldn't I just go away and promise not to tell?"

He laughed. Once. A horrible coughing/belching/sneezing noise. "You wouldn't believe me if I said 'yes'. You've lost your innocence already, through your own doing. The question is – what do you want to do now?"

The Crimson Trail
L.W. Underwood

Race reached the Jacobs farm sometime late afternoon and could tell something was amiss right away. There was an eerie feel in the air, a restlessness that made Lucky's hair stand on-end in a stripe down his back. Race felt it too, and he climbed off his horse as Lucky let out a low, mean growl.

"Easy boy," he said, tying off his horse on a fence post. As he and Lucky moved toward the house Race noticed the sound of crows cawing in the distance.

"Hello?" he called out. "Anyone home?"

He stepped onto the front porch and peered through the windows. Everything seemed in order inside, yet Race still couldn't shake that uneasy feeling. He walked toward the back of the house, Lucky padding along at his side, and then pulled up short when he reached the back pasture, gasping aloud. There in front of him were the decaying carcasses of an entire herd of cattle, lying scattered about the yard like lumps of coal.

The smell of rotting meat and decay was thick in the air. Race fought back the instinct to puke and pulled a handkerchief from his pocket. He held it to his face and moved closer. He guessed he was looking at the remains of twenty or thirty cows, their bodies bloated and bulging. A murder of crows covered the carcasses, picking and pulling at the foul feast. He could barely hear himself think over the excited cawing of the birds.

He wondered if some sort of infection had struck - some disease perhaps - but he'd never seen an entire herd affected like this. He made his way through the carnage to a large clearing. The grass was matted down here, like it had been crushed by the weight of something heavy. A trail of blood led off into the distance.

Race followed it away from the Jacobs house toward the woods, then over a muddy rise. As he topped the hill a lake came into view, spreading out in the distance. The rotten smell returned anew, hitting him like a punch in the face. The source was quickly apparent; another dead cow was lying at the bottom of the rise, the top half of its body submerged in the lake. Two turkey vultures were tearing away at its haunches, oblivious to his presence.

Lucky stopped at the top of the rise, whining and pacing. Race told him to stay and carefully made his way to the water's edge. The vultures flapped away as he approached, their meal interrupted. They reluctantly landed on a nearby tree where they could keep a beady-eyed watch on him. He glanced at the waterlogged heifer, no more than a couple years old, and wondered again what had happened.

Race caught sight of his reflection in the water, and paused momentarily. He was a big, broad shouldered man with a powder keg chest and the sun-browned skin of a man who spends most of his time outdoors. His reflection rippling in the water made him look larger, he noted - and older than his 30 years. His face was covered with stubble, as he hadn't shaved in the better part of a week. He took off his hat and wiped the sweat from his forehead, the wind soothing as it blew through his short, blonde hair.

He noticed the trail of blood and matted grass continued along the bank of the lake. He followed it along the water's edge, stepping carefully over rocks and limbs in the process, as water moccasins were bad this time of year. The crimson trail continued for thirty yards or so before abruptly halting. It didn't seem to lead anywhere in particular, it simply ended.

Race walked ahead a few yards, to see if the trail picked up again, without luck, then returned to the spot where the trail vanished. On one side was the lake, on the other a steep dirt wall. There wasn't room for a boat to pull up here, as the vegetation was too dense along the shoreline, and several trees had grown right at the edge, their limbs drooping down into the water.

Race was stumped. Maybe one of the cows had wandered down here, injured, and then stumbled along the lake line, until it died. But if so, where was the body?

He suddenly realized it was getting dark out. There was no way he could make it back to town tonight, and he still wanted to look around a bit more. He made his way back up the hill, Lucky wagging happily at his return. They walked back to the house, Race doing his best to ignore the rotting piles along the way. He tried the handle of the back door – it swung open at a touch.

"Hello?" he called hesitantly. Only silence answered. He could make out the shape of a lantern and box of matches on a shelf just inside the door. The hiss of the match was loud in the silence as he struck it and lit the lantern. As the darkness retreated he found himself in old man Jacobs' kitchen.

Holding the lantern above his head, he made his way through the rest of the house, the golden glow casting weird shadows across the walls and ceiling. It was a small place, only five rooms total. Jacobs was nowhere to be found.

"Might as well sleep here tonight and have another look around in the morning, I suppose," Race muttered to himself. He looked at Lucky. "Anyway, it sure smells a helluva lot better in here, eh boy?" The mutt tilted his head at the question, as if trying to understand what he was saying.

Race fixed a quick meal for himself and Lucky. Afterwards he tossed a blanket by the front door where he could keep watch for anyone entering. Lucky curled up next to him, and they settled in for the night. Race listened to the sound of crickets, their mating song soothing in the darkness, as his thoughts drifted back to what had brought him to this point.

Last Thursday Judge Shadinger had asked Race to stop by his office. Thinking he had another bounty to collect, Race hurried over, but this time it wasn't an escaped convict he needed Race to track down; instead it was Sheriff Reynolds himself that was missing, along with his Deputy. Both had been disappeared over two weeks ago, Deputy Franks first then Sheriff Reynolds a few days later. Race questioned the Sheriff's wife and learned that when she last spoke to her husband he was headed out to the old Jacobs ranch to look for his deputy, who'd ridden out there a couple days earlier to investigate a case of missing cattle. Neither had been heard from since.

Race ran over the conundrum in his head. The harder he thought the more questions came to mind. He decided to try and forget about it till daybreak. From where he was positioned he could see the night sky through the front window. He tried to clear his mind and relax, focusing solely on the shimmering stars in the clear night sky.

He must have drifted off at some point, because both he and Lucky woke with a start sometime late in the evening. Race thought he had heard something, but couldn't be sure he hadn't dreamed it. He sat still in the darkness, listening intently, waiting for the sound to repeat itself. Then he heard it again, clearer this time – a light scraping sound, like something moving around just outside the door.

Race grabbed his pistol and made his way quietly to the window. He watched for a couple of minutes, straining to see in the darkness, and thought he could make out a shape moving near where his horse was tethered.

Making his way back through the kitchen Race opened the back door as quietly as possible, and stepped outside cautiously. The air was humid and still as he made his way to the edge of the house and shot a peek toward his horse. Everything appeared normal, but just as he started to move closer Lucky began barking. He hurried back inside and heard a loud crash from

Jacobs' bedroom, where he found Lucky bent low, growling, looking under the bed. He grabbed a bedpost and pulled the bed away from the wall, wondering if maybe a raccoon or possum had somehow gotten into the house and was cornered under there. To his surprise he discovered a large hole in the floorboards.

Race relit the lantern to get a better look. The hole was about two-and-a-half feet across. The edges were ragged and rough, like they had been chewed, rather than cut, into the wooden floorboards. He held the lantern over the opening; there was a drop of about four feet into what looked like a tunnel of some sort.

Lowering the lantern into the hole, Race slowly leaned his head down to take a look. The tunnel started under Jacob's bed, and extended as far as the lantern's light would reach. He could hear the sounds of something scurrying off in the distance.

Why the hell is there a tunnel under Jacob's house, he wondered, and where does it lead? He patted Lucky on the head. "I'll be back before you know it, old feller."

He lowered himself and slowly made his way along the tunnel, carefully avoiding banging the lantern on the dirt walls. It was just large enough for him to make his way through, crouching. He was headed east initially, but quickly became disoriented, as the tunnel twisted and turned at odd angles and slopes. He would go no more than ten or twelve feet before it would change direction again, sometimes slanting up or down sharply in the process. He noticed several smaller offshoots from this main tunnel along the way, too small for a person to crawl through. As he advanced a horrible odor began to reach him, a sour, moldy stench that made his stomach turn.

The tunnel took a sharp, ninety-degree turn and opened into a small cavern. As the light of the lantern flickered across the interior of the chamber, Race beheld a sight that would haunt him the rest of his days.

The room was about twenty feet across and fifteen feet high. The floor was flooded with green water covered in thick algae. Rock formations pushed randomly out of the stagnant surface, and stalactites hung from the roof, slick and shiny with moisture. There were three separate entrances into the room, each about the same size as the one he had crawled through. It was stiflingly hot, and Race felt sweat break out throughout his body.

The stench of rot and death was overpowering; Race threw up, repeatedly emptying his stomach until nothing but bile remained. Once he composed himself Race turned again to the horrific scene. Through watery eyes he noticed a mud shelf lined three walls of the room, just above the water line. It was about four feet wide and was covered with shapes that he couldn't make out at first – or perhaps his brain simply couldn't comprehend what he was seeing.

The shapes were bodies, human and bovine alike, piled thick upon the mud embankment, each covered with numerous smaller shapes that looked at first like scabs, about a foot long. Race blinked away tears and stared harder, for he couldn't believe his eyes. The shapes covering their bodies were moving, and were in fact human in contour - like miniature people. They were covered in pink, mottled skin, crisscrossed with a hideous roadwork of blue veins. But worst of all was the fact that their heads were buried inside the flesh of the moaning victims!

Race took a half step back, stumbling, mind reeling from the scene of horror. His foot slipped on a loose rock and he found himself sliding over the edge of the mud shelf, into the stagnant water. As he hit the stinking stew a fresh wave of ghastly stench hit him, and he found himself waist deep in slime. His movement in the water stirred up a fresh batch of noxious vapors, as well as numerous shapes that came bubbling to the surface. Race recognized one as a human skull, grinning up at him through a layer of green gauze.

Overtaken by a sense of revulsion he scrambled out of the water and onto the mud shelf, face to face with the unholy banquet.

"My God! What the hell is this…" he muttered.

Race did a double-take, as lying just to his right was Sheriff Reynolds. He was naked and covered with a half dozen of the little creatures, each twisting and twitching in an effort to dig deeper into his flesh. He stepped over the body of a calf and knelt beside Reynolds. His eyes were half slits and he barely noticed Race.

Race felt sickened. He pulled a knife from his belt loop and poked it into the body of one of the creatures. It gave with a popping sound, green and red mucus spewing forth like a mini-geyser. The creature twisted in pain, but didn't release its grip.

Race had an idea. He looked over at the lantern, recalling a trick his Granddad had taught him to remove ticks. He would heat a straight pin with a match and press it against the tick's body. The little critter would pull out of the skin on its own accord.

He placed the tip of the knife into the lantern's flame, turning it slowly from side to side. A sizzling sound filled the air as he pressed it against the creature's pale skin, the smell of burning flesh joining the hellish mixture of odors in the room. It immediately started squirming and writhing in an attempt to escape the red-hot blade, then pushed away from Reynolds body as it released its hold.

Race gasped aloud as the creature slid out of the red gash in Reynold's side, not believing his eyes; for in place of a head was a series of tendrils, twisting and twitching in the torrid air. The creature left a red slime trail down Reynold's stomach as it slid toward the ground. Its legs began kicking as it made contact with the rocky surface, and Race brought the knife down just as it started to skitter away. It sliced deep into the foul being, nearly cleaving it in two.

He quickly began clearing the rest of the things off Reynolds, hacking them in half once they released their grip. Once they were all removed Reynolds started regaining consciousness, moaning.

Race stood up, momentarily dizzy from the sudden movement and heat. When he regained his composure he began moving cautiously along the ledge, searching for other survivors. He spotted a woman a few feet away, her skin wrinkled like an old peach, as if all the moisture had been drained from her body. He shuddered and kept going, spying another person a few feet ahead. As he neared he recognized it was Deputy Franks. He took two more steps toward him and stopped cold; Franks was dead, as wrinkled and shucked as his female companion.

Race shuddered and turned back toward Reynolds, accidently bumping Franks in the process. His corpse shifted and slipped off the ledge, splashing noisily into the green swamp water below. It floated for a moment, and then slowly sank below the surface. Race continued making his way back to Reynolds when he heard a churning sound behind him. He turned just in time to see the water heave and bubble, and a giant gelatinous shape rise from the murky soup, stretching into the air toward the ceiling.

It resembled a huge earthworm, except its skin was opaque, and covered in tendrils much like those sprouting from the smaller creatures. Within the monstrous body Race could make out the shapes of what appeared to be more of the smaller beings. Several were closer to the surface, and one was pushing its way out of the gelatinous bulk, twisting and burrowing with its mass of tendrils as it dug free.

Reynolds was on his feet, leaning against the wall with one arm, staring at the unholy beast before him. Race rushed to him, supporting him with one arm and scooping up the lantern with the other. He quickly headed for the nearest opening, dragging Reynolds into the tunnel, and scrambling along as quickly as possible. He heard a sucking and squishing sound behind them, and realized the worm creature was following them into the tunnel.

They took a sharp left turn then the floor dropped abruptly, dipping down about ten feet before making another sharp right. All the while the squishing sound was growing louder, as the thing was gaining on them.

"Hurry," Race yelled, handing the lantern to Reynolds and pushing him onward.

As they reached a long straight segment of the tunnel Race spotted the tip of the creature rounding the bend behind them. Its body completely filled the tunnel, contorting to the shapes of the walls. He pulled his revolver and fired into the monster, the roar of the gun deafening in the cramped quarters. The bullet found its mark and plunged deep into the soft tissue of the thing, a noxious yellow liquid spurting out of the wound. The thing stopped momentarily, withdrawing back around the bend.

"Go!" shouted Race, urging Reynolds forward again. As they started around the next turn Race could just make out the tip of the thing joining in the chase again. They made a few more quick turns, the squishing sound growing louder. As they rounded one final left hand turn the tunnel went straight for ten feet or so, then abruptly ended.

"Dead end!" shouted Reynolds frantically. "What do we do now?"

"I don't know," said Race. "Look for an exit of some sort."

Reynolds twisted his head frantically, searching. "I can't find one!"

The thing started around the bend and Race fired again. This time the thing hesitated for only a moment. Race emptied his gun, the remaining slugs burying deep inside the gelatinous mass. It continued advancing slowly towards him, its segments undulating in a grotesque rhythm. Race watched as the jellylike form quivered and rippled steadily, almost hypnotically, and found himself unable to look away, mesmerized by the fleshy dance before him. As it inched closer he became aware of a presence, an alien intelligence, and realized the thing was ages old, older than man. A malevolent ancient evil that existed for eons, sustaining itself on a hatred for mankind that radiated from the gaping pink maw in pulsating waves, crushing him, overwhelming him.

Reynolds scrambled as far away from the advancing horror as possible, pressing his back against the mud surface of the tunnel wall. He closed his eyes tightly, preparing for the worst, when he heard a scratching sound from behind him. Turning, he saw a tiny strand of light breaking through the mud wall. He heard a whining sound, followed by more scratching, and an enthusiastic bark.

Reynolds grabbed Race's shoulder and shook him, breaking the hypnotic trance of the advancing horror. "Race, look, a dog!"

Race turned toward him. "That's Lucky!" he shouted. "Dig, Reynolds!"

Reynolds began pushing and clawing at the mud wall frantically, gasping in relief at the flood of fresh air pouring into the fetid chamber. He pushed his way out of the tunnel, and then began pulling at Race, Lucky barking excitedly beside him. A tendril slithered across the ground and wrapped around Race's boot, yanking him back inside the tunnel. Race pulled his knife and swung hard at the tendril, cutting through it with a spurt of yellow fluid. Once free Race didn't hesitate; he scrambled through the opening and tumbled hard onto the ground below. He found himself on the bank of the lake, where the crimson trail had ended earlier.

He twisted back toward the opening and saw the thing poke its tip out after them, tendrils twitching into the air in all directions. He spotted a long piece of fallen driftwood and lifted it, raising it to waist level, and then charged the creature, like Don Quixote tilting a gelatinous windmill.

The wooden shaft split the soft skin and plunged deep inside the foul creature, causing it to quickly retreat back into the tunnel. It withdrew several feet and paused, appraising this new form of attack. After a few moments it began moving forward again, pulsating grotesquely as it crept toward them.

Race looked at Reynolds and saw that he still held the lantern. He grabbed and threw it at the thing with all his might, the glass shattering as it impacted against the driftwood barb sticking out of the thing's tip. It exploded into flames, thick smoke filling the corridor, obscuring all vision.

A putrid black fluid oozed out of the opening, dripping onto the ground below. After a couple of minutes the smoke died down enough that they could look into the tunnel.

Inside were the charred remains of the thing, no longer moving. The fire had liquefied the creature instantly. It looked as if someone had poured massive amounts of black tar into the tunnel.

Race turned back toward Reynolds, breathing deep of the fresh air. They made their way back to Jacob's cabin and found a fresh set of clothes for Reynolds, then headed back to town. Once there they made their way straight to Doc Branson's office, where his wounds were tended and he was put immediate to bed, with no protest on the Sheriff's part. After a few days Reynolds' strength returned to the point he could tell his side of the story.

"You see, Race," he started, "I pulled up on the Jacobs place and found it a shambles, dead cattle everywhere. I looked around, wondering what happened to the herd, much as I gather you did. I made camp a half mile or so from there, and sometime in the night I awoke to a sharp pain in my back. I rolled over and found a gaping wound on my lower back. I touched it and pulled back a hand wet with blood and some kind of green fluid. That's all I recall until I woke, sometime later, in that cavern where you say you found me. It was like something out of a nightmare. I recall something coming along every so often and sticking me again in that spot in my back. Then I'd hear it slither away – slither, I tell you. By God that's the only way to describe it... a slithering sound."

"I think I was being seasoned," he said. "So help me, seasoned like a side of beef, so those little abominations could feed on me, drain the life out of me like they did poor Deputy Franks. Whatever that thing injected me with must have paralyzed me, too. I couldn't move, and could only stare at him for days as they sucked him dry, unable to move a muscle or turn away."

Race shook his head slightly. "Horrible. And poor old man Jacobs was most likely taken by those things too. I figure those things must not have been able to fit the larger cattle into the tunnels. That's why they left them for dead."

"But one question keeps coming to mind," said Reynolds. "Why now? What brought that thing to the surface now?"

"I know it's hard to believe, but when it was advancing on us, there at the end, I could feel it reaching out to me with its mind. That thing was intelligent, and full of hate. I think it had lived, trapped, underground for ages. It's old, older than man, and those things were its children. One horrible image kept coming to mind, somehow transmitted from that thing into my brain. A horrible image I can't seem to shake no matter how hard I try, an image I'll carry with me for the rest of my life."

"What's that?" asked Reynolds hesitantly, almost afraid to know the answer.

"It's the image of that thing, in a giant chamber, covered by hundreds of those little creatures, and before them a group of humans, dressed in scant clothing of furs and hides. And these people are unafraid. They weren't trapped and scared as we were. They were there by choice, on their knees, worshipping the thing as a God.

The End of The Others
Charie D. La Marr

I remember the night Aunt Francis and the others from town came into my room and gently woke me. I was eight, and it was Halloween. They told me something terrible happened to my mother. Robert Gilman wrapped me in a blanket and carried me into Innsmouth to my aunt's house. We'd talk more when I was rested.

In the morning, my aunt fed me and sat me down in front of the fire to talk. My mother, her sister, was gone. Dead. After I went to sleep the night before, the demons that haunted my mother returned. Frantically, she ran from our tiny house on the hillside to the cliffs and threw herself into the sea. The tide was full, and the swift undertow carried her away. There was nothing left to bury.

My aunt and I returned to the house a few days later. I was allowed to fill a sack with my clothing and another with some of my favorite things—books mostly. The first time I cried was when she allowed the women of the village to come and take things they could use. I screamed in anger, ordering them to step away from the things that had been a part of my life since I was born. Clothing, dishes, even the woven rugs Mother made for the floors—rugs that kept my feet warm every morning of my life.

Wasn't it enough that I lost my father before I was even born? That he just walked away one day and left my mother alone to bring me into the world kicking and screaming? My mother was gone without a trace. Now the women of Innsmouth were carrying away the pieces of my life like I didn't even matter. How could they? They knew Mother. She was their friend and neighbor. It seemed so cruel.

Aunt Francis took me aside and told me it was insensitive of her. I should be allowed to own some of Mother's things. However, her house not that big, and there wasn't room for much. I took the photo of my parents' wedding and her favorite sewing box—the one that sat on her lap on so many nights while she mended our meager clothing. I carefully packed her wedding dress in a box, promising Aunt Francis there was room underneath my bed. And I took the quilt from her bed that smelled so much like her—the quilt I'd hidden beneath on so many stormy nights while she rocked me and sang to me. That we took to the undertaker who put it into a pine box and buried it beneath a stone bearing her name. Margaret Waite Harrington. It didn't occur to me then, but were no other Waites or Harringtons in the graveyard.

Gradually, I grew into my life with Aunt Francis. On the hillside, Mother schooled me. In Innsmouth I went to the small schoolhouse. It was a sad and quiet existence that smelled of fish. It seemed no one ever left town except for the occasional person who left and never returned. Supplies were delivered to our store monthly. Men delivered them, unloaded and left as fast as they could. We had a hotel, though it was seldom used. I read books, and learned about faraway places in school. I longed to leave our dreary little town with half its houses boarded up and falling to the ground and see the world.

As I grew older, I began to notice the differences between me and the others in town. There was something in their appearance unlike mine, although I'd never seen people from outside of Innsmouth and didn't know enough to realize there was a repulsion, a characteristic ugliness about the people. While I bore some of those features, I was different.

One day, I brought my parents' picture to my aunt and asked her about it. While my mother bore all the traits of my neighbors and classmates, my father bore none. And my last name —Harrington—no one else in the town had that name. There were other Waites I assumed were distant cousins. I wanted to know where I belonged and how I fit into Innsmouth—a sad little orphan who desperately wanted to see other places.

It took my aunt a few moments to compose her thoughts. She turned her back to me and put the kettle on the stove. Anxiously, I sat at the table watching her. When she was done, she put the teapot and two cups onto the table and poured us both steaming cups of peppermint tea. My favorite.

"Emily, I always knew this day would come. When you'd start noticing things and want to know. Your mother often anguished over how she'd tell you. This is exactly what we decided. She'd sit you down with a cup of peppermint tea and open her heart to you. Now the task falls on me.

A long time ago, something happened in Innsmouth. The best way I can describe it is to tell you Innsmouth sailors traveled the South Seas and returned with natives of an island they visited. There was something different about these people. They stayed and married the people of the town. There was a terrible illness that spread through the town, and many died. Children who were born after that were . . . different."

I looked at the photo of my parents. "My father doesn't look different."

"No, he wasn't," Aunt Francis said. "He'd been traveling from his home in Maine to Boston when he was attacked and badly beaten by robbers. Your mother found him and brought him here where she nursed him to health. The beating left him blind. He never set eyes on your mother, yet he loved her with all his heart and asked for her hand in marriage. Our father hesitated, but finally agreed. They married and moved into the house on the hillside. New blood, Father thought, might begin to turn around our repulsive appearance. When your mother became pregnant, we waited patiently to see. We rejoiced when you were born. The defects were barely noticeable. It was our hope if we could bring more men to Innsmouth to marry our women; our people once again live with the rest of the world. We wouldn't have to hide away."

I listened to what she said as I stared at my father's face. I'd never noticed it before, but there was a blank stare as he held my mother's arm and smiled. It was obvious he was blind.

"But where did he go, Aunt Francis? How did a blind man so in love just walk away when she was expecting a child? Why?"

My aunt took on a far away look. "No one knows, child. One day he was just gone. Not a trace."

After that, I went to the cemetary and used a stone to add my father's name to my mother's headstone. Maybe he slept under that quilt, too. I liked to think he did.

Then the night before May Day when I was seventeen, I awoke to the sound of arguing.

"No!" my aunt screamed. "Not her! Someone else! Hasn't our family given enough? They took everyone she had! If it must be a Waite, take me! I won't let you do it. She's only half-bred. Her father wasn't one of us."

"They took him anyway," Robert Gilman said. "They're asking for her."

"What choice do we have?" Silas Eliot asked. "We need what they give us, you know that, Frannie. It's never our choice—I wish it was. Do it myself if I could. What have I to live for? But it's the girl they want. When the moon's full, it's time. There's no more to say."

The next morning, Aunt Francis woke me early. She told me to pack my clothes into a sack as quickly as I could. Carrying her sack and a small wooden box, we left as quietly as we could. In the woods nearby, she'd hidden a wooden pushcart. She dropped the box into it. I could tell it was heavy.

We walked for days. When we were hungry, my aunt hid while I went into the nearest town to beg for food. Sometimes we were able to get rides in the back of trucks. Some kind people let us spend a day or two in their barn. We became gaunt and haggard. How far did we have to go to protect me?

Weeks went by. We passed through Massa chutes and Connecticut and into New York. Still we pushed on. We entered Pennsylvania heading west. I became worried for my aunt—she was tired and weak. I didn't know how much further she could go.

One morning, I found her struggling to breathe. We were not far from a city, I could go get help. Aunt Francis said no. She opened the wooden box and showed me the contents. There were several gold coins and a letter.

She gave me the letter. "This is your admission to Oberlin College. I've written to them and paid for your education. They're expecting you. For your safety, I enrolled you under your father's name, Edward Harrington. Cut your hair; find some clothing before you go there. Trust me, it will save your life. The rest of this is for you to live on. Find a bank near the school. Keep it there. You'll be safe in Oberlin as long as you remember this. There are rivers in Ohio. You must avoid them at all costs. You may feel water calling to you or even hear it. Pay it no mind, Emily. Go on with your studies. When you're done, you may stay there or to go somewhere else. But you must stay away from water. It took your mother and your father. And it will take you, if you let it."

She closed her eyes and breathed her last. I sat and wept for a long while. Then I knew I had to move on. I prayed over her body and covered her with leaves the best I could. I picked up the box and headed to see what life held for me in Ohio.

When I arrived at Oberlin, I'd cut my hair and gotten some men's clothing. As my deformity was confined to my legs and torso, wearing a long sleeved shirt and jacket at all times allowed me to go undetected. I was plain, almost ugly and practically invisible. I was comfortable with that. I had a room of my own. I chose to focus on biology. One day, I hoped to be a doctor so perhaps I could understand what illness caused the defects in me and those in Innsmouth. Naturally, I was shy and didn't make friends well. I kept to myself—attending classes and studying alone in my room. I kept my money in a bank and lived as frugally as I could. I cannot deny there were times when I felt myself drawn to rivers. I dreamed of an ocean I'd never laid eyes on.

My favorite class was human biology. We were studying Mendelian Genetics. Gregor Mendel, the father of genetics, discovered certain trait inheritances passed down from parents to offspring. Working with pea plants, he found traits he called "units of inheritance." He described them mathematically, using simple rules and ratios. In 1905, William Bateson, a follower of Mendel, coined the term "genetics" and within ten years, the chromosome and genetic linkage were discovered.

I was silent throughout my school days, but now I wanted to know more. I raised my hand, and using a soft but distinctively deep voice, I asked my question.

"Sir, hypothetically, if an entire race of people unconnected to the outside world—say living on an island—contracted an illness and then rejoined society, would it be possible their genetic background could alter society significantly? Enough that there was a difference in their physical makeup, and even appearance?"

The professor thought and then smiled. "Very interesting, Mr. Harrington. We know there are several diseases—even some childhood diseases—that can cause a change in human genetics to include defects in infants born to a mother ill during pregnancy. Assuming these people were so isolated their only choices in breeding were among each other, and all carried this gene due to some kind of catastrophic illness leaving none untouched, it would be possible as generations went on and they interbred, this gene would become stronger, and the defect would become more prevalent. Excellent question."

I felt I had the beginning of an answer. Those in Innsmouth bred with the South Seas creatures, and the results were striking. My mother married a man who was not carrying the gene. Therefore, I only received half the genes causing the defects—Father's genes were normal. That explained why I had only slight defects—insignificant enough that I was not considered a monster. Others from Innsmouth would be shunned and looked upon with horror with the way their genetics had been altered. That was why my aunt knew she could get me away and into college. It also explained why she wanted me to live my life as a man. I'd never have children and risk passing on bad genes. I'd stumbled on to my future. I could never know love. I felt I understood what happened to my mother. The water called to me and I wanted to run to the nearest bridge and jump.

"Edward Harrington? Stop! Wait for me!" a voice called from behind.

It was one of my classmates. A young man named Jonathan North. He was a quiet, studious man who didn't speak much either. It was the first time he'd spoken to me. I waited to hear what he wanted.

"I see you know, too," he whispered.

I could feel the lump in my throat. "Know what?"

"That place in New England. Where the people are monsters. Is there somewhere we can talk?"

Panic and anger filled me. Monsters? The people of Innsmouth weren't monsters. I wasn't a monster!

We sat in the corner a small café nearby. I asked him to explain.

"My grandfather talked about a place not even on maps. He used to go there and sell supplies every month. They paid in gold. It was their gold that paid to send me here. He said they were always very generous and paid much more than was necessary."

"What does that have to do with monsters?" I asked, trying to keep my anger under control.

"He said they were different. They didn't look human. They were horrific to look at, but the gold made it worth it and he went every month. He felt sorry for them. As he told the story, generations ago there was an outbreak of a terrible illness that struck the whole village. They were normal then. But afterward, the babies were born different."

"Like monsters."

"Yes," he replied. "We have a few weeks' vacation from school soon. I intend to go and see for myself"

I wanted to tell him how dangerous that was. The few people who stayed at the hotel disappeared. I knew of weary travelers stopping for the night and going insane. They fled into the night, leaving belongings behind. But I couldn't. I wanted to go back, too. I wanted to know what illness had befallen the people there. And what happened to my parents.

That night I had a dream. I was at our house on the hillside. I climbed down the cliffs and stood before the ocean in my nightdress. Never had I done that. My mother forbid it. It was low tide and there was only a small trickle of water coming ashore. I stood back, afraid for it to touch my bare feet. Then the darkness came and a huge full moon. The tides became wild and restless. I could hear the waves crashing on the shore in the darkness. I screamed and backed up until my back was against the wall of the cliff. And still the tides came. I could feel the water soaking my nightclothes. In a state of panic, I tried to climb the stairs carved into the cliff, but my feet kept slipping into the water.

Something was touching me. It didn't feel like a fish—more like a snake or an eel, maybe even an octopus. It grabbed me, wrapped firmly around my leg and pulled. I struggled to find something to hold on to but found nothing, not even the smallest bush. Slowly it pulled me into the surf and I went under. The riptide tried to drag me out to sea. I surfaced, screaming for my mother. It pulled me under again and I fought to find the surface, gasping for air as I screamed for help. Then I woke up, bathed in sweat and shaking badly.

I knew I had to go back to Innsmouth.

Would I be recognized? It was more than two years since my aunt and I left. During that time, I lived as a man. I learned how to walk and move like one. Not once at Oberlin had anyone questioned my gender. If I was careful, it could be done. We could pose as travelers who needed a place to rest and stay at Gilman House. Along the way, we'd gather as much information as we could—never letting on either one of us ever heard of this strange town.

We left Ohio on the tenth day of July 1927, venturing by train and motorbus toward the southern shore of MAs sachets. Our first stop was Newburyport on the pretense we were researching Jonathan's lineage. The ticket agent was talkative and knew a lot about Innsmouth. I listened as though I was hearing about the town where I spent my first seventeen years for the first time. I never knew anything of what this man seemed to know.

Newburyport had a large library and we spent most of that evening reading about Innsmouth. We paid a visit to the Newburyport Historical Society where we saw an item I can only describe as a tiara made from materials I'd had never seen before. The curator, Miss Anna Tilton, told us it came from Innsmouth. That wasn't possible! The people of Innsmouth were simple people living in dilapidated buildings and wearing little more than rags. She assured me they'd gotten it from a pawnshop who got it a man from Innsmouth who was killed soon after. I watched Jonathan's eyes as he stared at the precious object. The curator spoke of devil worship and a secret society called "The Esoteric Order of the Dragon". I lived there for seventeen years and never heard of such things! There was no turning back—we had to discover the secrets of Innsmouth.

After a sleepless night at the Y.M.C.A., we boarded a bus and headed to my strange and suddenly unfamiliar home. I didn't know the driver by name, but he bore many of the disfigurements those in Innsmouth had. There was no doubt he was one of us.

When we arrived a few hours later, I was shocked to see how much the town had decayed in two years. While I hid in an alleyway, Jonathan went into the grocery store and spoke to a young man from Arkham. He explained how to get around in the town. There was no library or chamber of commerce. When my companion told me the rest of what the clerk said, I gasped. It was insane! He told of the Marsh family, the Gilmans, Eliots and my own family the Waites. He said it was rumored those families harbored relatives too horrible for public view. I lived in the Waite house and knew of no one but my Aunt Francis living there. He said my mother Margaret was banished to the house on the hillside when she married an outsider.

Jonathan and I made our way around the village—me keeping my hat low and head to the ground. There was little to see. If the people of Innsmouth were unfriendly to me as a child who lived there, they were even less friendly to outsiders.

Then I remembered someone who might talk to us. Zadock Allen—an old-timer with a taste for whiskey. I hid in the shadows while Jonathan purchased a quart bottle. We found Zadock near the southern waterfront and showed it to him. As Jonathan doled out spirits, I remained obscured by my hat and listened to a story I could scarcely believe. A tale of the founding fathers of Innsmouth and their trip to the South Seas lead by Captain Obed Marsh. They returned with creatures who lived beneath the sea and thrived on blood sacrifice in return for gold. Old Zadock told of the terrible night when they came up the maw of the Mantuxet, thirsty for blood. Marsh took over—telling the people things were going to change. They were forced to take the Oath of the Dragon to breed with the creatures. The sacrifices began—twice a year on May Day and Halloween. Most of the Waite family went to the Other Ones. My mother and father among them.

Waves crashed against the docks. Zadock became mad with drunkenness and fear, begging us to run for our lives. We ran for the bus to Arkham, only to find it wouldn't start. We had no choice but to stay at the Gilman Hotel. Jonathan signed while I stayed back, lowering my hat and studying a book. For two dollars, we were given the keys to a room on the top floor. While I stayed, Jonathan went in search for food, returning to the room before dark.

We heard voices coming from next door. The handle on the adjoining door started to turn. Were they after Jonathan, or did they know I was a Waite? I remembered the night before Aunt Francis and I left. They wanted me. And they weren't going to wait until Halloween to sacrifice me. They intended to do it that very night.

We jumped to the roof of an adjacent building and began to flee for our lives. In minutes, we watched a crowd leaving the hotel carrying lanterns. The only chance Jonathan had was to separate from me. Perhaps I had some kind of a scent they were following. If only one of us could survive, it should be him. He was innocent. He was not of Innsmouth and not a party to the horrors of so long ago. Clearly, my family was. In the bank in Ohio was Aunt Francis's gold—clearly ill gotten from these horrendous creatures. She was the only Waite to survive because she belonged—she'd taken the Oath.

Jonathan refused to leave without me, and we ran until we could run no more, pursued by the hulking shadows of the people and that fish smell that made us both gag. I didn't recall smelling it as a child. Clearly it was there and I was just accustomed to it. Two years in Ohio had desensitized me to the stench.

I remembered the abandoned railway station and the tracks that ran through it. We followed them through a tunnel. There was a cut overgrown with weeds. We could barely smell the fishy smell there, and saw no lights in the distance. We hid, trying to catch our breaths, clinging to each other—afraid any second they'd spring upon us and drag us to the water. I could hear my aunt's voice telling me to promise her I'd stay away from water. Why hadn't I listened? I looked at Jonathan. He'd fainted. Getting as low as I could, I did my best to stay awake and keep watch, but sometime in the night sleep overcame me.

We awoke to a gentle rain and began our trek from Innsmouth. We made it safely to Arkham, where Jonathan became a man obsessed. He went to the historical society and with the help of a Mr. Peabody began to learn about his ancestors. There, he learned in 1867, his great grandmother was named Marsh. The name took all the color from Jonathan's face. She was said to have been an orphan from New Hampshire. There was no direct information on her parents, but he took pages of notes and planned to return home to Toledo to rest and see what information he could learn from his family. They welcomed me into their home and privately expressed concern for his well being. He was a changed man. After a few days, I left there, promising to see him in school when the semester began.

Back in Oberlin, I spent the summer working in the school library. Jonathan wrote several times. He'd gone to Boston for more research. His letters were filled with his desire to return to school and obtain his degree, but I sensed something else was going on. He was a Marsh, I was sure of it. And what's more, I was sure he knew it, too. In some way, we shared some of the same blood—the creatures from the sea who'd infected the people of Innsmouth and changed them forever had a hold on us both.

I dove into my studies, trying to forget what I'd learned. I told myself I wasn't one of them. I couldn't be. But dreams of my aunt haunted me. Could she have been party to such things? Jonathan was more affected than I was. He claimed he wasn't, but sometimes I noticed him drawing maps and pictures of the people in the margins of his notebooks. He became quiet, but when he did talk there was always that faraway look in his eyes. They were calling to him.

We parted ways at the end of the year. With his degree in hand, he returned to Toledo and a job with his father. I stayed at school, seeking an advanced degree in biology with the intention of studying medicine. He wrote to me for a while, but his letters began to be intense and confusing. He was at times extremely depressed and at other times frenzied and manic. Soon his letters stopped, and he drifted from my thoughts as I entered medical school to focus on the subject of genetics.

It was nearly two years later when a dream of Jonathan woke me and forced me to go to my advisor and request a brief leave of absence. I saw Jonathan holding a gun to his head. Then I saw him throw the gun away and slip into the ocean at Innsmouth with someone else. He appeared greatly changed—his features surpassed those of the people of Innsmouth. He was becoming one of them.

I had to stop him. I understood—truly I did. I'd noticed over the years my own deformities increasing. Sometimes I wondered how much longer I'd be able to hide it. But it seemed my father's genes were strong within me, and fought hard to stave off the inevitable.

When I arrived in Toledo I found Jonathan living alone on the outskirts of the city. When I knocked on his door, he refused to allow me in. A bottle hit the door and shattered. I smelled alcohol. He was drunk. The time had come to be truthful with him.

Knocking again, I shouted as loud as I could. "I know all of it, Jonathan. I was born in Innsmouth. I left there before I began at Oberlin."

The door opened and the man who stood before me stopped my heart for a second. It was more horrible than anything I'd seen before. He pulled me inside. The smells of fish and alcohol gagged me.

Twisting my wrist hard, he glared at me. "You were born there? What are you talking about? We were there together. No one recognized you. Not even Zadock. How would that be possible if you had lived there for so long? Tell me!"

There was a long pause before I pulled free of his grip. "Because when my Aunt Francis escaped with me, she had me change my appearance. I became a man. For all these years, I kept up the charade, but I cannot do it any longer. My name is Emily Waite Harrington. My mother was a Waite; my father was a man she found beaten on the side of the road and nursed to health. He was blind."

Jonathan shook his head in disbelief. "But all the years I've known you—you show no sign of this!" he said, holding out his arms. "It's everywhere now—look at my face. You don't have this!"

I opened my jacket and unbuttoned my shirt, letting both fall to the ground. Then I unfastened my pants and stepped out of them until I was standing before him naked.

"My God!" he whispered, not taking his eyes off of me in the dim light. "You're one of us!"

Tears welled in my eyes. "Yes, I am. I sensed you were when we learned about your Marsh ancestors. I'd almost forgotten about you until the other night when I had a dream. In it, you put a gun to your head and nearly pulled the trigger. I knew I had to come to tell you the truth."

"That was four nights ago. The gun's in the drawer beside my bed. I almost did it. My Uncle Douglas did. I can't live among humans anymore. My only choice is to join them. It won't be long before I'm one of them. I want to go there. Will you help me?"

He held out his arms and I slid into them. Already the biceps fused to his torso and his hands were becoming webbed. He kissed me. His mouth was large and wide and his nose had flattened significantly. I could see lines where soon gills would open and make breathing through his nose impossible. His eyes no longer faced straight forward—each looked to the side and appeared gelatinous. He had no eyelashes. His deformities were far more severe than any I'd ever seen.

Taking me by the hand, he led me to his bed. As he took off his shirt, I gasped. His skin was dry and scaly with an iridescence. I looked away as he finished undressing and slipped into the bed. I couldn't let him see the sorrow in my eyes. It was more than I could bear. His body was icy cold as he slid on top and entered me. I wanted this. I'd loved him since the day I first laid eyes on him, but when the lovemaking ended quickly, I cannot deny it was with great relief.

We stayed there for a long while. I listened while he talked. He told me what he'd learned of the Marsh family. There was one other—a cousin in a mental hospital. His plan was to rescue him and go to the sea at Innsmouth There were no other options. He no longer belonged in this world.

I couldn't believe it. Did he really want to become one of them? They were murderers! My own parents were victims. I was repulsed as I listened him. His human blood would strengthen and help them endure. He hoped he would retain his education and knowledge. It would be useful to them—he'd be able to teach them.

Next to me was the bed table with the gun inside. It broke my heart, but I knew he had to be stopped. They had to be stopped. I took the gun, and with tears in my eyes, I whispered, "I'm sorry, Jonathan. I love you. I've always loved you." I pulled the trigger. Dressing quickly, I wiped my prints from the gun and placed it in his hand. It would have been very difficult for him to pull the trigger, but nobody would question he had.

It took me months to find someone in the government to listen. Eventually, they sent people to investigate. As a result, they destroyed the town and its inhabitants and torpedoed the reef. Divers were sent down. There was nothing left. I finally ended the horror plaguing my life by locating Jonathan's cousin in the asylum. While I was alone with him I smothered him with a pillow, ending the madness forever.

Now I'm a doctor. After my studies and training, I worked at a children's hospital. Then the sea called to me once more. Only this time, I knew there was a good reason. A large hurricane tore a path through the Caribbean. There was much death and destruction. I left Ohio and began working in a small clinic in Haiti, caring for children who were left orphans of the sea—as I was. A local woman showed me a plant growing indigenously that helped to smooth my scaly skin. I'm brown as a berry and walk among the natives without notice. The water is so clear when I swim I see the fish below the surface. This is where I'll make my home—knowing I'm safe from the shadow of Innsmouth.

The Eye of Cthulhu
Neal Privett

Bryant was sitting by the fire as I walked into his study. The snow was falling outside on what should have been a beautiful February night. But I could tell from my friend's voice when we spoke on the telephone that something was very wrong.

I had pulled up at my friend's home and rang the bell. The servant had let me in. Bryant never glanced up when I initially appeared in his study. He sat in his chair with hands folded. Lost in the dark pit of deepest thought. His eyes remained locked on the crackling fire in his hearth. Somewhere in the orange-blue flames he must have seen the specter of an ancient god taunting him.

Finally he spoke. "Carroll. Sit down." He beckoned to the chair beside his. I slid into it, finding myself almost swallowed up by the cushions. Bryant had always had excellent taste in furniture. A man would do well to spend his evenings sitting by the fire there, comfortable, warm, and dreaming.

Bryant continued. His voice was somewhat monotone, as if he had not slept in a century or two. Something terrible had obviously obsessed him and worn him down to a state of total exhaustion. "A peculiar gemstone was discovered at Beaumont."

"Beaumont? The old abandoned mining town in Arizona?"

Bryant nodded. "This is a most peculiar stone…very strange. Some of the workers on the archaeological crew discovered it, buried far back in one of the caves there. The stone was well hidden. It was a miracle that we were able to find it even. Someone did not want that stone to be discovered."

"What an incredible find," I said. "What manner of stone is it? Is it very valuable?"

Bryant laughed, but there was no humor in his face. It was as if I were speaking with a ghost. "*Valuable*. How funny. Yes…I suppose you could say it was valuable. To certain parties perhaps. The stone was just the beginning. Beside the stone, in the same test pit, was a hand carved statuette of unknown vintage."

I grinned from ear to ear. "That's fantastic, Bryant. Do you have the statuette here? Could I examine it?"

Bryant nodded and reached down beside his chair. He brought out a small wooden box and handed it to me. I took the container and slowly lifted the lid. In my mind raced visions of ancient Indian art. But when I took out the small effigy my heart stopped beating and my blood ran cold. The night ceased to be beautiful and peaceful and became something ominous and dark. I held in my hands a remarkably vivid carving of a demon.

The thing's face was the stuff of nightmares…it was as if an octopus had been attached to its shoulders. Pupil-less eyes stared back at me…no doubt the very light of evil would have beamed through those portals, if the beast was a living, breathing entity. Tentacles writhed silently on the lower part of the creature's visage. Every detail…every muscle, vein, and scale was perfectly illustrated in the unknown artist's work. The ancient Greeks could have learned a thing or two from whoever produced this satanic paperweight.

Two great bat-like wings extended from the shoulders and waited there, folded behind its back…waiting to propel the creature through the blackest of nights when the time came.

To say that the monster was deadly in its appearance would have been an understatement.

And finally, both of its massive hands and feet were armed with razor sharp claws that could rip through the thickest of metals. Such a beast would have been unstoppable.

I tried to smile, but my facial muscles were damn near frozen with icy dread. "I don't understand, Bryant," I said. "What is this damnable thing and how does it relate to the mysterious stone you found in the cave?"

The stone is the talisman for ...*that*," Bryant said. A cold shiver came over him and he began to shake uncontrollably. I was about to call for the servant and a doctor until my friend got hold of himself and continued his explanation.

I held the statuette up in my hands and examined it again. "*This*? This horrible little thing of fiction? The possessor probably bought it in a curio shop in Paris or London. This block of soft stone rather smacks of a base carnival mentality." I didn't quite believe what I was saying, but I wanted to ease my friend's nerves nonetheless.

"That thing...is no *fiction*, Carroll," he said. His eyes were wide and a jolt of terror had shot through his body so that his face had become a colorless mask. "I have a journal...left behind by one of the townsfolk there at Beaumont in the late nineteenth century." Bryant reached down beside his chair again and produced a small, leather bound book. He handed it over to me. The outside cover was well worn with time and the pages inside were yellowed and brittle. They stuck together as I tried to flip through and examine the tome.

"That explains everything," he said.

The journal had belonged to one Silas McAlister, a rare breed of Old West miner who could also read and write. The first twenty or so pages were mundane details about his life in the burgeoning mining camp, which had begun as a tent city and had developed into an actual burg. He wrote about long days, excavating for silver ore back in the caves that surrounded the town. He even talked about his dalliances with a local prostitute named Kate.

And then his writing took on a completely different tone and became not a record of his life there in Beaumont, but a dire warning to whoever would read his journal in the years to come. One day, while digging with pick and shovel in the walls of the cave he uncovered the statuette. McAlister wrote: "*As I held I the damnable thing in my trembling hands, the superstitious lot present there in the cave with me fled for daylight. I took a torch from the wall and examined the artifact more closely. I have never seen anything like it. It looked like Michelangelo had journeyed down to hell to chisel out a demon's David from out of the tormenting flames.*"

"*I dug down a little more and found a strange gem...of such otherworldly colors that my mind almost stopped working. I held the stone up to the light of my torch and my mind began to swirl. The cave began to grow black. I nearly passed out right then and there, but I caught myself on the stone wall. I gazed into the gem once more and what I saw at that instant will haunt me forevermore. I saw...reflected in the brilliance of the stone...images of the very creature whose statuette I now possessed. The beast flapped its unholy wings and lifted its tentacle face to the burning stars above it. I knew right then and there that Hell awaited. I shoved the weird carving and the gemstone into my pack, shouldered it, and walked out into the daylight as fast as my trembling legs could carry me.*"

The statuette and the gemstone were all McAlister wrote about from that point on. As I flipped through his journal, it became evident that he was now possessed by something dark and unholy that he could not control. Undoubtedly the miner became *persona non grata* and the townsfolk shunned him from the moment of his discovery of the artifacts onward. Even his little soiled dove would have nothing further to do with him. But it seems that McAlister did not care much. He became more and more engrossed in his morbid discoveries. Until...

The last entry in the journal read: "*Something is calling to me from within the gem. I feel an overwhelming need to walk out under the cold stars of the desert, hold the gem up to the Heavens and call something down from other galaxies that will wreak havoc and destruction on my world. I know now that this simple gemstone is a portal, a mere veil to be lifted, and this awful beast will descend through the doorway to Earth, and it will be my doing."*

"I know now that I damned myself the day I found these accursed artifacts in the cave. Where they came from I don't know...but I do know that they are going back to the cave, where I will reinter them where they belong, hidden forever again from the eyes of man."

"If you read further, you will see that McAlister killed himself back in that cave...after burying this statuette and gem once again," Bryant said.

"And you re-discovered them," I said.

Bryant nodded. In his eyes was a look of terror that I have yet to see in a mortal since. "Man was not meant to experience such horror. These are things best left alone," he moaned. "And you know, the miner was right," Bryant continued.

I could hardly speak. *"He...he was?"*

"Yes. I took the gem out under the stars late one night. I was curious. I held it aloft for several minutes...my arm was growing tired...and then suddenly, the strangest feeling came over me. Something was passing through the gem...into my arm...emerging into the Earth night. It was as if a cold river of death was being slowly poured on me. The feeling stuck to my skin... penetrated deep into to my bones...and when I glanced back up at the night sky...a green light had begun to form around the Big Dipper. It wavered there...in the firmament...growing larger by the second. As the glowing green aura gained in size, the gem began to tremble and grow hot in my hand. My entire body felt like it had been dipped in the ice cold water of the Hudson from my youth."

"What did you do?"

"I threw the stone to the ground and broke the spell. Immediately the freezing sensation left my body and the green aura in the sky vanished. I was alone again...with the night."

I rose from my seat. "Where is the stone now, Bryant?"

"The stone is dangerous...no one can ever possess it again. The horrible truth is too much for any one mortal to bear," he said.

I moved closer to him. "The stone, Bryant...what did you do with it? We should destroy it somehow."

Bryant became frantic at that moment and he began to shout hysterically. "That beast...that horrible beast from the stars...it waits. The gem is its *eye*...it can watch us through the stone...it can see into this dimension and it hungers for what it sees. Don't you understand, Carroll? The stone is its portal...its doorway into this world...It waits for someone to use the gem and bring it to Earth. It will destroy and conquer...we will all die or become its slaves. I cannot let that happen."

"Bryant..."

"Do you hear me, Carroll? I cannot let *that* happen..."

"Then tell me where the gem is and we can dispose of it together...along with that horrid little statuette..."

Bryant slumped back into his oversized chair and grinned demonically. "Where is the stone? You want me to tell you where the accursed bloody gemstone is?"

I nodded. It was a terrible thing to see my friend this way. A haunted man with a haunted mind that was beginning to crack under the mental and psychological strain. Bryant proudly thumped his stomach. "It's in there, my friend...I swallowed the damnable stone. No one will ever get their hands on it now..."

My jaw dropped. I stood there...in stunned disbelief. My brain couldn't process all of this. It was uncanny. *"What?"*

"I swallowed the gemstone," Bryant shouted. "The damnable eye of Cthulhu..."

"*Cthulhu?*"

"You don't know? Cthulhu is the ancient god...the eldest of gods...the demon-thing that waits behind the pale of stars...waits in awful silence for someone to call him down to earth...but he can go on waiting! You hear me, Carroll? I stopped him! I swallowed the stone and now no one will ever be able to use it..." Bryant reached into his jacket and produced a pistol.

"*Bryant! What are you doing? Put that pistol away!*"

"And now that I've hidden the stone deep inside me...I am going to finish this." He held the gun to his temple and reached into his coat. He pulled out an envelope and tossed it over to me. "There are detailed instructions for my burial in there. My servant has been instructed to follow those instructions implicitly. I ask that you assist him. Goodbye, Carroll...I take this terrible secret with me into the abyss..."

"*Bryant...for God's sake...wait!*"

The gun's ear shattering report shook loose every nerve in my body and echoed harshly throughout the house. My friend's brains exploded from the back of his skull and he fell lifeless to the floor. The mortal terrors he had experienced could touch him no more. I stood there in shock, staring at the statuette of *Cthulhu*, drenched in Bryant's blood.

Bryant's manservant entered the study, grimacing in revulsion and fear. He reached down and wrapped Bryant up in the rug and calmly took the gore spattered figurine away.

My friend Bryant was buried in an underground tomb with a steel door. After his corpse was interred, the heavy door was swung shut and welded so that it can never be opened again. The tomb was then covered over with soil and the grave has gone unmarked ever since. Last I heard a grove of trees was planted over the site.

I have never spoken or written of this until now. My blood freezes each time I consider the possibility of an ancient evil, just waiting among the stars like a vampire from the old country... just waiting to be invited in from the cold reaches of space.

The Eye of Cthulhu, that damned gemstone, lies interred with Bryant's bones. I still mourn the loss of my friend, but I also acknowledge his sacrifice. With his death, he saved the universe. But what if there are other gemstones...other portals through which the elder gods can pass into our world?

I try not to think about these things. And I never look at the stars when I go out at night.

From Beyond Came the Key
Eric Tarango

Cold darkness, tinged by faded flecks of light was the passage. Where it traveled from, even it could not really recall, like fragments from a dream slipping away. It tumbled, and strained to remain in one piece, but it sped past planets and moons without any hesitation or need to rest. It would rest when its job was done, on Earth.

"Call that damnable fool to my table, Edgar, at once!" Captain Collins Jeffries demand of Edgar Baskins, his first mate. Captain Jeffries had demanded his steak be prepared medium rare, not medium well. The meat was too dry, and even ruined the taste of his wine.

"Right away, Captain," Edgar nodded and exited the cabin.

He was happy to stretch his legs, see other faces than just the captain's glowering face. Long sea voyages made the captain unbearable to deal with. He complained for the most unreasonable things, but there was nothing he could do, he was hired to do as he was told.

Once he stepped out of the door into the night sky his displeasure seemed to melt away. The wind was a high breeze, light sea spray accompanying the blow, refreshing against the skin. And the stars were shining brightly in the heavens, giving him the clarity of how vast the world truly was, humbling him.

"What does his majesty require now, Baskins?" Rozio jokingly inquired as he made his way to the ladder going up to the crow's nest. No one was permitted to remove it from the nest, and if you did and were caught, well then, you might as well pray to turn into a fish once you hit the icy water. The ship had no holding cell and no room for fools.

"Theodore over cooked the meat. And the captain is starving, saved his appetite for that steak."

"What an oaf. He has been sneaking extra pints of ale is my bet. See you later Mr. Baskins I need to get to me post on the double."

"Aye, don't go falling asleep up there." He joked.

"Piss on you for saying that. Like a jinx that is." Rozio smiled his crooked, yellow smile and scampered expertly up the ladder.

Edgar gave the sky one last look, then headed down to the galley to reprimand Theodore. He truthfully knew that the poor cook was not at fault, there was only so much you could do with food on a ship if there were no spices, or fresh meat to throw on the fire. All the meat was locked in cold storage and that had been a week before setting sail, two months ago.

The ship corridors was stuffier and smelled of rot more than the captain's cabin. Mr. Baskins let out a long breath to eliminate the gagging that he felt rise from his belly, he was stronger than the insulting aroma. He passed the crew man's quarters and couldn't help smile at the sound of snoring coming from behind the closed door. It did not feel it, yet over thirty years ago he was one of the men sawing away in a hammock. The ships then were not as spacious and were not very accommodating. When he had first stepped on a new ship that offered two crew quarters and the first mate had a cabin the size of one of the quarters he was astounded and disturbed. He felt as if he betrayed his roots, but he was too young to realize the benefit and that advancements would be the norm. He had has own cabin now, and he might feel nostalgic to his beginning days, he would not return to them. Had was not insane.

"Theodore you are needed by the captain." Mr. Baskins announced as he stepped into the cook's galley. Theodore was sitting at the table having himself a meal, it was not a hearty meal at that. Mr. Baskins considered bringing the plate to the captain and introduce him to the meals the crew ate while he whined about a steak that could have fed three of the crew.

"The meat is affected by the frost, Mr. Baskins. I did the best that I could, and his majesty is upset over conditions that is his own fault. The last stop at Cape Horn could have provided us with fresh supplies and vegetables if the tightwad had opened his petty wallet."

Mr. Baskins took a seat across from Theodore and laughed. He was not so eager to return to the captain.

"I understand fully my friend. He used to traveling Canadian waters, this is his first trip through the Cape Horn route. This is my fortieth. I have been trying to convince him to stop at one of the ports in Mexico to re-supply. He only grumbles his answer. He hates to deal with the Mexicans, think them a bunch of savages and thieves."

"I myself have been to Mexico twice. Once in the north toward California and another in middle of the country. Which I am glad for the second trip. I was convinced that it was a miserly country and would fall to desolation. The midst of Mexico is a sight, Mr. Baskins. Such beauty, and culture that I learned to enjoy. Not to mention the women."

"Yes, I would agree about that. I almost fell in love with young Mexican woman, but I could not bring myself to use her for my pleasure and then leave her. The day I settle is when I no longer feel the tug of waves."

"Then you will be alone until your bones are in the ground."

They both laughed at the statement, but Mr. Baskins felt a sadness in the back of his mind. If he had refused to set sail, he might be married to Laura, and have children. He was skilled at carpentry, masonry, and iron work. He could have made a living easily. The call of the ocean was way too strong though.

"Well, let us go see the captain and get this foolishness over with. I am not enjoying my dinner anyway. Maybe, his temper will give me my appetite back." Theodore smiled.

They were on their way up the corridor when a clanging arose on the deck. Theodore turned and looked at Mr. Baskins with wide eyes. The ringing of the bell either meant land or another ship, and not a friendly one. Yet, at this time of evening, not even Rozio's sharp eyes could make out the ship until it was right upon them.

They rushed out the doors, almost colliding with ship mates who sprang from the door, still pulling their clothes on in a frantic. The men arrived on deck to the sound of the captain shouting what in blazes the racket was. Rozio yelled down to them and pointed up into the sky. At first Mr. Baskins could not understand what the big deal was, when he noticed a bright shine he took for star was falling toward them. There were gasps from the men gathered, even the captain had no words. They followed the fall of the object with their eyes. They expected the object to fall into the sea and disappear in the distance. But, there was a loud echo and a flash.

The object had touched land! They were nowhere near land though, Mr. Baskins thought his mind was betraying him. Until, the men began to confirm that they too had seen what they believed an impact on land.

Mr. Baskins made his way across the deck up to the captain.

"Land out here captain. An island that has not been identified perhaps?"

"Not to my knowledge Edgar. This is my first travel this route. What do you think hit that piece of land?" The captain had a wild glint in his eyes, his mind was going over ideas.

"As hard as it hit. I would say that it was not a chunk of rock. Something harder and more solid."

"I agree. A new and rare metal if my luck is in favor. One that people of power would pay to accumulate. Scientist throwing their offers in, backed by universities. A lifetime payoff."

Mr. Baskins only nodded his head. He knew better than to dampen his captain's hopes of stumbling upon a treasure. The captain was a dreamer, one that dreamt of immense wealth. He wondered at times if the captain had forced into the sea faring employment. Jeffries seemed to regret having anything to do with his vessel, yet being the captain was better than being a hand. Mr. Baskins doubted that Jeffries could stomach the daily grind of manual labor, the few hours of sleep that could be taken, the food that may cause upset bowels, and the worst were the lonely nights. Wondering where your spouse was, and fighting to keep the mind from chicanery tied to fidelity. Men had driven themselves into rages over imagined affairs, and those men either were smart enough to find another trade, preferably without travel, or cause pain and violence in their marriage. There were stories floating about among the ports of men who crossed over to devil's murderous ways, and ending the lives of their families. Even the new born were not safe, as some men got it into their heads that the child was that of another man.

The captain gave the orders to make course for the island, he wanted his meteor and nothing could sway him. The wind was but a strong breeze, but the main sails were rigged down, as the captain stationed himself upon the poop deck. Before departing the captain handed Mr. Baskins the key to the powder magazine with the order to remove one powder hulk. The island may be inhabited by savages, or cannibals.

Mr. Baskins ordered five men to ready their pistols and to fill their flasks and ball bags. Only these five men, including the captain and himself, were capable of accurate firing. The other seven crew members could not hit the side of a barn.

The ship slid quietly along the ocean's surface, the waves were not aggressive this night. The only disturbance lay within the crew, their apprehension was apparent in their faces and their jittery manner. The captain gave the call to drop anchor a bit over a hundred yards from shore, if they ran aground they might never get free. Mr. Haskins had a foreboding feeling that if that happened the island would not relinquish them, pulling them down into the depths when it returned from where it came.

Mr. Baskins knew that he was volunteered from the beginning to attend the debarkation, the captain chose three of the best shots; Vincent, David, and the Duke, no one knew his real name and he did not want to share. The only surprise was that the captain stated boldly that he would be accompanying them. Mr. Baskins bit back his tongue, he did not think it was responsible for the captain to come along, yet the captain was the captain.

They carried few supplies, mostly water and a couple of short handled pick-axes to excavate if necessary. No one uttered a word as the Duke rowed the boat toward shore. Each was lost in his own fear, yet conditioning to handle extreme situations, mostly due to nature, kept them from giving that fear power. When they reached shore if one of them had spoken up and asked to return to the ship, they would have given up the quest as a lost cause; pride is what killed them, and one of them most of all greed.

The shore was unlike a sandy beach, the grains beneath crunched as if made of glass and crushed shell, ready to bleed the feet. Mr. Baskins muttered the first lines in the Lord's Prayer, but the rest would not come, completely forgotten. Damn Rozio and his sharp eyes! This was a foolish quest, whatever had fallen was not meant for them.

The captain, David and Duke lit torches to set off. Three torches should have given them plenty of light, but the islands shadows seemed to drink in the light. The encroachment into the sparse landscape was apparent, there seemed to be no life, not the call of a bird, not even a seagull or the buzz of mosquito wings. The island knew none of the sounds that its modern cousins shared, for that is how Mr. Baskins thought of the island, as more than primitive. It was far more ancient, a chunk that had never bothered to evolve with the rest of the world.

"This place does not feel right. As if it does not belong." David said.

"You are wrong about that. It is we who do not belong here. This was here before we walked out of Eden." Duke said. They looked at him in amazement. His thought was truly spoken, and not even the venerable captain could argue.

The islands interior was just as intense, there were monolithic pillars of rock pointing up wards, some so close together there was no way through and they had to go around; though, they did their best not to touch the structures. Or, even look at them. A few were smooth and cast their reflections back like damp mirrors, but even those reflections were alien, and what looked back was separate.

Nearly half an hour had gone by and they found no impact site. They wanted to turn back and rest at ease on the ship, pushing the islands images from their minds as they sailed away. Yet, the captain had this look of desperate determination. He herded them toward the midst of the island. It was there that they found a pillar that had been damaged by a puncture and had cracked but not burst apart. Though the pillar was not as enormous, the impact lie within ten feet above their heads.

"We will have to get up there." The captain said.

"Well we cannot shimmy up the rock, sir. It is too smooth, we will have to build a scaffold made of rock most likely." Mr. Baskins said.

They began to find large enough rocks to move, but not too heavy to pick up. It would defeat the purpose of obtaining the object if they threw their spines out. Once a man hurt his back in such a way, he was never the same, and only through medicines could he feel right, but he would die as an addict. Laudanum had helped with the pain, but refused to be divorced so easily.

"Let us hurry chaps! We are spending too much time upon this…land o' the lost. Even I am beginning to feel threatened by the air we breathe." The captain finally admitted. Yet, even his discomfort was not enough to call of the hunt for the object.

A quarter of an hour and they had their makeshift scaffold. It did not look sturdy, and the others were too large and bulky to try the climb, which left Mr. Baskins, much to his chagrin. Mr. Baskins rolled up his sleeves and with his stamina and agility he made way to the crest of the rocks, but was about three feet short from the impact entrance. He studied the opening, and determined that it would do no good to leap and catch the ledge, the surface looked crystalline and might only manage to slice open his hand.

"In my bag is a brand new belt, throw it to me."

David searched the bag and brought out the belt. He whistled at the sight, never seeing a slice of leather so perfectly tanned, and shined up. David felt envious at the sight of it, he had never owned anything to fine; but that was his fault, though he would never admit to spending his stipends on drink and companionship.

Mr. Baskins felt reluctant to use the belt, but he saw no other choice. Holding each end he looped the belt into the thickest part of the ledge and pulled himself up. It was not as easy he hoped, his feet barely found enough purchase to remain hoisted. He peered inside the opening and found the object, still glowing from the impact, yet Mr. Baskins knew that it had been over an two hours since arriving and the object should have cooled. He used his right arm to tuck into the opening to pull himself up further, and with his left tested the surface. His eyes had been deceived. It was not hot, the color was a burning crimson. He took hold of it and pulled it out, it was not large, disintegration from the fall had caused it to downsize. He tucked it into his back pocket and struggled to let himself down, but his feet slipped and before he could correct himself, his arm pulled viciously against a jagged edge, tearing away a slice of forearm. Mr. Baskins screamed and crashed down into the stones and almost smashed into the floor, but Duke was quick to the rescue.

The wound was ghastly, blood pooled out like a fount.

They bandaged it as tightly as possible, the amount of blood spilled had caused Mr. Baskins to feel faint. Yet, he had achieved their goal. He reached into his pantaloons and removed the object. It was queerly shaped, a shape that they all had seen before yet could not immediately place.

Mr. Baskins handed it to Duke to see, it was only right as they all had gone through the trouble to search for it. Duke stared at it, his eyes glazed over and his face grew pale. Next David and Vincent held the object, it still looked like no stone, and the same affliction came over them. The three stared at it when the captain took ahold of it, and his eyes widened and he made a grotesque mask of his face, baring wide his lips, exposing his teeth an almost a growl.

Mr. Baskins passed it over as his captain's greedy happiness, he tended to his wound. Putting as much pressure as he could to let the material of the bandage to staunch the bleeding, but could do nothing for the pain. He wished he had laudanum now.

"Can we leave now? This pain is becoming excruciating." Mr. Baskins held his arm up to make his point. The men only looked at him, but they did not see him, then their eyes returned to the object. Mr. Baskins felt a terror swim inside him and slowly causing waves, making him queasy. He took several steps toward the spot they had entered.

"Where do you think you are going, Edgar?" Duke asked. The way he spoke was monotone, but carried so much threatening weight.

"I need to get attended to."

"You need to take your turn to hold the key."

"Key?" Mr. Baskins had no idea what Duke was hinting at.

"The key, Edgar!" The captain said harshly, as if the key was a term he was supposed to be familiar with.

"Give him the key!" Vincent directed to the captain. Mr. Baskins expected the captain to scold Vincent for giving him an order, but the captain only smiled obscenely, all his teeth exposed.

"I would rather not. Let us be off. We have found the object-," he was cut off.

"Key!" David impressed the word on him.

"Key, then. We can examine it when we are safely aboard the ship, there is more light and tools to view in greater detail."

"Take the damn key!" The three said in unison. Mr. Baskins choked back his words of wisdom, there was no talking to them, and they were bewitched by the "key." How it was a key to them he could not figure, it had fallen from space.

He held out his bloody hand, from holding the soaked bandage, to take the key. When the object fell into his hand, the world seemed to explode, or his head. The object was a key, but not the kind that opened any door he had ever laid eyes on. It pulled the blood from his palms and fingers into itself, and pieces began to fall away, slowly stripping the course rock revealing the true form beneath. A heart.

The island vibrated with a lustful intensity, awakened by the true form of the key, and the key in return answered back by filling Mr. Baskins mind with images of an ancient world filled with indescribable creatures that occupied a desolate and Godless realm. Mr. Baskins tried in vain to release the key to the floor, but it wanted him and for that he had a purpose. The three chuckled at how he cried in agony to be rid of the key, begging them to aide him in be free of it. They though answered to it and took him by the arms and led him further into the island's center.

There began a quickening in the key, at first he believed that it was his frightened nerves, yet it increased until the key began to slowly beat with a rhythm. The heart and a place on the island called to each other. He wished he was struck dead here for he did not want to know anymore, his body was cold and the only part that remained with warmth intact was his soul. He knew it to be his soul, for no natural born part of the human body was made to withstand such monstrous fear.

Mr. Baskins stumbled as he was being led, but the strength of captain and Duke held him up. The reflections in the stone pillars shifted in radiance and surging definition. The reflections followed them with vicious smiles, eyes like pools of oil, and they vibrated in anticipation; the earth slowly parted to allow them easier access to the destination. Mr. Baskins was forcing himself to build courage, to take them by surprise and flee, but the plan was too radical, because the heart remained fixed to him.

Damn his willingness to produce excellence in his work, it was his downfall, to oblige the captain without sway. He was paying the ultimate price now, and there would be no rescue for him, where he was going would be his last venture.

He had expected to be led to a pit, or chasm of some kind to be sacrificed, yet they marched him to a single pillar in an open space. The pillar was robust, three or four sizes than the others, but it was smaller, still about twenty feet high. This pillar did not shine with smoothness, or reflect. The heart was drawn directly toward it nonetheless, and with it took Mr. Baskins without consent; he felt like his body was being hauled powerfully by an invisible rope, tugging him as if he were a boat being hauled to shore with no resistance from wind or water.

They stopped before the Northside of the pillar, and engraved into the rock were runes and images of creatures that thrived in shadows and dark voids. It was laying eyes upon the structure that Mr. Baskins understood fully what was to transpire. The heart he held was a key, and it was used to open the pillar, the carvings were a doorway ready to open and summon ancient leviathans that had walked under the sky eons ago. There was one who had sacrificed one of its hearts in preparation of this day, it had pulled its heart from its throat and commanded a minion to fly into space and release the heart on a course that would bring it back in the future. The minion had devoured the heart and sped forth and though it was a beast it required air, and it died in space, petrifying as it streaked through the galaxy. If there were eyes on other planets to witness the trek, would they have wished upon it as did the children on earth? Mr. Baskins had no idea but the thought of other life in the galaxy was not so preposterous now.

The air and earth felt alive around him. Mr. Baskins was begging with his for assistance from the others, as his throat would not sound a single letter. Dear God why had he been ignorant enough to venture here, when he knew that the cause was insane? He slowed his mind, he was Edgar Baskins, and after growing up at sea he had encountered plenty of dangers, from man and nature; now here was the supernatural, how he would survive this ordeal was up to his wits. He was known as a smart man, nearly brilliant, and for that he was well respected. Could he find a way to solve this hostile puzzle presented to him now? He knew that there was one way, his mind had handed it to him directly as soon as he studied the door without allowing the fear to consume him. *Lord, my Father, forgive me, but I see no other way. If the time comes that you return and this door is open, please send the angel Michael for me, if it is in your favor.*

His three friends took to his sides and one behind him, but he gave them one last look. Though they were strangers at this moment, he still recognized the friends he had come to know. It was for them and the world that he was strong enough to move forward.

He reached for the door a lightly pressed the heart to the rock, a small amount of his blood pushed from the organ, similar to the way a sponge pushed water out. The blood spread out into the crevices of a few runes and the door parted but a crack. Mr. Baskins pressed harder on the heart, filling more runes with his blood. The door opened a foot. There was nothing but darkness behind the door, but the air was putrid, containing no breathable oxygen, and with it came the voices of beasts crying to be released, surging toward the door.

Mr. Baskins pressed the heart once more but not as hard as the second time, and prayed that his plan succeeded. The door swung in a few centimeters more, and that is when he took his leave. Mr. Baskins slipped into the door way and before he could be stopped by the captain and crew mates, he shoved with all his will against the door and sealed it once again. He had no idea of what to do then, but there was nothing he could do. He was seized in the darkness by angry tentacles and hauled away into the deep. But death was too good for Mr. Baskins, he suffered there, until what was human was no longer human, but a twisted corpse that wanted to destroy anything in its path, raging in the darkness, waiting for the door to open.

No one ever spoke of that voyage to the island. The captain and crew had been logged in the books as being washed overboard in a storm. The island had sunk back into the sea, and those aboard the ship that witnessed the return to the fathoms, understood that speaking of it would bring bad things, and whatever lived there could get to you in nightmares.

The Shoggulators
Benjamin Sperduto

The remnants of the city came into view as the lander dropped out of the bloated stormclouds. A steady sheet of rain pelted the urban graveyard, keeping the skeletal husks of fallen skyscrapers and tangled heaps of twisted highways slickened and black.

"Hell of a sight, ain't it?"

Javier Santego had never seen a city before, at least not one like this. Would have been home to three, maybe five million people at its height. That had been long before he was born, though.

Before everything.

"Yes, sir."

Karasov pointed out the husk of an old high rise half-submerged in the sluggish, polluted river.

"Had family that lived there," he said. "Mother's cousin, I think."

Dutton laughed humorlessly.

"Everybody had a cousin or two here, man. Cousin or an aunt or a grandma or something."

Santego didn't know if that applied to him. His mom never talked about how things were when she was young. Never said much of anything, really. There were days when she'd go for hours on end without a sound, just staring at the wall of their bunk, a smile sometimes tugging at her lips.

"Might be you've still got a few relations down there, the lot of you," Corporal Surizaki said. "Not that you'd want to have them over for dinner."

A voice crackled over the intercom.

"No sign of patrols. Touch down in seven minutes."

Surizaki withdrew from the viewport and clapped his hands.

"Gear up," he said. "Ready in two."

Santego knew the drop prep routine after a year of training, but he followed Karasov and Dutton's example anyway. They were the veterans, the sort he ought to be imitating if he wanted to become the same.

"How many this make for you?" he asked

Karasov scratched his chin.

"Seventeen," he said, "I think?"

Dutton grunted and reached for her helmet.

"Don't listen to that shit," she said. "He couldn't count his fingers if you spotted him a glove."

"Fuck you."

Dutton ignored the retort.

"This makes twenty-five on the nose, for both of us." She turned to Surizaki. "And, what, fifty something for you, right, sir?"

The corporal had already donned his helmet and slung one of the flamer units over his shoulder. He checked Santego's equipment quickly, adjusting a strap here and there.

"Fifty-two total," he said. "Twenty-eight in command capacity."

"Right," Dutton said. "Good mix for your first time."

Karasov shoved a flamer unit into Santego's hands. The weapon felt heavier than the ones he'd used on the training course. He looked down at the fuel indicator. The tank was nearly full.

"Just remember not to melt whoever's in front of you, alright?" Karasov said.

"That's enough chatter," Surizaki said. "We're inserting about five blocks from the old stadium, which is being used as some kind of a temple. Once we secure the perimeter, we find a way inside, burn the place out, and take down the high priest. Then we haul ass to the extraction point before our window closes. Forecasts say the storms will kick up again in about three hours, so time's already moving against us. Any questions?"

"What do we know about the high priest?" Dutton asked.

"Ichthymorph, most likely. Whatever it is, it's pretty damn powerful. We've tried to bomb the temple six times in the past year, but nothing can get through its psychic shielding. That's why command is sending us in to deal with it."

"What kind of resistance should we expect?" Karasov asked.

"Hard to say," Surizaki said. "The storms keep interfering with the scanner sweeps. Could be anything from some inbred scavengers to a whole ichthymorph nest. That's why they sent us, got it?"

Santego and the two veterans nodded.

The corporal grinned with the mischievous glee of a child ready to break something.

"All right, Shoggulators, let's go wake the wolves."

＊＊

Santego took up position in front of one of the three large capsules in the cargo hold. The containers weren't part of the hold's original construction, nor was the pile of bulky equipment clustered around them. Thick tubes pumped liquid coolant into the main cryogenic system to regulate each capsule's internal temperature. The machinery emitted a low, steady hum that filled the cargo hold.

A single word was stamped upon the capsule's poly-steel hatch, scarcely visible beneath a sheet of white frost.

Typhon.

Karasov and Dutton stood poised over the two other capsules just a few feet away, each of which had a label of its own.

Rahab.

Echidna.

Santego kept the flamer's barrel trained on the hatch while the corporal punched an access code into the capsule's control panel. A cloud of freezing vapor escaped as the hatch hissed open.

Something inside the capsule moved.

He struggled to keep the flamer steady. He hoped the corporal wouldn't notice how much effort it took.

A tall, naked man stepped out of the capsule, stopping only inches from the flamer's barrel. His black eyes had no pupils, like small droplets drawn from the endless, dead vacuum of space. The man's skin appeared unblemished, his face unwrinkled by age or worry.

Santego had interacted with shogg troopers in the last stages of his training. Before that, he'd learned everything there was to know about them, learned how researchers had awakened the traces of alien genetic code buried deep within human DNA to create something more, and less, than human. Something that could salvage the war effort if only it could be controlled.

By all rights, then, he should have been accustomed to the sight of a shogg trooper, but something about this one made his skin shiver. Those black eyes seemed to pin him down, smothering his thoughts and weighing down his limbs. Looking at the shogg made him feel like he'd fallen into a pool of tar.

When the shogg trooper finally broke eye contact to glance down at the flamer pointing at his chest, Santego realized he'd been holding his breath since the hatch opened.

Surizaki reached over to push the weapon's barrel down.

"Good morning, Typhon," he said.

The shogg looked at the corporal and raised an eyebrow.

"Surizaki, is it? What's the occasion?"

"Dinner for three. Seafood. Hope you brought your appetite."

Typhon glared at Santego. The world slowed down again, but Santego at least remembered to breath this time.

"I don't know this one."

"Private Santego will be your handler today. Go easy on him, all right? It's his first time."

Typhon smiled, his ebon eyes shimmering.

"Welcome to the war, kid."

***

The lander touched down on an intact rooftop just north of the old stadium. Karasov took point with Rahab, the biggest and meanest looking of the three shoggs. Dutton followed close behind escorting Echidna, the lone female shogg. Corporal Surizaki went next, toting along the spectral scanner and motion tracker, while Santego brought up the rear with Typhon. Once they cleared the loading ramp, the lander took off, its grav-thrusters making scarcely a sound even at full power.

Surizaki consulted the spectral scanner.

"Building's clear. Rahab, go check the perimeter."

The shogg grunted. Then he ran to the edge of the roof and leaped off the building.

Santego activated his helmet's tactical display. Each shogg carried short range nanite transmitters in their bloodstream, allowing their handlers to track them at all times. He watched Rahab's signature move quickly around the building's perimeter, far faster than any human could manage on foot.

"There's a certain beauty to it, don't you think?"

Typhon's voice stabbed into Santego's ears like an ice pick. The shogg stood just a few feet from his handler, but his gaze remained fixed on the broken horizon of the shattered city. A few spears of starlight managed to puncture the dark clouds overhead, glimmering off the wet expanse of rent metal and glass that once housed millions of inhabitants.

Santego took in the sight. If he let his eyes unfocus, the landscape took on a mutable, dreamlike quality. There was something serene about the sight, something…

He turned away and shook the image from his mind.

Less than two minutes in the field and he'd nearly forgotten the first rule of dealing with shogg troopers.

Don't talk to them.

Ever.

"That's enough chatter," he said, mustering his sternest voice.

Typhon shrugged.

"Have it your way."

Santego was relieved to hear Rahab's voice come in over the radio.

"Perimeter clear."

Corporal Surizaki pointed to the stairwell.

"Echidna, take point. Let's move."

The team made it to the outskirts of the temple before the shoggs caught the scent of something nearby. Surizaki checked the spectral scanner and spotted a cluster of humanoid figures gathered inside one of the partially intact structures surrounding the temple. He relayed orders silently through the team's tactical displays. Rahab and Echidna would engage the targets on the ground level while Typhon provided support from above.

They moved into position quickly and silently, splitting up as they approached their target. The building looked like it might have been a church of some sort before the great cataclysm demolished the city. Half of its roof had collapsed, but the walls remained in place.

Santego and Typhon circled around to the rear, where the roof seemed most stable. The shogg scaled the twenty-foot high wall with ease. Once he attained the roof, he reached down to Santego, his arm reshaping into a slithering, fleshy tentacle that stretched all the way to the ground. The appendage wrapped around Santego's waist and hoisted him up to the roof effortlessly.

Typhon greeted his handler with a smile.

Santego refused to acknowledge the expression, instead pointing toward the hole in the roof nearby.

They crept over to the opening and peered into the building. A group of men, women, and children stood before a crude cement altar. Even from high above, Santego had no difficulty making out the crude idol resting atop the shrine. Fashioned from a rotted chunk of wood and adorned with lengths of rebar bent into the form of writhing tentacles, the makeshift icon formed an unmistakable visage.

Cthulhu, lord of R'lyeh. The doom of mankind.

The people gathered within the profane chapel looked only vaguely human. Patches of scales besmirched their waxen skin and their shoulders slumped forward. Their overlarge eyes stared dumbly ahead, unblinking and soulless.

Santego shivered. But for a bit of chance, he might have been born into such a monstrous existence.

The monster beside him nudged his arm.

He glanced over at Typhon, careful to avoid looking at his soulless eyes.

"Here they come," the shogg said.

Rahab and Echidna stormed into the building from opposite sides, ripping through the concrete walls like they were made of wet cardboard. Moving in for the kill, they retained few traces of their humanity. Bundles of ropy tendrils extended from their uniform sleeves in place of arms, each one barbed with hundreds of sharp thorns. Rahab's jaw opened wide enough to swallow a grown man's head while Echidna's tongue stretched into a five foot long tentacle covered with dozens of biting mouths ringed with fangs.

Typhon waited until the other shoggs fell upon the wretched creatures before diving through the roof to join them. His hands changed into snapping jaws as he fell, and two sets of sucker-covered tentacles sprang from his back when he hit the ground.

A few of the degenerate worshippers reached for makeshift weapons, little more than rusty metal implements cobbled together from the ruins, but none managed to put up any meaningful resistance. The shoggs moved too quickly, whipping through the confused melee in a lethal mass of tentacles, fangs, and talons. Most of the congregation tried to escape, but there was nowhere to run. Blood, entrails, and shards of bone exploded against the walls to the sound of their panicked screams.

The slaughter took only a handful of seconds, but to Santego it seemed to last an hour. Again he realized that he'd been holding his breath.

Once the shoggs finished, the rest of the team moved inside the building. Typhon and Echidna had already returned to their human form, but Rahab had yet to retract all of his barbed tendrils. When he caught sight of Dutton and Surizaki on the far side of the room, he made a foul, gurgling sound and lumbered toward them.

Karasov stepped into the room and leveled his flamer at the shogg trooper's back.

"Stand down, Rahab!"

The big shogg stopped, then turned to glare at his handler. Even looking down from the roof, Santego could see the blue pilot flame glowing at the tip of Karasov's flamer. One squeeze of the trigger and a gush of superheated plasma would incinerate the shogg's mutable flesh.

For several tense seconds, no one moved.

Typhon broke the silence.

"Rahab," he said, his arm stretching out to form a long tentacle that touched his comrade's shoulder. "Enough."

The shogg grunted, then shrank to take on a recognizably human form.

"Sorry," he said. "Blood was up."

Karasov lowered his flamer, but kept his attention fixed on Rahab. Santego noticed that he hadn't extinguished the weapon's pilot flame. He'd be watching the shogg even more closely from now on, something Santego should be doing with his own charge as well.

That was the second thing to remember about shogg troopers.

Don't take your eyes off them.

Ever.

Typhon withdrew his tentacle from Rahab's shoulder and whipped it across the room to yank the grotesque idol from the altar. He smashed it against a nearby pile of rubble until it shattered.

Echidna spat on it.

"His stink is all over this place," she said. "Ought to burn it all."

Surizaki shook his head and consulted his spectral scanner.

"Waste of fuel," he said. "Let's get moving, people. We don't want to miss our ride out of here."

***

The team regrouped outside and set off toward the stadium. Rahab and Echidna led the way again under Karasov and Dutton's watchful eyes. Santego trudged along the muddy street a few yards behind Typhon.

He kept his flamer at the ready, focusing all of his attention on the shogg's movements.

"So what do you think of the big city, kid?"

Don't talk to them.

"Keep walking, Typhon."

The shogg looked around, his gaze sometimes lingering on a portion of the ruins.

"My parents used to live here, back before the big squid took a shit on the world."

The comment piqued Santego's curiosity. Shoggs weren't supposed to remember anything from their lives before the DNA infusion procedure that awakened their alien genetic code.

Santego couldn't keep his curiosity in check.

"You remember your parents?"

"Not much," Typhon said. "Some broken images here and there. But I know they were here. Every now and then I see something that looks familiar, like an echo from somebody else's dream."

Santego stopped walking and tightened his grip on the flamer. Typhon shouldn't have been able to remember his own past, much less access the genetic memories of his parents. He knew he was supposed to scorch the shogg at any sign of irregular behavior, but this was something different.

Typhon turned around to face him.

"Are you going to shoot me now or what?"

Santego swallowed, sending a cold lump of anxiety down to his stomach.

He should burn the shogg now, just a singe to an arm or leg to remind it who was in charge. That was what Santego's training told him to do when a shogg stepped out of line, but something about Typhon's defiance flummoxed him.

It was too… human.

"I haven't decided yet."

The shogg smiled, and Santego realized he'd made a horrible mistake.

"Well, let me know when you do. I hate waiting. Come on, we don't want to get left behind out here."

They resumed walking, each one acting as though the conversation never took place. Santego found it hard to think about anything else.

The stadium loomed into view as the team left the chapel behind. Although not as enormous as the city's fallen skyscrapers, the building still took up most of a city block and stood over two hundred feet tall. Its great domed roof had partially collapsed, and the crumbling walls had been reinforced by scrap metal and stone from nearby structures. Rubble covered the original entrances, but a large hole torn into the building's side had been framed with rusted girders to form a makeshift entryway. Beyond the gaping threshold, darkness reigned absolute.

Rahab and Echidna moved to either side of the opening while Surizaki checked the motion tracker and spectral scanner in turn.

"No movement," he said.

A slender appendage slithered out from Echidna's sleeve. It probed into the darkness beyond the door. After a few seconds, she reeled the feelers back in with a hiss.

"What is it?" Surizaki asked.

"Seafood."

The corporal checked his spectral scanner again.

"The scanner's still negative."

"It's wrong," Echidna said.

"Structure could be interfering with the scan," Dutton said.

Surizaki nodded.

"Maybe. Keep a sharp eye. Let's move."

The team stepped into the darkness one by one, but Typhon paused on the threshold. Tentacles extended from his arms and neck to probe and sniff at the air.

"What is it?" Santego asked.

Typhon shook his head.

"I don't know. Air tastes funny. Could be nothing."

"A lot of people died around here when the storms hit," Santego said. "Could be they left some kind of psychic signature."

He probably wouldn't buy the explanation himself if he thought about it for very long, but he preferred it to the alternatives lingering on the edge of his mind.

"Maybe."

Typhon retracted his sensory tendrils and moved inside.

Santego took a deep breath and followed.

***

The stadium's interior reeked of brine and decay.

Santego activated his helmet's night vision display and immediately clamped his hand over his mouth to keep from vomiting when he saw what was inside.

A long walkway led down to the swampy mire that covered the temple floor. Rows of rickety catwalks clung tenuously to the walls, and many of the ceiling's reinforced bracings had already collapsed. Water ran down from every nook and cranny with maddeningly irregularity, each drop echoing clearly throughout the open space.

Clusters of rubble formed small islands in the muck throughout the vast room. On one of the larger islands, a statue made of bent and twisted lengths of iron towered above the water. Even at a distance, its tentacle-faced likeness was unmistakable.

Santego's attention, however, went not to the statue, but to the gigantic piles of human bones before it.

He realized he'd been holding his breath again. When he took a gulp of the temple's rancid air, his lungs rebelled and his stomach threatened to join the protest.

Someone touched his shoulder.

"Close your eyes," Typhon said. "Nice and slow."

Santego took the advice. The first few breaths were a struggle, but his lungs adjusted to the foul air quickly.

Another voice joined them.

"You okay, Private?"

The corporal?

Santego nodded and opened his eyes. His stomach quivered, but he managed to force the bile back down his throat.

"Yeah," he said. "Fine."

Apparently satisfied, Surizaki went back to studying his spectral scanner.

Typhon watched him go the rest of the team, then gazed at the ghoulish statue in the center of the temple.

"You should never have come here," he said.

Santego turned to face him. The shogg's eyes looked even blacker in the helmet's night vision display.

Don't talk to them.

"Can't you smell them? Taste them? Feel them?"

Don't talk to them.

"Of course you can't."

Don't talk to them.

"Because you don't belong here anymore."

"Enough!"

Santego pointed the flamer at him, but he couldn't quite manage to keep the barrel still. Typhon glanced down at the weapon, then back at him.

"Well?"

"No more talking," Santego said, marshaling as much authority into his voice as he could manage. "You open your mouth again and I fucking melt you down, got it?"

127

The shogg stared at him for several seconds before taking a step back and raising his hands. Santego lowered the flamer slightly.

"Good choice. Now let's catch up with the others."

Typhon obeyed without any objections, but Santego would have felt better if he'd done it without smiling.

Rahab and Echidna led the team down the ramp. Karasov and Dutton followed close behind with their flamers. Santego found himself at the rear once more, trailing after Typhon and Surizaki. The shogg seemed increasingly amused as they descended, but he kept his mouth shut.

Echidna gave the signal to halt when she reached the edge of the water. A tangle of writhing antennules extended from her eyes, each one poking and prodding at the air.

"What is it?" Surizaki asked.

"He's here," she said. "Somewhere in-between dimensions."

Surizaki looked at the scanner readout again, then packed it away and lit his flamer's pilot light.

"Scanner's negative. Can you pinpoint his location?"

Echidna pointed at the statue.

"There."

"Alright, then," Surizaki said. "Let's move."

Rahab smiled for an instant before his face split open right down the middle to form a vertical, fanged mouth the size of his head. His arm muscles rippled, the flesh flowing downward to gather into two bony cudgels where his hands had been. Echidna's arms split into a bundle of tentacles again, each one ending in a talon shaped like a meat hook. Her jaw distended, dropping down to the base of her neck and sprouting row upon row of razor sharp teeth. A tentacle the size of a man's arm and covered with suckers sprouted from the center of her mouth.

Typhon remained unchanged.

Santego lifted the flamer a few inches, just enough to get the shogg's attention.

"Go on, then," he said. "Do your thing."

Typhon raised an eyebrow. A small, ropy appendage no wider than a finger shot out from his neck and coiled around the flamer's barrel like a whip. Santego tried to pull the weapon free, but Typhon held it fast. Then the shogg's tongue stretched from his jaw and sprouted a wide flap of skin to clamp tightly over Santego's mouth.

A small orifice on the tentacle moved, whispering in a mockery of speech.

"Or what?"

Their eyes met once again and Santego wished he could turn the flamer on himself, anything to escape that monstrous gaze.

"Santego!"

By the time the corporal's words reached his ears, the terror had passed. Santego rubbed his mouth and moved his flamer freely while the rest of the team stared at him. For a moment, he wondered if he'd imagined the whole episode.

Then he saw Typhon smile.

"Yeah," he said, fighting to keep his voice steady. "I'm ready."

"Good. You and Typhon cover our ass."

Santego closed his eyes and cursed.

When he opened his eyes, Typhon stood mere inches from his face. He staggered back, but the shogg caught him by the arm.

"Let's go see who's home."

Santego nodded before his brain could even process the words. The shogg turned him free and stepped back, smiling.

Typhon sprouted four sets of tentacles from his back, each one nearly six feet long and covered with serrated hooks. His fingers, writhing like serpents, extended to twice their normal length, each one tipped with a fanged mouth. The lower part of his jaw split in half to form a pair of rending mandibles.

Santego should have torched him, but it was too late for that. Losing a shogg now would put them in even more danger.

He'd had his chance to assert control and he lost it.

His life was in Typhon's hands now.

If the shogg decided to end it, Santego would have little say in the matter.

Trembling, he followed Typhon into the water.

***

Santego stayed as far back as he dared, trailing about a dozen yards behind the shoggs up on point. The frigid air contained so much humidity that his helmet's display fogged up within seconds. He couldn't go more than a few steps before having to wipe the helmet clean, though the hazard-ridden water made it difficult to move quickly anyway.

The shoggs moved unimpeded, easily slithering over obstacles and probing the waters before them. Karasov, Dutton, and Surizaki struggled to keep up, which eventually forced Rahab and Echidna to wait for them. Typhon moved more slowly, carefully probing the air and water with various appendages as he went.

They were about halfway to the statue when Surizaki's motion tracker screamed to life.

Santego saw the corporal look down at the device just as a huge figure burst out of the water beside him and tore him in half.

It moved too quickly to make out through the night vision sensor, but it stood twice the height of a man. Karasov wheeled around and hit it with a burst from the flamer before it finished ripping the corporal to shreds. The flare compensators dimmed Santego's display as the fireball washed over the creature, preventing him from getting a better look at it. Nothing could have blocked out the thing's scream, however, which filled every inch of the room before being answered from every direction by similar shrieks. When Santego's display normalized, he saw similar monstrosities rising from the water everywhere he looked.

Ichthymorphs.

Somewhere between the creatures' screams, he heard Dutton's voice.

"Light 'em up!"

He took aim at the nearest horror, but Typhon got to it first. The shogg snared its legs with a mass of tentacles and sliced its head off with a single swipe of his bone-bladed arm. He reshaped his other arm into a studded club to stave another monster's skull before turning toward Santego.

"Watch your back!"

He turned to find two of the fish things rising from the water behind them. They were smaller than the others, only a bit taller than a man, but their thick, muscular limbs looked more than capable of breaking every bone in Santego's body.

A single, sustained blast from the flamer incinerated both of them. More and more of the creatures joined the attack, and Santego soon found himself sweeping the flamer back and forth like a hose, torching everything that moved in a torrent of superhot napalm.

The ichthymorphs' dying cries quickly became deafening. When he chanced a look over to the rest of the team, Santego saw a great writhing mass of limbs and tentacles swirling around a plume of fire. The flare compensators made it difficult to make out details, but even if he could have seen perfectly, he doubted it would be possible to determine who was winning or losing.

Before Santego looked away, he caught a glimpse of something else. Beyond the conflagration, a huge figure flickered in and out of sight. It came into full view only once, a winged terror perched atop the great statue like the monstrous lord of some alien kingdom. When the wretched thing blinked into view, a rush of psychic energy flooded the room. Santego felt a million tiny daggers stab into his skull, and he fell to his knees screaming.

A rush of images flashed through his mind. He saw Karasov's liquefied brain running out through his nostrils, saw Dutton turn her flamer on herself rather than let the squid-faced giant take her in its grasp. Rahab's last tenuous link to his humanity snapped, and he raged as a powerful, invisible force ripped his morphing body apart molecule by molecule.

For a moment, the high priest of Great Cthulhu, a spawn born off the horizon of some unfathomably distant and ghastly planet, seemed almost irked by their presence.

Then Typhon and Echidna fell upon it, and the timbre of its psychic barrage changed.

Annoyance gave way to alarm.

And then to fear.

The pain in Santego's head intensified as the shoggs clawed, bit, and rent the monstrously alien being with such fury that the building threatened to collapse on top of them. He tried to force his eyelids open, but the psychic assault overwhelmed him. A cold, shivering shock raked down his spine and he lost consciousness.

***

Heavy drops of water splashed against Santego's face, slowly dragging him out of his stupor with their stubborn insistence. He opened his eyes to find himself beneath the open sky, far removed from the dark confines of the stadium's interior. His head still felt ready to burst open and his body ached all over. Fighting both pain and fatigue, he sat up and tried to get his bearings. He seemed to be on a rooftop some distance from the stadium, which crouched menacingly several blocks away.

"Thought you'd never wake up."

Santego turned toward the familiar voice.

Typhon knelt just a few feet away from him. Beyond him, Santego saw Echidna standing near the edge of the roof. There was no sign of the rest of the team.

"What happened?" Santego asked, rubbing his still aching head.

"Found you passed out in the water," Typhon said. "Brought you to the extraction point."

"Karasov? Dutton?"

"Dead. Rahab too. But you already knew that."

Santego lowered his head and nodded. He'd seen it all in those brief mental flashes. Part of him hoped it might have been a hallucination.

"What happened in there?" he asked.

Typhon stood up.

"More than any of you could handle. Echidna and I took care of it."

Echidna stepped away from the edge of the roof to join them.

"Lander's two miles out," she said. "We need to get moving."

"What are you talking about?" Santego asked. "We're already at the extraction point."

Typhon looked at Echidna.

"You go on. I'll catch up."

Echidna nodded, then ran to the edge of the roof and jumped off the building.

Typhon turned back to Santego.

"We're not going back with you," he said.

"What?"

"Back to cold storage until you need us to kill something you can't handle yourselves? No thanks. I'll take my chances out here."

Santego shook his head.

"If you wanted to skip off, why not just leave me in the temple?"

Typhon smiled.

"Because maybe I'm not ready to let go of that last bit of humanity yet?"

"What am I supposed to tell command? They're not going to take kindly to a pair of shoggs on the loose."

Typhon shrugged.

"Tell them whatever you want."

"They'll want to track you down."

"After what you saw today, do you think that scares us?"

Santego shuddered at the memory.

"No. No, I guess not."

Typhon stepped away from him, black eyes glistening.

"A word of advice," he said. "Sooner or later the rest of the shoggs will get the same idea. Some of them might not be so accommodating. When you get back to the ship, you should either burn them all or turn them loose."

"But how are we supposed to take anything back without them?"

"Take what back? Look around you. This place isn't meant for you any longer. Every day your numbers dwindle while things decay a little more. Without us, you might already be gone."

"No," Santego said. "We're not done yet. We can reclaim cities like this. We can—"

A tendril snapped out from Typhon's collar and wrapped around Santego's head. It twisted him around to gaze out over the devastated cityscape.

"Take a good, long look, kid. This world is a corpse. Maybe the world that comes after will be worth fighting for, but humanity will never get to see it. The sooner you accept that, the better off you'll all be."

Typhon withdrew the tentacle and jumped off the building, leaving Santego to stare blankly at the ruins.

By the time the lander swooped out of the clouds and closed on his position, he was no longer sure if Typhon had done him a favor by not leaving him for dead in the temple.

Trach's Death Ray
Benjamin Welton

I met Frank for lunch at a drugstore two blocks away from my new apartment. I had barely set down the leather sofa I had bought in the Financial District when my telephone rang.

"Hi ya, Jake. Heard you just got back from Shanghai. Tell me, how many of them Chinese warlords did you duke it out with?"

"Not many. It's best to be sober during battle, and I didn't spend a dry minute in port. What's going on, Frank?"

"Not much, old buddy. Well, there is this one thing I want to talk to you about. Can you meet me at the corner drugstore in a half hour?"

"Sure, thing. Can't you at least give me a hint?"

"No can do. Besides, I know you like mysteries. All I'll say is that this little sweetie of mine might net us $750 each."

I put my lips together and whistled.

"You can do that little number until the cows come home."

"Or until the boats return to San Francisco Harbor. See you in a few, Frank."

Frank was seated at the far end of the lunch counter. He had a cup of coffee in front of him and a white plate that had until recently held what looked to be blueberry pie.

"Sorry, pal. I got a little peckish. Pie's good here, so is the beef stroganoff. That is if you like Russian food."

"Can't be much worse than the chow I was lapping up a month ago."

"I can't imagine. Tell me something, is it all really opium dens and tiger women over there?"

I had to laugh. Poor Frank - he'd only been to two places in his whole life, and neither was more east or west than northern California. To him, my life was something splendid, something akin to the adventure magazines that he loved to read so much. He loved to riddle me with questions about foreign places, and when he wasn't asking me about African jungles or Arab deserts, he was asking me about the war.

"I saw plenty of weird stuff over there. Then again, I've seen plenty of weird stuff in the Tenderloin."

Frank put his head back and laughed.

"Gee, you're some kidder. Do all soldiers of fortune have such a wonderful sense of humor?"

"I dunno. They might be funny if I could ever understand a word they say."

"Yeah, a bet a lot of those guys you deal with are foreign crooks hiding out from justice back home. Sorta like the Foreign Legion or something."

"I knew Legionaries in Flanders. They all seemed like idealists to me." After a pause, the waitress came over and asked me what I wanted. I ordered coffee, ham, and eggs. After the waitress left, Frank put his hands on the table and started talking business.

"Here's the thing, Jake. I called you down because I have an in with the Continental boys."

"I knew that already, Frank. It's hardly news."

"Yeah, sure, but did you know that the Continental agency is currently looking to hire a special detective for the purposes of a one-time deal?"

"No, I hadn't heard that. I'm guessing this special detective is supposed to be me, right?"

"Right, and I'm getting in on the action too. I already told them to split the dough between us. Mind you, I'm a pure reconnaissance man. You're here for the hard stuff."

"Okay, I don't like the sound of it already. 'Hard stuff?' What, are we going to bump off a labor organizer or start a war between tongs?"

"No, no, no. It's a simple job. It's like this see: there's this weird inventor by the name of Julius Trach, or von Trach if you prefer the old world pronunciation. He's supposedly some kind of White Russian scientist who's working on a highly secret operation that he runs from out of his apartment. The Continental boys have been on to him for a while, but they can't pin anything down for sure. Now, all the men they had following Trach have either quit or can't do it anymore because he recognizes them."

"What does the agency think the guy's doing? Illicit liquor? White slavery? Dope?"

"Nothing that simple. For my money, I think the guy is some sort of smuggler. You know, diamonds, rubies, and emeralds. My guy at Continental thinks Trach's the man behind a private army. He thinks that old boy Trach is stockpiling weapons and cash in order to send it all over to some friends in Europe for the purposes of taking the Motherland back from the Reds. Frankly, anything's possible at this point."

"And Continental is going to pay us to do what, exactly? Follow him around?"

"Yes, but they want solid proof that Trach's doing something seriously nasty. We're to get as close as possible. Maybe we'll even show ourselves into his house. Whatdya say?"

By this point I had eaten my ham and eggs. I was on my second cup of coffee and I wanted more. Too bad I was down to my last dollar.

"Right now I can't say no to money. I still haven't gotten paid from my last job overseas, and those sort of things take some time to process. I guess I have to say yes, even though I don't like it."

"What's not to like? It's just watch, tail, and report back. Easy and simple."

Frank cleaned the nonexistent dirt off of his hands to emphasize just how little the problem was going to be.

"I don't know, Frank. There's a lot of unknowns with this one, and besides, it's never a good idea to break into a guy's house when you suspect him of gun running."

"Hey, what's to worry about? You're the best shot in the Western world, and the East too. I'd drop you into any situation involving firearms and feel completely certain about your safety."

"That's the thing: you're dropping me into the fire, while you're safe outside, right?"

"Naturally."

Frank put his hands behind his head and relaxed his body. The grin on his face was impish, and when he added the cigar to his mug, he looked as content as the cat who ate the canary.

Later that afternoon, Frank showed up at my apartment with a stack of books and papers underneath his left arm. In his right he had a flask full of illegal hooch. I put the reading material on my coffee table, then Frank lobbed the flask at me. I caught it, drank enough to make Frank a little sour, then picked up the first book on the table.

"It's Ruski writing. Why did you go and get a book in a language neither of us can read?"

Frank shook his head like a disappointed school teacher.

"Tsk, tsk, Mr. Breakiron. You've been to Russia and you never bothered to learn the language?"

"The boys I was working for didn't pay me long enough to stick around. Besides, when I got there all the fun was gone. The Reds have turned the place into one giant church. The really preachy kind, too. It's pretty funny when you consider that they made atheism the law of the land."

"And enforce it, too."

"And how!" I grabbed the flask again and took another pull.

"To answer your question, my lush of a friend, I will say simply that you're too damn impatient. Yes, it's in Ruski, but I got an old timer at the public library to translate some of the juicy stuff for me. Here's the kicker: the author's name is Julius von Trach."

"So our boy writes books, eh?"

"You got it, blotto. Originally published in Trach's hometown of Riga in 1911. The book is called The Great Beyond: Exploring What's Behind the World Using Non-Euclidean Geometry and the Secret Mathematics."

"Well, Trach's short on brevity."

Frank liked that joke a lot. He threw his head back and let out that hyena laugh of his.

"Even for an egghead tome, this title's a humdinger. Seems to be a theme in Trach's life, though. Those papers there are copies taken from Russian journals from about 1912 until the end of the war. Trach is in all of them, and he's usually playing defense."

"'Playing defense?'"

"The old man at the public library wrote out Trach's commentaries and his one essay that they let slip through while the editor was napping. To put it bluntly, our man Trach is a lunatic."

"How big and how bad?"

Frank clapped his hands together, then slowly pulled them apart. When he was done, his palms were facing each other from about a shoulder length distance.

"About that bad, Jake. You could fly to Japan with how much hot air this guy has. Get this: the one essay and the entire book is about how Trach believes there are multiple worlds besides ours."

"What, like planets?"

"No, no. More like different realities and whole new ways of living. Trach believes that these worlds can be explored by creating machines that are based on his highly specialized version of advanced mathematics. Sounds kinda rummy, right?"

"Not only that, but the guy's billing himself out to be Harry Houdini and Einstein rolled into one. Besides, how can you buy a guy who's selling an idea that is both crazy by itself, but is even crazier when you realize that it can only be pulled off through some extraordinarily vague and idiosyncratic branch of arithmetic?"

"You sound a lot like Trach's detractors in there," Frank pointed at the pile of papers. "They all called him some really nasty names. Most asked him to shut up and stop pretending to be a serious scientist. One guy even called upon the czar to send him to Siberia."

Frank inched closer to me from across the coffee table. He dramatically splayed his fingers and held them aloft in some kind of gesture that I didn't immediately comprehend.

"Here's the thing: I think of lot of them were scared of Trach. You see, he not only called into question their assumptions that there's only one 'real' world, but he likewise admitted that the worlds surrounding ours aren't exactly friendly to our existence."

I cocked one of my eyebrows at him to show my confusion.

"I'm talking outright mean, hateful even. Those things that live in the other worlds want to harm ours. They want swallow us up and forget about such a thing as Western civilization. The 'why' is never explained by Trach."

"Boy, that's dour. But now I don't understand why the Continental agency would be interested in some academic kook."

"This kook has been very active. The one English book in the pile is a catalog of occult organizations throughout the world. It gives these little rundowns of where these groups are, how big their membership is, and what they believe in. Trach not only spent time in one of Russia's biggest occult societies, but he was also the president of the Harbin chapter for a year."

Frank was growing really restless now. He had drained the flask and loosened his tie. He had his hat cocked back on the crown of his head. He pulled out a cigar from inside of his coat and began blowing heavy, foggy rings. He told me the story of Trach's group with the cigar in his mouth.

"The group calls itself the Army of Olkoth. The group is a hodge-podge of students, their professors, ex-military men, bar fighters, and true nuts like Trach. The Army of Olkoth are decidedly paramilitary and even more decidedly right-wing, but the Whites want nothing to do with them. This is partially because the Army of Olkoth cares nothing about reestablishing the monarchy. At times, they've been known to fight White militias, so they have little friends there.

"Of course the Reds don't like them either. Consider them half-conjure men and half-con artists. Only members like the Army of Olkoth, and they aren't the type who recruit. Besides, who wants to join an armed group that actively tries to bring about the end of the world?"

It took me a while to swallow that one. A personality cult is one thing, but a death cult is a whole different ball game.

"Okay, Frank. Let's shoot completely straight at least this one time: are you implying that somehow, here in San Francisco, a mad Russian scientist is leading a group of apocalypse chasers?"

"I just might, Jake, I just might. That's ultimately up to us to decide, and I have an idea too."

Frank reached into his breast pocket and pulled out a letter. I thumbed it and found that it too was written in Russian.

"It says that our old pal Trach is to meet a certain Mr. Orlovski of the Greater White Movement Organization at 10 p.m. tonight. While he's making a social call, we'll slip into his apartment and see what we can see."

"Let me guess: your old timer at the library again?"

"Elementary, old gunner, elementary."

At 9:45, I met Frank in a restaurant beside Trach's apartment. He'd gotten the address from his contact in the Continental agency, who said that the best way to enter was through a back window. While drinking coffee near the restaurant's front door, Frank nudged me and pulled back his coat. Inside was a crowbar and a chisel. He made a nod with his head as if asking a question. I pulled back my own coat and showed him my .38 Police Positive. I rolled up my right sleeve in order to show him my wrist watch, too.

We waited until we saw Trach leave. It was 10:05. Apparently, he was a man who was not afraid to make others wait, even if it was the president of a fake organization. When Trach was out of sight, Frank and I left the restaurant and walked down into the alley behind Trach's apartment. Frank handed me the crowbar and chisel and pointed to a first story window.

"That one leads into an empty apartment. Despite this house being cut up in order to include multiple residences, only Trach lives here. The whole place is mostly empty rooms, except for the very top. That's where our friend lives."

I slid the crowbar between the sill and jamb. I tried to be as delicate in my movements as possible because the glass looked fragile and about the shatter at any minute. When I finally felt the stile rise, I handed the crowbar back to Frank and pushed the window up with my hands. It moved the slow, dirty trudge of a barely used machine.

"Okay, Jake. It's all you from here. I am going to stay out in the cold and play dodge with the street and the alley just to make sure Trach doesn't get any cute ideas about turning in early."

"And you're just going to brain him with the crowbar if he does?"

"No, I'll yell too."

"You're going to need this more than me, then."

I handed him the gun, but kept the chisel just in case. I asked him if he knew how to use it and he nodded his head.

"Point straight and pull. Easiest thing in the world."

I called him a dirty word and stepped into the empty room.

In the darkness, I couldn't see much. The place was covered in dust and had the unpleasant smell of mold and decay. I gagged quite often while trying to find a light switch, which didn't work anyway. I was then forced to struggle my way to Trach's room in utter darkness. I used the peeling wallpaper as my guide, and when I finally found the stairs, I hunched down on all fours and climbed them like an animal.

Near the top of the stairs, the thumb on my left hand found an exposed nail and was summarily impaled. The blood first spurted, then oozed at a steady drip. The wound left red droplets in the dust as I scrambled to find some sort of bandage or wrap. In the painful chaos, my body hit every wall and unattended object. I was positive that Frank was outside wincing himself silly because of the racket I was making. Finally, after pitching forward due to my feet finding an unexpected rug, I found Trach's room on the top floor.

The interior was lighted by candles. In the low light, I managed to find a robe. I took the belt from the robe and tied it around my thumb and hand. After letting the pain settle in, I started taking in the room around me. It was massive. On the far left side was a large window surrounded by burgundy curtains. To the right of the window was a lever that was connected to a simple pulley system that was in charge of opening and closing the gigantic window. Underneath the glass was the city of San Francisco and one could see the Pacific Ocean in the distance.

On the opposite side of the room sat a tiny, unmade bed. Next to it was a washroom and a roll-top desk made of dark wood. Above the desk was a large map with several pins stuck strategically across the globe. Most of the pins were stuck in Russia and the eastern half of Europe, but many were also scattered throughout the United States and Canada. Most of the American pins were in northern California. Beside the map and desk was a bookshelf, which itself stood directly across the room from another bookshelf. The bookshelves were in a state of disorder, with various loose papers carelessly thrown on top of almost every row. Next to the bookshelf on the left was a cathedral-style radio with a pair of headphones attached to the side. Upon closer inspection, I found that the radio had once belonged to a Danish vessel called the Wild Hunt.

Overall, Trach's room gave off the impression that its owner was an eccentric scientist who cared little for the niceties of good housekeeping. Of course, even with this impression, everything would have seemed normal if not for the covered thing that stood in the middle of the room. Placed above some elaborate floor drawing that had been done in white, red, and black chalk, the object was a cyclopean monstrosity with a single eye that stretched towards the large window. From underneath the sheet, which was made out of grey wool, it looked like an exceptionally large telescope.

As a general rule, I am a curious man, so it took no time for me to start the process of removing the large sheet. It proved surprisingly heavy, and I soon found that the ends were weighed down with metal balls of some kind. After a few minutes of vigorous pulling, I managed to uncover the thing.

It was a type of telescope, but not quite. It's long body did end in an objective lens, but it contained along its sides various tubes that moved with translucent liquids that alternated between the colors of blue and green. The base of the object reminded me of naval artillery. The object even had what I presumed to be a blast shield and an enclosed mount which contained a type of seat. Most startling of all, however, was the peculiar lock box near the mount. Illuminated by another translucent fluid (this one being orange), the lock box was fronted by a piece of glass. Behind the glass sat a book that looked to be very old and was bound in black leather. With my chisel, I broke the glass and retrieved the book. I placed the chisel on the ground and began to read.

Unfortunately, the book was written in some unknown language. But the book did contain several disturbing sketches that could only be compared to the Danse Macabre etchings of the middle ages. I soon became so engrossed in these images that I failed to hear the door open behind me.

"Mesmerizing, no?"

The voice had a heavy Slavic accent and an implicit malevolence that jolted me awake.

"I could tell you about it, but I'm sure such knowledge would be wasted on you, Mr. Breakiron."

I slowly turned around to face the voice. It was Trach, but he was holding something in his hand. It was a gun. Even in the semi-darkness I knew it was my .38 Police Positive.

"Where's Frank?"

Trach partially smiled and mumbled the word "Swimming."

"I've been to Russia and I live in America, and I know that murder is illegal in both, Trach."

"So is breaking and entering. But let us dispense with such legal talk. After all, we are not mere cops and robbers. No, rather you and I are on the cusp of witnessing something truly great. For that, I thank you, Mr. Breakiron."

With the gun outstretched, Trach took the book from out of my hands and placed it back in its former position.

"I suppose I'll have to repair that glass, but it'll have to wait. You see, your participation is all-important."

"What are you hinting at?"

"Oh my, don't you know?"

When I shook my head in the negative, Trach began laughing.

"So they really don't know about this then, do they? Please tell me, do they still suspect that I am some sort of gun runner for the Tsarists?"

This time I shook my head in the affirmative.

"Those fools! As if the great Julius von Trach would be concerned with something so trivial. I'll admit I did throw my lot in with the Whites for a time, but that was only because I knew the Bolsheviks would come for me in order to seize my equipment and my estate. When they labeled me a reactionary of the old regime, I knew it was time to flee. So, using a White militia as my unwitting guards, I escaped using a private train heading east.

"Along the way I met a rather mad general who was leading his men into Mongolia in the hopes of establishing a private empire. He and I spent many pleasant evenings together talking about any number of esoteric subjects. It was through him that I found out about a secret organization in the Chinese city of Harbin."

"The Army of Olkoth."

"Quite right. Very brave men, dumb, but very brave. They are the only Russians left who still have the old curiosities of our pagan ancestors. Still, until my leadership, they were more or less nihilists without a purpose. Most of them just wanted to fight and kill, while the more serious among them saw themselves as the vanguard of a revolution - a revolution based around the pre-human religion of the Earth. These men proved steadfast in their desire to bring about the end of the world as we know it, and for my purposes, they proved effective propagandists. Through them, I convinced the rank and file to submit themselves to the will of my new machine.

"Few suspected that they were mere cattle, for my machine only desires their blood and nothing more. Although they thought that they were volunteering for a ritual that would grant them greater powers as warriors, they were in fact marching towards the dinner table for those things that live in the space between worlds. I took great pride in my job of delivering their bodies up to the invisible beings, but sadly some members of the exiled Russian community were under the impression that I was in fact a murderer. It was they who chased me from Manchuria all the way to San Francisco.

"Because of them I cannot find any peace, and undoubtedly some Harbin Russian with an Orthodox cross firmly around their neck was the one who first put you and your private detectives on my trail. Thankfully, only I know about the machine and its true power.

"Until tonight, I was worried that I had let its strength flag for too long. Because of the intense surveillance, I have not been able to feed the beings who animate the machine for a while. I have been forced to provide them with only the most minor of sustenance."

In the gloom, Trach raised his other hand. It was missing three of its fingers.

"I was pondering whether or not I could go through life with one leg when I found out about you and your friend. A word of advice: don't let on about your plans to drunks with loose tongues. All told, it only cost me two American dollars and fifteen minutes of my time to learn that you would be here tonight."

As he spoke, Trach and the gun inched closer and closer to my position. Throughout his oratory, he had been circling me, thus forcing me to slightly adjust my body towards the middle of the room. As he drew closer, I began to realize that he was trying to place me directly over the symbol on the floor.

"With each new body, the beings between the worlds grow stronger, and the stronger the meal, the stronger they become. With the Army of Olkoth, I almost succeeded in culling the beings forth, but I was ultimately thwarted. Now, with one more kill, I will finally be able to not only bring the beings into our world, but also harness their energy via my marvelous machine."

"What's the point then, Trach - the end of the world?"

"I think of it as more of a rebirth or rather a reawakening. All the old gods need is a clear signal to interrupt their long slumber. As for me, I will become a new god."

At the word "god," Trach thumbed the hammer back. He was so close that I could feel his breath on my arm. Instinctively, I threw out my right foot, which landed squarely on his knee. I felt him buckle, but to my surprise, the strike did not completely destabilize Trach. Knowing that I now only had a second before Trach would right himself and fire the pistol, I rushed his legs and forced him onto his back.

While falling, Trach managed to squeeze the trigger once. The bullet came so close that it burnt the top of my ear before embedding itself in the opposite wall. Using my left hand, I pinned the gun and Trach's right hand to the floor, while with my right I began digging my fingers into Trach's eyeballs. Trach fought with the desperation of a wounded animal, but his mangled free hand could not halt my advances. Within minutes, I had blinded him. Then, while he screamed in pain, I pried my gun from his hand and fired off two shots while straddling his upper torso. Trach was dead.

Before the police arrived, I did what damage I could to the machine. I used the chisel to fray several wires, and I fired the remaining rounds into certain sensitive-looking areas on the machine. In particular, I opened up the oddly colored tubes and found that upon contact with the air, the translucent liquid evaporated. Finally, I removed the book once again and began tearing its pages out. Then, using a set of matches which I had rediscovered in my back pocket, I set the pages alight. This action somehow caused the few candles in the room to flicker, then go out completely. The temperature sank as well, and in the cold room I discerned the sound of wind despite no window being open.

Amidst all the confusion, my ears began to pick up certain sounds. At first I thought I was just hearing the blood pounding in my wounded ear. But, as the noises began to increase in volume, I realized that what I was hearing were howls of pain. They were hollow and unnatural cries that seemed to come from everywhere all at once. Then in an instant they became an unbearable cacophony that drowned out even my own shouts of pain. In order to muffle the hellish choir, I placed my hands over my ears, but had to drop them again due to the tenderness of my one ear and the soreness in my wounded thumb. As I moved my hands back to my sides, a series of two shapes moved into the room. All I could see through my tears were two vaguely humanoid outlines dressed in blue. Out of habit, I tried to reach out to them without realizing that I still held my .38 Police Positive.

The last thing I remember was the feeling of several sharp pains hitting my abdomen and upper thighs.

The Rain in Eksley
Brian Hamilton

It was raining.

That was something I had forgotten about the sleepy little village of Eksley, out deep in rural Massachusetts. It never mattered what the forecast said about the surrounding areas. Eksley was, for the fall season, permanently overcast with swollen gray clouds. The rain could be anywhere from a light drizzle to a torrential downpour. But it was always, always raining.

This morning it was somewhere between the two extremes, with the sound of soggy fingers drumming against the roof of the small bed and breakfast at which I had rented a room for the weekend. I laid in bed, staring at the fold where the two sloping sides of the roof met overhead until there was a soft knock at the room's door. A voice drifted softly over the sound of the rain. "Mr. Griggs?"

"I'm up, Martha, thank you," I responded, tossing aside the covers and getting up. The floorboards on the other side of the door creaked as the building's owner moved away. I dressed quickly after realizing how late I had slept in. I put on my hat and coat last since they were still slightly damp, even after spending the night in the attic's near stifling heat. But better that than Eksley's cold, damp air.

I decided to skip the complimentary breakfast, instead grabbing a couple of apples out of a bowl on the dining room's table as I said my goodbyes to Martha. No one else was in the small room, either because they had already left or, as I suspected, there was no one else staying there. It made sense, I thought, as I stepped out of the bed and breakfast and immediately felt my clothing grow heavy with moisture. No one in their right mind would want to spend a week in this weather. Better to come in the summer or spring.

I slid into my rental car, immediately turned on the heat after the engine had started up, and pulled out onto what was, sadly, called Main Street. As I bit into an apple I noticed that there weren't many people out the street, and many of the stores either had their lights turned off or signs reading "Closed" in the windows. I guessed that no one had wanted to go out that Saturday morning. Honestly, I wished I hadn't as well.

I drove out of the center of little Eksley, towards the reason why I had come back.

As I drove towards my destination - which, according to my phone's map, would take some time - I thought over my purpose for being here. My parents had moved from Eksley when I was a child, wishing to get away from the periodically soaked village that had been home to their families for generations. I had grown up in sunny Austin and had opened up a relatively successful consulting firm in one of the better areas of the city. It made enough of a profit that I was able to help my parents move into a nice little retirement community, the kind with nicely manicured lawns and little houses suited to fit a couple getting on in their years.

Eksley had been so far removed from our lives that the death of Isaac Griggs, my father's uncle, had come as a complete surprise. The old man had never attempted to contact any of us after we'd moved away. Apparently Isaac had never gotten married or had any children, legitimate or otherwise, since everything he'd owned - property included - had gone to my father, his only living relative. And Dad, knowing he'd never be able to get to "Uncle Griggs'" estate, even with his new knees, had asked me to go instead. "Just to see what's there," Dad had said.

And so there I was, driving a rented car up a long gravel driveway, flanked on either sides by impenetrable phalanxes of thick New England woods, the trees a riot of browns, yellows and reds. Every so often I saw a patch of green holding on despite Nature's endless crawl onward.

The trees eventually gave way to an overgrown clearing, and the driveway led up to a cabin that, I realized as I pulled up, was in a serious state of disrepair. The most obvious piece of damage was the collapsed roof, which had exposed the left side of the cabin. Blocks of chopped wood lay in a pile, likely knocked over when the roof came down. A blue, plastic tarp lay on the ground next to the woodpile. What had been some kind of front porch had also fallen apart, rotting planks of wood jutting up like crooked teeth. The paint on the outside had peeled until I could see more brown than white - and what white remained was mostly stained until it was some kind of tepid yellow. I couldn't see any glass in the windows, and I imagined how much moisture must have seeped its way into the interior.

There was a police car out front, and as I turned my car off Sheriff Owens stepped out. He walked up briskly as my window rolled down. He tilted his head to look at me, but used one hand to keep his wide-brimmed hat up, saving me from a faceful of rainwater. "Mr. Griggs. Nice of you to show up."

I shrugged in reply. "Sorry, Sheriff. Overslept." I nodded towards the cabin. "Not much of an inheritance, is it?"

Owens turned around. "Not really, no."

"When did the roof collapse in?"

Owens scratched at his head. "Sometime between when we found Isaac and when you came up. Seems like it had been rotting away for some time now."

"I bet that happens often enough, with all the rain."

"You're right about that. Our local church just had a few structural supports replaced. And there was the Mason's barn that fell apart when they decided to skip repairs for a year." Owens shook his head. "Some people live here their lives and they still don't seem to get it."

"I bet they learn fast, though." Owens chuckled, but didn't reply. We both stayed silent for a time, listening to the rhythm of the rain, increasing and decreasing in intensity seemingly at random. Thinking I'd show some kind of camaraderie in the face of our mutual enemy, I rolled the window up, got out of the car and stood next to Owens in the rain.

After another few moments, I asked, "Did you know my Granduncle, Sheriff?"

Out of the corner of my eye, I could see the gears turning in Owens' head. "Not really," he replied. "Old Isaac was around even before my time. He was always a bit of a recluse, and we saw even less of him after your father Joseph moved your family away. He came into town regularly, if not that often, to get food or to get a package or two that had come in to the post office."

"And that's how they realized something was wrong?"

"Right. Came a time when someone realized they hadn't seen Isaac come in for a couple of his regular visits. I got called up, asked to come out here to check on him." Owens gestured towards the decrepit building. "Wasn't in such bad condition when I came out here, like I said, but I found the old man dead in a chair. Looked like he had been there for a couple of weeks, passed in his sleep."

I shivered when Owens said that. It was from the kind of chill that cut far deeper than any autumn weather. I never liked the idea of going into a place where someone had definitely passed away. Call it a phobia. Rumors could be dismissed, but finding a body? I'd probably run screaming out of a room and take the first window I could find if that happened to me. I got jittery just visiting the hospital my doctor practiced out of.

But I wasn't ready to leave just yet. "Should we go in now, Sheriff?"

Owens nodded, walked back over to his car, produced a pair of black metallic flashlights and handed one to me when he returned. "You don't have to do this, you know. The home's probably not worth saving anyway."

"You're right about that, although the property around it will probably get a good price. But we should check to make sure we haven't missed anything." With that, I started towards the cabin, Owens to my right. I could have sworn that, with every step I took, the rain grew in intensity, until it was pounding hard enough on the wooden overhang of the front door that I was momentarily worried the water would drill straight through the rotted wood.

Owens stepped up to the door and opened it with a little effort. The wood was swollen and had become partially stuck in its frame. The door swung in on rusted hinges, protesting every bit of the way until it thumped to a stop on some inner obstacle. There was, for a brief moment, a rush of cool air, somehow colder than the outside temperature. It was like a sort of exhalation, carrying the stench of rotting wood and other worse things. Owens and I both froze for a second, the twin beams of our flashlights throwing up shadows down the receiving hallway.

The sheriff threw off his hesitation first and walked into the structure. I followed.

It quickly became apparent to me that the house was far smaller than it had seemed from the outside. As soon as we walked in I noticed that the central hallway led to two other rooms on either side. To my right was some sort of sitting room, occupied by an old, sagging couch that had been torn into by some animal. The floor, beneath a well-worn, faded rug, was equally sagging and was probably best left alone. Although something about the downward curve seemed off to me.

The room on the left had been some sort of study, but the collapsed roof made it inaccessible Papers were scattered on the floor, but they quickly came apart in my hand, and the ink had run on the pieces large enough to read. Rain drizzled in from the hole in the roof. "Any idea what Isaac did as a job?" I asked.

"I not sure he was employed," Owens told me. In neither of the rooms had we found any indication of modern technology - no computers, televisions, phones or even heating ducts.

Owens and I moved to the end of the hallway and found ourselves in a small kitchen. There was no refrigerator, but a small wood burning stove squatted in a corner. I guessed that Isaac had used it to keep warm. "He didn't cut the wood for the stove himself, did he?"

Owens turned from the empty cupboards he had been inspecting. "No. He had someone from town come out to chop the wood down and then stack it up for use during the colder months. I couldn't imagine someone as old and thin as Isaac Griggs wielding an axe." I imagined a caricature of a scrawny old man swinging an axe around, and couldn't decide if it scared me or made me want to laugh.

We concluded the search of the premise. Isaac seemed to have been a boring old man. Dad would be glad to know we could get rid of the property quickly, without worrying about the need to tear down a perfectly good house. Bulldozing the cabin would probably be an act of mercy. Owens took back his flashlight from me as we walked out of the cabin and back into the rain. "You sure you can find your way back?" he asked.

I waved my phone as I said, "My reception's pretty good out here, and I've got a map saved just in case. I'll been fine, Sheriff. Thanks."

Owens look satisfied with my answer. "I'll tell Martha you're on your way back when I reach Eksley." He got back into his patrol car. Owens waved as wheels switched from gravel to tar and the car went out of sight. As the sounds of the motor started to fade, I turned back around to face the cabin. The rain had quieted back down to a drizzle. My breath came out in long, slow exhalations of steam, curling thickly in the afternoon air. I watched Isaac's home and, strangely enough, it seemed to watch me back, it's broken windows seeming to be sunken, haunted eyes. I shivered as cold water finally dribbled off the back of my hat and down into the collar of my coat, racing along my spine.

It was then that realization hit me. The curve in the floor of the one room sunk further than the cabin had been raised off the ground. Even what little remained of the front porch hadn't been that high up. So there must be some sort of lower level. A quick walk around the perimeter showed that there was no hidden cellar door, not even beneath the fallen pile of logs. Owens and I had missed something.

I walked back up to the door, which I hadn't bothered to close after following Owens out. Anything of worth had already been collected. But Owens had also left with both flashlights. I used my phone's screen light, which paled in comparison to what I had used before. Even worse, the lowered brightness seemed to cast more shadows up on the walls of the hallway.

Regardless, I walked back into that place, turning right and stopping just at the threshold of the room with the sagging floor. The rug was still there, still faded and fraying at the edges. But the light of my phone revealed, after my eyes became used to the dimmer light of my phone, a square shape at the center of the rug. Owens and I hadn't noticed the slight difference in our cursory check of what we had thought to be a boring but potentially dangerous room.

A sort of morbid curiosity came over me, then. Isaac Griggs had something he wanted to hide. The only thing I could imagine being under that rug was some sort of trap door, and below it another room that couldn't be entered through by any other means - at least, near the cabin. Maybe there was an exit somewhere else. I briefly thought of an impossible series of tunnels down below Eksley, filled to bursting with centuries of rainwater.

It must have been during that daydream that I took a step forward. It was a mistake. The rot in the wooden floor had spread further than I could have guessed. With a creak that quickly ascended to some sort of roar, the floor gave way to a yawning black hole that sucked down the rug, wooden planks and the torn couch. I lost my balance, startled by the suddenness of the room's transformation, and tipped forward into darkness.

I rolled, bounced, flailed, fell. My hand, of its own volition, kept a death grip on my phone, the only source of light. Brief glimpses revealed stone walls, stone stairs, and bits of debris. I landed, miraculously, on the couch that had fallen before me. Great clouds of dust and dirt billowed in the smothered light of my phone. Despite my relatively soft landing, I groaned in pain. I wasn't sure if I had broken anything, but I was able to move my fingers and toes.

I rolled off the couch, coughing and choking. I spat out a mouthful of splinters, dirt and whatever had been inside the couch. Looking around, I dimly realised I had been right - underneath Isaac's cabin had been some sort of basement. Steps led down from what had been the floor of the room above.

I stood up, using the light from my phone to get a better understanding of my surroundings now that my head had stopped spinning. Whatever this room was, it had originally been some sort of cavern. No walls could be so smooth, or transition to ceiling or floor with such a gentle, almost unnaturally perfect curve. But there was evidence of human hands - the stairs leading down, of course, and the wooden door opposite of them on the cavern's far side. Thinking it was some sort of storage room, I walked over and reached out.

For just a moment, the door seemed strange. It almost felt like I had misjudged its distance, as though my spatial reasoning was gone. The knob seemed a mile away, and yet loomed in my vision. But then the door was just a door, and my hand closed around the knob. I twisted, yanked the door open, and recoiled, the hairs on the back of my neck standing up.

More darkness greeted me, and after my heart had stopped racing, I felt my face flush with embarrassment. I was acting like a child, jumping at things in the dark. I walked into the room, knowing just by intuition that it was smaller than the room before. I brought my phone up and checked the battery life. A stylised battery showed a sliver of red bar left. I needed to get out quickly.

This room contained only two items - a small wooden table and a compact book with a leather cover. I put my hand on the table and found it dry, almost at odds with the surroundings upstairs. The leather book was almost as unremarkable, apart from the faded golden lettering on the front that signified it as a journal. I guessed that it was Isaac's, and wondered as to why the man had kept this particular book down here, when so many others had suffered upstairs.

Not thinking, I picked the book up. I immediately dropped it, yelling in pain. The damned thing had actually writhed in my grip, as though alive, and it had cut me as well. I could see the thin line of blood forming on my thumb. Sucking on it, I looked down to the book to find it had opened to what were the last few entries.

What I read then, I had thought to be the ravings of a madman. Isaac had clearly been hallucinating at some stage. It spoke of rituals performed and promises made. It told of things outside, intelligences looking in, but stymied in their search. I couldn't make any sense of it. But it was the last few lines that drew my full attention. At some point Isaac had slipped back into lucidity, and his handwriting had lost its manic, chicken-scratch form.

I am now too weak to finish my work, it read, *but the ritual only requires blood that is in some part related to its originator. Having left my estate to my nephew, I hope that either he or his son will travel here after my death. The ritual will bring them to this journal, no matter where I place it. With my death as the primer, it will only take a few drops spilled to accomplish my goals.*

With the ritual complete, the clouds will disperse, the rain will end, and the path to the Watchers will be clear. No longer will Eksley be a salve for this wretched world's existence.

If you have bothered to read this, my dear nephew William - or perhaps Alexander, who I expect to no longer be that young brat you took away from our legacy thirty years ago - I thank you for your part in this.

I stood back up, my eyes moving from the last page of the journal to my thumb, where the small cut glistened in the low light. Something in my gut twisted, and there was a sense of general wrongness in the then-stifling air of the small room.

So I turned and ran. Ran out of the room, past the couch, almost tripped halfway up the stairs, scrambled up the edge of the hole, hauled myself to my feet and nearly fell face first as I left the cabin. I stood there, hunched over, trying to catch my breath with my hands on my knees.

But even as my breath swirled out in front of me, I realized something still felt not quite right. The hairs on the back of my neck weren't just standing up, they were nearly jumping up and down. My panic-stricken mind took a moment to realize what was missing, what should have been there.

The rain had stopped.

That constant, ever-present sound of rain falling, dripping, running everywhere at every second was gone. I could even see, out from the corners of my eyes, that the slight haze that had accompanied the rain was also gone. I licked my lips, which were surprisingly dry.

I had to look up. I needed to. I had to look up and see. So I did. I stood straight up, my head tilted back and I opened my eyes. I hadn't realized I had closed them.

I looked to the heavens.

And saw someplace else.

What I saw isn't entirely describable. There were stars, yes, but they were wrong somehow - some sort of sickly, wasting green and yellow instead of the normal twinkling spectrum. And I saw what I thought were planets, maybe moons. But planets and moons don't look back. Planets don't have eyes the size of oceans. Moons don't have mouths comparable to continents, filled with teeth that could dwarf the tallest of Earth's mountains. You've never looked at Mars and felt even the smallest indication that it wanted to devour you whole and keep you screaming for all eternity in the darkest pits of its never-ending stomachs.

I believe that's what I saw. I believe that's what Isaac wanted to see. And somewhere in some hell or another, Isaac shrieked and laughed and jumped with joy.

And then the clouds returned. They rolled back across the sky, swirling, pushing close the portal through which lay the death of every single living creature on our planet, and perhaps the extinction of our universe. I couldn't move as droplets of rain began to mix with my tears, rolling off my trembling body.

I stood like that for some time. I eventually came to my senses and, when my hands stopped shaking so much, got into my car. I drove back down the gravel path, away from the sinkhole that had taken Isaac's cabin at some point. I slowly drove back to Eksley.

What I found in Eksley wasn't much better. There have always been stories about abandoned ghost towns that are the result of some disaster, like the mining town in Pennsylvania with its underground fire, or the little city in Maine that's perpetually covered in a thick fog. That's Eksley now. That's what happens when everyone in a little rural town disappears overnight. I remember passing by Sheriff Owen's car, which had crashed into a ditch on the side of the road. No one was inside. The same was for the bed & breakfast - there had been a dinner set up, still warm, but no one to eat it. I may have heard someone - or something - scream wordlessly somewhere off in the distance, on the outskirts of the town. Or I might have been the one who screamed. But I packed my belongings and quickly drove back towards Boston and the safety of home.

As for being questioned about what happened? I guess that Eksley was one of those incidents that everyone who's vaguely important wants to keep quiet about. I told my Dad the land was worthless, which was true enough. He promptly forgot about it. I'm not sure how much he knew about Isaac and the plans the old man had.

I still spend some nights sleeplessly wondering why my Granduncle's ritual failed. I try not to think about why he did it - that's too far in the deep end for me, and I now know that there are things down in those depths I never want to know in detail. I can only guess that at some point, some component went wrong. The clouds came back. The Watchers, as Isaac called them, could only watch as their chance to invade our reality - if that is the right way of thinking about it - was foiled.

By a simple, unknown mistake, washed away by the rain.

The Summoning
Jason S. Aiken

I

Zeki eyed the tall foreigner with great suspicion. He mistrusted sorcerers, but he was not going to turn down a lucrative opportunity before hearing all of the details. Nahuel, his guest, cleared his throat, and Zeki nodded at the dark man to continue.

"To the west is an island reachable by small boat. A gathering is being held there, a conference of men and women with talents in the mystical arts. Their number will be small enough that they won't be tripping over each other, but large enough that an extra body won't be noticed. Especially when there is precious work to be done and little time to do it in. If one had the ambition, certain items of immense value could be liberated during the process without detection."

A smirk crawled up the corners of Zeki's mouth, but he was quick to hide it. "Just a moment. I enjoy making extra coin as much as the next man, but I make it a point to avoid crossing anyone who can turn me into a toad. I have stayed in business a long time by avoiding this type of risk. Something tells me stealing an ancient artifact would not be worth the wrath of the owner."

Nahuel laughed. "Right you are, my good man! It most certainly would not! That would be quite dangerous! That's why the plan involves leaving the priceless artifacts unmolested. Oh no, we aren't after anything that would be the death of us." He touched a long finger to his temple for dramatic effect. "We will be smart. You are a merchant—well, at least you pretend to be. I trust you know which items are your most lucrative?"

Zeki swallowed and looked around his store. While it was true he owned the place, he let his wife run the day-to-day business operations. It allowed him the time to take care of the rougher clientele during the night, where a fence makes his coin. He knew what the wizard was getting at, though. "Low risk, high reward."

Nahuel clapped his hands together and beamed. "Exactly! Exactly! That is indeed the essence of our plan! I have just the item in mind, too! Kirin powder!"

"Kirin powder?"

"Yes! We are in the prospering port city of Guspar, where wealthy merchants sleep on silken sheets and have beautiful wives...and mistresses. What man wouldn't want a little extra help in the bedroom?"

Zeki rubbed his eyes, his interest waning. "You're losing me wizard. What's a kirin and why should I care about it?"

"Ah, I forget you are ignorant of the mystic arts. Allow me to educate you! A kirin is a rare beast that dwells in the mountains far to the east. It has four legs, but its exact appearance differs from specimen to specimen. Some of the creatures have one horn, others two. If one can capture a kirin, the horns can be harvested and ground into a powder. Add this powder to any drink and the results are instantly noticeable to any man who isn't a eunuch, if you take my meaning."

Zeki was about to question Nahuel's sanity over risking life and limb for such a vain prize, but he stopped and thought about it for a moment. He thought back to his own nocturnal activities —or lack thereof recently. The wizard might be onto something. "So this powder increases...virility?"

Nahuel smiled and his white teeth gleamed. "Oh yes, very much so. Virility and...more. I think you can figure out the rest. The Eastern Mystics have a technique where the captured beast remains unharmed and is then released back into the wild for its horns to regrow. This has created a surplus, and the wizards always bring a generous supply to the annual gathering on the island. However, for our purposes we would only need a small flask of the powder. We obtain the powder and sell it to a select clientele, then live out the rest of our days without a care in the world."

Zeki was practically drooling as the foreigner laid out his master plan. In his mind he was already in the noble quarter, in a mansion surrounded by beautiful women waiting on him hand and foot. He then noticed the look of triumph in Nahuel's eyes and wondered if he were being taken for a fool. "That all sounds well and good Nahuel, but what is your place in this? Why would you steal from your own kind?"

"Why not? Anyone can steal from anyone. Are wizards that different from normal men? I think not. Besides, I wouldn't really consider them my people. A rather gloom-and-doom lot they are. My membership is what you would call on a trial basis, and I've never really been much of a joiner. No, I think I've set foot on that island for the last time. That's where you come in Zeki. A man in your position must know of a thief up to the job."

"I know plenty of them, but I still don't understand where you fit in. As far as I can see, the piece of the pie, so to speak, is getting smaller and smaller. Once the profits start coming in on this investment, the honorable thing to do would be to split them three ways after all." Zeki raised his eyebrows up and down, as if testing Nahuel.

"My good man, there's no need for that! I thought you were a business man. No, we'll pay the liberator a generous fee on delivery of the powder. I have some extra coin on hand, and I'm sure you do as well. The profits....we split between the two of us."

Zeki grinned widely. He felt he no longer had to hide anything from the wizard, that he was talking to a man after his own heart. "You have a deal, my friend. That is exactly what I was thinking. I know just the man we can use."

II

Kasar was cornered and outnumbered three to one, but he refused to back down to anyone. He had just as much of a right to frequent the tavern as the three oxen staring him down. He picked out the ugliest of them, the one in the middle and shot a haymaker of a right straight towards his jaw. His aim was true and he felt bone give way... in his own hand. His opponent bent forward and with his big bull of a neck, propelled his own skull into Kasar's face. Kasar flew backwards into the wall, knocking over the scimitars hanging there.

Standing just above five feet, and barely weighing over one hundred pounds, he wasn't much of a physical threat to anyone. But he had heart, and thank the gods he had that. He sure didn't have brains. Well, when it came to fighting, anyway. Writing, painting, sculpting, languages —he was quite good at all of these things. Sadly, he wasn't born into the appropriate social caste to take advantage of these talents. Growing up as an orphan on the streets, he had seen the limits of his station on a daily basis. He didn't feel sorry for himself, though. He had accepted his lot in life a long time ago. The life he led could be categorized as fight or flight. Two guesses as to what his favorite option was.

Kasar scrambled back up to his feet, shaking the cobwebs out of his head. It didn't matter which of them he went after, just as long as he got a piece of one. Kasar could take a punch and beating with the best of them, and he wasn't one to give up after one try.

The oafs laughed at his show of fortitude. "Give it up, you smelly runt, you aren't welcome here. Walk out that door or we'll throw your scrawny ass out!"

That's all it took. Kasar was back in the fray. He launched himself at no one in particular, but the next thing he knew he felt tight grips on his left arm and leg, and he was flying towards the entrance.

Lucky for him the door was partially ajar to let the outside air in; otherwise, he may have broken his neck on impact. The door sprung open and he saw the street come up to meet him. He broke his fall with his hands, but he still lost consciousness.

He came to with his face in the dirt and choking on dust. He turned over on his back and looked up into the blurry, twilight sky. He felt a warm lump in the middle of his spine and realized he had just rolled onto a pile of horse dung. He didn't care, though. He wasn't done, not by a long shot. He would set those three straight before the sun rose.

His vision cleared and two forms appeared over him. One he recognized as Zeki, his fence. Kasar liked the man. Zeki was always giving him work and paid him well enough to keep him from living on the street like in the old days. So what if he had to spend the occasional week in jail with a precious stone sequestered away in the only place the guards refused to search. It was all a part of the job, and he didn't hold it against Zeki. The dark man he didn't know, but something about him looked menacing to Kasar. Until the man's lips parted and a mouth of gleaming white teeth warmly greeted him.

"Zeki, my friend, you are correct as always! Correct as always! This is definitely the man we're looking for!"

III

At Nahuel's insistence, Kasar waited until nightfall before anchoring the skiff and swimming to the sandbar surrounding the island. He clutched at the green rock he wore around his neck just to reassure himself that it was still there. According to the wizard, the spell cast upon it would allow his approach to go unnoticed. When he asked the wizard about sentries, the dark man just laughed. Apparently sorcerers felt they had no need for sentries. Nahuel did tell him the concealment spell would only be effective on the fringes of the island. Once he made it to the inner court he would be on his own.

Kasar thought Nahuel was kind of eccentric, but he seemed trustworthy. So he decided to take Zeki and Nahuel up on their offer. The fact that they would pay him such a large fee upon delivery didn't hurt their cause either. The way Kasar figured, he could live off that for most of the year.

He made sure to secure the mask covering his face and lifted up the robes he was wearing before stepping off the skiff and onto the sandbar. Nahuel had modified the ceremonial outfit to fit him, and Kasar thought he did a pretty good job. If he ever lost his magical powers he would make a fine tailor. He pushed thoughts of the wizard to the back of his mind, as he knew he had to focus on the job. This wasn't one of Zeki's normal robberies—he was up against powers beyond normal men. He knew he had to take extra caution.

Following the route Nahuel laid out for him, he nonchalantly strolled across the sandbar and onto the island itself. The island was exactly as the wizard described it to him. He reached into his robe and pulled out a small container holding the map. Kasar had illustrated it himself with Nahuel's guidance. As a matter of fact, the wizard was quite impressed with his skill. Together they had planned Kasar's movements within the inner court.

He unrolled the parchment and examined it. The island was in the shape of a large circle. His destination, the inner court, was shaped like a circle as well. A series of gray stone buildings formed the perimeter. These buildings were made up apartments, temples, and storehouses. The remaining open space in the center was flat and covered with smooth black stone. The only means of entering and exiting were four alleys located at the compass points. The plan was for him to enter via the eastern alley and make his way towards the northern storehouse to liberate the powder.

As he entered the inner court it was evident he was no longer among normal men. The architecture of the buildings was unlike anything Kasar had seen before. They had a malevolence in their design. There was something threatening about the way they towered over him. He got his wits back when he locked eyes on the first of the island's visitors, a muscular magus with broad shoulders. The man paid Kasar no attention. He was busy muttering to himself as he carefully transcribed strange glyphs onto the ebon floor in green ink. As Kasar continued on his route towards the north storehouse he observed a diverse selection of sorcerers performing the same task. Luckily, there was also a fair amount of them who were walking around the grounds as he was.

Kasar carefully weaved his way through the crowd, taking extra care to not draw attention to himself. Luck was on his side this day, as he made it to the northern storehouse without incident. He entered the building and immediately descended the steps into the basement. According to Nahuel, the kirin powder was always kept in the same location: a large barrel stored in a room at the end of the hallway. The room was straight back the hall, but doors lined the sides of the hall as well, so he was mindful of these. Kasar made it halfway down the hall when he began to hear strange noises coming from the last door on the right.

He stopped and listened intently. In his mind there was no doubt the sounds coming from the doorway were of an intimate nature. He could make out at least one male, and two, perhaps three females in there. Kasar was unsure how to proceed from here. The plan was time sensitive, and he knew he shouldn't delay. But, how would he explain his presence here if he were discovered? He finally made the decision to quietly and quickly walk past the door. In his mind the occupants sounded like they were enjoying themselves enough to shut out outside stimuli.

Kasar lunged forward and performed three quick strides. He didn't bother to peep into the other room. He was afraid if he made eye contact with one of them it would all be over. Kasar stepped into the storeroom and found himself directly in front of the barrel. He stood still for a few seconds, but the sounds from the other room continued. He was safe for now.

He circled around the barrel until he found the symbol Nahuel described to him, confirming this was indeed the kirin powder. He quietly raised the lid and then removed an empty flask from his robes. He filled the flask to the brim and corked it. While putting away the flask he had an idea. Why not take more? Especially when he had a canister containing a map he no longer had any use for. Kasar popped out the canister and removed the rolled up parchment. He searched for a place to dispose of it and found another barrel containing a boiling substance. He decided this was as good a place as any, so he dropped the map inside. The parchment evaporated on contact and Kasar immediately stepped back out of caution. He turned around and made his way back to the barrel of kirin powder. Kasar filled his canister and knew it was time to make his exit. The thief felt he had dallied in the room a bit too long. Inching toward the doorway, he could still here the sounds emanating from the other room.

From this angle he could see it quite clearly and couldn't resist having a look. He saw a portly brown man on his back, with two women sitting on top of him. One on each end, so to speak. Kasar was used to seeing some pretty rough women in the city slums. He had never seen women this attractive. The thief couldn't take his eyes off of their supple, ivory bodies. He watched them, mesmerized. Then he thought his mind was playing tricks on him. For every few seconds he thought he saw their faces change. The change didn't last for more than a second, but he could have sworn one had the head of a fish and the other a squid-like being. This didn't stop him from watching, though. The well-built wizard he had seen before appearing seamlessly out of nowhere in front of him sure did though.

The large man looked at Kasar then craned his neck into the next room and shook his head. "Alright, time to get back to work. I have a portion of stone that could use your touch. Let's go."

Kasar did the only thing he could do in this situation. He followed the giant back outside into the inner court. The big man led him back towards the eastern alley, but stopped as soon as the exit came into view. The man pointed at the ground. "Here, you're responsible for this section. Make sure you inscribe legibly, now isn't the time for errors. But make haste, the hour approaches. I don't care what you do with your leisure activities, but the work must come first. Now get to it." The magus shoved a brush and large pot of green ink into Kasar's hands. He then turned his back and began walking towards the northern storehouse, loosening the belt on his robe while doing so.

Kasar watched the big man enter the storehouse. He placed the brush and ink pot on the ground and was about to make for the eastern alley when another large form stood before him. Where the other man was tall with broad shoulders, this man was short with a broad waistline. "Those glyphs are not going to paint themselves. The Great Old Ones are awaiting the completion of our work. Let us not disappoint them my friend."

Kasar did the only thing he could think of—he nodded and got down on his hands and knees. The chubby man waddled away. Kasar knew if he tried to leave again without completing this work he would most likely be discovered. He had no choice but to inscribe the black floor. But with what? Whatever language these wizards were inscribing was foreign to him.

It should have been. The language was ancient even in the times of Atlantis, Lemuria, and Muu. However, Kasar was excellent with a brush; although he had no idea what the glyphs actually meant, he could copy them quite easily. He started at the outside edges of his assigned space and took time to observe the glyphs others had placed in there sections. Blessed with a good memory, Kasar was able to memorize dozens of them and apply them to his own section, although not quite in the same order. Luckily for him, his section wasn't very large, so he was able to complete this task without much trouble.

Once he had inscribed his last glyph he stood up and looked over his work. His chest actually puffed out a bit, he was so proud of himself. Kasar put the stopper in the ink pot and tucked it, along with the brush under his robes. He saw the sun begin to peek up over the horizon, and realized he had been here far longer than he thought. It was now or never: he had to make his exit. Zigzagging his way through the crowd, he saw how focused the mages seemed to be on their tasks. Kasar was wondering what could be so important. He let this thought slip his mind, as he reached the eastern alleyway and was home free, when he felt a hand on his shoulder. He stopped turned around and saw a tall, supple, female magus towering over him.

"Keep this in mind worm, the next time you feel the need to watch." His nether regions exploded with pain as she shot a knee into his groin. Kasar fell to the ground, but luckily the magus walked away and left him there writhing in agony. Evidently word had gotten around about him peeping in the storehouse. Kasar couldn't afford to stay on the ground for too long, though. No good would come of the extra attention. He managed to make it to his feet and waddle down the alleyway to the beach. From there, Kasar gutted it out and waded into the sea, where he crossed over the sandbar and collapsed into the skiff. He laid in the boat for a few minutes before the pain subsided enough for him to operate it and begin his return voyage to Guspar.

IV

Arlak, high priest of the Order of the Great Old Ones, stood in the center of the inner court surrounded by green glyphs. The midnight hour approached. The members of the Order formed a circle around him, their hands joined together. Some of them appeared to be a bit unsteady and inebriated to him. Arlak found it difficult to cast judgment on them, for he also enjoyed the celebrations earlier in the day. He was not concerned; the Order has been preparing for this day for centuries. The stars and planets had aligned and all earthly and celestial bonds and locks could be shattered. He was confident the summoning ceremony would be successful.

Arlak raised his arms into the air and with his deep, booming voice roared to his followers. "Let us begin!"

The Order chanted in a dark tongue, and the glyphs on the floor began to glow. As they continued, the glyphs actually began to rotate around them, moving faster and faster. The star-filled sky began to darken as black clouds began to form over the island. The surrounding sea began to churn and torrents of water shot high into the sky. The chanting continued and the phenomena only intensified. As the Order recited the conclusion of the incantation, an audible boom should have been heard and the ground should have quaked at the arrival of the masters.

Arlak heard nothing, and felt nothing. When he opened his eyes it was to the same star-filled sky he had witnessed at the beginning of the summoning ritual. He broke through the members of the Order and ran to the beach to observe the sea. When he arrived, he saw only calm waters. He fell to his knees in agony. The ritual had failed and they had missed their opportunity. By his estimates, another chance of summoning their masters wouldn't come for quite some time.

The high priest stood up and faced his followers. "Nobody breathes a word of this to anyone. The return of the Great Old Ones is still forthcoming."

V

Zeki had his shop locked up tighter than a fortress. The fence had not moved for hours, he couldn't bring himself to take his eyes off the profits. High stacks upon high stacks of gold coins littered his desk. He thought of how he was going to spend his share of the fortune. Then he thought about Nahuel. Just where was that damn sorcerer? The wizard had said he would only be gone for a few days, but it had been almost a week since Nahuel had departed. Zeki had decided he couldn't wait forever, and went ahead and made some initial sales of the powder without Nahuel. The sorcerer had told him to wait for his return, but what if he never came back? Yes, a dangerous life, that of a sorcerer. Zeki thought if that were the case he could just keep all of this for himself.

"Oh! Well done, my good man!"

Zeki just about fell out of his chair upon hearing Nahuel's voice coming from behind him.

"Nahuel! It... is so good to see you back. I was worried something must have happened to you."

"Oh just a bit delayed is all! No need to worry! Oh and look at this golden hoard! Oh how I love a partner who takes the initiative! Bravo! I knew you were a quick study and would be able to dilute the powder properly. I just knew it! Well done, Zeki!"

Zeki felt his stomach drop. "I'm sorry? Dilute the powder? You never mentioned that before..."

Nahuel sat down and rested his chin on his fist while contemplating. "I didn't? Hmm, that's most unfortunate, most unfortunate. You see, the kirin powder is quite potent. Unless you cut it with another substance, there will be some adverse side effects. Not only that, but when mixed we would be able to sell more of it. Just how much pure kirin powder have you sold Zeki?"

"Well...I sold about a quarter of what was in the flask. But don't worry, Kasar was most clever. He used the map canister to smuggle even more powder off the island. I doubled his rate for this as a bonus, which is nothing compared to these rewards you see before us. Between what's left in the flask and the entirety of the canister we have plenty left to dilute and sell."

Nahuel eyed Zeki suspiciously. "And how much have you taken for personal use, my friend?"

Zeki put his hands out in front of him. "Oh, not a lot, just enough to support my nightly activities. After all, a salesman must be able to stand behind his product, right? I have to say the results have been amazing!"

The wizard shook his head and looked down at the floor, "I'm sorry, good Zeki, then I'm afraid it is too late for you."

The fence's heart skipped a beat and he began to perspire as he stared dumbfounded at Nahuel. Then Zeki felt the muscles in his back and neck begin to spasm and heard popping sounds coming from all over his body. He felt his jaw bones separate and push outward. He fell to the floor and clutched the sides of his head.

Zeki looked up into the eyes of Nahuel, pleading with him to do something. Then his vision of the wizard became a shade of red. It was the final thing Zeki would ever remember seeing.

VI

Kasar was walking through the streets, his head down and his hands in his pockets. They were gripped around what was left of his earnings. Zeki paid him fairly well, but by the time he settled his debts and paid in advance for his lodgings, he hardly had any gold pieces left. He cursed his luck, and decided he had better go see Zeki about another job.

However, as he turned the corner and passed by the noble quarter, he saw chaos personified. Buildings were on fire and bodies lay in the street, broken and bloody. To his horror, some of them appeared to be women, but some were members of the City Watch as well. Kasar looked farther down the street and saw dozens of watchmen battling what appeared to be a pack of large apes. Oddly enough, the muscular simians were dressed in fine clothing. While Kasar was no coward, he was not equipped to handle a sight as unusual as this. He was about to turn around and run when Nahuel appeared behind him. Blood caked the wizard's ebon robes. Kasar took a step back.

"Oh! I apologize for surprising you, my friend! No need to worry, this isn't my blood. But I have grave news to report: our stalwart friend Zeki has perished. I tried to save him, but alas I was too late." The wizard brought his hands to his eyes and mimed wiping away tears. Then he pointed to the heavens and smiled. "However, we are in luck! With his dying breath Zeki declared you to have half of his share! The other half will go to his wife, but he felt you deserved a proverbial piece of the pie too! Here is an initial installment!" The magus reached into his robes and produced a large bag which he extended out to Kasar.

Kasar took the sack of gold coins in his hand and nearly dropped it. The bag was so heavy he needed to use two hands to hold it. "Th-Thank you sir! I always knew Zeki was looking out for me! Now I'll have to carve out a hiding place in my floorboards to store this."

Nahuel raised an eyebrow, then poked Kasar in the chest with a bony finger. "You will do no such thing. Tomorrow you will head to the counting house and make a deposit first thing in the morning."

"But sir, I'm afraid they'll rob me blind. The counting house is only for the city nobles."

The wizard shook his head and pointed at his own chest. "Young man, I own the counting house. Open an account and tell them Nahuel sent you. Keep depositing your payments and buy yourself a nice space in the noble quarter."

Nahuel turned and began walking away from the scene, but then stopped and turned back around. He flashed Kasar a big smile. "From what I hear there is going to be a large number of vacancies. It's a buyer's market!"

The Speaker
Taylor Foreman-Niko

I.

The clock tolls, a doleful sound that echoes through the vastness of my home. Marie looks up as the chimes follow, as if frozen in that moment of announcement. I see the fear seep into her, a trickle at first that I'd spotted hours earlier in the mild hurriedness of her attentions, so different from the Marie of daylight, now made into a trembling desire to flee. She knows what day it is. She remembers.

The chimes cease and Marie lets out a long, quiet breath, then leans over and pours me a cup of tea. The amber liquid steams as it fills the China, assaulting my nostrils with the herbaceous musk of the Orient. It is said to increase the acuity of one's mental faculties. I rarely drink anything else.

She finishes pouring and straightens, a pleading in her eyes.

"Thank you, Marie. You may go."

Relief. She mutters her goodnight and begins to walk away.

"Marie?"

She stops, anxiety in her young face. "Yes, Sir?"

"You left the front door cracked open, as instructed?"

"Of course, Sir."

"Good. Leave quietly. I shall see you in the morning."

She inclines her head in a slight bow and walks from the room. I hear her clean up only briefly before the door to the servants' quarters closes.

And I am alone.

I sit in the study. I don't call it my study, for it is not mine, nor was it my father's, or his father's before him; the same could be said for this house. We are merely occupants, placeholders; that three of our line have dwelt in this place is both an honor and a curse. For the role of incumbent Speaker comes with this house. Or at least it has for the last seventy years.

The house itself carries no value to Them. I asked my father why once. The answer was predictable. In this business, vagaries and half-truths are rampant; it is not the house, it is this point of cursed geography upon which it sits that matters, imbued with cosmic significance both arcane and unknowable to all but the most ancient of beings.

For forty-two years I have held vigil here, as the world has aged around me, as the forests shrank and the horizon became marred by tall buildings and billowing smoke. Yet in a manner I have been fortunate. My Grandfather spent most of his sixties scouring the Philippines for the Meeting Place, consumed with triumph one day, only to know desperation the next. To locate the Meeting Place is as fickle and inscrutable an art as dowsing for water, taking a number of artifacts and time to locate. These artifacts are now arrayed about me in cases or upon stands, awaiting the day they will have to be used again, if all does not come to darkness in the meantime.

That the point of the Meeting Place has remained here from the years of my study until now has been fortunate, affording me the opportunity to train the next Speaker in a relatively controlled environment, devoid of the dangers of the more exotic places of our world. Her name is Hollis and I think she will do well in the times to come for hers is a heart so consumed by love for the human race that she will sacrifice all, as I have, to see it continue.

It shames me to know that her well-meaning optimism will one day be broken. She is a good girl. Intelligent, exacting, thoughtful. Kind. I have never known a better Candidate. Not even my Peter.

I have learned from my mistakes with him and she is not here this night. The servants have also been sent home. I sit in the study, the walls festooned with the exploits of my fathers: animal heads, ivory horns, curving swords, ritual masks, and athames of dark and terrible origin. The floor is covered with exotic skins pulled from the bodies of beasts from places I have never been, places I will never see. Oil portraits of my father and grandfather look down upon me from above a crackling fireplace. I look at their eyes as I often do, searching for meaning in those enigmatic, neutral expressions. Do they judge me worthy despite my sheltered life? Do they doubt me even though I had no choice? Do they pity the man who has grown older than both of them, now bent by the inexorable assault of time?

The grandfather clock tolls once more and I return to myself. Another hour has passed. My tea is cold. I sip it anyway, welcoming the bitter tang upon my tongue. Any moment now, it will begin. I think I am ready. I know I am. The tomes that line my shelves have served me well in my vigil, being both friend and mentor after the disappearance of my father and later the death of my Peter.

Some I found in the forgotten corners of university basements; others I paid for in gold; some were bought with blood. Yet all of the sacrifices have been worth the knowledge held within their pages and I would not undo any fell deed that has come to pass at my command. Mine is the work of a savior, not encumbered by the bounds of human religion. For I know the terrible truth of the universe and of the unfathomable darkness that lurks in the yawning beyond.

A knock sounds at the door of the study.

It is here.

II.

"Come in," I say. I do not stand, for this is more a meeting of opposing forces than the greeting of an old friend.

The door opens and it enters. This year it appears in the guise of a young man, no older than twenty-five. He has only recently been taken, for his movements are jerky and irregular, like a marionette in the hands of a novice.

"Speaker," he rasps. He mouths the words, but the movement is all wrong. The teeth seem too big, the lips too red, like some livid gash in pallid flesh.

"Emissary," I say. I do not hide my disdain. We are far beyond niceties.

He, for that is what I shall call him, shambles stiffly to the large leather chair set opposite mine, looking as if with each step he is struggling not to be pulled into the air – perhaps his body wants to return to where he belongs, no matter his mission. He falls into the chair rather than sits, a jumble of gangly limbs, his neck lolling. I nearly spit at this macabre puppet display. The foolish part of me wants me to demand that he shed this insulting deception. However, I do not know if I would survive bearing witness to his true form and we have a game to play.

"Thomas," he says.

And it begins. The conversation that will prolong our existence or bring it all to a cataclysmic end.

"What?"

"Thomas," he repeats, his tongue sounding thick in his mouth. "That was his name, this acolyte of the Truth. He gave himself willingly." He smiles a rictus grin and the look sends a trickle of hot fear spreading in the back of my chest. "He knew without knowing. He believed."

"We call that 'faith.'"

He laughs, a sepulchral gurgle that sounds like someone drowning in earth.

"I know of your faith, Speaker. Misplaced as it is."

"I have no faith, you know this."

"Perhaps," he says, regarding me with brown eyes, stained black in the dim light of the study. The firelight gleam in them gives his face a hellish aspect and I question whether or not he purposefully chose a man that looked like Peter.

"Or perhaps not," he continues. "Religious faith, no. But in something...greater?"

I think for a moment. In the years of my vigil I have grown accustomed to these prologues. I wonder if they have purpose or are merely the indulgences of a weary ancient that has awaited the fulfillment of prophecy for far too long.

"I have faith in potential."

"Potential," he repeats, as if mulling over the taste of the word in his mouth. "Explain."

I keep my answers short. I know him. He likes the sound of his own voice.

"Potential in the goodness of humanity."

"Potential, like the future, is immaterial."

"Immaterial, yes, but the thought holds value."

He ponders this for a moment, his odd eyes drifting about the room. Absently, I think of what is happening behind that mask of human flesh, what peculiar logic and intuition guide a being so foreign, so intrinsically *other*.

"Like faith." he says at last, his gaze returning to me. I'm uncertain whether or not there is a question in his voice.

"Like faith," I say, doing what I can to assuage him. I do not like this monster from another world, but the rules have always been nebulous. I have never known how much of my success is dependent upon his judgment.

A rumbling noise rattles in his chest, a sound which I've come to know in our years of parley as a sigh. Ponderous this time, instead of bored. That's good.

"Is that why you continue?" he asks.

"Yes." It is a simple answer, but the truth.

"Continue, despite what happens beyond?" He makes a vague gesture towards the tall, shuttered window on the wall opposite the fireplace. "I have wandered far and seen much, Speaker. Your optimism fascinates me."

"Why?"

"Because it is so wholly blind to the sad reality of this place which you think is yours, but is not yours."

"Ignorance is not the fault of the people, especially when your master and his kin have not revealed themselves to us."

"And would your people follow, regardless?"

It's a good question. In my experience humans are often capricious, illogical beings. The familiar comforts them. The new is often shunned, no matter the evidence that exists to support it.

"I do not know."

"I walked the trenches of the Great War," he says, a sickening relish painted across his unnatural visage. "There I saw death unfathomable. Thousands upon thousands given to the void, and for what?"

The answers to this question are innumerable, yet all I know is this: many good men died; some of them had been friends from my university days abroad in England. They'd joined up in their advanced age because of a sense of duty, the very same feeling which beats within me now, not nearly as storied, nor dramatic, but just as important. All of this passes through my mind in an instant; I do not let it reach my face. I wait for the answer that I know he will give me.

"Land. People. Dust. Dust upon dust." He licks his lips and there's something feral in the movement, despite the youth and handsomeness of his body. "If only they knew about the Tide of Ending that approaches even now. That this world will be made an abattoir of suffering, immeasurable and everlasting. And in this great pyre the Old Ones shall cavort upon the bones of your foolish people, so dedicated to their own destruction that they did not see the chaos which already lingered upon their doorstep."

My fingers have sunk into the arms of my leather chair, knuckles white, the veins in my hands bulging. I hate him. I hate him with all that there is of me for what he has done and will do should I fail, for all that he represents. He looks at me with a predatory gaze: the bloodthirsty look of anticipation, of hunger. I know this is the end of our prologue. The true test is about to begin.

"I've had enough of your eschatological drivel. You have come to the appointed Meeting Place, Emissary. Shall we begin?"

The creature that occupies the body of Thomas leans forward, excitement contorting its abhorrent face in a parody of glee.

"Let's."

III.

"I think you will enjoy this one," he says and cold fingers of dread worm their way into my limbs, an anxious itch that cannot be scratched.

"Get on with it." I tire of his words. His dead smile. Though I know a world exists beyond this room, that trees sway, smoke rises, and a gibbous moon hangs high, it matters not. My reality has been reduced to four walls and two chairs. And I the only human in the room.

"Speak the primordial name of my master."

The command nearly strikes the air from my lungs and my jaw clenches. *Don't*, I tell myself, *don't give him the satisfaction.* I know he has done this on purpose. I know because he asked the same question of me as Peter looked on through the peephole beside the bookshelf.

"I hope there are no fledgling Speakers about this time," he says and I do not need to look at him to see the smile in his words.

The primordial language. The blackest speech. I have studied tomes of this foul tongue, bound in human flesh, scrawled in an abrasive hand that undulates and writhes beneath my sight. To see is one thing, to speak another.

"You know that I cannot speak his name fully with my human tongue." I try to not let desperation seep into my words; I fail.

"The attempt will suffice," he purrs.

The room has grown quiet. The fire, still lively in its hearth, flickers without crackling. The wind outside has ceased. The creaking of this ancient prison has abated, if only for a moment. It's as if the whole world has taken a breath and now waits upon me. Peter's face flashes behind my eyes and I remember the sound of him choking in the passageway adjacent, the crushing helplessness I felt as I knew the Emissary had outsmarted me. The first rule I learned as a Speaker is that one must complete the test. The Meeting Place cannot be left or the trial has been failed. On that dark night, I spoke the words, yes, but with each moment, my son kicked and spat his way further into oblivion, unable to survive their otherness.

"Well?" he says.

This time he has faltered. This time there is no one to lose. Only my life, which is inconsequential. I only need pass the Third Trial. Hollis has instructions should I perish. *Yes, everything will be alright.* I think this, because I must, because the agony of what is about to come.

I open my mouth and speak His name.

The primordial tongue explodes from me; the syllables pass like jagged shards of glass, scraping up my esophagus, and lancing across my tongue and the insides of my cheeks. A single utterance seems a lifetime, each nanosecond charged with white-hot pain. Each letter exits from me in a torrent of black bile, thick and viscous. It spurts into my lap and onto the tiger's skin beneath my feet, too much for a human body to have held. I feel like bursting, pain wracking my chest and back, crackling through my head. My ears are wet and my eyes sting, but I do not stop. I will not. For my father and my father's father, for Peter, for Hollis, for the whole damn world.

The last syllable leaves my torn lips and it is done. The torrent of filth abates and I'm left sodden and stinking in my chair, trembling, feeling as if I'm bruised both inside and out. And through it all, I force myself to smile. Peter would have liked that.

The thing inside Thomas is not amused. That much is clear on his face. He thought he had me. Not this Meeting. Not yet.

"Commendable," he says, the word tinged with annoyance.

"Indeed," I say, a trickle of blood sluicing over my lip. I tongue a ragged hole in my gums. I think I've swallowed a tooth. "What is next?"

He glares at me and I bask in the hostility of his attention. My body aches. I wipe absently at my face. My shirt sleeve comes away blackened by ichor wept from my eyes. I wonder what I look like to him and almost laugh. Perhaps I am going mad. Yet even insanity I cannot enjoy, not until my task is complete. I push down the giddiness spawned from my victory and await the Second Trial.

IV.

When he speaks, there is no longer any mischief in his voice. The smirk is gone, replaced by the air of haughtiness I first witnessed through the peephole at the age of ten as my father sparred with him.

"I am the great lie," he says. He is no longer leaning forward, instead reclining in the leather chair like a judge passing sentence. Only conviction marks his words, which are uttered through the too-big teeth of his vessel.

"I am the poisonous balm," he continues. "Where I dwell, foolishness dwells also. Where I sing, so do the hearts of men. In the hands of deceivers, I have assuaged the hordes with promises of an after. I give strength to the futile and the doomed. The irony of the death throes of those I fuel feed oblivion, from which none can hide. I am immaterial. I am false. I am a cruel joke, given unto you only to be taken away."

His dark eyes regard mine.

"What am I?"

I ponder his words in silence and wonder at how the whole of the future of this tiny planet, sequestered in a galaxy among innumerable galaxies, depends upon the words I next speak. *Oblivion,* I think, the word echoing deep in my mind. He likes to use this word. I imagine it ugly and black upon his tongue, the color of the deep, eternal dark beyond the realm of time and space, where the Old Ones dwell. I remember Peter's face when I first told him about those dread sentinels that watch and wait to destroy us. His face fell and tears sprung to his eyes. A paternal pang twinged inside my chest and I leaned forward, comforting him. I told him that we could stop it. That there was a way we could save everyone.

He looked up at me and a smile broke upon his face. That image warms me to this day and fills me with...

"Hope," I say.

A guttural growl sounds from within him; I can see his nails digging into his palms. One of his eyes, slack and malformed to whatever lurks beneath it, twitches, as if hearing the word pains him. Yet he does not strike out, nor voice his disappointment. No. He has one more chance this Meeting. One last Trial of his choosing that will see us either to a new day or cataclysm.

"Shall we proceed?" I say.

He wets his lips with a pale tongue and begins to speak.

V.

The words whisper out of him like a death rattle, laden with the unfathomable weight of his dread purpose.

"I am the deep dark, the slow decay. I am the cancer at the heart of paradise, insatiable, unthinking. I believe I am the New God, but this is a lie. Ignorance spurs me to violence. Greed leads me to squander. Fear goads me to hate. I am weak. I am petty. In me, darkness is made manifest. In me, all ill things come to pass. In me, there is only ending; for every addition I make, a score must be subtracted. For every boon, a tragic cost. I am the great devourer."

He quiets, a challenge in his glaring eyes.

"What am I?"

Silence but for the beating of my heart. Sweat trickles down my temples, mingling with the black ichor. I think on his words and can only see red. Red in my mind and in my heart. The color of blood.

My eyes pull from him, sweeping across the study, taking in the trophies that are scattered about the room, the work of my father and grandfather. A tiger's skin. A rhino's horn. A stuffed bird now said to be extinct. So many precious things. Have we always killed to show our worth?

A framed picture on the mantle shows my grandfather standing in front of a group of young, naked men with ebon skin. He smiles as he holds up his kill for the camera. My gaze settles on their eyes in the background. What do I see there? What lies did he tell them when he bought their services? What lies did so many others ply as they put manacles about wrists and set chains to free people?

The chains turn into tank treads in my mind, gnawing their way across European soil, pulping meat and bone beneath their titanic weight. Screams fill the air along with the buzz of bullets and the crack of gunfire. A man yells in one language as he's mounted by another who speaks in his own tongue; they cannot understand one another. They wrestle in the gore-soaked earth, *dust upon dust*, like he said. Two forms, the same, but different, separated by earth and ideology, governed by their fears, their ignorance, and sometimes their greed...

"Humanity," I say and I know I have won, yet there is no victory in my words.

He examines me with a long, thoughtful look, as if he's surprised.

"Yes," he says simply, "that is what you fight for." A small frown parts his lips and he shakes his head in disbelief. "Is it really worth it?"

The question surprises me and for a moment I see just how ancient he is, how sad and eternal his mission has been. Something cool and melancholic fills my throat and I fight the urge to pity him.

"It is," I say.

"Why?"

Now it is time for me to smile.

"Potential."

His eyes narrow, but he does not speak. He stares at me for a long time and then—

VI.

It's morning.

I am sitting in my chair, still covered in the mess of my unnatural vomit. I groan as I stand. The embers burn low in the fireplace. My father and grandfather look at me from their portraits and what is that I see? A slight smirk of acknowledgment? No, perhaps not.

I cross slowly to the shuttered window and throw it open. A clear, glorious day assaults me, washing me in light and warmth. Trees sway about the mansion grounds. Beyond, smoke puffs into the sky from dirtied stacks alongside the growing towers of industry; the sounds of the city drift over the forested countryside, melodic in their distance, reassuring. The sun blazes high in the sky.

I smile as I take it all in: the good, the bad, and all that lies between. A new day has come and the Earth remains. The Old Ones will have to wait for their cataclysm.

I stand in the sunlight for a long time.

Mosaic
Mark Sims

The southern slopes of the Himalayas are bathed in starlight as the time hewn alabaster peaks glow an effervescent indigo over distant, rocky and lightly forested foothills. In jagged ravines of sparse growth and precarious entry, ancient caverns lie hidden and rarely seen. One such cavern lies dark and hollow, empty but for the form of an aged and withered Sufi chanting weakly in the pitch black. At the end of a winding narrow passage, the mystic squats on haunches in utter darkness, a reed textile basket of small square tiles sits by his side. He mutters and whispers as he reaches into the receptacle and swirls bone thin fiercely nailed fingers amid the gem fragments therein. He picks a tiny jade square from the bin and holds it before his face. He peers at it from scarred and empty sockets whose orbs were stolen long ago in a ritual much like this one. From a patterned combination of signs and shapes that are keys to dimensional locks, celestial pathways and windows into the unperceivable are constructed. His eyes he had willingly removed as a trade for true sight, the spiritual vision that transcends the five senses as we know them- cognitive comprehension beyond the material.

The jade square is rolled and examined between soil stained, calloused fingers. The long matted beard sways from his chin, a grimy gray flag of disapproval, as he shakes his head and replaces the tile to search for another. Humming in the inky enclosure reverberates from ageless crystalline formations and thin calcite columns as the loosely turbaned, filthy wool cloaked magician smiles in wizened toothless pleasure at a find in the loose bound fibrous basket. A ruby square of blood red milk shade is produced from the lot and without examination is placed in a spot on the floor before him. It clicks into place between two others positioned together to form the final piece of a vibrant hexagram inlaid with hexagrams upon hexagrams, folding and bundling into each other in an impossible hornet's nest of lines and angles that baffle the observer in its endless pattern of complexity and near unbelievable arrangement of an uneasy absolute perfection.

Miles away a lone rider takes shelter from a rain deluge that has his mount struggling through foul sections of washed out trail and the constant birthing of new rivulets. The horse's hooves make way up a ravine amid a downpour that has the rider completely cloaked in a sweeping olive green poncho that does little to keep the dampness from his bones. Lightning strikes and illuminates a crumbling stone structure on the hillside offering a small depression into the cliff to take refuge from the downpour and the traveler takes advantage of the rare cover amid the sparsely treed hills. He appears a bulky mass in the saddle as he dismounts and enters what was left of a small overhang. Removing the poncho, he unstraps a wood stocked automatic rifle and drops a pack off of his back to easily access a GPS from a satchel at his front. He waits for it to power up hunched in the corner with his back to the storm outside. Water drips down his forehead from his soggy turban and he mops his brow with an even wetter arm. Once ready, he locates his position and finds his destination. According to his device, he is right atop his goal. Finding this crumbling shelter is a good sign that he is on track and it is a good place to leave his mount. He shall walk from here.

To Rashid Azeem this was but a nuisance. A wet and soggy exploit into the vast and empty wilds that he loathed. Rashid had been groomed by the mosque since his birth as he was born into a wealthy family with strong ties to the faith. He had been educated at both Oxford and MIT, his post graduate studies were done in the Netherlands and his travels tended to take place amid paved streets and marbled hallways. This scrambling through the mud was not fitting to him in any way but he shook off the cold and headed in the direction of the coordinates. The blinding rain and thick cloud cover made the task a hazy ordeal with difficulty in finding firm footing. To his dismay, the direction was up a sharp slice ravine that offered a heavy stream of water and very little room to either side. He waded up the first cascade while holding fearfully to the sides and when he made it to a bend ahead, he beheld his destination. The amber stream flowed down a ledge concealing a wide hole in the earth just behind the storm inspired falls. He cursed beneath his breath at the soggy muddiness of it all and cut through the sheet of brown water to enter.

The wide hole opened up nicely into a broad chamber where he could feel its emptiness and the sigh of cool air from beyond. Taking a glow stick from his satchel, he cracked it and held it up as he nervously swept the area with his rifle barrel.

The chamber dazzles and glimmers in the soft glow of the luminous chemical light. There is gold lace twisting through patterns of onyx, pearl and alabaster interlaced with myriad shards of precious gems and volcanic glasses. Rashid Azeem was blinded momentarily at the sudden assault on his senses but was quickly able to identify a gold trimmed intricately swirled iron door across the way cut into the living rock and sided by an alcove containing a large rectangular brass gong and metal ringer,

His only instructions from the Clerics that sent him here was to ring the gong and present the information they supplied to the Sufi that answered. There was honor in this task as this site was one of the most hidden, archaic and holy places in the tradition. The place was unknown, unspoken of and privy information to a loose handful of practitioners of an ancient sect that was attached to the very pinnacle of the clergy. The rites and customs of this sect were even more mysterious than the location of their temples and the messenger's imagination reeled with images of Djinn and devils in the eerie green glow stick illumination. He squeezed his thick black beard like a sponge and his head wrapping was awkwardly heavy from its soaking and he longed to take it off and wring it out but such an act in such a place was surely blasphemy. Having severely examined the room around him, he found courage to step forward and approached the door to ring the gong.

Rashid tried to wipe the mud from his hands before he grasped the cast iron ball ended bar that hung at the gong's side mostly for his own satisfaction rather than respect for the holy instrument before him. He raised the ringer and was reluctant to swing it hard in the solid silence of the subterranean arena so he tapped it. The noise was deafening. Reverberations from the initial tap rose to an ear splitting din which caused the loose tiles in the intricate decor to rattle madly and chime shrilly as their vibratory trembling caused gems to twinkle and sparkle with cosmic intensity. Rashid covered his ears and fell to his knees, struck dumb and rigidly frightened by the sensory violence he experienced and then it stopped abruptly leaving only a fierce ringing in his head. He eyed the entrance he had came through and minded a quick escape but fought the urge off as he thought he heard motion from behind the door.

His suspicion was confirmed as metallic fumbling could be heard behind the gold swirled steel plate before him. There was heavy clanking and the soft exhale of a broken seal as the door swung slowly inward with grinding patience. His glow stick barely scratched the darkness of the revealed chamber and the white of the walls where he stood aided in darkening the open doorway. He saw motion and stepped back as a ghastly and withered old man shuffled from the inky darkness. The old mystic was hunched and slow as he ambled forward on earth blackened, talon twisted arthritic feet. He was soiled from head to toe from life in the cave dust and a solemn gray over toned his gnarled skin and tattered robe. His turban was a filthy cloth saturated with ages of grime. The most disturbing sight, to top it off, was the utter absence of eyes, the sockets of the wise man were sagging slots of scar tissue and dirt crust, dark and hollow in the vague glow of the chemical stick.

"Alas you have arrived" he said,"I have waited long."

Rashid Azeem replied through nerve dry lips " The journey was horrible. Mud slides, tree falls and the ever pouring ran. It is a miracle I made it. I fear that with the continuing rain, my passage back may be impossible as the creeks and gullies were rising before my eyes as I crossed."

"There is plenty of time for return," the old man said, "I trust you have brought the new coordinates with you? Please, let us have a look at them."

Rashid was humored by the man's choice of words. Having no eyes would make "having a look" quite difficult, he mused. Regardless of the absurdity, he produced a lap top computer from his bag and proceeded to load a flash drive. The old man and he sat at a stone carved bench slotted into the dazzling wall and waited for the information to load.

The old Sufi spoke, " I have been here since my youth, creating the pattern and following the cosmic avenues that lead to eternity. I have seen the beginning and end of all creation from the eyes of the creator yet still I long to see more."

There was the "see" word again. Perhaps the old man had been blind for so long that he had lost its meaning. As the screen came to life, its added light doubly illuminated the entry chamber. The digital glow revealed deep crevices in the old man's face a he leaned towards the device appearing to view it impossibly from an eyeless visage.

"What do you have there?" he asked, "Bring up the star charts, I want to know if my work has been accurate, it is very important that we track its movement."

Rashid moused and clicked about the screen to bring up the information. He had no idea what was on the flash drive and the old man was making very little sense. What was he talking about? What was being tracked? Finally the screen came alive with an animated star map of some vague section that Rashid could not identify off hand, there at the center of the screen was a darker spot, it appeared to be an emptiness or void, the old man placed his finger on the dark spot on the screen.

"There!" he exclaimed, "So it is true, the old one returns despite our efforts at disrupting the celestial streams, our cosmic barriers are in the wrong place!" He stood up and paced the room, Rashid remained motionless and veritably confused by the old man's mad talk accompanied by an apparent ability to see the screen.

" Young man," he said, " The mosaics and the sacred geometries I design are manipulators of the galaxy, the Sufi tradition is to experience the creator through ourselves, very few of us can. When one experiences Him in this way, one becomes a part of Him and in conjunction with proper devotions and the sacred combinations devised through the patterns, that distant realm can be reached and through union with the creator, altered and influenced"

Rashid found this hard to believe, he was well aware of his faith and its mysticism but he was an educated man that found these things to be less literal and more symbolic ideas from a crudely civilized and superstitious age. His education had not damaged his devotion, in fact it was the opposite, he found the wonders of creation in algorithms and chemical reactions which solidified his belief in a more rational God created world. He preferred belief in a maker of rational order over a maker of ghosts and genies. His thought was that it was man's duty to discover the world's wonders and understand them thereby coming closer to understanding the mind of the creator. Caught in this surreal situation, he hoped his task was nearly over for the jeweled chamber and the gristly mystic made him uncomfortable.

The old man had him read off numbers and celestial positions in great detail. He carried on in explanation, " Long before the Earth was formed there were others, great and unimaginable Old Ones, the dwellers of the void that where vile corruptions of emptiness and nothingness incarnate. Denizens of the non-existent realms, these horrors ruled the vastness of space in utter dismal cold and darkness.When the creator uttered the word that became light, these horrors suffered a fearsome extermination, but not completely, for the creator's design in absolute perfection allowed for the darkness necessary to counterweight the light to its fullest potential. Horrid things fled to shadows and extra terrestrial subterranean lairs to slumber and hide from the light. One found the depths of the Earth's oceans to be its home and made its rest in the coldest darkest chasms of deepest recesses. The dreams of this Old One caused madness and delusion to mix with the night sky bringing fret and sorrow to all who slumbered on the surface. Life was in turmoil and those that suffered through this age were exposed to unfathomable misery. Eventually, powerful Djinn found its lair after eons of searching and following a cataclysmic confrontation they were able to drive it into the farthest reaches of the universe. The patterns and geometric complexities laid out in the great chamber deep in this mountain are critical in keeping the atrocity away. "

Still Rashid was skeptical and having a difficult time following the old man. He was fully capable of reading the star charts and understanding the nature of the universe as best one could. To his understanding, the spot on the screen was simply an area of space that was less dense than the other, or maybe an effect of something like a black hole. So far as he knew, there were no astrophysicists publishing papers on ancient interstellar deities.

"Please," he thought, "Be done with me so I can go home." He longed for a shower, a decent meal and lush lodging.

The wizened mystic went on and on about the nether realms and the thin fabric that separates time and space from utter chaos and eternal night. His oration continued for quite some time and Rashid begin to drift into sleep when the mystic clapped his hands and cried, "Come now! It is time for you to see!"

Rashid Azeem rose to his feet wearily and reached for his rifle that leaned against the tile wall.

"Leave it." muttered the old Sufi and he then pointed at the glow stick. "You mustn't bring that either, I will lead you."

Reluctantly, Rashid grabbed on to his guide's filthy sleeve and was lead beyond the ornate archway into the black beyond. Nervous at first, he gained composure as the floor proved to be of smooth tile and the mad mystic was a gentle escort. In complete surrender, he allowed the aged wise man to take him for several minutes down a long straight passage. He saw nothing, the utter darkness was impermeable, but he became aware that they had come into a huge open space. The echoes of the cavern gave hints of a spacious amphitheater and a lofty ceiling. His guide bid him sit and so he did, his hand feeling for assurance that he squatted safely on the smooth ground.

"Watch," whispered the mystic,"There are things that cannot be seen in the light," he began to hum low and chant softly. Rashid was not aware of what he was supposed to be watching in utter darkness so he sat quietly and waited for the old man to finish. The humming continued in guttural harmonic tones for quite some time and the observer felt the threat of sleep upon him once more, that is when he saw the Djinn.

Ahead of the two men, far in the center of the chamber, a lithe and thin form began to come into focus, faint and pale. it appeared to be lightly awash from inside with subtle starlight. Hardly a contrast to the darkness, the implied figure grew in height and girth until Rashid was stunned to see a mighty figure standing in plain view. Twisted ram's horns, mighty lions paws and sweeping outstretched wings appeared faintly in an eery glow against the ink backdrop. This fearsome apparition raised itself to a full, tall stance and raised its arms to the ceiling to throw its head back and emit a horrific howl. The echo quivered Rashid's neck hairs and he nearly wet himself as hundreds of Djinn dropped from above and surrounded the first. The rapid filling of the chamber with these figures gave testament to the vastness of the cavern as they neither crowded one another or ever allowed even the tips of their wings to meet.

The ground beneath each began to glimmer with the same faded star light and Rashid was able to make out the forms of different patterns at their feet. The tiles laid for generations by ancient masters emitted a dull shine in the darkness and each began to spin, roll, gyrate and twist at the feet of the Djinn. The Djinn began to swirl along with the patterns, a Dervish whirlwind of fluttering wings, wild manes and barbed tails appeared in front of the soggy messenger and he was fearful beyond his comprehension. The clicking and scraping of hooves and claws on the tiles was maddening, the spinning undulations were dizzying and uneasy as the whirling mass continued a howling chorus directly in front of him.

The maddening commotion was soon accompanied by the sound of rattling tiles as the patterns underfoot began to shimmer fiercely now and the watcher covered his eyes and gasped as each design burst into a brilliant light show of celestial wonder. Each ghastly Djinn now twirled above novas, galaxies, nebulae and brilliant star clusters. Comet tails dotted the scene as stars died, planets were born and the whole universe reeled sickeningly before him.

"This is the universe" began the ancient man beside him, "These are the doorways of celestial influence and astrological manipulation. From here we can stop the Old One from returning but the task is not complete, the Djinn whirl among the wrong stars...the pattern needs another life time and my time is nearly over. "

Rashid trembled in the darkness, the vast mind altering realization of what he observed had his intellect reeling and questioning every assumption he had ever had about anything. This was truly unreal. But it was real. Impossible. He thought this must be some sort of trickery. It would be very simple to conduct a play of lights at his expense. Perhaps his superiors and cohorts had executed a prankish rouse. He was able to momentarily gain hold of rational thought when the Sufi spoke once more.

"Another lifetime is required to complete the angular composition and it should be yours. You need to finish the mosaic. You must complete the pattern that detours the Old One."

This statement caught the young man off guard, he had no intention of staying in this dank hole in the ground despite the honor of the task's reverence. It was undoubtedly a chore that he was not suited for. He preferred silk divans and a leisure ordained with comfortable attributions. Furthermore, he preferred sunlight.

"You must continue the work laid before you, the toil is relentless and the danger is immense, do not falter," A thin bony hand grasped his arm, " You must begin at once."

The entire scene was more than he could take, the strange vision before him and the suggestion that he remain here compounded into an urge for him to run. He fumbled in his bag frantically and reached for a glow stick. He needed to find the exit and remove himself from the mind scathing scene as quickly as possible. The old man heard the crack of the chemical capsule and he cried, "No! No light here!" but it was too late, the sight that Rashid Azeem beheld froze him in his tracks and caused his mouth to gape.

In the light, the Djinn did not appear and the chemical stick exposed a vision far more terrifying. Those twisting tumbling patterns that covered the floors and walls were composed of dimensions and non-euclidean degrees that eyes could not comprehend and the visual cortex could not register. They held the mathematics of Hell, the angles of the abyss and the weight and measure of the demonic. Their composition defied reality and blasphemed the conformity of creation. To have laid tiles to compose such insanity would drive one mad unless one was blind, Rashid wished for temporary blindness now.

His lids were pried wide open by the sight, he could not close them, all he could do was view. The vision he endured assaulted his psyche violently and soon it consumed him. He felt as if the vision had entered him, as if he were understanding it now, as if he could almost see, but not quite. He felt sight now, literally felt it, like a caress on his mind, soothing and rational. The angles were beginning to make vague sense and their subtle comprehension induced a cognitive satisfaction unlike any he had ever experienced. He wanted to see them further. He wanted to experience them more. The overpowering lure of the promise in seeing beyond and the ecstasy of what he was experiencing gave him cause and reason to do what he did next.

He fell in reverent worship before the vision. Truly he was one with creation to experience this, if only he could see more. The passion drove him to rip, bare fingered, his own eyes from their very sockets as he knelt and sobbed at the beauty of the vision while surrendering to the true sight. The sight that transcends seeing.

The gristly old man that dwelt in the jeweled cave put a hand on his shoulder and said, "You may begin."

Hours later the gold swirled iron door is sealed once more and the heavy clanking of its mechanism assaults the silence of the empty cavern.

At the end of a winding narrow passage, Rashid Azeem squats on haunches in utter darkness. His soggy turban, thick beard and damp robe are heavy with cave dust. A reed textile basket of small square tiles sits by his side. He mutters and whispers as he reaches into the receptacle and swirls filthy fingers amid the gem fragments therein. He picks a tiny square from the bin and holds it before his face. He peers at it from blood caked and empty sockets whose orbs were stolen in a ritual much like this one.

Far down the trail, an ancient and withered Sufi braves the storm on horseback. Sunlight filtered through the cloud cover offers the first rays that have touched his skin for decades. He has done his duty for a lifetime in an unrivaled devotion and now he returns to take his last few breaths in retirement reclined upon silk divans, patiently awaiting a passing of leisure ordained with comfortable attributions.

The City of Stars
Robert Trska

I breathe heavy, throttle in hand as my arm shifts slightly. The onboard speedometer spits out 31.20 in bright blue LED lights, its photons scattering across the interior of the chamber in a dim glow. I am focused on a small view screen in front of me as digital objects appear and disappear from the display. Tiny pixelated shapes and polygons slide in from all directions, outlined in orange-red on a black background. The main HUD glimmers brightly with numbers, indicating the distance of each of the transient shapes. I glance once more to the blue light and my muscles tense, the numbers rapidly spinning down to an even 30.00. With a sharp exhale; I use my free hand to slam an overhead toggle, locking the LED.

I release the throttle, and the rhythmic, mechanical whirling of an engine dies down. A sense of relief washes over me and I break my sight from the screen. Its once black display was now littered with glowing shapes and geometries. Fixed in the center is a large, torus-shaped object, dwarfing the other items. I glance once more to the LED before switching another toggle on the mainboard in front of my seat.

"Bravo Zulu Alpha Sixty, we are locked at a travel velocity of 30 000 kilometers per hour. Our altitude remains a steady 400 clicks, but will require correction within the next hour or so."

"Copy that. And for God's sake Andy, just call me Jim."

"Copy, Jimmy."

I lean back in my seat, grinning, and take note of the surrounding instruments. Their dull hums resonate throughout the cockpit. Or at least what could be called a cockpit. Its tiny interior would be best described as closet with a chair. Crammed with wires and electrics, the small chamber held a switchboard littered with knobs, dials, and screens. The faint blue light of the speedometer idled at a steady 30.00, illuminating an assorted variety wires and junk. Despite its clutter the main focus of the cockpit, however, was a small aperture above the seat: a tiny porthole of glass and rivets, revealing the never-ending night outside.

Stretching my arms out, I lazily palm for a small packet from my left-breast pocket. My hand brushes across a small metal tag reading 'Cpt. Andy Summers- Astrocore Removal'. A slight frown creases across my face as I pull a cigarette from the packet and place it in my lips. Andy Summers, captain of the salvage vessel, 'Ragpicker', I mused to myself. Not the most prestigious of positions, though the ship has a suitable name for an equally dingy job at least.

Looking up to the porthole, I see the emerging crest of a beautiful blue and white sphere come into view. There it is, I thought. Earth. The only home we have, and here I am four hundred kilometers away in a metal tub, collecting garbage. Sighing, I pull up a lighter and start the end of my cigarette. Immediately a pitched alarm whines from the dashboard as a small 'No-smoking' light stutters on with a buzz. Leaning forward with a loud smack, my hand topples down on the sign as the last bits of electrical holding it together dislodge. With a jittering hiss of static, the light and sound fade.

Never was one for loud noises, I muttered to myself.

As the cockpit filled with a thin veneer of smoke, the ventilation fan whirred into life, struggling like a broken record. A thin plume of smoke wafts into the oxidized shaft, where its carbon and carcinogens get scrubbed through ancient filters and outdated purifiers. My eyes drift away from the vividly blue oceans and pearly clouds of the nearby planet as I pull another drag from the cigarette. Focusing back onto the small screen, the large orange-red torus lingered in its center. Must be some sort of abandoned satellite, or discarded scrap leftover from a larger vessel.

The world would of gone to shit had we stopped looking to the stars, I thought. The competition for asteroid mining near the inner belt brought new life to the space program over the past few decades. But as more and more demand for vessels increased, so did the amount of debris left in orbit, and that stuff doesn't go away. It wasn't until after the incident with the Prestige that a real effort was made to clear the night sky of leftover materials.

I remember that day, so many years ago. It was an outgoing supply ship set to provide materials and components to mining endeavours. On the cusp of breaking from Earth's gravity, there was a reported sensor malfunction of some sort. A piece of debris travelling 40 000 kilometers an hour collided with the Prestige. No bigger than a tennis ball, the hunk of scrap metal punched a hole through the hull and set the ship off course. In a matter of minutes the vessel was sent screaming back to Earth, crew and all. A shudder crept through me at the thought, as I cautiously glance at the view screen for any small orange pixels. A nervous feeling grew within me, and I find myself rapping fingers on the throttle next to the seat, the LED still idling at 30.00. Finishing the last puff of my cigarette, I lean forward and flick the communication switch on the mainboard.

"Jimmy, you there? We've got a big one about two hundred meters away, looks like a satellite."

"Yeah, I got that Andy. Can we harpoon this thing and be on our way?"

Rubbing my chin, I check the status of the onboard collection units. For medium sized debris, a magnetic-tipped rod is typically fired outwards to harness and reel it over. Alternatively, the course of debris can be changed towards the Earth, in hopes it will burn up upon reentry. For bigger operations, the target can be broken up into smaller pieces; however, this requires a finer touch. I pause and input a command for a diagnostic on the mainboard. Keying in several lines, a small terminal computes some algorithms and estimates the size of the debris in plain text: W10, L5, 1000Kg. I consider the next move. Hauling debris isn't exactly the safest job, but it's one that needs to be done.

"Negative, Jim. Debris is too big. We will have to do this manually. I'll pull us in closer."

I place my hand on the throttle and flick the overhead switch. The blue LED brightens once more as the numbers begin to fluctuate. 30.01... 30.05...I ease on the throttle and begin pulling closer to the object, minding the orange and black screen. My free hand clasps around a nearby control stick as I begin to orient to the floating debris. I feel the ship vibrate slightly from the thrusters as its mass adjusts course.

"Now would be a good time to suit up Jim, we are approximately seventy meters away. Just keep an eye out for any shards, my screen is starting to look like a Christmas tree."

"Copy. I'm heading to the airlock now."

I push the throttle up a notch, the engines whirling up once more for a quick pulse of speed. Within moments the distance of the object closed. Guiding the ship downwards, I maneuver its bulk around several lingering pieces on the screen. Whatever happened here left a lot of junk.

"Alright Jim, we're about fifteen meters out. I'll keep an eye on any shards or clutter."

Still clutching the control rod, I hesitantly wait for Jim to exit the ship and move towards the debris. A dull warning tone echoes in the cockpit as the exit airlock depressurizes. I flick another switch on the grubby mainboard, prompting a nearby screen to spring to life. Bits of noise distort the image, but I clearly recognize Jim tethered to the ship, floating towards the object. On the view screen, a polygonal green figure moves towards the large orange torus as the computer tracks his movement.

"What do you see, Jim?"

"Just like you guessed, Andy. Fried satellite. Its panels are beat to all hell, but there looks to be a decent amount of salvage on it. I'm moving in to find any hard points that I can connect to."

With his approach the screen increased in static, the sporadic rhythm of white sound and grain interfering with the instruments. I give the screen a slight nudge on the side and lean back into my seat, looking to the porthole above. The pearly clouds of Earth weightlessly part in spirals to expose the vast ocean beneath them, its deep shades of sapphire and azure washing together in unfathomable depths. I take a deep breath and lower my sight at the display as a rapid and oncoming orange blur registers to my mind.

In a sudden clangor the mainboard lit up. Frantically I look about, a sudden fear welling in my stomach. My ears ring in pain, preceding a jarring impact that curved through the hull of the ship and into my body. Heaving in my seat, the harness digs into my chest, pulling the wind from my lungs. I gasp for air as the alien shriek of twisted metal and depressurizing cabins chorus through the vessel and electrical instruments short on and off. The view screen of Jim went black.

Looking above, I see the Earth spin uncontrollably, its blue oceans becoming a blur with the clouds. In the pandemonium, the automated system detected a loss of oxygen and hull integrity, and began to partition the cockpit from the main cabin.

My ears pop from the immediate pressure change as the chamber sealed itself with an intimidating hiss. Gathering my wits, I grab the throttle and control stick in attempt to stabilize the ship, as the electronics balanced between life and death. Bathed in the blue light of the LED, the steady 30.00 ran rampant from the power surging and shorting within it. I feel an intense vibration beyond the sputtering engines and realize we had been knocked into a rapid descent.

I wrench and pull on the controls; the rapid spin had evened out yet the ship was unable to escape the gravitational pull. We were falling towards Earth. Panicked I opened all communications in attempt to reach Jim.

"Ji---m do yo- co---py? J---im"

Static. Shit. Shit. Shit.

With no response, I sat in silence as the ship lurched and plummeted towards the ocean. Minutes passed and the vibrations grew more turbulent, the atmosphere becoming denser and denser. In the cockpit the blue light had died out, replaced by the warm glow of friction heating the outer ring of the porthole.

Tearing into the stratosphere, I feel the cabin gradually burning up from the outside in. The groans and creaks of warped metal sing a farewell tune amidst my frantic struggles to get some power back into the ship. Flipping switches and routing circuits, the immense gravitational forces pressed upon my body. Nauseating and sweltering, my vision began to tunnel as the blood pulled from my head and made mush of my brain. I clench my muscles and tighten my body, breathing hard and rhythmically to force the blood back in.

Focusing on the possibilities, I flip several switches. In a brief moment of hope, the light stammers on a nearby sign: 'No-smoking'.

I slam my fist on the mainboard in desperation and fear, the turbulence rocking the entire cabin violently. In a tried instance of percussive maintenance I slam the mainboard again. Another battery of lights activate, highlighting the emergency chute lever and a global positioning system. Immediately, I pull the lever and pray to whatever gods listening that the chutes deploy. With a high- pitched siren and a sickening yank, the descent slows and my stomach churns. The porthole suddenly flipped upwards to the night sky as the Ragpicker reoriented its mass. Jerking savagely upon my seat, my vision rapidly tunneled once more. My senses go numb, and I begin to drift in and out of consciousness.

Smashing into the ocean, the hard sound of water breaking against the exterior panels fall on my disoriented ears. I hear the flow of water filling the cabins below, and I struggle to undo my seat in vain. A heavy ache throbs through my leg and back, shackling my body to the chair. The night sky becomes dimmer as water crests and wells above the porthole. Rapidly sinking, all remaining electrical begins to short out. I glance to the last remaining scrap of light from a flickering GPS monitor. For a brief second its coordinates beam 97-9S, 126-43W before snapping away. With the last lights gone, all becomes enclosed in pitch darkness. In moments, the haunting groans of steel and metal echo in the cockpit as the dark depths press inwards. Sinking deeper and deeper the pressure built with the sound of stressed metal. With a metallic snap and whine, all became blank.

***

In the dark I dreamed of places beyond the black. Spiraling figures and forms danced in my periphery as all sense of time and space dissolved into nothingness. I contemplated if this was the experience of death, or racing towards some notion of oblivion. The inky black warmth of an unknown presence pressed upon my unconscious mind, and I melted between layers of reality and illusion. For whatever time I was here, my mind felt disconnected and turbid. My body drifted and oozed through mired cerebral states, feeling separate yet whole. Lost in the void, consciousness stretched thin as bizarre and abstract thoughts of alien and foreign places shone randomly like a projector. In segmented glimpses and visions, imagery of an unfathomable evil quashed all rational sense and instilled a primal fear within my being. In the depths, an ancient malevolence lurks, its blasted figure split across all planes of geometry and time. And though it waits beyond the cosmos, it turns its eyes upon me and sees...

I awoke from the nightmare with a violent scream, and the stinging scent of brine pried me from the deepest of dreams. A cool breeze wafts over my face, and I shut my eyes tighter. Deluded senses betray my innate perceptions though I feel the rough hardness of stone pressed against my back. From whatever dream I emerged, the solid material felt comfortable and real. I was uncertain if I had experienced such terrible images, though the lingering dread of what I saw lurked in the dark corners of my mind like a repressed memory.

I lean upwards and run a damp hand over my face, the uncertainty of reality still consuming my thoughts. The stinging salt of seawater bites into my eyes, and I rub them in an awkward surprise. Blinking in reflex, tiny streaks of white trickled into my vision like tiny comets darting through the night sky. Groggy and confused, I make a candid attempt to rouse my awareness back to life.

I slowly gaze about and squint in a blue-green darkness. Tracing my eyes along the floor, the room was small and tinged with the colour of seaweed and rot. The walls sloped upwards to elegantly form a pointed dome, the ambient trickle of water dripping from a nearby source. Blinking a few more times I run a hand through my hair and begin to stand up.

Wincing, a pain shoots along the length of my leg and into the base of my skull. Sharp and poignant, the sensation staggers me slightly, reminding me of the catastrophe from before. A panic wells within my chest and I whirl about looking for any clue of where I might be or what had happened. I remember a fiery collision and the descent into the ocean depths, and a large satellite high above the Earth. I remember Jim and the dead silence from the communication system. A growing nausea spreads through my stomach, as the room suddenly becomes claustrophobic. I begin to feel enclosed, the walls moving in closer and closer, smothering my mind with effluvial grime and pungent stenches. My breath becomes erratic, and from the corner of my eye a faint beam of light shines dimly into the room.

Heading to the source, I set my teeth into a contorted grimace and tough out the pain. My hand braces the slick surface of the wall as its contours shift beneath my weight in a bizarre and fluid fashion, chilling my fingertips. I look to my hand and notice the material coiling into various patterns and shapes, as if it were responding to my touch. Swirling for a brief moment, the stone petrified into random fractals and alien sigils. I rub my eyes and stare at the material in attempt to comprehend what had just occurred. In the silence a sudden blast of sound churned throughout the chamber.

A low, rumbling tone vibrated across the floor, rippling the small puddles of water around my feet and scattering loose pebbles. Drawling out for several seconds, the immense sound ceased, and I found myself quickly pacing towards the light source.

Rounding the corner I stopped short of the threshold to gape in wonder and bewilderment. Far off in the distance, sloping into a valley was the unmistakable shape of a sprawling metropolis. Marred hues of green and blues illuminated a thick fog lingering throughout the city. Its domed structures spiraled in odd angles and shapes, coiling inwards to a shell-like pattern. Pathways of streets and alleys cut through the buildings in an erratic and schizophrenic manner. In the center appeared to be a large courtyard obscured by thickets of seaweed and rubble, its open area dwarfed by a massive chapel behind it.

Lingering above the ruinous shape of the antiquated city was a darkened sky. No single star shimmered or glowed in its form, though hints of deep blue and greens reflected downwards upon smooth domed surfaces. Engulfed in its seemingly infinite depths, I followed its breadth down towards the horizon. It's peculiar curvature following my gaze until it abruptly ended beneath the city grounds. In an almost spherical fashion, a shadowy cloak hangs over this city. Panning its blackness, a small pinpoint began to form within its folds. Expanding and swirling, the pinpoint grew as a familiar sound echoed throughout the valley. The skies above the chapel suddenly churned and frothed like a riptide. Swirling and thrashing about, an immense whorl spun into existence as a deep rumbling shuddered the city once more.

I clasped my ears and watched in disbelief as the whorl parted larger and larger. Its mass grew, dispelling the darkness above the chapel until the eye of the storm was revealed. Faint glimmers of light speckled from behind the chaotic veil, revealing the night sky like that seen on Earth. Constellations of stars beaded a matte black skyline as dark emerald and sapphire torrents swirled around the rim of the whorl. Petrified in wonder and fear, I gaze upon the supernatural, and disappearing as fast it had arrived, the phenomena collapsed upon itself like a breaking wave.

In silence I stood, unable to comprehend the magnitude of whatever had occurred. Against all rational or conventional thought, my basic instinct ushered me towards the center of the city and to seek what lay below the stars. A drawling sigh whistles from my throat, and I proceed down a set of stairs, hoping that this was all but another horrible dream.

Winding this way and that, the stairs leveled off into an elongated pathway, its sheen stones an invitation beneath ancient archways and tunnels towards the city. Through the mist-filled streets I traversed, navigating abandoned limestone buildings and catacombs, giving the impression of a torturous maze. Gazing upon the stonework of the ancient metropolis, horrid statues depicting grotesque fish-men and aquatic monstrosities plagued my mind. Cold and unnerving, I felt their deadened gaze follow my every direction, though I swore it to be nothing more than paranoia. A creeping dread nestled within the confines of my mind as I questioned the reality I was in. All these seemingly impossible events render the conclusion that I had died within the crash, yet it all seemed so vivid and real. The sting of pain and pangs of thirst festered in my body, and I felt alive wandering the maze of a forgotten and forbidding city.

Mixed with a sense of frustration and desperation, I trudged onwards, my wanderings interrupted by the periodic formation of the whorl. Such terrible noises churned from its spirals, though against my better judgment I continue to pursue the inner city. It was after the fourth whorl did I break past the maze and into new territory. The scent of brine faded, and the ornate and preserved statues of demigods and devils crumbled into disarray. From beyond a thicket of dried seaweed and collapsed pillars I spot a large iron gate leading towards the inner courtyard. The crunching dirt packed beneath my feet as I cautiously slide towards the gate, stealing myself into its inner sanctum.

My eyes widened at the sight before me. Lingering without gravity, a massive and marred object bloomed with barnacles and blight. Suspended several feet above the ground, I held my breath and began to recognize this shape and form. It was my ship, the Ragpicker.

In wonder, I circle around its large frame and see the rumpled steel around the point of collision. Shredded metal and debris hang off frayed wires and melted filaments, as a gaping hole sits where a panel used to be. Looking about in suspicion, I reach upwards and find a good grasp to pull myself in thorough the breach. With a jump and pull, I scramble on board. Pooling water and detritus wafts an abhorrent stench from isolated pockets within the cabin. Dark and upturned, I blindly paw my way through the interior, until I find the service ladder leading towards the cockpit. Blue green rays filter through an encrusted porthole window, but there was another, dimmer light up ahead.

From above, a blue LED shone.

My heart raced and I began to scale the ladder. Clasping the final rung, I peered precariously over the edge to see the light blue glow of the speedometer flickering 30.00. I stared in disbelief as I pulled myself up towards the mainboard. Approaching the pilot seat, a burst of electricity whirls all the apparatus to life. In unrestrained excitement, I begin flicking switches, and the grinding pulse of engines began to vibrate the ship. Lost in the moment, a burst of static flared across a display. Startled, I lean forward and squint to make out the details upon the screen. Beyond the static and noise, an image of the ship exterior was displayed, yet for a brief moment a figure walked past on the courtyard. I wait breathless as a figure once again walks past and looks to the camera. Donned in a spacesuit, I recognized this as Jim.

My stomach sinks and I turn rush out of the ship into the courtyard. Frantically I searched among the engine sounds, but there was no sign of anyone else. I attempted to dismiss the reality of witnessing my dead crewmate, yet in this nightmare nothing is impossible. I turn to circle around the ship, but my foot snags on something. Stumbling downwards, I see the ship's tether wrapped around my leg, its length leading deeper into the courtyard, towards the massive chapel.

Standing to my feet, I unwrap my leg and look to the Ragpicker. The dull hum of its engines began to pick up in strength and power. If there was a shot to leave, this was it, but I could not go without finding what was on the other end of the tether. My mind hung with guilt and responsibility, I had to find out what happened to Jim. I swallow my fear, and start down the courtyard, looking back at the Ragpicker. Even when covered in barnacles and swill, it was still the most beautiful thing here.

Tracing the snaking cord across pale stone, the entrance of the chapel loomed menacingly. Three great archways descended into shadowed corridors as I squinted and peered further ahead. Hefting the tether, I began following its route but held it close as a lifeline to the ship. For several minutes I walked, perturbed at the distance. The length of the tether has already far exceeded its normal stretch, yet it continues to wind in the dark. I look back and see nothing but blackness and ponder if I had condemned my only means to escape. I trudged onwards, the feeling of guilt and remorse burning away at my conscious like wildfire. Lost in thought and wandering aimlessly, the corridor opened up towards a colossal amphitheater. I looked ahead and witnessed a massive shape.

With naught but an errant glance upon its hideous and incomprehensible form my mind raked in agony. In an insurmountable panic, I turned to flee, stifling discordant laughter as my eyes welled with tears. Casting down the tether, memories long past flashed before my eyes in nonsensical arrangements. The collective summation of my personal sensory experience melded together in a hemorrhaging mass of modalities. Maddening images of taste perfumed my ears with sounds of colour, and a phantom limb flopped rigidly next to my side. Gritting my teeth, I shut my eyes and ran, the gibbering sound of my own voice playing back within my skull as the colour gold and green played a musical pattern within the inside of my lids. Breathless, I slam into the courtyard and recall the distinct sound of the whorl as I feel fingers not of my own prying my eyes open to gaze at the open sky.

From above, thousands of stars speckle the darkness, as the whorl churned once more. In my last rational act, I lunged into the Ragpicker. Movement and time shuttered in stop-motion as I thrust myself into the seat, my body acting on its own. Clasping the control rod, I hammered the throttle downwards as the engines powered to full capacity. With a magnificent boom the thrust propelled the ship upwards and towards the eye of the whorl. In moments, I passed through the threshold, the dull groan of the whorl fading into the distance. A feeling of weightlessness accompanied a sudden alarm, as the automated system slammed the cockpit door shut. From the grimy porthole the black of space returned to view, and I breath in gibbering excitement. Looking down, I once more see the beautiful crescent of a blue and white planet. Shuddering with spasms, I grin and wipe a tear from my eye. Flipping several switches I broadcast a cryptic distress signal across all channels, and the Ragpicker's last known GPS location: 97-9S, 126-43W.

Satisfied from the final transmission, I return to madness. Overriding the airlock command, I turn towards the door. The hiss of depressurizing air fills the cockpit…Sorry Jim…

The Crossing of the United
Jacob Farley

Black water lapped hollowly at the hull of the cargo ship *United*. That sound, more than the sudden absence of engine noise, disturbed Cookie's dreamless slumber. The low rumble of the engines was so familiar to him that it took a moment to notice its absence but once he did, he was suddenly and completely awake.

He swung his legs over the side of his bunk and grunted as he stood. Absently running his hand through what was left of his thin grey hair, he listened intently for any sounds of motion from elsewhere in the ship. Hearing nothing, Cookie paced nervously back and forth in his small room. There was no reason for the engines to stop in the middle of the night, halfway across the Atlantic.

Cookie eased the bulkhead doorway open and stepped into the hall before realizing he was only wearing his undershirt and shorts. He stepped back and found his trousers crumpled on the floor and struggled into them, sucking in his gut as he buttoned them up. This accomplished, he proceeded out the door of his cabin and up to the main deck.

***

Cookie wasn't his real name, of course, but he'd been a ship's cook for almost his entire life and sailors were nothing if not traditional. He'd been on the *United* for four years now, following short stints here and there on smaller freighters after the war had ended (as well as a brief attempt at marriage he tried not to think too much about) but Cookie liked it here. Captain Walker was easy-going, as far as sea captains went, and the crew was never so large that Cookie felt overworked. All in all, it had been a mostly agreeable time.

When the ship had stopped in Boston to unload and take on more cargo in preparation for the long trip to the European continent, Cookie had taken the opportunity to find a motel and get himself good and drunk for a few days. By the time he returned to the ship, the captain had hired on ten new hands, all strangers to Cookie. He later learned they had all come to the captain together, claiming to be family, though they bore no resemblance to one another that Cookie could see.

***

Cookie stepped onto the *United*'s main deck, his breath pluming in the cold Atlantic air. The cargo containers were stacked all around him, looming above him like a a wave of frozen steel. Cookie shivered and wished he'd thought to take his coat.

He walked farther out onto the deck, but nobody seemed to be on watch. Cookie started to call out for a deckhand, but the words seemed to dry up in his throat. Finding himself unaccountably nervous, Cookie moved through the spaces between the containers, his footsteps the only noise on the deck.

Rounding a corner, Cookie saw that several of the cargo container doors were open, revealing empty blackness within. Someone must have opened them, but Cookie saw nobody nearby.

As he moved closer to one of the open containers, Cookie stumbled over something in the gloom and fell hard onto his knees. Blinking tears away, he peered closer at the shapeless mass that had tripped him up. He reached out to touch it and recoiled when he realized it was a person, crumpled on the deck.

Heart thudding painfully in his chest, Cookie rolled the body over. It was Edgars, a simple seaman Cookie had known for several years now. The young man's eyes were wide and staring, and when Cookie tried to pick the man's head up, his hand came away wet with still-cooling blood.

Cookie scrambled to his feet, his breath coming fast and shallow. He couldn't pull his eyes away from the pallid face now reflecting the dim moonlight. Cookie had never seen a dead body before- even during the war, he'd been lucky enough to avoid combat. Seeing one now, his mind reeled. He knew he had to find the captain. He had to find someone.

He turned and half stumbled back the way he'd come, making his way to the bridge.

***

The new crew, all of whom claimed the last name of Marsh, were sullen and uncommunicative. They kept wholly to themselves, gathering in a corner in the mess together during meals. When they could, they preferred to work their shifts together, and when they couldn't they communicated only in the briefest of phrases- affirmatives, negatives, grunts. They knew their work, though, so the rest of the crew mostly ignored them after the first few days at sea. Sailing families were nothing new to them. Only Cookie seemed to mislike what he saw in them, and even he couldn't put a finger on why.

The day they'd embarked, Cookie found himself on the bow, looking out over the ocean.

"Beautiful," said the man Cookie hadn't realized was beside him. It was Jedidiah Marsh, the oldest of the clan, a whip-thin man with a deeply lined face. "The source of life and death. The source of...everything."

"I suppose so," replied Cookie.

"It's good to be going home," said Marsh.

"Are you, uh, from Spain?" Even as he spoke, Cookie felt foolish for asking. Marsh said nothing, though. Instead, he continued to gaze out onto the horizon. After a moment, he turned and strode away. Thinking on it later, Cookie couldn't even say for sure that Marsh was speaking to him. The more he considered it, the more it felt like Marsh's words were spoken for his own pleasure. It was the longest conversation he would have with one of the Marshes.

***

Cookie's feet stomped up the stairs leading to the bridge. He'd seen nobody in his panicked flight to the upper decks. He burst into the bridge and found it empty. Nobody at the helm, nobody in the captain's chair. Cookie put his hands on his knees and tried desperately to catch his breath. Pain tore at his side and his head swam and he wasn't sure how long he'd been standing there before he heard the scream.

His head snapped up and, looking out from the bridge to the deck below, Cookie realized figures were moving around. As he watched, one stopped in front of a seemingly random cargo container. Visibly straining, the figure opened the outer latch and from within the container poured a dozen more figures. They spread out and moved farther up between the containers.

Cookie spun back and sat heavily, his back pressed against a bulkhead. His mind raced- what was this? Mutiny? Piracy? It had the flavor of neither. Another scream pierced the strange silence that had settled over the ship, this one cut off almost immediately after it began. It was coming from the main deck. Cookie suddenly knew, somehow, convinced in his heart, that this was the doing of the Marsh clan. Why they would do this, what their goals were, he had no idea, but he knew he had to find the captain. Captain Walker would know what to do.

Cookie struggled to his feet, trying to suppress the tremor in his hands. Looking at the ship's controls, he realized they had been attacked and badly damaged, apparently with the fire ax kept on the bridge, which was discarded nearby. He could see that the anchor had been deployed, but it would be impossible to retrieve, and the ship certainly couldn't be steered anymore.

He stood above the ruined controls for a moment before picking up the ax and starting back down the stairs.

***

When he wasn't working, Cookie liked to just wander the deck. The ship was large and he was on friendly terms with most of the crew, so there was always someone to chat up. Five days into the voyage, Cookie was doing just this when he passed a cluster of four of the Marsh boys.

They were speaking in low tones to one another, but stopped as soon as they saw Cookie approaching.

"Fellas," Cookie nodded amiably at them. They stared back at him. The youngest, a boy who couldn't be more than eighteen, turned and spat onto the deck next to him. One of the older men smacked the boy hard on the back of his head with a flat palm and turned back to the chef.

"Cookie," he nodded. The others each made a halfhearted wave or shrug of greeting, though the boy just rubbed his head and stared sullenly.

When it became apparent that no more conversation was forthcoming, Cookie nodded again and walked on further up the deck. As he went past the container they had gathered in front of, Cookie could have sworn he heard something moving within it. That was just foolishness, he decided.

***

Moving as quietly as he could, Cookie's eyes darted from side to side. Terrified of being discovered by one of the figures he'd seen emerging from the container, he slowly made his way towards the captain's cabin at the aft of the ship. Twice he ducked into alcoves and behind corners when people he didn't recognize strode down the passageways. He heard doors slamming open and shut farther off in the guts of the ship, and occasional muffled voices. Once, another shout.

His palms slippery with sweat, Cookie kept his left hand tightly gripped around the ax handle and, with his shaking right, reached for the latch to the captain's door and pushed it open.

"Captain?" he whispered. Inside the cabin was dark, but there was a coppery smell pervading the air. "Are you in here?"

Too terrified to move any further into the room, Cookie's hands fumbled for the light switches. Finding them, he clicked the overhead light on and let out a small sob.

The captain wasn't here. His bedclothes were crumpled on the floor and the white linen was stained a deep red. A smear pattern on the floor led from the bunk to the door and out. Nothing else appeared out of order, and the incongruity of the bloody sheets next to the otherwise meticulous cabin impressed itself deeply on Cookie.

Shaking his head back and forth as if to deny what he saw, Cookie backed out of the doorway into the passageway beyond. He tried to come up with a new plan, but he suddenly felt so old and so tired. He had moved beyond terror, it seemed, to a new place where the only rational thing to do was to go back to bed and wait for the morning.

He stood like that in the passageway until a shout from behind him snapped him back to consciousness.

"Here he is," the voice shouted. "Cookie, we've been looking for you!"

Cookie turned the other way and ran.

***

Earlier that evening, Cookie had noticed several of the crew hadn't turned up for dinner. He asked Edgars where they were and Edgars told him that the whole night watch had taken sick with some kind of stomach complaint. The Marshes had volunteered to fill in, even ones who would thus be pulling two shifts in a row. Everyone else, glad of the opportunity to take a full night's sleep, had happily let them.

After dinner, Cookie tried to stop by Henry Gafford's cabin to check up on him. He was one of the men who was supposed to be ill, and Cookie liked him, but there was no answer when Cookie knocked on the man's door.

"Henry," he called, "It's me, Cookie. Open up if you want some soup!"

There was no sound from beyond the door and, after a moment, Cookie shrugged and walked away. Best to let Henry sleep.

***

Voices rose all around him now as Cookie's feet pounded through the passageways of the *United*. Turning one corner, he saw two men racing towards him. He lowered his shoulder and charged through them, knocking one to the floor.

The voices were loud, shouting and screaming in a language Cookie didn't know or didn't recognize. He could hear them behind him, getting closer. He was not a young man, and not used to running in any way. His side ached and his breath came in difficult wheezes as he stumbled up to the deck.

If he could get to one of the lifeboats, he might be able to get away. He thought briefly of trying to find other members of the crew who might not have been discovered yet, but thought better of it when he heard more shouts from other corners of the deck, converging towards him.

He stumbled across the deck, crouching low and trying to be as quiet as possible. He found his way to one of the lifeboat stations and set the ax down next to him. With desperate fingers, he fumbled at the knots and pulleys keeping the small boat attached to the *United*. Throwing glances over his shoulder, he grabbed the nearby rope and began lowering the boat over the side. The pulley system let out a metallic squeal that was audible even over the shouts of whoever the men were behind him.

"The lifeboats! He's at the lifeboats," called someone nearby.

Panic gripped Cookie and the rope slipped out of his suddenly nerveless fingers, crashing to the water below. He leaned over the rail and saw the boat undamaged, bobbing in the gentle waves.

Cookie was just climbing over the side when hands gripped his shoulders and pulled him back over. He looked up into the eyes of Jedidiah Marsh, who smiled benevolently. There was a great white pain at the back of Cookie's head, and then nothing.

***

Cookie knew lots of superstitious sailors, of course. It was practically a requirement of the job. Bananas are bad luck, cats are good luck, whistling is either good or bad luck depending on who you ask. None of them, though, compared to Jock Nevin and his unwillingness to cross the Atlantic.

They'd known each other a few months aboard a ship making supply drops around the Pacific Rim. The captain announced that the ship would be making a long run through to the Atlantic and onwards to the continent. That night on shore leave, Jock confessed to Cookie that he'd be jumping ship first chance.

"I'm never crossing that that blasted stretch of water again, so help me," Jock had said.

"What, the Atlantic ocean? Why not?" asked Cookie, draining the last of his beer. He signaled to the bartender for another.

"Because He's waiting down there. Waiting for me, waiting for you, waiting for whoever calls Him on up, that's why," Jock had muttered. They had been in the bar together for hours now, and Jock was barely able to open his eyes.

"Who?" asked Cookie, but Jock only shook his head.

"Don't ask me things you don't want to know about," Jock had replied. "You don't want to know about this. Hell, *I* don't want to know! If it wasn't for my pappy, maybe I'd be going along with you. But I ain't. Take my advice and do the same." Jock got to his feet unsteadily and threw down a wad of bills, then weaved his way out the door as Cookie watched, unsure of what to say.

True to his word, when the ship had disembarked the next day, Jock was nowhere to be found.

***

The cold metal of the ship's deck pressed into Cookie's face and brought him back to wakefulness. His head throbbed and the back of his neck felt sticky. Lifting his head, he realized he was last in a line of unconscious or kneeling men spread across the main deck. He recognized all of them as crewmen he'd served mess to over the past few days. Some were weeping, others pale in the reflected moonlight, others lay still on the ground. At the other end of the line, he saw the captain, staring vacantly into the distance. Cookie thought the man might be drooling.

Climbing painfully to his knees, he saw that they were surrounded by a ring of robed figures, dozens of them. Cargo containers lay open all over the deck and the figures seemed to line the entire ship, their voices raised in a wordless baritone song. In front of the supplicating crew stood Jedidiah, the oldest Marsh, dressed in a long purple robe. He saw Cookie sit up and smiled at him.

"Glad you could join us, Cookie," said Marsh, and raised his hands above his head.

Abruptly, the men ceased their singing.

"Brothers!" shouted Marsh, "His moment draws near! His time is nigh!"

"His time is nigh!" repeated the ring of men.

"We bring forth the water of life!" Marsh gestured to one of the robed men, who stepped forward. Cookie saw that it was the youngest Marsh boy, his eyes feverish and wide. The boy produced a long, curved knife, stepped up behind the captain, and drew it across Walker's throat. The blood looked strangely colorless in the pale moonlight, and Cookie found that he couldn't look away as it splashed to the deck and pooled around the captain.

The ring of robed men were singing again, higher-pitched and faster than before. The youngest Marsh made his way down the line of crewmen, slitting the throat of each. As the pool of blood grew larger, tendrils of it began to snake towards Jedidiah. His eyes were closed and arms still raised to the sky, a rapturous smile on his face.

Cookie's heart pounded in his chest as the boy got closer and closer. When the boy stepped behind one man, he struggled to his feet, but two other robed men stepped forward and grabbed the crewman roughly by the arms, forcing him back to his knees. They did not cease singing while the young Marsh killed the man.

The blood continued streaming of its own accord towards Jedidiah, encircling him in a moat of gore. The last crewmen between young Marsh and Cookie were sobbing now, one screamed, but none of the robed figures took any special notice.

A frigid wind whipped across the deck, so loud and so sudden in its arrival that it temporarily halted the singing men. They picked their wordless song back up, faster and yet more shrill again.

Cookie's brain went blank as the young Marsh killed the man next to him and, finally, stepped up behind Cookie himself.

Without thinking, Cookie swung his head backwards, directly into the boy's groin. The young Marsh wheezed in surprise and crumpled to the deck, the knife clattering next to him.

Scrambling to his feet, Cookie grabbed the knife. The robed figures nearest him jumped out of line to try and moved towards him. Cookie slashed at one and the man fell away, clutching at his face. The other hesitated and Cookie sprinted through the gap between them. Behind him, he heard the oldest Marsh crying out. "Stop him! Stop him! Without all forty sacrifices-"

The singing had stopped now, as all the robed men converged on Cookie. The wind raised its tempo, howling strong enough to rock the massive cargo ship in the water. As Cookie ran towards the side, he realized that the water around the ship was bubbling and lit from below by a faint white light that seemed to be growing stronger commiserate with the wind's increasing intensity.

Having no thought but the frantic desire for escape, Cookie reached the railing. Figures grabbed at him from every angle, but he slashed and stabbed at them with the boy's long knife and they could not hold on to him.

Cookie threw himself over the edge and the water rushed up to greet him. He was stunned by the impact, but the cold water brought him back to his senses. From the decks above him he could hear more confusion and anger. Looking around, he realized he had landed very near the lifeboat he'd dropped earlier and, thanking whoever was listening for small miracles, swam towards it.

As he climbed aboard and wrapped himself, shivering, in a tarp from under a seat, he could hear other lifeboats being dropped off the side. Weeping, he reached desperately for the oars and splashed them into the water. With the last of his strength he rowed away from the *United*.

He was some forty yards from the ship when the light glowing around it suddenly darkened. He could hear the men pursuing in the other rafts shout in alarm when, suddenly, impossibly, something enormous, a blackness silhouetted against the night sky, reached out from the sea and wrapped itself around the *United*'s midsection. There was a great creak and snap of metal like Cookie had never heard before and the ship seemed to bend in the middle. Faster than should have been possible, the enormous cargo ship was sinking. *No, not sinking*, decided Cookie. *Being pulled down.*

Still weeping and shivering, Cookie clutched the tarp tighter around himself as he witnessed the terrible death of the *United*. When the ship finally vanished under the waves, Cookie found himself alone in the Atlantic, black water lapping hollowly at the hull of his tiny boat.

About the Authors

Craig E. Sawyer, born of Scottish MacKay highland and Irish stock, is a direct descendant of the McCoy family that famously feuded against the Hatfield clan for many decades over a stolen pig. Craig left his small town in Middle Tennessee at an early age, and traveled much of the United States before settling on the West Coast, where he currently lives with his beautiful fiance Valerie, big-eared dog Cisco, and their calico cat Ivy McT. He brings his unique experiences and knowledge of the supernatural to his writings and films. His stories typically combines elements of crime and horror with the weird and unseen.

Carl Thomas Fox

Born and raised in Swansea, Carl lives with his fiancée, Samantha Smith, and their two daughters, Amelia and Nevaeh. Carl also works with children, a teaching assistant in the Reception area of a Primary School, in which he runs a creative writing club to help children write stories.

As a pagan with a deep interest in the occult and ancient mythologies, Carl tries to use as much of this as he can in his writing. All his stories will be part of what is known as the Wellworlds mythology. A singular mythology that all work focuses on, almost mirroring the Norse idea of Yggdrasil, the tree that all worlds are connected to. This is a life-long work that he is deeply focused on.

You can follow Carl on:

Facebook at https://www.facebook.com/carl.fox.5454
https://www.facebook.com/carlthomasfox
Twitter at @CarlFox49
Amazon Author Page: http://www.amazon.co.uk/Carl-Thomas-Fox/e/B00HR6HT40
Website: fox492.wix.com/ctfauthor

Kevin Wetmore is an actor, director and stage combat choreographer who also writes horror. He is the author of Post-9/11 Horror in American Cinema (Continuum) and Back from the Dead: Reading Remakes of Romero's Zombie Films as Markers of their Times (McFarland), among others. He also has short stories in such anthologies as Enter at Your Own Risk: The End is the Beginning (Firbolg), History and Horror, Oh My! (Mystery and Horror), Dark Tales from Elder Regions (Myth Ink), Moonshadows (Laurel Highlands Publishing), and Midian Unmade (Tor).

Kevin Henry lives in a small town in Ohio, USA, where he builds diesel engines for a living. He has been publishing his horror, sci-fi and fantasy fiction for the past year. He hopes to one day land a publishing deal for his in-progress epic fantasy series, The Soul Forge Saga.

John Kaniecki is a published poet and writer. His poetry has appeared in over six dozen outlets and he has about half a dozen stories out.

He is the author of..

Words of the Future: https://www.createspace.com/5208167

And *Murmurings of a Mad Man:*

http://www.electiopublishing.com/index.php/bookstore#!/Murmurings-of-a-Madman

Josh Phillips is an applications developer for a mid-sized bank in Denver, Colorado where he currently lives with his wife, who introduced him to the horror genre, and a myriad of pets both furry and scaly. He graduated from Colorado State University with two degrees completely unrelated to writing and attends the Pikes Peak Writers Conference in Colorado Springs on a yearly basis to compensate. During his final year at CSU he wrote a weekly opinion column for the university newspaper and was subject to all the scrutiny and mockery such a position brings with it. When he isn't hiking in the Rocky Mountains, training for 5k mud runs, or taking alligator wrestling classes in southern Colorado, he spends his time writing and playing the electric guitar.

Owen Morgan lives in Vancouver British Columbia. He is an avid reader of Science Fiction & fantasy with a particular fondness for Dungeon & Dragons, and is the author of The Angel's Lamp found in Warlords of the Asteroid Belts, Splicers from the anthology, 2113 An Oral History of the Last God, and The Loyalist Washington found in Altered America.

Matthew Wilson has had over 150 appearances in such places as Horror Zine, Star*Line, Spellbound, Alban Lake, Apokrupha Press, Space & Time Magazine and many more. He is currently editing his first novel and can be contacted on twitter @matthew94544267.

Spencer Carvalho has had short stories published in various literary magazines and anthologies. His stories have appeared in the anthologies Undead of Winter, Tales of the Undead-Suffer Eternal: Volume 3, Horror in Bloom, Nightmare Stalkers and Dreams Walkers Volume 2, Moon Shadows, Sanity Clause is Coming, State of Horror: North Carolina, and others. To find out more about him check out his Goodreads.com page.

Phil Morgan is a published author, artist, and standup comic. He lives and works in central North Carolina.

James Pratt lives in southern New Jersey and enjoys writing horror, fantasy, and weird fiction. His influences include H.P. Lovecraft, Jack Vance, Clive Barker, William Hope Hodgson, Clark Ashton Smith, Michael Moorcock, Roger Zelazny, and Stephen King. James's stories have appearing in a number of anthologies including Canopic Jars: Tales of Mummies and Mummification from Great Old Ones Press, Dark Hall Press Cosmic Horror Anthology, Alter Egos Vol. 2 from Source Point Press, How the West was Weird Vol. 3 from Pulpworks Press, Tales from the Blue Gonk Cafe from Thirteen O'Clock Press, and Barbarians of the Red Planet from Rogue Planet Press.

Stephen R. Wilk is a Physicist and Engineer who writes both fiction and non-fiction. His non-fiction includes the books Medusa: Solving the Mystery of the Gorgon (which shows what happens when you let a physicist loose on Classical Mythology) and How the Ray Gun Got Its Zap! (A book on weird and interesting optics, including chapters on edible lasers and on the History of the Ray Gun), both published by Oxford University Press. His articles have appeared in Scientific American, Weatherwise, Parabola, Classical World, The Spectrograph, and Optics and Photonics News. His fiction includes Science Fiction, Fantasy, Horror, and Historical Mysteries, and has appeared in Analog, Tales of the Undead, Fiction Vortex, and will be in the forthcoming anthology Live Free or Dragons. In addition to working at research labs and optical companies in the northeast, Steve has been a Contributing Editor for the Optical Society of America for over a decade. He had also written on Pop Culture for the e-zine Teemings under his nom de internet, CalMeacham.

Larry Underwood hosted late night Creature Features for the better part of two decades on the Middle TN scarewaves as TV horror host Dr. Gangrene. Now he writes about them, too, with stories published in a handful of anthologies. He currently lives in Hendersonville, TN (Johnny Cash's home town), just North of Nashville with his 3 sons and 3 dogs, and still makes appearances from time to time as the Physician of Fright hosting live events.

Neal Privett lives on a farm somewhere in Tennessee, where he goes on coffee binges, listens to a lot of rockabilly, punk, and jazz albums, writes furiously, and keeps watching the skies for the Elder Gods' imminent return.

Eric Tarango grew up in Marfa TX, known for the famous Marfa Mystery Lights. Currently he resides in Odessa TX and is busy working on several short stories in the fantasy, horror and contemporary. This is his first published story outside of Kindle.

Benjamin Sperduto is a history teacher and has also worked as a freelance editor and writer for roleplaying games. Some of his short stories have appeared in Red Skies Press's *Techno-Goth Cthulhu* anthology, *Bastion Science Fiction Magazine*, *Encounters Magazine*, and ACA Books's *Rejected* anthology. His first novel, *The Walls of Dalgorod*, is available from Curiosity Quills Press. A graduate of the University of South Florida, he lives and works in Tampa, Florida. For a full list of publications and fiction updates, visitwww.benjaminsperduto.com or follow him on Twitter (@bensperduto) and Google+ (+BenjaminSperduto).

Benjamin Welton is a freelance journalist and short story writer based in Boston. His work has appeared in The Atlantic, VICE, Crime Magazine, Sanitarium Magazine, and others. He currently blogs at literarytrebuchet.blogspot.com.

Brian Hamilton is from Philadelphia, Pennsylvania, and is a recent college graduate, freelance writer, and fan of horror literature - especially anything Lovecraftian. "The Rain in Eksley" is one of his first published short stories.

Jason Scott Aiken is the host and producer of Pulp Crazy (http://pulpcrazy.com), a video blog and podcast dedicated to classic popular literature, characters, and themes. Jason enjoys penning fantasy and horror tales, especially sword & sorcery and weird fiction. The Summoning is his first published work. He can be found online at http://jasonscottaiken.com.

Taylor Foreman-Niko is a writer currently residing in Orange, California. Ever since he was a child, he has been enthralled by the power of stories. He began seriously writing when he was sixteen and has endeavoured to create compelling art ever since. He graduated from Marist College in May of 2014.

Mark Sims:
Raised in the Sierra Nevada Range of California, *Mark Sims* is a lifelong mountaineer and chef that now resides in the La Plata Mountains of Colorado. Married with two grown up kids and a grand daughter, he is an avid backpacker that enjoys long distance trail running and mountain biking as diversions and plans on living well passed one hundred. After a long, fast paced career spanning the West in the high end corporate food industry he has now chosen to take the mellow route of mountain life and spinning tales.

Robert Trska was born and raised in Ontario, Canada. Currently living in Halifax, Nova Scotia, he now holds a Bachelor of Science degree from Dalhousie University. Having studied a double major in Neuroscience and Biology, Robert has always taken a vested interest in the sciences. In particular, the mysteries and functions of the human brain and consciousness hold his curiosity. With experience in neuroimaging laboratories, his current focus is on studying human error processing and neuroeconomics. Presenting data at previous conferences, he hopes to expand his research into medicine and rehabilitation.

Outside of the academic and laboratory setting, Robert takes time from the scientific rigors of reality to venture the realm of fiction. Participating and dungeoneering in various tabletop campaigns, crafting unique characters and themes are his hobby. Through immersion and vivid imagery, the exploration of new worlds and scenarios entwine both the critical and creative mind.

Reading different genres of fiction from Lovecraftian horror to modern science, many authors and stories have held a place in his memory and heart. It is also across different mediums that Robert has taken inspiration and influence, such as cinema and digital gaming.

With his scientific background, Robert hopes to continue writing creative stories across all genres, and pursue a future career in Medicine.

Previous works of Robert include the tale "Chains in the Dark", from the first volume of the "Fall of Cthulhu" anthologies.

Jacob Farley lives in Seattle, where he writes fiction, theater, and scripted burlesque shows and futilely attempts to wrangle two small dogs.

Distantly related to Mary Shelley, **Charie D. La Marr** is currently working to establish herself as an author in her own name after years of ghostwriting for athletes. She has created a genre called Circuspunk (listed at Urban Dictionary) and writen a collectio of short stories in the genre called Bumping Noses and Cherry Pie and a horror novel called Laugh to Death. She also has written her first Bizarro book (or Nyzarro as she calls it—the New York version of Bizarro), Squid Whores of the Futon Fish Market for JWK Fiction She also participated in many anthologies including the heavy metal anthology Axes of Evil , James Ward Kirk's Memento Mori, Bones and Ugly Babies 2, In Vein for the benefit of St. Jude's Hospital, Ripple Effect for Hurricane Katrina relief, Oneiros Books' CUT UP! and other anthologies. She was selected to participate in the 2014 Ladies and Gentlemen of Horror—as one of 14 new voices in the genre. She is known for writing in many different genres from crime to bizarro to erotica and even Seussian. She is most proud of working with an Iranian translator, translating Booker Man Award Winner Vernon God Little into Persian—which became a bestseller in Iran.

A redhead with a redheaded attitude, she lives in NY (where sis is a busy member of the HWA chapter) with her mother and son and fur children Bailey Corwin, Babe Ruth and Casey Daniel.

CPSIA information can be obtained
at www.ICGtesting.com
Printed in the USA
LVOW01s1542140716
496336LV00020B/684/P